PENGUIN CLASSICS

CROCODILE'S TEARS

Amado V. Hernandez (1903–1970) is one of the most famous nationalist writers in the Philippines. His poetry, fiction, and plays stoked the flames against the US imperialism, the workers' poverty and a feudal land-tenancy system.

Born in Tondo, Manila, on 13 September 1903, Hernandez began his career in journalism in the 1920s, when the initial Filipino massive resistance against the US military rule had declined. He became an editor of the Manila daily *Mabuhay (Long Live)* from 1932 to 1934. In 1939, he won the Commonwealth Literary Contest for a nationalist historical epic, *Pilipinas (Philippines)*; and in 1940, his collection of mainly traditional poems, *Kayumanggi (Brown)*, won the Commonwealth Award in Literature. During the Japanese occupation of the Philippines (1942–1945), Hernandez served as an intelligence officer for the underground guerilla resistance, an experience reflected in his first novel, *Mga Ibong Mandaragit*, which has been translated into English by Danton Remoto as *The Preying Birds* (2022).

After the war, Hernandez assumed the role of a public intellectual: he organized the Philippine Newspaper Guild in 1945 and spoke out on national issues as an appointed Councillor of Manila from 1945–1946 and again from 1948–1951. It was during his presidency of the Congress of Labor Organizations (1947), the largest federation of militant trade unions in the country, that he moved from the romantic reformism of his early years to militancy.

An allegorical representation of the sociopolitical crisis of the country from the 1930s up to the 1950s, can be found in Hernandez's realistic novel, *Luha ng Buwaya (Crocodile's Tears)* and the epic poem of class struggle, *Bayang Malaya (Free Country)*, for which he received the prestigious Balagtas Memorial Award, named after Francisco Balagtas (also Francisco Baltazar), the foremost Tagalog poet of the nineteenth century.

Tarred and feathered during the Cold War which also reached the Philippines, Hernandez was arrested on 16 January 1951 and accused of complicity with the Communist-led uprising. While in jail at various military camps for five years and six months, he wrote the satirical poem, '*Isang Dipang Langit*' ('*An Arm's Stretch of Sky*') and the play, *Muntinlupa*.

After his release from prison, Hernandez wrote countless stories under various pseudonyms for the leading weekly magazine, *Liwayway* (*Dawn*). He also wrote columns for the daily newspaper, *Taliba* (*News*) and edited the radical newspapers *Ang Makabayan* (*The Nationalist*) from 1956–1958 and *Ang Masa* (*The Masses*), from 1967–1970. He participated in the Afro-Asian Writers' Emergency Conference in Beijing, China in June–July 1966, and at the International War Crimes Tribunal, where he joined Simone De Beauvoir, Bertrand Russell and Jean Paul Sartre in November 1966, emerging as an outspoken voice for freedom of expression and human rights worldwide.

His numerous honours culminated in the Republic Cultural Heritage Award (1962) and National Artist Award given by a grateful nation in 1973. Up to the day he died (24 March 1970), Hernandez was writing a column and giving advice to the leaders of the massive rallies that rocked the Philippines at that time. In the uncanny situation of a novel being prophetic, his *Mga Ibong Mandaragit* (*The Preying Birds*), prefigured the Marcos dictatorship that would soon descend upon the land and stay for fourteen long years (1972–1986). *Luha ng Buwaya* (*Crocodile's Tears*) was his second and last novel. Both novels are required readings in Philippine high schools and universities, and lines from his nationalist poems have reached the realm of pithy proverbs and sayings, quoted often in classrooms and everyday conversation.

Danton Remoto was educated at the University of Stirling (British Council Scholar) and Rutgers University (Fulbright Scholar) as well as at the Jesuit-run Ateneo de Manila University (Association of Southeast Nations Scholar) and the University of the Philippines. He has worked as Publishing Director at Ateneo, Head of Communications at the United Nations Development Programme, TV and radio host at TV 5 and Radyo 5, President of The Manila Times College, and Head of the School of English at the University of Nottingham, Malaysia. He was the first Filipino to head the

School of English of a British university. In 2015, he was awarded the Gawad Balagtas Award, a Lifetime Achievement Award in Literature, by the Writers' Union of the Philippines. He has been writing for the Philippine press since 1986 and has published more than 10,000 columns, feature articles and editorials. At present, he is the news editor of *The Manila Times*, the Philippines oldest newspaper, founded in 1898, and continues to teach as a Senior Professorial Lecturer at the Department of Communications, Ateneo de Manila University, and in the Department of Languages and Literature, San Beda University. He is also the producer and host of the daily radio show, *Pinoy Konek* (*Connected Filipinos*) on Radyo 5 True FM. The highly rated show deals with overseas Filipino workers as well as Philippine arts and culture.

He has published a baker's dozen of books in English, including *Riverrun, A Novel* and *The Heart of Summer: Stories and Tales*, both published by Penguin Random House Southeast Asia. He also translated the 1906 novel by Lope K. Santos, *Banaag at Sikat* into English as *Radiance and Sunrise* and *Mga Ibong Mandaragit* as *The Preying Birds* for the Penguin Southeast Asian Literary Classics series. His work is cited in the *Oxford Research Encyclopedia of Literature*, *The Princeton Encyclopedia of Poetry and Poetics*, and *The Routledge Encyclopedia of Postcolonial Literature*. He has been a Fellow at the Cambridge University Summer Seminar, the Bread Loaf Writers' Conference, and most recently, at the MacDowell Arts Colony in New Hampshire, USA. He is now writing his next novel, as well as a new collection of essays and poems. He divides his time between Southeast Asia and the United States.

Praise for *Luha ng Buwaya*

'The novels of Amado V. Hernandez are paradigmatic of committed literature. They offer a picture of a just society that shall give birth to Filipinos. When that time comes, then the Filipinos' sense of humanity will be complete and they can hold their heads high ...'
—Citation for National Artist Award for Literature, 1973

'The *Tanglaw ng Lahi* (Light of the Race) Award is given to those who have dedicated their lifetime to promoting Filipino identity and have succeeded in steering the national consciousness towards a clarification of the Filipino image ... Amado V. Hernandez avoided the affliction common to most intellectuals, known as miseducation. His words reflect the revolutionary consciousness that runs through the literary tradition of national hero, Dr Jose Rizal.'
—Citation for the *Tanglaw ng Lahi* Award,
Ateneo de Manila University, 1970

'The creative self of Amado V. Hernandez was forged by more than fifty years of struggle for Philippine nationalism, democracy and social justice. His life and writings seem to be one, both marked by deep love of country and the possibilities of hope.'
—Dr Rosario Torres-Yu, Critic and Former Dean, College of
Arts and Letters, University of the Philippines

'Amado V. Hernandez is the grand old man of Philippine literature at whatever age.'
—Ninotchka Rosca, Author of *State of War* and
Twice Blessed, Winner of the American Book Award

'Like his fellow anti-colonial writer James Joyce, Amado V. Hernandez forged the uncreated conscience of the race ... The movement of his writing was from an arm's stretch of sky, as seen from his narrow prison cell, to the vast hopes of a free country.'
—Dr Epifanio San Juan, Winner of the Asian
American Studies Outstanding Book Award;
Emeritus Professor, University of Connecticut

'Amado V. Hernandez is both a creator and a destroyer. His writings recorded the heroism of the race ... He gave words to the poor and the voiceless, and his works awakened the indifferent. His life was a testament to the Filipino genius.'

—Andres Cristobal Cruz, Novelist and Winner of
the Don Carlos Palanca Prize for Literature

'Amado V. Hernandez showed deep love of country in his life and in his art. He did not only use the novel to spread his pro-masses stance, he also wrote essays, short stories and plays that showed his involvement in the nationalist movement.'

—Dr Soledad S. Reyes, Author of *Nobelang Tagalog,
1905–1975: Tradisyon at Modernismo*; Emeritus Professor,
Ateneo de Manila University

'Although *Mga Ibong Mandaragit* (*The Preying Birds*) has clear political intent, the fact that it was originally serialized in the popular *Liwayway* magazine is an indication that Hernandez also intended it as entertainment, or that the politics should go down easily ... There are some aspects of the novel that might surprise. Mando's politics are hardly radical: he's more social democrat than socialist. He believes in democracy and education; state ownership is only one solution of many and it requires ... its leaders to be honest. He doesn't avoid violence, but neither does he consider it a solution to the problem he details. His vehicle of choice is (perhaps not coincidentally, given Hernandez's own career) journalism ... In its simplicity of language and a tendency to bend the novel to direct political and philosophical ends, the novel is reminiscent of the work of Turkish novelist Yasar Kermal and (somewhat later), Thai writer Pira Sudham. While *The Preying Birds* can and should be read as an important milestone in the history of Southeast Asian literature, it can also fortunately be read and enjoyed as a saga of adventure and social derring-do ...'

—Peter Gordon, *Asian Review of Books*

Praise for *Danton Remoto*

'Lush, limpid and lean, Danton Remoto is a stylist of the English language. Read him.'
—Bernice Reubens, Winner of the Man
Booker Prize for *The Elected Member*

'I am a fan of the works of Danton Remoto.'
—Junot Diaz, Winner of the Pulitzer Prize and
the National Book Critics' Circle Prize for
The Brief Wondrous Life of Oscar Wao

'Danton Remoto is an accomplished writer whose fiction is marked by elegant and intense language. I am also impressed by the social concern in his language, wrought well in images so clear, it is like seeing pebbles at the bottom of a pond.'
—Sir Stephen Spender, Winner of the Golden
PEN Award, Poet Laureate of the United States

'Danton Remoto's books are vivid, well-written and enthralling. He is an adroit writer: his works form part of the Philippines new heart.'
—James Hamilton-Paterson, Winner of the
Whitbread Prize for *Gerontion*

'Danton Remoto is one of the Philippines' best writers.'
—*The Age*, Melbourne

'Danton Remoto is a smart and sensitive writer whose works ask many questions about our complex and colourful region.'
—Jessica Hagedorn, Shortlisted for the National
Book Award for *Dogeaters*

'Danton Remoto is such a wonderful writer. In *Riverrun, A Novel*, he writes about the tropical Catholic magic that saves and destroys.'
—Tiphanie Yanique, Winner of the American Academy
Arts and Letters Award for *Love and Drowning*

'Danton Remoto's *Riverrun, A Novel* is one of the most anticipated books by an Asian writer in the year 2020.'

—Bookriot

'The works of Danton Remoto are like the quick strokes of calligraphy. The meanings are not just found in the words but also in the white spaces, the silences between.'

—Edwin Morgan, OBE, Lifetime Awardee
for Literature, Scottish Arts Council

'Danton Remoto is a noted poet, fiction writer and newspaper columnist whose books have reached a wide audience in the Philippines and in Southeast Asia. Self-affirmation is highlighted in many of his writings.'

—*The Routledge International Encyclopedia of Literature*

'The fiction of Danton Remoto is part of Asia's literature of dissent. He writes with clarity and compassion about growing up in a region that is in a never-ending ferment.'

—*Asiaweek* Magazine

'His fiction points to a new direction in Southeast Asian writing in English. It is intimately personal yet utterly political, the prose polished like marble, and his profound reflections are caught in the cold eye of memory.'

—Nick Joaquin, Winner, Ramon Magsaysay Award
for Literature, Asia's Nobel Prize; Author of *The Woman
Who Had Two Navels and Tales of the Tropical Gothic*

'I like the passion and the intensity in the fiction of Danton Remoto. But most importantly, I like the fact that he writes with heart—which is the only way to write.'

—Bienvenido N. Santos, Winner of the American
Book Award for *Scent of Apple and Other Stories*

'I only have admiration for the fiction of Danton Remoto. The vessel of form and the fluid of content are fused in one organic whole in his works.'

—N.V.M. González, Winner of the Republic Cultural
Heritage Award for *The Bamboo Dancers*;
Creative Writing Scholar at Stanford University
under Katherine Anne Porter; National Artist
of the Philippines

'One of the best writers of his generation. His words have wings.'

—Kerima Polotan, Winner of the Republic Cultural
Heritage Award for the novel, *The Hand of the Enemy*;
Fellow for Fiction, Bread Loaf Writers Conference

'Danton Remoto's fiction is full of marvels. Deep insights spring out at the reader from harmless-looking paragraph corners, keen observations startle the reader into looking at everyday reality with more alert eyes, and the unexpected placement of words make the prose exciting. Quite simply, one of Asia's best writers.'

—Dr Isagani Cruz, Visiting Professor, Oxford University;
Emeritus Professor, De La Salle University

'Danton Remoto is an outrageously good writer. He writes with substance and style, and he knows history—the context that shapes fiction—like the lines on the palm of his hand.'

—Carmen Guerrero Nakpil, Winner of the Southeast Asia Write
Award; Author of *Myself, Elsewhere* and
The Centennial Reader

'Danton Remoto can capture curves of feeling and shapes of thought in his writings. His language is chiselled and lapidary, musical in its control and tonality. His eye and ear are perfect.'

—Professor Rolando S. Tinio, National Artist for
Literature and Theatre, Philippines; British
Council Scholar at University of Bristol

'When Danton Remoto joined the worlds of radio and television, I began to tease him as looking like a studious film star. He did appear in *Boy*, a controversial and prize-winning film by Aureaus Solito, where he played a difficult role—a poet and a creative writing teacher! But don't let that cheerful face deceive you: he is one of our most exquisite writers. His structure is impeccable, his language is lyrical, and his heart—especially his heart—is in the right place.'

—Gilda Cordero-Fernando, Awardee for Literature and
Publishing, Cultural Centre of the Philippines;
Author of *The Butcher, The Baker, The Candlestick Maker*
and *A Wilderness of Sweets and Other Stories*

'Danton Remoto is a professor of English, a prize-winning writer and a veteran journalist. He is one of the best chroniclers of the contemporary scene in Asia.'

—*People Asia Magazine*

'The Ateneo de Manila University has produced some of the finest Filipino writers in the last three decades. One of them is Danton Remoto, who writes poetry and prose of the highest order.'

—*Manila Chronicle*

'Danton Remoto is a gifted writer. His works have a contemporary flavour, dealing with topics that show delicately but thoroughly the Filipino heart.'

—*Philippine Daily Inquirer*

'The poetry and fiction of Danton Remoto are a sight to behold. He is raising a body of work that will be vital and enduring.'

—*The Evening Paper*

'Danton Remoto is the child of modern Asian literature in English. He studied well the American and British literary canons, and then he used that excellent training to write his own stories in a strange and beautiful English.'

—Father Joseph A. Galdon, S.J., *World Literature Today*

'Danton Remoto is a novelist with the heart of a poet.'
—Dr Edith Lopez Tiempo, National Artist for
Literature, Philippines; Fellow at the Iowa Writers'
Workshop under Robert Penn Warren

'*Riverrun* is a fine novel and Danton Remoto is a literary heavyweight.'
—*Vogue Australia*

Crocodile's Tears

Amado V. Hernandez
Translated by Danton Remoto

PENGUIN BOOKS
An imprint of Penguin Random House

PENGUIN CLASSICS

USA | Canada | UK | Ireland | Australia
New Zealand | India | South Africa | China | Southeast Asia

Penguin Classics is part of the Penguin Random House group of companies
whose addresses can be found at global.penguinrandomhouse.com

Published by Penguin Random House SEA Pvt. Ltd
9, Changi South Street 3, Level 08-01,
Singapore 486361

| Penguin
| Random House
| SEA

First published in Penguin Classics by Penguin Random House SEA 2023

English Translation Copyright © Danton Remoto 2023
Copyright to the original Tagalog text © Amado V. Hernandez

ISBN 9789815017854

Typeset in Adobe Garamond Pro by MAP Systems, Bangalore, India

www.penguin.sg

*This translation is dedicated to
the National Artist for Literature Virgilio S. Almario,
Lualhati Bautista, Jose F. Lacaba and Rogelio Sicat
who taught us all
that roots can give us wings
and that memory is the mother of all writing*

Translator's Introduction

Like the Indonesian writer Praomedya Ananta Toers and the Thai writer Pira Sudham, the novels of Amado V. Hernandez recreate the spiritual geographies of a nation, the soul of a race. Hernandez wrote the outline and first draft of his first novel, *Mga Ibong Mandaragit*, while in jail. It was the middle of the Cold War, whose unfortunate effects also reached the American neo-colony that was the Philippines. He was charged with the alleged crime of complex rebellion, which was primarily rebellion against the state, along with arson and robbery. He was shunted off to various military camps and detention centers for five years. If Oscar Wilde said that writing is the best revenge, then Hernandez did just that. He wrote three books while in detention at the National Penitentiary: an epic poem, a play and his first novel.

He wrote his second novel, *Luha ng Buwaya* (*Crocodile's Tears*), when he was acquitted by the Supreme Court and either editing or writing for various newspapers and magazines in Manila. The National Artist for Literature, Bienvenido Lumbera, ascribes the more reformist tone of the second novel to the fact that Hernandez had just been released from jail, and was advised by his wife, the late National Artist Honorata 'Atang' de la Rama Hernandez and his friends, to tone down the militancy in his writings. He was also appointed as a councillor twice for the City of Manila, and he wisely channelled his advocacy in the direction of political reforms.

Lope K. Santos, who was Hernandez's teacher and also a newspaperman and fiction writer like him, published *Banaag at Sikat* in 1906. *Radiance and Sunrise*, my English translation of this novel, was published as part of the Southeast Asian Literary Classics series by Penguin Random House Southeast Asia in December 2021.

Nationalist feelings still ran high in the early twentieth century, and poetry and fiction were being published in the daily newspapers. They were placed side by side with the news, editorials and columns to highlight the premium then placed on literature. They were frankly anti-American and the new colonizers stemmed these sentiments by passing anti-subversive measures into law—and calling those who opposed them 'bandits' and 'outlaws'; words that would later morph into 'Communists'.

Hernandez was born on 13 September 1903, in Tondo, Manila, the cradle of heroes and revolutionaries. His birth seemed propitious, for the Americans were just beginning their benevolent assimilation of the Philippines. He was hurtled immediately into the vortex of the times. Listen to Hernandez talk briefly about his education:

'I studied in Gagalangin, Tondo, at the Manila High School and the American Correspondence School, where I finished the third year of my Bachelor of Arts. I wanted to be a lawyer and a defender of the working class at one time, and I almost became a painter. But I turned into a poet instead, because my aunt hit me on the head for painting a portrait of her with horns.'

The worlds of poetry and images led him to work as a reporter at the *Watawat* (*Flag*) newspaper, a columnist at *Pagkakaisa* (*Unity*) newspaper, and editor of *Mabuhay* (*Long Live*) at the age of thirty-two. In his long and storied career as a journalist, he also edited the following newspapers: *Pilipino* (*Filipino*), *Ang Makabayan* (*The Nationalist*), *Sampaguita* (*Jasmine*) *Weekly*, and *Mabuhay Extra*. While editing news and features, and writing columns and editorials, he was also crafting his own poems and short stories. He was a prolific writer with a vast and admiring readership from among both the intelligentsia and the masses.

When the Japanese came, he worked as an intelligence officer for the resistance movement. But he was disillusioned after the war. He said, 'I saw the rapacious self-interest of those around me, people switching their allegiance. What happened here was a contrast to an English bakery incident I read about, where the bakery was turned over to the community. If you go to the Quinta Market now, you will see food rotting in the stalls, and yet, the people are hungry.'

After the war, he resumed his newspaper work, where he helped organize the Philippine Newspaper Guild in 1945. This paved the way for his work with the labour movement. He later helped found the Congress of Labour Organizations (CLO), which was suspected of being a Communist front. He was tarred and feathered in a Philippines that was also part of the Cold War in the 1950s. He was thrown in prison, and from the depths of that prison came his first novel, *Mga Ibong Mandaragit.*

While still in prison, he sent an essay to the *1952 Yearbook of the International Longshoremen and Warehousemen's Union (Local 37)* edited by the Filipino expatriate writer, Carlos Bulosan. Hernandez wrote, 'During the dark days of the enemy occupation, the Filipino workingman realized that labour must speak only one universal language. It has to rise above national and racial barriers, that labour everywhere has one common struggle, and that it must march toward one goal: the liberation of all the peoples from the chains of tyranny, fascism and imperialism.'

When he was released from prison, he published the novel in serial form and rejoined the labour movement. He was also appointed for two terms as City Councillor of Manila on a pro-labour platform. From 1962 to 1967, he also worked for *Taliba* and *Ang Masa*, while continuing his work with the labour movement.

During the last years of the 1960s, which happened to be the last years of his life, Hernandez revised the serialized 1959 version of *Mga Ibong Mandaragit* and finally published it in book form. Shorn of some of the romantic and touristic asides that catered to the weekly *Liwayway* audience, the revised version was leaner and bolder. Hernandez also updated the novel to include the latest shenanigans of the corrupt powers-that-be, true to his training as a journalist, whose job was to hurry history. His second—and final—novel was *Luha ng Buwaya*. It had lesser pages than his first novel, was more conciliatory in tone and less grainy in texture than the first novel.

The setting of *Luha ng Buwaya* is the town of Sampilong, lorded over by the powerful Grande husband and wife, Don Severo and Donya Leona. Their ancestors had grabbed vast tracts of land and Hernandez shows the landlords in a fatal embrace with the Church, the political leaders and the police of the province. The poor farmers and the people who live in the slums are led by Bandong, a young and idealistic schoolteacher. As in his first novel, *Mga Ibong Mandaragit*, Hernandez seems to say that the cooperative movement is one way for the farmers and the slum-dwellers to improve their lives—but only if they forge a common alliance. Education is also implied as a way out of the massive poverty that stalks the land.

Hernandez was a major poet and he painted vivid images of the lack of equality in Philippine society—the grand feast of the rich counterpointed with the empty plates of the poor, the sad death of Sepa and Teacher Putin and their funeral wakes, the slimy way the tentacles of power grip the necks of the poor, the noise of the packed courthouse and the cracks in the land as the farmer refuse to plant rice anymore. The images are startling and powerful.

The skewed power play in the Philippines is shown with eloquence and as well as the tight hold of the foreigners on local businesses. Sacks of rice are hoarded in the granaries and warehouses of the landlords, bearing an uncanny resemblance to what still happens in twenty-first-century Philippines. Colonial mentality is also shown through wonderful set-pieces, as well as the uncritical acceptance of all things foreign, especially in matters of culture. But in the end, hope gleams in the novel, as it sketches a horizon of possibilities that is vast and alive for the Filipinos who want to secure a comfortable life in their own country.

Dr Bienvenido Lumbera won the Ramon Magsaysay Award for Creative Communication and Literature, which was the Asian equivalent of the Nobel Prize. He wrote, 'Amado V. Hernandez is a major novelist who has contributed to the vitality of the Rizal tradition in the period of the Republic ... His two novels are a vigorous reflection of the political and economic troubles of the times. They were a far cry from the stereotypical novels that were published in the weekly magazines and merely read to while the time away ... *Luha ng Buwaya* (1963) depicts the plight of the peasantry, how the rich landlords exploit them and how they fight back in order to win for themselves a better life ... The novelist's secure grasp of social realities makes his novel a passionate work on the exploitation that Filipino peasants and workers are still trying to shake off ... Later, the figure of Hernandez took on the dimensions of an institution from whom young writers were to draw inspiration and guidance in the creation of a new nationalist literature.'

In late 2022, GMA 7, a major Philippine television company, produced *Maria Clara at Ibarra*, a fantasy and historical drama, that shook the nation. The story deals with Klay, a Gen Z nursing student, who is transported into the world of national hero Dr Jose Rizal's novels after reading *Noli Me Tangere*. Towards the end of the hugely successful TV series which is now on Netflix, the main character muses which novel she would read next, thinking that perhaps she could also enter its pages as well in the future. *Mga Ibong Mandaragit* comes up.

The sales of Rizal's novels, in their Filipino and English translations, shot through the roof when this series was being telecast. Perhaps, the same might happen to *Mga Ibong Mandaragit* and also to *Luha ng Buwaya*, in the same strange way wherein a form of mass media, aided by social media, propels old books onto bestseller lists. Dr Lumbera seemed prophetic when he said that then (and certainly even now), Hernandez was and is a lodestar for the Filipino writers' nationalist aspirations.

Let us give the last word to the poet and critic Dr Epifanio San Juan, who has devoted a lifetime championing the cause and the writings of Amado V. Hernandez. 'In his novels, Hernandez has given the country his vision of the good in life, in the human community, so that from this example, at once a mirror and a symbol, may be born a future in which every Filipino can realize his full personality face to face with his fellow men, no longer darkly but luminously with his god.'

When all is said and done, there is in Amado V. Hernandez's work a repetition of Dr Jose Rizal's imaginative act: a Western form (the novel) has been made part of the native landscape, infused with a local habitation and name.

References

Abueg, Efren R. 1974. 'Ang Sosyalismo sa Nobelang Tagalog'. Sampaksaan ng Mga Nobelistang Tagalog (Quezon City: Ang Aklatan, University of the Philippines).

Agoncillo, Teodoro A. 1970. A History of the Filipino People (Quezon City: R.P. Garcia Publishing).

Batnag, Aurora E. (Ed.). 1984. Panunuring Pampanitikan: Mga Nagwagi sa Gawad Surian sa Sanaysay (Manila: Surian ng Wikang Pambansa).

Cruz, Andres Cristobal. 1970. Panata sa Kalayaan ni Ka Amado (Manila: Keystone Press).

Cruz Reyes, Jun. 2015. Ka Amado. (Quezon City: University of the Philippines Press).

Guillermo, Alice and Charlie Samuya Veric (Eds.). 2004. Suri at Sipat: Araling Ka Amado. (Manila: Amado V. Hernandez Resource Center).

Hernandez, Amado V. 1979. Philippine Labour Demand Justice (New York: Far East Publishing).

Hau, Caroline S. 2000. Necessary Fictions: Philippine Literature and the Nation, 1946-1980 (Quezon City: Ateneo de Manila University Press).

Hernandez, Amado V. 1974. Luha ng Buwaya. (Quezon City: Ateneo de Manila University Press).

Jurilla, Patricia May B. 2008. Tagalog Bestsellers of the Twentieth Century: A History of the Book in the Philippines (Quezon City: Ateneo de Manila University Press).

Kintanar, Thelma B. 'Tracing the Rizal Tradition in the Filipino Novel'. Tenggara. 25. pp. 80–91.

Lachica, Eduardo. 1971. Huk: Philippine Agrarian Society in Revolt (Manila: Solidaridad Publishing House).

Lumbera, Bienvenido. 1967. 'Rehabilitation and New Beginnings: Tagalog Literature Since World War II'. Brown Heritage: Essays on Philippine Cultural Tradition and Literature (edited by Antonio G. Manuud). (Quezon City: Ateneo de Manila University).

Lumbera. 1997. Revaluation: Essays on Philippine Literature, Cinema and Popular Culture. (Manila: University of Santo Tomas Press).

Mallari, Luisa J. 2002. From Domicile to Domain: The Formation of Malay and Tagalog Masterpiece Novels in Post-Independence Malaysia and *the Philippines* (Bangi, Malaysia: Penerbit Universiti Kebangsaan Malaysia).

Maranan, Edgardo B. 1985. *Ang Usapin sa Lupa sa Mga Nobela nina Amado V. Hernandez, Rogelio Sikat at Dominador Mirasol. Galian 6.*

Mojares, Resil. 1983. *Origins and Rise of the Filipino Novel: A Generic Study of the Novel Until 1940* (Quezon City: University of the Philippines Press).

Reyes, Soledad S. 1982. *Nobelang Tagalog 1905-1975. Tradisyon at Modernismo* (Quezon City: Ateneo de Manila University Press).

Schumacher, John. 1973. *The Propaganda Movement, 1880-1895: The Creators of a Filipino Consciousness, the Makers of a Revolution* (Manila: Solidaridad Publishing House).

Schumacher. 1991. *The Making of a Nation: Essays on Nineteenth-Century Filipino Nationalism* (Quezon City: Ateneo de Manila University Press).

Yu, Rosario Torres (Ed.). 1997. *Magkabilang Mukha ng Isang Bagol at Iba Pang Akda ni Amado V. Hernandez* (Quezon City: University of the Philippines Press).

A Note on the Translation

The translation is based on the 1974 edition of *Luha ng Buwaya* published by Ateneo de Manila University Press under the guidance and personal supervision of Honorata de la Rama viuda de Hernandez, the widow of Amado and herself a National Artist in Theatre and Music. The book has become a required reading in high schools and colleges, and is still in print today.

When I began translating this novel, I followed the principles that I employed when I translated *Mga Ibong Mandaragit*, which was to be as faithful as possible to the original text written by Hernandez. Unlike Lope K. Santos, who self-published *Banaag at Sikat* in 1906 using a very flowery, repetitive and discursive prose style, Hernandez used a brisk and vigorous prose style that lent itself well to English translation. He was a writer in Tagalog who had read Ernest Hemingway and Jean-Paul Sartre, and was thus conversant with the literary modernism and existentialism of the age. But always, in his heart and mind, he wedded this training with his acute reading of Philippine history and his sharp study of its many social and political ills.

Aside from being a journalist, Amado V. Hernandez was also a novelist. He was a journalist writing a novel, which was both a boon and a bane. It was a boon because he sometimes employed the staccato style of writing news and magazine features, and this made for easier reading. It was a bane in the sense that he sometimes assumed that the readers knew the background (economic, cultural, social, political) of the issues in the story. What I did was to flesh out some details, adding a phrase here or there to clarify the expression of an idea.

Also clear in my mind was that I was writing a translation that would try to approximate the way the characters spoke—if they had spoken in English. Thus, I avoided the wooden, textbook prose that passed for the translation of some classic works of literature. I also used a late twentieth-century prose style, which I thought would be appropriate for the audience of this translation.

Moreover, I used the English equivalents of words (jasmine for *sampaguita*). In many cases, I have retained the names of places and proper names (Donya). I retained the original spellings that Hernandez used. I retained as well the 'fragmented' English spoken by the characters in the game of *juega de prenda*, the game of fines played during the funeral wake scene in the novel.

I also retained the same 'fragmented' English as well as the dialogues of Mr Henry Danyo, the principal installed by the landlords. Unfortunately, the dragonfly-thin Mr Danyo is a graduate of one of the diploma mills that produced half-baked teachers, and Hernandez had a roaring great time satirizing him in this novel.

One technique I used to have the novel read briskly is to use contractions in both the passages and the dialogue. This technique has been used more often by fiction writers in the last twenty years, and I also opted to use this to make this novel a page-turner.

I would like to thank the family of the late Amado V. Hernandez for giving us permission to translate this novel.

I would also like to thank Nora Nazerene Abu Bakar, the Associate Publisher of Penguin Random House South East Asia, for entrusting the English translation of the Philippine literary classics into my hands, as well as her fine and capable editors.

I would also like to thank my sister Nanette Remoto, whose house in Los Angeles is a haven and a home when I want to write deep into the night or late into the afternoons, before the sun went down.

My gratitude also goes to Bellarmine Global Education Centre and Saint Robert's University in Bangkok, Thailand, where I stayed for two months during the translation of this novel. My forever thanks to the Galindez family for their kindness and hospitality. The well-done Filipino food at Toto's Inasal, run by Doctor Jong and Sir Lawrence, nourished me while I was translating this novel. The conversations of Eunice Barbara Novio and G.V. Bhuyo, as well as the respite afforded by my travels with them in Bangkok and Korat, energized me and pushed me to finish this translation.

And finally, I would like to express my gratitude to my partner, James, for taking care of me when I was doing this translation in Cebu— despite, in quick succession, a motorcycle accident, a super typhoon, an Omicron Covid-19 virus infection and a cataract operation.

As with *Banaag at Sikat* and *Mga Ibong Mandaragit*, I would sometimes have vivid dreams about some of the scenes in *Luha ng Buwaya*. Even if I was, in another wit's words, a mere translator, I also lived inside the world of the novel I was working on. This also happened to me when I was writing my book *Riverrun, A Novel* at Hawthornden Castle in Scotland many years ago. I guess when you're writing or translating a novel, you have to dream it, so you can write it.

World, please welcome the second and last novel of Amado V. Hernandez, the Philippine National Artist for Literature.

CROCODILE'S TEARS

(Luha ng Buwaya)

Amado V. Hernandez

Translated by Danton Remoto

Authorized English translation

1

1

'Sampilong! Those who are getting off at Sampilong!'

The bus conductor called out in a crisp voice as the vehicle stopped on one side of the narrow road. Two, no more than three passengers, would get off. After a while, the bus would continue on its route.

Sampilong was a small town, far from the national road in a province in Luzon. It had no train station and you had to wait the whole day for the bus to arrive and leave. Only a few jeepneys and horse-drawn carriages came here.

Nobody amongst the old-timers knew why the town was called Sampilong. Old records that could have provided factual information had been either lost or burnt.

Even Ba Inte, who had almost forgotten his age, could not provide the information. According to him, one of his female ancestors had said that Sampilong is the contracted name for San Teofilo, shortened to San Pilo or Sampilo, like San Pedro that became Sampiro. Sampilo later became Sampilong.

One quality of the Tagalog language was to shorten what was already short. One could see these in the signages for jeepneys: Maypajo became Pajo and Divisoria became Soria. Sometimes, the latter would be abbreviated only to Soria, especially when the driver would cut the trip short and turn onto a wider road. Then, he would bring the passengers back to their original destination.

About Teofilo, nobody knew why that saint had been chosen to name the place after. Although it was known that Teofilo came from the Greek word meaning 'one who loves God,' the learned remember that a famous Teofilo became the bishop of a town in Asia Minor. But according to legend, this man consorted with the devil.

3

However, according to others, as related by Ba Inte, Sampilong didn't come from the name of a holy man, but a word original to the Tagalog language, which meant a slap or a slap on the nose. Allegedly, a native man refused to kiss the hand of the first Spanish friar who had come here—as a sign of respect—so the annoyed master opened his five fat fingers and let them land squarely on the face of the disrespectful native. But the crazy native really didn't recognize the friar, so he drew his machete, causing the frightened friar to fall to his knees, begging for forgiveness.

That is the converse of another story, which related that the friar wasn't the one who unleashed a slap, but instead, it was on his face that the swift slap of a woman from the village landed. The friar had allegedly invited the woman to his convent after she had made her confession. Whatever the reason for her slapping the friar, it wasn't known, but it must have been that the woman discovered that the priest was also human and not an angel.

Before the Second World War came, Commonwealth President Manuel Luis Quezon fanned the flames of nationalist feelings, and many towns changed their names. Some people had planned to change the names of Bataan, as well as Tayabas and Cebu. While many people agreed to change the names of places from the heavenly saints to the great Filipinos, trouble brewed amongst those who discussed whose names should be picked.

One proposal came to change the name of Sampilong to Captain Melchor, in honour of and as homage to the father of Donya Leona, who had left her an inheritance of vast lands. Perhaps, this proposal must also have come from Donya Leona herself. However, the farmers quickly protested against this. What's virtuous about that shameless soul? they asked. Is it because he was a curse on this town? Stealing everything through land-grabbing and usury? Is it because of his miserliness—he who even if rich, did not want to spend on his haircut? When his hair grew long, he would just get a bowl and put it over his head, then look at the mirror. Then he would cut the hair that was not covered by the bowl. Is it because of his greed? Whenever he saw someone cutting trees on his land, he would drive him away by firing his gun. Truly, many souls have already gone to rest and yet could not forget what Captain Melchor had done.

The name of a politician from the province was also floated, but when the Second World War came, he quickly shifted allegiance to the Japanese. On the other hand, the town of Sampilong was indeed conquered by the Japanese, but they did not stay long, because they failed to win against the guerrillas. They were forced to return to the capital after the school house—which they had used as their quarters—burnt down. That was why the townsfolk who could not agree on whom to name the town after, just decided to keep to the name Sampilong. They also agreed that when the history of the town was finally written, they would honour the memory of the village maiden who had slapped the foreign friar.

One man alighted from the bus when it stopped in the plaza at noontime. His quick body, five feet and eight inches tall, quickly jumped off the bus. He must have been around twenty-seven years old. He was wearing formal white native wear made from spun pineapple fibres and khaki trousers, and he was carrying a purple box.

He greeted those he met and slowed down his steps upon reaching the barber shop.

'You must have come from the capital, Teacher Bandong?' asked Tinoy, the barber, who at that time, had no other client. By the door of the barber shop, two men were playing Chinese Checkers.

'He's already a principal,' said one of the players before Bandong could answer the barber's query.

'Please stop by here first,' Tinoy invited him.

'I can't, it's already noontime,' answered Bandong. He got a handkerchief and wiped the sweat from his forehead. 'I'll go ahead,' he then said.

'Are you really a principal now?' asked Tinoy hurriedly.

'That is just a barbers' tale,' Bandong said by way of avoiding an answer, but before he left, he added with a smile, 'Perhaps!'

Indeed, Bandong had just come from the capital, where he had had a meeting at the office of the superintendent of the public schools. The principal at Sampilong needed to take a vacation because he was ill, and Bandong had been assigned to cover for him. Bandong was the role model for teachers in the school.

Teacher Putin had wanted to finish the last semester, which was anyway nearing its end, but his illness had worsened. That was why he had asked the superintendent to give him a sick leave so he could rest. He had requested that Bandong cover for him, since he had already worked with the younger man.

Bandong was in a rush to reach his home in the village. While walking, he gazed at the rice stalks now filled with fat yellow husks, bowing low in the whistling wind. He could smell the air already fragrant with the smell of ripening grain. The rice would be harvested in one to two more months, Bandong thought. With his eyes, he measured the width of the rice field whose stalks looked like countless hands made of gold, offering him immense comfort and happiness.

There was the house of Mang Pablo—of Pina. It had been Bandong's wont to slow down his steps whenever he reached the front of this house. It was as if he was waiting for the curtains to part and find the happy face of the village muse there.

'It's already noontime,' Pina greeted the young man with a smile as soon as their eyes met. The woman knew where Bandong had come from, because they had already talked earlier, as he was leaving for the capital.

'I'm already hungry,' said Bandong and teased her. 'Do you already have lunch prepared in your house?'

'Rice and dried herring,' Pina said, followed by laughter. 'Please come inside and spend some time with us.'

'Thank you,' said the invited one, 'but my auntie is already waiting for me.' Then, he quickly added, 'Will you be here later?'

'Why?'

'I want to visit you.'

'But our door is never bolted.'

'We'll never know. You might have a visitor and I'd just be a nuisance,' he made a snide remark.

Indeed, they were suddenly interrupted by the loud honking of a horn coming from a rushing jeepney. When it reached Bandong, it even raised a thick cloud of dust that flew and reached the window where Pina was. Dislaw was driving the jeepney and it carried the owner of the wide farmlands of Sampilong. They were going to the rice fields.

Because Donya Leona had rushed to the rice fields at noontime, it must have been for something important or she would have had to solve a problem that needed her personal presence. Perhaps, she would discuss the coming harvest with the tenants.

Dislaw was the overseer of the Grande family, but he also served as the driver and collector, as well as the bodyguard of Don Severo. While Dislaw was in-charge of ensuring that the landlords' rules were followed and he also collected the loans, the Donya did not trust him when it came to large sums of money.

'When the jeepney was gone and the dust had settled,' Pina spoke again from the window.

'What were you saying before that braggart passed by?'

'I said you might have another visitor later and I'd just be a nuisance,' repeated Bandong. 'I thought your acquaintance would run me over.'

'Him?' Pina pointed her lips and followed this with a movement of her hand. Then she made a snide remark, 'Perhaps, this isn't the place you're supposed to be visiting.'

'You know there's no one else.'

'I don't know about that,' the woman said with a smirk.

'If that is so, then I'll see you later.'

'What time?'

'Like before.'

'I'll wait for you.'

The afternoon had flamed and Bandong still had a long way to walk, but he did not seem to mind the heat and his feet seemed to be floating above the ground. He was already far but Pina still kept on looking at him, and she only went to the dining table when she heard the call of her father, Mang Pablo.

'What's happening to you, Pina? The food's already gone cold.'

Nana Oris, Bandong's auntie, was waiting for him. After changing his clothes, Bandong went to the dining table to eat. While eating, he was relating to her what had happened at the provincial capital. He had been assigned as the interim principal of the only public school in Sampilong.

'Oh, poor Teacher Putin,' said Nana Oris with sadness in her voice.

'He might be well after his vacation,' answered Bandong.

'Now that you're in his place, you should take care of your health,' his auntie advised him. 'It's easy to get sick, but difficult to recover one's energy.'

'Being a principal is a big responsibility,' said Bandong. 'I used to teach full-time; now, I've to be in charge of the teachers and the school as well.'

'Perhaps, they'll also increase your pay?'

'I don't know.'

'Well, bigger pay for more work.'

'I hope so,' agreed Bandong. 'But when there are no public funds, what can people like me do? Just be patient. One who serves the government should serve well, whether he earns a lot or a little.'

'You're right, my son, but how many in the government believe in that?' said the old woman. 'More rice?'

'I'm already full, auntie.'

Nana Oris raised Bandong and sent him to school as well. She and her husband had their own farm, like Mang Pablo. Bandong was the only child of Nana Oris' brother. When Bandong became an orphan, his aunt cared for him. She could not have a child of her own because of infertility. She raised Bandong as if he were their own flesh and blood. Nana Oris was widowed during the war, but she took care of Bandong and sent him to school until he finished a teaching degree at the highly rated Philippine Normal University. In the meantime, the old woman rented out her farmland, because nobody else would take care of it, and Bandong's Education degree would just have gone to waste if he tilled the land. Life was not as comfortable as it was when her husband was still alive, but Nana Oris' farmland yielded more or less 150 sacks of rice. This was more than the needs of the aunt and nephew. Then, Bandong was hired as a school teacher, and even though his salary was low, he could still manage to save some money.

After eating, Bandong went to his room to do some reading while he rested. He always read because it was part of his continuous education. He had a small library, and even though he had a limited budget for food and entertainment, he did not hold back when buying good books. He had various books on history, the sciences, politics, philosophy, sociology and literature.

When the day cooled down, he went downstairs to chop firewood. He was carrying an axe when his fellow school teachers arrived and greeted him.

'We heard about it,' they told Bandong, and they congratulated him one by one. 'We want to give you a blowout.'

'You shouldn't do that,' Bandong told them. 'Thanks, but that's not what I was waiting for. Just help me; let's help each other improve our school. Can I count on you?'

The teachers' voices rose as one when they made a promise to their new head. Bandong buried the blade of the axe deep in the hardwood he was trying to chop, and he invited his guests to go upstairs.

2

The moon was red as the face of a drunken man peering from the bamboo groves, rising above the rooftop of Nana Oris' house, when Bandong went downstairs. He was wearing a grey polo shirt.

Mang Pablo's family had just finished dinner when the young man called out his evening greetings. The old man met him and bade him to go upstairs.

'Please sit down, Bandong,' Mang Pablo's wife gently told him. After sitting down, the guest looked around the house.

'Pina is still changing her clothes,' he said, then added, 'I heard the good news. You're now the principal.' Mang Pablo was the president of the Parents' and Teachers' Association (PTA) of Sampilong.

'Yes, indeed, while Teacher Putin is on sick leave.'

'That will take a while,' said the old man. 'He has a lung problem, right?'

'Yes, that seems to be the diagnosis.'

'I should call a meeting of the PTA,' Mang Pablo suggested. 'Our members should meet the new principal,' he added with a smile.

'Our school has problems—'

Bandong stopped when Pina came over and joined them happily. The young man stood up to show respect.

'I'd like to greet the new principal,' the woman said.

'Thank you,' Bandong sat down again.

'If we didn't hear it from others, we wouldn't even know,' Pina said in an accusing tone.

'It wouldn't be nice if it came from me.'

'You're really secretive ...'

In a small town like Sampilong, the appointment of Bandong as interim principal was something out of the ordinary, that was why news of it had quickly spread. In fact, news like this would spread even before it actually happened.

Mang Pablo stood up to give the two of them privacy and then he repeated, 'Don't worry about it, I'll call for a meeting.'

'It seems Aling Sabel isn't here?' Bandong asked.

'She's finishing something in the kitchen,' the man said and then went into the kitchen.

Bandong fixed his gaze on the beautiful face of Pina when they were all alone.

'How are you?' were the only words that came from his lips.

'I'm okay, but I'm not like you,' she said. 'You're now a big shot.'

'Big shot? Hahaha!' the new principal laughed out loud. 'The new responsibilities won't make my nose any higher,' he said. 'If it brings additional honour, then I'd add my happiness to the other humble gifts I want to offer to you.'

Pina gave him a moist gaze, but did not say anything.

'And I think,' the man continued, 'that perhaps this is a step closer to my dream.'

A cloud fell on the woman's face and she answered in a tone filled with doubt.

'You seem to want more responsibility,' she said. 'You just said that being a principal means additional work for you. Now, you want more responsibilities to be given to you.'

A question could be seen on Pina's face and it seemed that now she was the one waiting for a reply.

'Yes, additional responsibilities,' admitted Bandong, 'but with a different reward. The reward will come from your love and my happiness.'

'You're counting your chicks before they're hatched.'

'What I mean, Pina, is that this responsibility is something that can be lightened. It will be, if both of us help each other out. If two become one—'

'When will Teacher Putin return to work?' asked the woman, deflecting.

'Nobody knows. If all goes well, he should be back in six months.'

Pina wanted to imply something by talking about timelines.

'Six months—that's not a very long time,' and she added, almost in a whisper, 'If Teacher Putin heals in six months ...' She let the thread of her thoughts hang, stood up and went to the window. From there, she looked at the moon whose red face had turned to yellow.

Bandong was thinking of what Pina had meant when she returned to her seat.

'What if Teacher Putin heals in six months?'

'Let's talk more about your added responsibilities.'

'What if he doesn't heal?' asked Bandong.

The woman's eyes widened, she smiled and then spoke, 'Could the six months be lengthened or shortened?'

Gladness filled the young man's whole being, for he had been courting her, but he restrained himself.

'Yes, Pina,' his voice was bright. 'For someone like me who'll love you for a hundred years, who's almost dying from the waiting, six months will feel like six years.'

Pina was happy with what she heard, but before she could answer, Aling Sabel had already entered. She was carrying a tray with a bowl of dessert and a glass of water. Pina got the tray from her mother and put it on the table between her and Bandong. She took several spoonfuls of the dessert, transferred them to the saucer and offered it to her guest.

'Please have some of this mango dessert I've made,' she said with pride.

After tasting a morsel, the young teacher said, 'I'd be filled with happiness if the way you feel for me is as sweet as this dessert.'

In the whole of Sampilong, Pina was considered the most beautiful, although she also had other good characteristics, too. She was good at making desserts and pickled papayas, at sewing and making decorations for the house. When it was time to plant rice and harvest it, Pina did not mind if her fair skin got burnt by the sun, and she worked in the fields like everyone else.

When she returned to the village after taking a vocational course in Manila, she already had a sewing machine and things needed for her work. The best dressmakers in the capital could not hold a candle to her skills. Even men would come to her to ask her to make their polo shirts and native formal wear, and consequently, Bandong and Dislaw became two of her customers.

People liked to compare Pina and Ninet. The latter was the only daughter of Don Severo and Donya Leona, while Pina was the only daughter of Mang Pablo and Aling Sabel. Even if they grew up in different conditions, they were both the centres of attention, especially for the men. Ninet was beautiful, but it was the sort of beauty created by layers of makeup, with dresses that followed the latest fashion, a body adorned with expensive jewellery.

To avoid comparing the two women would lead to issues no one wanted to have, so Ninet was compared to a lovely flowerpot made of porcelain, while Pina was compared to a jasmine flower that was blooming, planted in the earth, with a beauty not shaped by the hands of any man but by sunlight and wind. A diamond with many facets, Ninet had a blinding brilliance; a pure pearl, Pina was demure and offered a cool comfort to the eyes that gazed at her, bright as the sound of raindrops falling, and clean as white silk.

Nobody in Sampilong could go to the stone house of the Grande family to court their daughter. No young men dared to do so, not because they feared the ferocious dogs in the backyard or the sharp tongue of Donya Leona. They avoided doing so because it seemed to be such an act of bravado. Moreover, Ninet was uncomfortable dealing with the mere mortals of Sampilong.

On the other hand, the house of wood and thatch in the village had no barking dogs, nor a sour face that a visitor would fear. Mang Pablo often told Pina that she had already come of age, that was why she could decide for herself on matters of will and of the heart.

'The door of our house is always open,' Mang Pablo said. 'If they come here as human beings, then we'll treat them as such.'

In truth, Pina held no secrets from her parents. Both of them knew who the men courting their daughter were. It would be uncommon for any young man in the village and the neighbouring areas not to be attracted to Pina's beauty, but rare was the man who had enough courage to declare his intentions openly. Only two, Bandong and Dislaw, could be compared to two knights who had declared their intentions to Princess Pina, whose real name was Pilipinas.

Mang Pablo was telling the truth when he said that their house was open to any suitors. Oftentimes, those who would go there needed something from Mang Pablo. It was because he had almost taken over the work of Ba Inte, who counselled the people in the village and they, in turn, went to him for help because he was younger than the sickly Ba Inte. He was also the president of the PTA and had been teaching for many years as well. The members did not want to replace him, although Dislaw harboured a strong desire to lead the group.

Bandong and Dislaw took turns visiting Pina. It seemed that they were in silent agreement to not go to her house at the same time. Other young women would also visit Pina, but they mostly came to her to have their dresses made.

There were nights when they would be disturbed by singing. But it would only be a moment of light-heartedness on the part of some of the young men, who were friends of the family. They would be ushered into the house and they would stay for one, two hours, playing the guitar and singing. They would also ask Pina to sing, for she also had a good voice. The house always had preserved mangoes, jackfruit or cotton fruit in store for everyone; that was why the last part of the merrymaking would be eating the food that Pina had prepared.

Sometimes, Bandong would be there unexpectedly, and upon seeing the group, would spend time bonding with them. But it never happened that this group serenaded Pina when Dislaw was around, formally offering his proposal to her.

Mang Pablo also avoided showing partiality to any of his daughter's suitors. He treated them both very well indeed. In truth, he was partial to Bandong, but he did not drive away the trusted man of the Grande family.

Mang Pablo's philosophy was that it was Pina who would live with the man she would choose. Love was strange. Mang Pablo knew that the heavy became light, if truly desired, while the good became as burdensome as a cross, if undesired.

Mang Pablo had witnessed times when parents forced their daughters into marriages not of their own accord, to men whom the parents wanted them to marry. He saw the bitter fruits of these forced marriages. While following the dictates of those to whom she owed her life, the daughter's wedding day would turn into the day her happiness would be buried. Mang Pablo loved Pina and he wanted her to be happy. And that would only happen if she were given a choice as to whom she could love for the rest of her life.

On the other hand, Aling Sabel was a bit partial to Dislaw. The man would often come to her, since the very beginning, but the old woman did not let on that she favoured him. She knew that her husband would not like it. She was pleased at the thought that the trusted assistant of the richest clan in Sampilong was courting her daughter.

Dislaw came in his jeep. He made it appear that the vehicle was already his, and he could freely use it anytime he wanted to do so. He would often talk about the Don and the Donya, their children, Jun and Ninet, the friends of the Grande family in Manila, and his place in the abovementioned contexts. He said he would bring the money to meet the children's expenses, he would pay for their tuition and dormitory fees; he would do this and he would do that.

And he always slung his revolver in his belt and showed it to the world. He also boasted about his skill at firing a gun, that was why he was never afraid to go anywhere in the village, the capital, or the city itself. Aling Sabel liked what she heard, but Mang Pablo noticed that whenever the brash Dislaw visited them, the usually cool wind would turn hot and humid.

Pina would face him and she never failed to be at her best behaviour. She tried her best to listen to Dislaw, even if his boasting grated on her ears. Sometimes, Pina was like someone who was reading a book whose contents she never fully understood.

In truth, she treated Bandong differently, even if the young teacher kept on complaining about her treatment of him. But that must be typical of the behaviour of someone who was in love and knew that he had a good chance.

Before Bandong left at ten o'clock, Mang Pablo and Aling Sabel joined them. Their talk veered towards the forthcoming rice harvest. Bandong asked when would this be.

'We must do it before the rains come,' said Mang Pablo. 'Maybe in the coming week.'

Bandong noticed that the rice plants grew well this year and the harvest might be good. But Mang Pablo expressed his thoughts that a good harvest was not enough to uplift one from poverty. Enough irrigation, supply of fertilizer and continued progress were also needed.

'The landlord only cares about his profit,' said the young man.

Before Pina walked him to the stairs, Mang Pablo said, 'Our country isn't for the handful who own the land, nor for the handful of foreigners who live here. Our country is for us, its native sons and daughters who work on the land and make it produce wealth.'

Bandong walked down the stairs, deep in his own thoughts.

3

The villagers woke up earlier than the sun that Saturday morning, the start of the harvest time.

The people had already prepared on the previous night the things they needed to bring to the fields. Sharp scythes and machetes, pails and jars of water, food containers and native woven bags, banana leaves, amongst other things.

They came in groups but they all went into the rice fields together. Men and women and a cluster of children, those who got paid in harvested rice, the few who owned small parcels of land, the tenants, those who were requested to help, those who volunteered, as well as those who were paid. Light-bodied and firm-armed, they were ready to work the whole day, then the next day, even for a week. They were excited to harvest what they had worked hard for in the past year.

It was noticeable that there were more women than men among the harvesters. They were also more numerous when the rice saplings were transferred at the end of May and the beginning of June, the previous year. Farming was men's work. Cutting the wild weeds, plowing the field, piling up the earth to serve as raised pathways for people, digging canals for the water to flow, as well as transferring the rice saplings— one handspan tall, from the seed beds to the fields, all were jobs for men to do. Thorns got embedded into their hands and leeches sucked the blood from their legs.

But on this morning, the women indeed were more numerous than the men, that was why the work atmosphere was noisier and happier. Many of them carried food containers on their heads and wide winnowing trays filled with things, but these were all level on their heads.

The tenants of the Grande family comprised the biggest group. They were led by Beteng, his wife, and their daughter; Tomas and his wife; Tasyo, Simon, Blas and their children. Behind them were Julian and his two children, who, while still too young to use a scythe, could already run errands, if asked.

While walking, Julian remembered that he was with his wife, Sepa, when they transferred the rice saplings last year. But when they arrived home after the second day, Sepa was already burning with fever and the poor woman could hardly move. The next morning, she was wracked with cough and when she expectorated what was tightening in her chest and throat, they saw a stain of blood. From there on, she was bedridden, and dried up like a tree losing its sap.

And today, Sepa could no longer join them in the fields.

'I can't help you anymore,' she said sadly when Julian was about to leave.

She remained at home, along with their daughter, who was twelve years old and took care of her mother, and the youngest child who could not be kept apart from her. Sepa just looked out of the window and watched the noisy group venture into the fields.

She was not healing but rather, taking a turn for the worse, Julian thought. He walked at the end of the group, with his head bowed. He was still thankful, though, that Sepa could still taste the newly harvested rice, whose sowing had caused her illness.

Mang Pablo's group included Aling Sabel, his brother-in-law, his sister-in-law, Pina, her brother Dinong and other people, whom they had asked to help. Bandong was also there, along with another teacher, as well as Andres and two squatters who lived on the hill overgrown with cogon grasses. Mang Pablo and Andres were conversing. Some of the people walked fast, but Bandong and Pina were taking their sweet time. They were happily conversing as they walked.

Pina wore a lilac shirt with long sleeves; the hem of her long dress reached all the way down to her ankles. In her right hand, she carried a shining scythe, while on her left, she carried a pointed hat. The other women wore the same outfit, except those who would not cut the rice stalks. The others wore kimono-like clothes made of cotton, with the sleeves folded.

Bandong noted Pina's attire, which he compared to a believer following the procession on Holy Thursday. Her feet were unshod.

'Whatever you wear can't detract from your beauty,' said Bandong.

'The believers who follow the procession of the Three Times When Jesus Christ Fell,' explained Pina, 'have a lifetime vow to keep. They wear clothes like those worn by the disciples of Jesus Christ, and they walk on bare feet.'

'What the believers wear don't usually look good on everyone,' Bandong butted in, 'but you look even prettier today.'

'You just stop that now,' the woman said, even if what she heard pleased her. 'I was talking about vows. The women in the field,' she continued, 'also take vows to help with planting the rice, harvesting and winnowing it. And this is what we wear while we fulfill that vow.'

Bandong saw a window of opportunity and went for it.

'You've been following that vow for a lifetime,' he said in accusing tone, 'but you still leave me high and dry.'

'Excuse me, Mister, but I haven't promised you anything yet,' Pina corrected him.

'That's what hurts me. You've been asking me to wait for a long time.'

'Six months,' the woman reminded him. 'Didn't we agree on that?'

'The long time needed for rice to grow and be harvested.'

'The short time needed—that's what you should say.'

And they continued to walk in silence, as if each one was discerning if six months was indeed too long or too short a time.

When they were near the rice fields, Pina asked Bandong, 'Have you seen any films about rice harvesting?'

'Yes, several times,' answered the man.

'Aren't they funny?' said Pina and laughed a little.

Bandong first decided what Pina meant and when he knew, he answered with a smile.

'Oh yes,' he said, 'the clothes of the film stars who would harvest the rice ... They're not even wearing underclothes,' and then he looked at Pina's attire.

'They're wearing a native formal dress, wooden clogs with designs and keeping their hair up in a bun, covered with a silk bandana. So funny. Those who make these films, have they not seen how rice is really planted and harvested?'

'Yes, it seems as if they only want the film stars to look ravishing,' Bandong explained.

'I even saw a film where women were doing laundry by the river bank,' Pina said. 'They were also wearing native formal wear, as if going on a picnic.'

'Nothing can beat the reality,' said Bandong. 'Film is a representation of life. Like drama and novels. It's annoying when they make something that is so far from reality. Believe me, when I saw them, I was thoroughly annoyed at our films that show fake cowboys and bandits.'

They finally reached the rice fields without seemingly becoming aware of it. The sun's rays were now at eye level and hitting the bowed sheaves of rice that were swaying in the wind. The grains of rice looked like shimmering waves of gold, offering some kind of wealth.

The reapers put on their gloves to protect their hands. Some of the gloves were made of leather, the others of soft fake leather, and the rest of white cloth. They also put on their wide-brimmed hats, and some of them even put on sunglasses.

The paddy and the footpath lay beside each other, but the rice fields to be reaped had different owners, and also different reapers. The biggest of them all was owned by the Grande family, with its group of tenants; the other rice fields belonged to Mang Pablo, and the others owned one-hectare lots that they farmed themselves. And the rest of the rice fields, which were also substantial, had been rented out, even if the owners had left Sampilong a long time ago.

The Grande family did not rent out their vast lands and they had a slew of tenants. They deemed this was the best way to make the most profits. The other property owners who had moved to Manila and Quezon City when the Second World War began in 1941, rented out their farm lands. They did not want to sell their lands outright and when they visited, they assigned caretakers who would collect taxes from *them* after the rice had been milled. Nana Oris also rented out to Mang Pablo the farmland that she had inherited from her late husband.

That was why Bandong, her nephew, was there to help harvest the rice from the field.

When the sharp scythes had begun to lop off the ripe grains of rice, Donya Leona would arrive in her jeep. Dislaw was behind the steering wheel. Usually, the landlords just stayed at home while the harvest went on in the rice fields and waited for the rice milling to begin. That was also the time when the rice grains were divided between the landlord and the tenants. But Donya Leona was different. If she were not ill, she could be found there from the start of the rice harvest to the winnowing, even until the milling. If it were at all possible, she would prevent the stray rice grains from falling to the ground, lest they be picked up by children and old women.

The moment she got off the jeep, she would tell Dislaw to announce what she wanted should happen. She would indicate where the harvesters would go, where to gather the stalks, where to cluster the stalks to form the mound, whose location she chose as well. The tenants were usually the ones who decided all of this, but even on these matters, Donya Leona expected to be followed. The real reason she was there was to show to one and all that it was she and not the tenants who owned the vast lands, and all of them were simply working for her.

Her actions annoyed most of those who had come there as unpaid labour and had just been requested by the tenants to help out, but they knew to keep their mouths shut. The farm workers always gave way to the landlords, if they could help it.

'Those who rent the land are luckier than us,' Simon said with a sigh.

'Indeed, because they're not under Leona's thumb,' snapped Tasyo. 'Sometimes, I just want to test the sharpness of this scythe on her tongue,' he said in a teasing tone.

'Your scythe will become dull,' Simon answered back, 'because her tongue is sharper.'

Two young men, one of whom carried a guitar and the other a harmonica, began to play as the farmers began their harvest. They played the folk song 'Planting Rice Is Never Fun'.

This caught the attention of Donya Leona and she said, 'If instead of doing that, you were working with your scythes ...'

The two young men stopped playing, but they didn't touch the scythes. They were students who were there to just observe. They thought that the guitar and the harmonica would liven things up.

'Killjoy,' one of them said with a smirk. The other one made the holes of his nostrils bigger, imitating the one who could not tolerate the pleasure of others.

The whole morning passed as slow as a water buffalo tethered to a tree. But it could not be denied that noon had come, for the sun blazed on the farmers' napes and the stomachs of some, and had turned the fields into a furnace. It was also the time when the food arrived to be shared amongst the different groups.

Some of the tenants insisted that Donya Leona eat with them, a gesture that was a testament to the goodness of their hearts. Even if the landowner's acts annoyed them, they were still the ones who humbled themselves further, so they could share a meal with the proud woman.

'I'll stay with Beteng,' Donya Leona decided. 'The food is good here and I don't want to move anymore.' With that, she sat on a chair and rested her back.

But the others still offered their food to Donya Leona. Tomas' wife brought her grilled catfish, Blas' sister-in-law brought her steamed shrimps, and another one offered her boiled eggplants and a dip made out of vinegar.

Mang Pablo and Pina also came to her and invited her to share a meal with them.

'We've included your share in our lunch, Donya Leona,' and Mang Pablo's words were true. The rich landowner thanked them.

'How about you, Dislaw?' she turned to her assistant. He also wanted to join them because Pina was looking at him, but he had already had his share of grilled catfish.

Pina waved at the two students and invited them to eat.

The reapers took off their gloves and began to eat the food arrayed on the low bamboo tables covered with fresh banana leaves. Everyone ate well, and in truth, only fish bones and meat skin were left after lunch was finished.

After the food was cleared, Donya Leona heard again the ringing of the guitar and the sighing of the harmonica. Suddenly, in the air, floated the sweet voice of Pina, singing a song about life on the farm.

The women and men came closer to the spontaneous programme. Even Dislaw joined them, and later became one of those standing close to the two students playing as the woman sang. But he was irritated when he saw Bandong seated beside Pina, cooling her with a fan made of wide, dried anahaw leaves.

When the chorus came, everyone began to sing with such joy:

'Planting rice is never fun
You bow your heads the whole day long
You cannot stand
Nor sit down.
But when harvest time comes,
Its joy fills up everyone;
How fragrant is the rice,
What a thrill it is to eat.'

4

Donya Leona was stricter than usual when it came to collecting the debts that people owed to her. For this harvest, she immediately got back the money due to her, and even deducted the loans taken for this and that purpose. She got her share of half the harvest, followed by the rice seeds that the farmers owed her, then the money she had loaned them so they could buy clothes, appliances on installments, medicines and cigarettes, amongst other things. Donya Leona did not only lend the rice seeds, she also lent money for all the things they needed, with interest.

Those whom she collected from were filled with sighs and complaints.

'After Donya Leona receives her share, nothing's left for us anymore,' said one of tenants who was filled with despair.

Donya Leona almost stayed the whole time in the fields when the rice was being harvested and later, milled. The farmers rarely saw Don Severo, but the woman was a constant presence the whole day long.

The farmers knew Donya Leona better than Don Severo, even though both the husband and wife came from Sampilong, born of parents who were also landlords. That was why they already knew the rich woman's ways.

Leona inherited the vast lands from her father, Captain Melchor, whose ancestors were pure Spaniards. The captain was notorious for his shrewd and wily ways, which he forced on his tenants. He became astoundingly rich while the peasants became poorer. And it was said that there was no tenant who was spared by his cruel hand.

'Captain Melchor was like a curse upon the earth,' said Ba Inte while narrating to the younger farmers what their ancestors had gone through. 'If the tenant borrowed five sacks of rice at harvest time, it would immediately balloon to ten sacks of rice. If he loaned money, the interest was always at least one-third more than the amount loaned.'

'And what does "mortgaging" mean?'

'Ah, that refers to loans on the land,' Ba Inte clarified. 'For example, if you borrowed fifty pesos, you would use your land as collateral. Let's say your land is worth 400 pesos. After one year, if you still haven't paid, the loaner will get your land. That's what pawning-buying means.'

'How did Captain Melchor die?' came a meaningful query from a farmer who was also listening. 'Did he die from an illness?'

'One afternoon, he was walking by the river bank but he never returned. A rumour went around that a crocodile had eaten him.'

'From one crocodile to another.'

'Seems like it.'

'What did the leaders do to protect the people from undue suffering?'

'What did they do?' Ba Inte said, repeating the question. 'In this country, Atong, you can count on your fingers the leaders who are not beholden to the rich.'

Ba Inte also mentioned the name of Captain Baltazara, the mother of Leona.

'She was the first woman I had seen who wore trousers,' he said. 'Leona got her courage from her mother, added to which were some characteristics that were her own.'

According to Ba Inte, Captain Baltazara had a notebook in the left hand and a big whip in the other. The notebook was where she listed down the names of those who had taken loans from her, along with the amounts owed. Those who made the mistake of questioning her accounts suffered the lash of the whip.

'And how did her life end?'

'Violence. A water buffalo mauled her to death.'

'May God forgive their souls.'

When Leona grew up, the young woman took over the management of the accounts. The heiress also had her own notebook, but she had transferred the information about the accounts of those who owed money to her parents, into it. On the farms, loans were inherited as if they were properties to be parcelled out.

Don Severo also came from a rich family, but he had lived away from Sampilong. He studied in Manila. When he was a young man, his father forced him to return to the old town. His parents had discovered that he would rather look at the faces of the four queens on the playing cards than the pages of his textbooks. He came home and did not finish his studies. He was then trained to manage their farmlands in Sampilong. Later, he got married to the only daughter of Captain Melchor and Captain Baltazara. Pascual, Leona's brother, was almost a priest by then.

'It would have been better if Severo finished his studies,' some of the old men in the town centre said.

The tongues of angels must have dictated that something good would come from Severo's marriage to Leona. Because of her, Severo was able to renovate their family's stone house and rebuild the rice granary. Don Severo insisted that they rent out their farmlands and return to Manila, where they would live.

'The children are already studying there and they shouldn't be separated from us,' the man insisted.

'It would be worse if we're parted from the source of our livelihood,' Donya Leona reasoned.

She didn't want to end up like the other landlords who left their lands in the hands of their tenants. Aside from that, the rich people who had left Sampilong had started other kinds of businesses.

The woman expressed her distrust for some of their tenants.

'Some of them are already making fools of us while we're still here, who knows what more might happen when we're gone?'

And as usual, Donya Leona's decision was followed; Don Severo agreed.

With the passage of time, she became bolder and more persistent in her ways. She was like a rock that could not be cracked by the rain. The tenants who owed her money just wasted their time in going to her house and pleading. She squeezed them dry without mercy and the tears of the tenants' wives came to naught.

'Donya Leona, please take your full share later; my wife Sepang is ill,' Julian pleaded.

'No.'

'I beg you. I'll spend a lot on her medication, which is only available in the capital.'

'If there's no other remedy, then the doctor is useless and the medicines would just go to waste,' she snapped.

'Donya Leona, may I just pay you half, first?' pleaded Tasyo. 'I've to send my two kids to school.'

'Impossible!' she said, her eyes widening.

'Donya Leona, it's beginning to rain and I've to fix our house. Our roofs are already full of holes,' complained Tomas. 'Maybe you could allow me—'

'Allow me first to get my share, okay?'

'My water buffalo died and I need money to buy—'

'What do you think I am, the Philippine National Bank?'

'Our youngest child has to be baptized.'

'You can't even pay your debts, why are you thinking of a baptism? Are you crazy?'

Like the lid of a jar, Donya Leona always suppressed the requests of the poor under her harsh words and accusations. Instead of helping them out, she blamed them for what happened to them.

'What else do you want?' she would say, her arms open wide. 'I've already advanced the cost of the rice seeds and your other needs, but we share half of the harvest. When the harvest is done and sharing is about to begin, then you all start complaining.'

The tenants could hardly put a word edge-wise, feeling as if they were being tried by a cruel judge. Then Donya Leona would continue with the lash of her words.

'How many times did the land taxes increase since the American liberation in 1946?' she would ask in a grating tone. 'Do you even know that? And why would you even care? Do you share the taxes for the land with me? What's your capital? Your hard bodies?'

No one amongst the tenants could answer her, so she continued adding to her sermon.

'I'll tell you your defects,' and then she mentioned the names of some tenants. 'You're loose with your expenses. Julian's wife is ill, Tasyo's sending two kids to school. Tomas will fix his leaking roof. Someone's going to have a baptism and that's why a feast has to be prepared. But you don't talk about your vices, cockfighting, gambling—'

'But I'm not a gambler, Donya Leona,' Beteng countered.

'If you're not, then why don't you have enough money?'

'Our situation is really tight,' Blas said.

'Because you don't save money.'

'How can we save when there's nothing to save?' Blas said. 'Like me, I harvested 150 sacks of rice from two and a half hectares of land. You got half of that, so I was left with seventy-five. Then you got my loans, which amounted to forty-five more sacks. How many were left? Thirty sacks of rice.' Blas drew a deep sigh and then continued speaking, shaking his head, 'Even if you don't deduct my loans, will thirty sacks of rice be enough for a family of five for one year?'

'Why not?' swiftly answered Donya Leona. She thought about it quickly, then she faced Blas. 'Look. Thirty sacks of rice are equivalent to fifty gantas of rice. In short, you have two gantas of rice per day. Could a family of five consume the whole of that? You must be eating like water buffaloes then.'

Some of those present laughed, while Blas almost lost his cool.

'But people don't live only on rice,' he reasoned. 'They also need a dish. Sugar, petrol, soap. Medicines when ill. Clothes for the children. School expenses.'

'Aha, that's where the fault lies then,' Donya Leona snapped. 'You're the ones increasing your expenses. Like your food. Why do you need to buy food when you can plant it? Is it bad to eat vegetables? You just need to pick from your backyard. You want to eat fish? The river is right there. You want meat? Don't you have chickens and pigs in your backyard? This is what's wrong with you,' and she spoke slowly, as if each word was a nail being driven deep by a hammer, 'you take care of roosters for cockfighting, instead of hens that lay eggs. Don't deny it, Blas, as well as the rest of you. Dislaw has given me a report.'

A collective grunt rose from the men at the mention of the report that came from the Grandes' caretaker.

5

Blas knew that things might come to a head if he continued to reason against Donya Leona. That was why he stopped, even if had wanted to say more things. He and the rest of the men knew that they would never win against her, because in her mind, she was always correct. Whenever there was a heated discussion, they would just stop and admit defeat. The rich woman always had the last word.

Insisting on their points, whether right or reasonable, might just lead to a falling-out. Donya Leona could deliver hurtful insults. She was hot-tempered and easily angered. She could easily provoke anyone she scolded. She threatened to get back the land and expel the tenant who brooked a heated argument with her.

The pitiful ones were afraid that they would suffer the same fate as Adam, when he angered God and was thrown out of paradise. But even if the tenant was not in paradise but in purgatory, he thought that purgatory was better, since he had awakened there and knew no other life. Who knew what greater sufferings lurked outside the farms?

Those who lost the right to farm would also have to leave the estate of the Grande family. Donya Leona did not allow anyone who wasn't a tenant or worker to stay on the estate. All of the people there worked for her. They should come when called and work when ordered to do so.

She also did not accept squatters on her land, even those related to her tenants. She had given strict orders to Dislaw to report if there were any strange faces on her estate. That was why she wanted to drive away the squatters even in a place called Tambakan, near the boundary of her estate. But she had no authority to do so.

Those whom Donya Leona rejected just kept their ill feelings inside themselves, and left the resolution of their problems to the mercy of time.

'If my wife dies, it will be on her conscience,' Julian said.

'But does the crocodile have a conscience?' said Ba Inte's constant companion.

'Donya Leona doesn't want our kids to study in school,' said Tasyo, 'because if they learn something, they'll look for other jobs and she can no longer enslave them. Pwe!'

'She doesn't want to lend me money to replace my dead water buffalo,' sighed one man. 'How then can I plow my field?'

'Then plow your you-know-what,' teased Simon, and was the first to laugh.

'She even called me a gambler,' Beteng said. 'Do I gamble? Is there anyone who goes as often to the cockpit as her assistant, Kosme? But I won't report that because my name is Beteng and not Dislaw. I'm not a spy.'

Someone let out a hiss before revealing his hurt.

'Why, she even prevented the baptism of my youngest child. Which would have been fine if her brother, Father Pascual, did not charge fees. Will I raise a child who isn't a Christian?'

And then they concocted reasons as to why Donya Leona had turned more savage in collecting back their debts. They had different opinions and reasons for her behaviour. Someone surmised that she must have lost a large amount of money due to contraband. 'That's why she collected our debts.'

'Don Severo lost several thousand pesos in a gambling session,' another pointed out.

However, Beteng, who had heard it from his wife who often worked as a housemaid at the stone house said that Junior and Ninet were going to have a big party on their graduation. The return of the siblings would bring great joy to the family.

Someone thought that, perhaps, either Jun or Ninet was going to get married.

'Perhaps,' answered Beteng, and told them another morsel of news he had heard from his wife. 'Jun's girlfriend is the daughter of a rich Chinese family. On the other hand, Ninet has a lawyer for a boyfriend.'

'Both have money.'

'Where else would they go?'

'Of course, the rich would only associate with the rich.'

'If they're rich, why do they squeeze us so?'

'Hey, can a leech ever really have enough blood to suck?'

'More wily than a monkey that won't share even the skin, if it's tasty.'

And the tenants remembered that if there was a celebration at the big house, they would get very tired helping, along with their families. But they could not taste even the leftover food—even if there was a lot of it.

'The food for the guests is different from the food for the servants,' said one man who looked like Tomas.

'Why, you could also sniff the aroma of delicious food, so that's your consolation, right?' teased another man.

'Am I a cat?'

And laughter drowned out their sadness.

But after several weeks, after she had done an inventory of her granary and updated her accounts, Donya Leona would lend money again. She knew that the business of usury worked better when the needs of the poor had become more intense. They would just bite the bullet. Usury was like a saw that went forward and backward, biting in every direction. Dislaw and Kosme would then go around the village and spread the good news that the grand lady now had a cool head.

But there was a hidden trap in the new direction of the blowing wind. The price of rice had increased since after the harvest. Dislaw and Kosme monitored how many sacks of rice were still left in the huts of the tenants. And they knew who needed to sell their rice in exchange for their basic necessities—petrol, soap, sugar, cigarettes, clothes, coffee, canned goods, amongst others, the things that Blas had mentioned when he had had a discussion with Donya Leona recently.

How strange the price of rice was, in the hands of the needy farmers. They sold it cheaply, even while the investment for growing the rice was heavy. Especially so when it was borrowed or paid in installments.

And these basic necessities were bought not from the capital or the grocery owned by the Chinese middlemen in the town centre, but from the warehouse of Donya Leona.

Soon, the farmers' share of the rice harvest would be reclaimed by Donya Leona. When she already had all the sacks of rice stored in her granary, the price of rice would suddenly increase. The farmers would be left holding only their empty jute sacks and cheap woven bags. The hay in the fields and scattered grains in the mills could be fed to the water buffaloes, or used to start and keep a fire for cooking.

The Chinese middlemen also went to the village. They would buy the sacks of rice at a price higher than the prevailing market price, and they offered a better deal than Donya Leona. However, they could not operate in Sampilong, because they would be driven away by the minions of the mayor and the chief of police. Mayor Bartolo was a first cousin of Don Severo, while Chief of Police Hugo was Donya Leona's godson by marriage.

In truth, the two men did not oppose if the Chinese middlemen came and bought the rice, but they did not want them to deal directly with the farmers. They wanted to be the middlemen, under the guise of helping the farmers, and for the Chinese middlemen to have a debt of gratitude as well. Thus, they profited both ways.

In addition to this, they also got a share from Donya Leona, who believed that the two men kept the foreign traders at bay. Dislaw would announce this to the Grande family, but shut his mouth in the presence of Mayor Bartolo and Chief Hugo. He knew that these two men could deal with him in other, more dangerous ways.

Has anyone ever touched a clay pot and not left with dirty hands? he said to himself.

Meanwhile, the fields that had been harvested were not yet clean, but the villagers were already facing problems with their food. They felt they lay between a rock and the sea—Donya Leona and the Chinese middleman on one side, and their poverty on the other.

'So how much did Dislaw pay for your rice?' Tasyo asked Simon when they met at the barber's shop.

'Six pesos,' Simon answered.

'Just last week?'

'Last Monday.'

'But you can't find rice in the capital that would sell for seven pesos.'

The other farmers who had also sold their rice at the price dictated by the buyer joined in the discussion.

'When it begins to rain in the village, we'll start eating congee again,' said one man in a despairing tone. 'Seven pesos for a small tin of rice.'

'Those who planted and pounded the rice, end up hungry,' said another man. 'The cycle has started again. All of our sacks of rice are now back in Donya Leona's granary.'

The day was hot and the wind coming from the dry fields was humid. The fields lay fallow and nothing grew in them, except small shrubs that didn't get wet in the rain. But rain had not yet fallen in the last two months.

Simon let go of the words that had tightened inside him like a fist. They later served like small embers that also burnt inside the other people gathered in the barber's shop.

'It's true that all our sacks of rice are now in the granary of the greedy,' he said, in agreement with what had been said previously. 'But when the time comes when people no longer have food to eat, that granary will be the lightning rod for the hungry.' And something sharp flashed in the eyes of Simon.

'What happened during the time of the Japanese invaders shouldn't be repeated here,' said Tasyo. 'It shouldn't be, but—'

'May God not allow it,' Simon said in agreement.

And with that, the men gathered there went their separate ways.

6

The wide yard surrounding the house of the Grande family had been busy for the last few days. People cleaned, arranged and decorated. It was rare to have a celebration inside the big house made of stone and surrounded by high walls. But every celebration there was forever imprinted in the memory of Sampilong's residents. Don Severo and Donya Leona were notorious for being cunning and miserly, but on an occasion like this, they opened their palms and spent their money freely. This was one of those rare occasions.

The Grande family wasn't the richest in the town of Sampilong. Other families richer than them, whether in terms of land or money, had moved to Manila and Quezon City after the guns had stopped firing in the Second World War. Be that as it may, because they were the only ones left, they were different from those they worked with and those who worked for them. Don Severo was the first cousin of the mayor. Donya Leona's brother, Father Pascual, headed the Catholic Church in Sampilong. And the Chief of Police was their godson by wedding. They were cheek by jowl with the few foreign businessmen in town. Their assistant, Dislaw, was the treasurer of the PTA.

They also cultivated close relations with the provincial governor, the treasurer, the engineer, and the judge of the Court of First Instance, and they were also friends with the municipal judge and the commander of the Philippine Constabulary.

That was why in their celebration, they gathered together all the stellar personalities in the town and the province. Some guests would even come from as far as Manila.

The rich couple expected the celebration to be a joyful one. It would be a homecoming and a homage for their two children, their only children, who had both just finished their university programmes of study. Junior, or Jun, the elder one, received a diploma in Medicine at the age of twenty-six, while Ninet, the younger, was already a pharmacist. Jun was older than Ninet by two years.

According to an earlier message from the siblings, they would come home immediately after classes closed on the twenty-first of the current month. Today was already the twentieth day.

Don Severo and Donya Leona faced each other in the hallway on the first floor. The man was leaning on the back of an ornate wooden chair and reading the newspaper. Swirls of tobacco smoke were floating from his mouth. The woman, who had just taken a bath, was sitting down on her rocking chair.

At first glance, Don Severo looked older than his fifty-two years, while Donya Leona looked younger than her forty-nine years. The man wore a faded pair of pyjamas, while the woman wore a blue dress with embroidered violet flowers on the front of her blouse. Her fingernails and toenails were painted with a hint of colour.

Later, Donya Leona looked at the thick carpet that had been laid on the ground the day before. It was still new and the colours of the rainbow had not yet faded.

'Look at that, Berong, if I had just left that carpet somewhere, it would have turned into a doormat by now,' the woman said with pride.

'Indeed,' agreed Berong, without taking his eyes off the newspaper. 'Even if you got it second-hand.'

Donya Leona just ignored the word 'second-hand'.

'You know the number of people who come to this house,' she continued. 'Especially the villagers, they just walk in here even if their feet were caked with mud.'

'Just let them be. Anyway, they're meek as lambs in front of you.'

'Because they want something.'

Donya Leona stood for a moment, gazing at the chandelier hanging from the ceiling like the big earring of a gigantic woman. It could also be compared to a jellyfish with its tentacles splayed, and at the end of the tentacles were the electric bulbs' wide-open eyes.

Donya Leona returned to her chair and spoke again to her husband, who was still reading the newspaper.

'That chandelier is beautiful when all the bulbs are lighted,' she said, again with pride in her voice. 'It lights up the whole living room. That was why when the priest saw it, one night, he said it would look good in his church.'

'Did you tell him that it came from a church?'

Don Severo put down his newspaper and lit the end of his tobacco.

'Who would know? If I followed you, we wouldn't have owned it. You said you didn't like it because it came from looting.'

'Wasn't it looted from a church in Manila?'

'But did we loot it?' asked the woman in a loud voice. 'In times of war, it's free to loot. We were also looted. We lost sacks of rice, appliances, clothes.'

'But you got all those things back, because you bought a whole granary.'

'It would have been better if I bought two granaries. Even now, the farmers are still paying me in installments.'

'You're really superior, Leona. Your brother, the priest, can't hold a candle to you.'

'You can say that.'

'I'm lucky, and our children are lucky as well.'

'We spent a fortune sending your two children to the university.'

'Thank God that they've finished.'

'Indeed, let's thank God first, and ourselves second,' and the woman let out a deep sigh that seemed to lighten her load. 'But the expenses aren't yet finished. Not yet,' and her forehead furrowed a bit. 'After Jun's medical studies, he has to open a clinic—expenses. Meanwhile, Ninet will also start a drug store—expenses.'

'That's all right, because they'll soon make money.'

'If it's the same as my business, then it would be stable,' said the woman. Her lips were twitching, as if she were measuring some profits. 'But the doctor and the pharmacist in this town are of the poor and the ignorant! Jun might even give them free medicines. And Ninet's pharmacy might close because of unpaid loans.'

'Is that possible?' asked Don Severo. 'Talk to your children. If the patient doesn't have money, then there will be no consultation.

If there's no cash, then don't give any medicines. They didn't just pick up their university degrees off the ground. You just said that we spent a fortune sending them to school.'

Donya Leona nodded, as if to assent to the logic of his words.

'In this celebration, Severo, we'll spend two, even 3,000 pesos,' she said with a bit of disappointment, but then she immediately took it back, 'but it needs to be done.'

'When will the children arrive?'

'If not later today, then tomorrow morning. They also invited some friends and classmates.'

Donya Leona seemed to remember something.

'Wait a minute,' she said. 'What happened to the invitations that I asked Dislaw to deliver?'

She asked her servant Iska to fetch Dislaw, who was in the garden, monitoring the work of the tenants.

'Good morning, Don Severo and Donya Leona,' Dislaw greeted them with politeness.

'I almost forgot. What happened to the invitations?' Donya Leona asked.

'They've been delivered,' the caretaker quickly answered.

'What did they say?'

'They will all come.' Dislaw was referring to the very important people who had been invited. The provincial judge, the treasurer, the commander of the constabulary in the capital. The mayor, the chief of police, Father Pascual in Sampilong. The teachers were also coming, bearing gifts.

'But Bandong still said he will see if he can come,' Dislaw announced.

'He hasn't decided yet?' Donya Leona said in an annoyed tone. 'Like rice bran for a pig that wants to increase its price. Does he think his absence will be our loss?'

'Do you get along well with Bandong?' asked Don Severo.

'We have both agreed to disagree,' he answered, which left the husband and wife laughing. 'We often clash at the meeting of the PTA.'

'He looks like a nitpicker,' noted the old man.

'He wants to be correct all the time,' added Dislaw.

'But maybe your problem with him doesn't concern the PTA, but the daughter of Pablo, right, Dislaw?' asked Donya Leona. 'What's her name?'

'Pina, ma'am, for Pilipinas.'

'A beautiful name for a beautiful woman,' the old woman said in praise. 'I looked at her closely during harvest time.'

Dislaw was glad to hear that and felt himself being lifted.

'How was your trip?' repeated Donya Leona.

'I was able to see her.'

'You saw her, but you didn't enter her house,' teased Don Severo.

'How about Bandong, your rival?' the old woman queried.

'Well, he was behind me. He was also trying to enter her house.'

Donya Leona laughed at Dislaw's short but meaningful description of the love triangle he was in with Pina and Bandong. Then, Dislaw turned to Don Severo and plied him with gossip.

'Bandong is a consultant to our tenants as well as the squatters.'

'I've heard of that,' and then Don Severo raised his hand and warned, 'It's up to him. He should know his place. But if he makes a mistake, then he'll have to deal with me.'

Dislaw was happy to hear his master's warning, because in his mind, the way things were going, they would turn out in his favour in his courtship of Pina. That was why he kept on feeding information to Donya Leona.

'Mang Pablo and his daughter will be there as well.'

'Of course, because of you,' teased the old woman.

'It's because of your invitation, according to Mang Pablo. Ba Inte is the only one who can't make it, on account of his arthritis.'

'He should see Jun for a consultation about his arthritis,' said the mother of the new doctor. 'Herbalists can't cure it.'

The conversation between the three was cut short when Iska came in with the information that a man wanted to meet with Donya Leona.

The man was a musician and he was carrying a letter from Jun about the orchestra that would play during the celebration. The letter also contained the cost of hiring the orchestra.

'That's expensive,' haggled Donya Leona while handing the letter to Don Severo.

'That's also our fee at the nightclub,' the musician explained. 'We didn't add any additional cost except for the bus rental.'

'Nightclub?' accused Donya Leona. 'You met my son at the nightclub?'

'No, ma'am,' was the musician's quick reply. 'Jun and I had met at the university. I'm also a student but I work at night as a musician at the club.'

Donya Leona then paid the musician and told him to arrive at the correct hour.

'You should be here before seven o'clock. Guests in the province arrive early.'

'Yes, ma'am, you can count on us.'

But while on board the bus bound for Manila, the musician was laughing when he recalled his conversation with Donya Leona about Jun and the nightclub.

'Cookie is on his table three times a week at the nightclub,' the musician said to himself. Cookie was the half-bred mestiza who was the lead singer of the orchestra.

Donya Leona was worried about Jun's habit of going to the nightclub; that was why she pestered her husband.

'Do you believe in that?'

'In what?'

'That your son doesn't go to the nightclubs?'

'Perhaps. He finished Medicine, right?'

'Jesus, would the santol tree bear a macopa fruit?'

And with pouted lips, Donya Leona left Don Severo.

7

Donya Leona and Dislaw were talking on the terrace. From there, they could see the tenants working in the yard.

'Did you see the expenses?' she told her caretaker. 'Money just slipped from my fingers like water.' She was referring to the payment for the orchestra, food and other expenses.

'Prices will still go up.'

'When rice is expensive, everything becomes expensive. Good we bought the rice when it was still cheap.'

'If I were not quick—'

'You should also be as quick at getting back the loans. Those who don't have money, get their rice. I prefer rice.' Donya Leona thought for a while and then she asked, 'But is there still rice in the village?'

'Many of them are now eating congee,' reported Dislaw. 'That's the reason why some of the tenants are now mad at me.'

'Really?'

'They said that I'm stricter than you, ma'am. They call me "The Eagle" behind my back.'

'Why "The Eagle"?'

'They said I look like one.'

Donya Leona tried to control her laughter when she took a closer look at her caretaker. Hollow face with high cheekbones. Nose like a parrot's beak. And eyes always blazing, as if in perpetual hatred. Donya Leona admired the acuity of those who called him The Eagle. *Perfect comparison*, she said to herself. But she decided to humour Dislaw.

'Don't mind them at all. They just envy you,' she consoled him.

'After this celebration, I'll turn my focus to them,' warned the caretaker.

'Well, you may drop by the village first,' the woman gave out her orders. 'Check the roasted pigs as well as the turkeys and chickens.'

'Yes, ma'am.'

Dislaw was about to leave when Don Severo quickly descended the stairs, wearing his Sunday best.

'Dislaw, bring out the car. We're going somewhere,' he said.

'Oh, where are you going, Severo?' asked the wife. 'I ordered Dislaw to go to the village.'

'That can be done later. I'm going to the capital.'

'For what?'

'There's still a query on our taxes,' the man answered.

'Is there no end to these taxes? the woman said in an annoyed tone. 'Or maybe you're just going to gamble ...' Donya Leona knew that there was a big gambling session in the capital that was held on a regular basis. Sometimes, even Mayor Bartolo and Father Pascual went there to gamble.

'The government levies layer upon layer of taxes,' the man complained, dissembling the suspicions of his wife. 'What do they do with the money? It's just being wasted by the government officials and functionaries.'

'And yet they squeeze us dry?'

'Who else but businessmen and proprietors like us? Would the employees and farm tenants pay taxes? It would've been better if I gambled the money. At least, then there's a chance of winning.' Don Severo draped an arm around Donya Leona's shoulders and said, 'What's worse is we already pay taxes and we still have to bribe them.'

'Why do you have to pay bribes?'

'Would our papers move if there's no grease money?'

'But didn't they say they would clean up the government? The winners gave us their solid promises. We even helped them win, right?'

'Leona, don't act as if you're not used to politics,' reminded the man, who had more experience in dealing with these things. 'They're all the same. They all have the same faces. They promise the moon and the sky when fishing for votes but once they've won, they'll just abandon you.'

Dislaw was already honking his horn and that was why the husband and wife hurried down the stairs of the terrace.

Before he climbed into his car, the woman even reminded her husband to see the governor, along with the judge and the treasurer, and remind them to attend the celebration on the next day.

'See?' the husband told the wife. 'That's why those in positions of power act like this. Whatever happens, they're still like saints to whom we pay homage.'

'Just let it be,' the woman said to calm him down. 'You never know. Maybe one day, Jun might become a politician. It's good if we already store up capital for that.'

'Very well then,' said Don Severo, and then Dislaw started the car.

When they were already on the provincial highway, Dislaw asked if they were going to the capital.

'What time is it?' Don Severo asked and then looked at his formal watch. 'It's not ten o'clock yet.' He ordered Dislaw to drive first to the number two politician in the provincial government. 'The governor isn't usually there in his office at this time,' said Don Severo.

Dislaw knew the house that his master was referring to. It was a bungalow located on a street past the provincial post office, ten minutes away from the capital.

Dislaw knew many secrets, because aside from being the farm caretaker, he also served as the collector, driver and bodyguard of the family. He received a salary of 150 pesos a month, which was already high by Sampilong standards. Many people thought that Dislaw had found his golden opportunity. More than anyone else, it was he who gave importance to himself. He was no different from a peacock that preened and displayed itself while walking on the street or attending a celebration. His revolver never parted from his body; if not tucked inside his belt, it would bulge at his side.

He was the eyes and ears of Don Severo and Donya Leona. He had a house outside the wall of the Grandes' stone mansion. He used to live alone, but when his sister Cely became a widow, he took her in. Many young men in town envied him, and many mothers asked their daughters to vie for the attention of the aging bachelor if they wanted to get married.

Be that as it may, many people disliked Dislaw. The tenants' blood would boil at the mere mention of his name, and the squatters in the hilltop overgrown with cogon avoided him as if he were a drunk soldier.

There were several rumours surrounding Dislaw, but many of them were unfounded. According to Ba Inte, Dislaw was Father Pascual's son, sired before he became a priest. His mother was supposed to be a servant of Captain Melchor's. She simply vanished after Dislaw was born, and Pascual was immediately forced to enter the seminary.

The origin of the other stories wasn't too clear, but Dislaw didn't bother about them and neither did Father Pascual. Dislaw was close to Donya Leona, but never to Father Pascual.

Donya Leona was filled with gladness as she flitted from the yard to the mansion, supervising the work of the servants. Sometimes, her shouts would rattle them, or she would wring their ears or flick a finger on their heads, if she caught them making a mistake or not focusing on their work.

She changed the way the bamboo arch was initially placed and also the way the lanterns were hung. The bamboo stands were placed outside the big door so that the incoming visitors could be spotted. The lanterns were hung on the low branches of the tree to resemble big fruits, especially when lit up at night.

She ordered the cutting of the thick grasses and the trimming of the shrub overgrowth. She had the dead branches cut and the dried leaves burnt.

She reserved a space in the yard to serve as the parking lot for the cars of the very important visitors. The governor's car was to be parked in their garage, she ordered.

She also chose the spot in the yard where the dining tables would be set up. They should not be placed too close to each other; some should be put here and the others there. All the visitors didn't know each other and were of different ages as well. That was why it was important to have spaces where people could gather together, so that they could enjoy the celebration better.

She also ordered that a trellis be set up above the two long tables where the food would be served. The trellis was made of wide anahaw leaves and coconut leaves. Even if the rain fell, the food would be

spared. The dancing was to be held in the big hall on the first floor of
the house. The orchestra was to be set up on the terrace, so that the
dancers could hear every song.

Donya Leona called for Iska, and ordered her to cook food
separately for the tenants and their families.

'Don't cook the rice we eat for the servants and the tenants,' she
reminded Iska.

'Yes, ma'am,' Iska reassured her. 'We still have the red rice covered
with husk for the servants.'

'What dish will they eat?'

'I bought a basket of small fish.'

'One basket?' asked the surprised woman.

'There are a lot of them.'

'Even so, leave some for their dinner. Some of them might stay
longer to finish the work.'

'Yes, ma'am.'

The dog was barking at someone outside the door in the yard.
The housemaid checked. Two women entered, along with a young girl.
They looked poor and had certainly come from the farm. They were
all related to one of the tenants. Everyone on the farms knew that a
celebration was imminent at the big house, and the tenants knew it was
their responsibility to help. Whether or not they were asked to help,
they were expected to offer their services.

That was why for the last two days, two groups of men and women
had been working on the yard and inside the big house. Some paved
the road while others cut the grass and trimmed the shrubs. Others
set up the decorated bamboo arch and hung the lanterns, while some
scrubbed the floors of the big house. Still others wiped the tables,
chairs, sofa sets and the other pieces of furniture, and some worked to
scrub the dull forks, spoons and knives until they shone.

The kitchen was filled with tenants helping out as well.

When the three women entered the living room, they greeted the
rich woman profusely.

'Why did you come just now?' she asked in a sharp tone.

'We're sorry we're late, ma'am,' the eldest of the three said humbly.

'Did you come here just to have free lunch?' she said accusingly. 'Aren't you Beteng's wife?'

'Yes, ma'am, and this is my daughter,' pointing to the young girl. 'The other woman is Tomas' wife.'

'He should be here as well. Why didn't you bring the eggs and the chickens?'

'They'll arrive this afternoon, ma'am.'

'How about the pigs?'

'They'll be slaughtered in the village and roasted there as well.'

'How about the goat stew?'

'Oh, we got fat goats.'

'I don't like stinky ones, okay?'

'They only stink when not thoroughly cleaned with scalding hot water.'

'Very well then. Iska—' the old woman said.

Suddenly, she noticed the two stalks of pepper leaves that the young girl was carrying and trying to hide behind her.

'What will you do with those pepper leaves?' she asked rashly.

'Those are ours, ma'am,' the girl's mother meekly said, which meant they intended to use the leaves for their lunch.

'Oh, look at these spawns of thunder! They would even dare to eat well here!'

The girl bit her lower lip and the two older women looked embarrassed. The faces of the men who were working at the back of the house turned sour when they heard the words.

'Iska, bring them to the kitchen,' the rich woman finally said in a shrill voice.

The three women quietly followed Iska into the kitchen. There was a separate route going towards the kitchen from the back of the big house.

Iska looked at the two stalks of pepper leaves held by the young girl and said, 'That would make for a really good dipping sauce for fish cooked in coconut milk.'

8

The men at work immediately heard the honking of the car's horn, so they opened the main door that led to the yard. This door was usually closed, and opened only when someone came or left the house.

A big gleaming car entered the garage.

'Our young masters are here!' screamed the one who opened the door, upon recognizing the passengers inside the car. They had arrived before lunchtime on the day of the dinner celebration.

Donya Leona and Don Severo met the guests with agility, and confirmed they were indeed their children, upon seeing the expensive car. The two old parents had been feeling bored waiting for their arrival. The breakfast had turned cold in the dining room.

Dislaw and the other servants also ran across from one end of the yard to welcome the children.

Jun and Ninet embraced their parents and shook the hands of their servants and tenants. Everyone went into the grand hall. Dislaw and the male servants carried their baggage and escorted them into the house. Iska picked up some of the boxes and placed them on a table in the hallway.

Jun introduced his friends.

'This is Marybee,' he said in a sweet tone, holding a young woman by the arm and bringing her closer to Donya Leona. The old woman kissed Marybee and asked, 'How are you, my dear?'

Marybee was a Chinese Filipina studying Banking and Finance at the university where Jun studied.

'And this is Bining,' he said, gesturing towards an attractive woman with brown skin. Bining was finishing a course in Education at the university as well. Donya Leona put an arm around the young woman's shoulder.

Jun turned to his sister and said, 'It's your turn, Ninet, to introduce these teenagers.' And the women laughed at his words.

'This is Pil,' Ninet said, gesturing towards a slender man who was wearing sunglasses. 'He's also a doctor now. He graduated at the same time as Jun.'

'I don't know the next one very well,' Ninet said. 'I heard he'll soon be a lawyer and his name is Dan.' Bining and Marybee laughed aloud.

Dan was healthy and good-looking.

'There's something else about Dan,' added Pil, while winking at Ninet.

'Off the record,' the young woman butted in.

Even if their qualities were not described right there and then, the two parents began to get to know their young guests better, as the hours passed. Marybee, who had an unusually beautiful face and slim figure, owing to her mixed bloodlines, was the daughter of a rich Chinese Filipino merchant and a woman from the province of Pampanga. She and Jun were in a relationship and the parents knew about her since Ninet had mentioned her to them several times. Dan owned and also drove the car that they had used to travel to the province. He had a great future carved out for him. He was courting Ninet, but the two were not yet in a relationship. Ninet sometimes mentioned his name in her letters to her mother as Jun's best friend. Bining, who was studying to be a teacher, came from a wealthy family in southern Luzon. She was Pil's girlfriend, and they had already reached an agreement on getting married after they had both passed the board examinations.

All in all, the six belonged to the upper crust of society. Even if they were not born with the proverbial silver spoon in their mouths, there was no doubt that they now cooled themselves under the shade of the great wings of luxury. Don Severo and Donya Leona were happy.

After a few pleasantries and updates, Donya Leona asked Ninet if they would like to have lunch. Or, if not yet, then they could have some snacks.

'We dropped by a kitchenette by the highway to eat, Mom,' she said. She still asked her companions, 'Are you hungry?'

'Instead of losing weight, Bining should be gaining weight, since—' teased Jun, but the young woman just smiled and glanced at Pil.

'I just want a glass of cold water,' Marybee said. Jun whispered to her, 'Don't you want a warm kiss?'

The young woman pouted and said, 'Why not?'

Donya Leona then invited them to the dining hall to eat or have some refreshments.

In the middle of a long table in the dining hall was a big plate of sandwiches, a crystal pitcher of pineapple juice, gleaming silver service for coffee, and aluminium pitchers of ice-cold water. There was also a wooden tray laden with fresh fruits. Glasses, cups and saucers were placed at one end of the table.

Without waiting for an invitation, the guests helped themselves to their fill of the food. They conversed loudly while eating and drinking.

Afterwards, Donya Leona took the women to the second floor, to the big guest room reserved for them. Even though Ninet had her own room, she decided to stay with Marybee and Bining.

The men stayed on the first floor. There were two rooms separated by a library. One of the rooms belonged to Jun. During his vacations, when the young man visited Sampilong, the people in the house often didn't know whether he was in the house or had left, except if his car or the jeep were missing.

The three women arranged their clothes, retrieving them from their baggage. Ninet asked Iska for help with ironing the clothes they were to wear that night.

They never stopped talking.

'I'll wear my native formal wear tonight, right, darling Ninet?' Marybee asked in a sweet tone.

'Nothing doing,' Ninet shook her head. 'I'll wear my native formal wear, but I'll change clothes midway through the party, sis,' she told Marybee. 'You know, once I was the queen of the festivities during the Rizal Day celebrations here. I was also the queen during the Flowers of May festival in the capital. We were walking in the procession, wearing our beautiful clothes, when the rain suddenly started falling—ay! We all got wet—what a waste it was!'

'But the mestiza gown is really grand, huh!' Marybee insisted.

'Especially when worn by a mestiza like my sis here,' teased Ninet.

'The advantage of that dress is that it doesn't get wrinkled,' added Bining.

'Even if the one wearing it is already wrinkled,' said Marybee, and laughed at her joke. Bining was forced to defend herself.

'Oy, please don't imply that something is going on between Pil and I. We haven't even used the pill, because he hasn't fed me anything.'

Their laughter rose even louder in the air.

'Can anyone compare to my darling sis?' Marybee said, turning to Ninet. 'She keeps on playing coy with Dan. The poor attorney is just left high and dry.'

'That's true,' Ninet said, happily. 'My trick is the one used on all the serpents, from Eve to the Duchess of Windsor. You make it appear as if the one courting you is running after you, even if in truth, you're just being coy with him. When he has won your heart, he'll feel like he has snared you, when in truth, he's the one who's been caught in a trap.'

Bright laughter filled the room, and even Iska laughed with them, even though she didn't hear what Ninet said.

Marybee made a quick addendum.

'The Chinese have a different method,' she said. 'You accept his gifts, but don't be rude; you accept his money, but don't be rude; talk to him and charm him so you don't lose him.'

And their laughter resounded in the room again.

Another thing, Ninet clarified, 'I won't get married until I'm twenty-five years old.'

'You'll be twenty-five next year, you naughty girl,' Bining reminded her. 'Don't follow the ways of one of the teachers in my town. She said she won't get married until she's twenty-five years old. But now when I look at her, I think she's already turned forty, if not older.'

Meanwhile, the three men were also arranging their things in the two rooms on the first floor. Kosme, the servant, shuttled between the two rooms. Then he went to the library with Jun, carrying a bottle of whiskey. One of their pieces of luggage contained nothing but bottles of Scotch whiskey.

'Kosme, please bring three glasses with ice.'

'And soda as well,' added Pil.

'If you're going to drink anyway, why not drink it straight?' Jun boasted, and then he delivered a speech. 'According to the statistics, only 5 per cent of all the drinks in the world can be guaranteed to be genuine, that's why I don't add anything anymore—I drink it straight. I don't want to ruin the pure taste of good liquor.'

'I can only take cocktails,' Dan admitted. 'It was America's greatest invention. I mix my whiskey with something else. If not, the whiskey will be the one to drink me up.'

'Many people aren't used to drink. They're already groggy before they can even finish their glass,' said Pil. 'It would be better if they were just groggy, but some behave worse than mad dogs.'

Jun continued as if he neither heard nor took notice of them.

'Liquor is the oldest proof of civilization, and he looked with admiration at the golden gleam of whiskey in his glass. Didn't Ernest Hemingway say that this gave him the deepest pleasure, better than anything that gold could buy?'

'What did Cleopatra have after she melted her expensive pearls into that drink?' asked Pil.

'An aphrodisiac called cantharidin,' snapped Jun.

'That's what she made Julius Caesar and Mark Antony drink,' Dan corrected.

'He made him drink it, and then he drank it as well,' insisted Jun.

'Cleopatra was really a great woman,' Pil said, 'but Cookie in the nightclub is much greater.'

'She'll be with the orchestra tomorrow, right, Jun?' asked Dan.

'Nardy can't assure it. He got the advance payment from Mom yesterday.'

'Better if she doesn't come here,' said Pil. 'The three musketeers might skin her alive.'

'Marybee is a sport,' said Jun. 'It would be worse if my Mom noticed it. She might not give me my allowance for America.'

'You'll leave Marybee?' Dan said the words without intending to.

'I'll undertake specialist studies in Medicine for two years,' said Jun, as if in answer to Dan. 'This is a must, he added. Here in the

Philippines, a professional may be good but he's still nothing without a postgraduate degree from the United States or Europe. That's the painful truth, isn't it? Even if the only thing you do there is to become an expert in their vices. That's why we should just dance to the tune being played, my brothers.'

Pil said that he wouldn't go with the flow and that he and Bining had already made their plans.

'Bining has agreed that we'll return to the province,' said Pil. 'I'll start my own practice there and she'll teach. I want to start at the grassroots level. We don't have hospitals and clinics in the villages, and that I think is the first mission for a doctor to accomplish. I'll work there and get experience as well.'

The conversations on both the floors of the house stopped when Kosme and Iska announced that Don Severo and Donya Leona were waiting for them in the dining hall. It was already past one o'clock in the afternoon when they had lunch.

Soon after lunch, the six visitors were given a tour of the yard and a dress rehearsal of what was going to happen during the celebration that night.

Afterwards, they went to a part of the yard where the trees grew thick and close to each other. There were mango, pomelo, chico, star-apple, jackfruit, guava and santol trees. Dan and Pil competed against each other at trying to climb two short trees. They picked the fruits and threw them down at the three women who were looking up at them.

Jun quickly got bananas and hurled them at the two young men holding onto the branches of the trees.

'Kura! Kura!' said Jun to the two men, and when they looked at him, he threw a banana each at them, as if offering them to monkeys. The two men peeled the bananas and ate them up, then proceeded to throw the peels at Jun.

The stomachs of the three women almost ached from all the laughing.

9

The sweaty afternoon had taken off its golden shawl and it was replaced by the grey silk of twilight. However, the darkness of the approaching night could not be found anywhere in the yard of the Grande family, since electric lights blazed forth and shone in every corner.

The tenants in the fields were already conveying cooked food in the early hours of the afternoon. Roasted pigs still skewered on bamboo poles, stuffed turkey wrapped in cellophane, fried chicken covered with fresh banana leaves, stewed goat meat still smouldering in the big vats, steamed crabs and shrimps just lightly salted, basins of pickled papaya, and a native dessert made from molasses that only the village maidens could offer—all to be offered to those with refined tastes.

Dislaw and Kosme coordinated the transfer of the food from the village to the big house. The jeep driven by Kosme went to and fro, carrying the wares. In the kitchen, Donya Leona proved herself a true general and Iska, her trusted assistant.

The Chinese ham was prepared in the stone house; perch and grouper fish three handspans in length, were also steamed, and a white sauce was poured over them. The chicken pastel was cooked in a traditional hot stove, while the salad was chilled in an ice box.

'You don't know how to cook these,' Donya Leona said in an insulting tone to the servants from the villages, whom she caught staring.

To humour her, one of the women said, 'But we also know how to eat that kind of food, madame.'

'Your stomachs will turn bad,' the rich woman scared them. 'It's not good to eat food that you're not used to.'

An hour before Dislaw announced to his master the arrival of the first guests, all the food had been prepared and set in their appointed places on the buffet tables. The arrangement was neat, like five buttons that fit perfectly into the holes of one's shirt.

'After this, I'll end up in the hospital,' Donya Leona complained before she rested her back against the lazy chair. But she was happy and not disappointed at all. Her words were just her way of implying that she was the night's festivities were a success because of her.

She faced Don Severo, who still seemed to be taking his time.

'Hey, you've to change your clothes. The guests will be here soon.'

Then she told Iska, 'Tell Ninet to be ready.'

The orchestra arrived early and Nandy immediately met up with Jun. The musicians were served an early dinner. After having their fill, they began to play, and in the air floated the strains of a sexy foxtrot, followed by a graceful waltz. Kosme had two assistants, and they stationed themselves at the bar. All kinds of drinks could be found there. On top of two long tables, under covered trellises, different kinds of food were served, along with the steaming white rice and sliced bread. On both sides of the table were placed plates and utensils, glasses and cloth napkins. Many servers went around offering food and drinks to the guests.

The guests invited by the Grande family always accepted the invitation and not just because of the varied and delicious spread prepared for them. They were also delighted at the way they were served. At these times, the looks, gestures and words of the rich old man and woman were different. They would leave behind their ill tempers, disrespect and sharpness, and don an affectionate look, sweet smiles and winsome ways. They were no longer the Don Severo and Donya Leona whom the villagers feared, but the Grande family who were friends with the governor and the other high officials at the capital and in the town. Long after the celebration was over, it would still linger as a topic of conversation on the lips of the guests, as well as those who had just heard about it.

The house and the yard were teeming with people when the guests finally arrived. Those who came from the capital and nearby towns arrived in their cars, while those from Sampilong came aboard horse-drawn rigs or just walked. Four town mayors met at the celebration, along with the judge of the Court of First Instance, the provincial engineer, treasurer, superintendent of schools, the commander of the Constabulary, Father Pascual and other illustrious gentlemen. Hugo, the chief of police, had already arrived with his wife.

Also present were several teachers and a group of men and women who were better off than the rest in Sampilong, along with two or three Chinese merchants who had already sent their gifts in advance. The councillors and the lieutenants spoke loudly, while in the corners, a few people from the town were present, even if they were not invited.

Bandong arrived with Mang Pablo and his daughter, Pina. Mang Pablo had his own farm and was in a constant tussle with Don Severo, especially regarding the way the farmers were treated, and politics. But Don Severo had invited the president of the PTA to show off the success of his celebration and the importance of his guests. On the other hand, Mang Pablo had accepted the invitation to show that he was also a gentleman and did not want to humiliate someone who had invited him, whether friend or foe.

Before Mang Pablo and Pina could greet the owners of the house, Dislaw had already met them.

'It's as if this is Dislaw's party,' Bandong said to Pina in a teasing tone.

'Just let him be so he can have something to boast about,' Pina whispered.

They paid their respects to Don Severo and Donya Leona, before greeting Jun and Ninet, as well as the siblings' guests from Manila.

'Dan, Pil, please meet the most beautiful woman in our town,' Jun said while introducing Pina. 'Hey, Bandong, I heard that you're now the principal,' he greeted the young man with whom he had grown up.

When the three guests had turned their backs, Pil teased Jun, 'Why did you let that chick go? She looks so luscious.'

'I'll get to her after my driver is through with her,' Jun boasted.

Bandong greeted the superintendent, who enquired about the school in Sampilong. Bandong said that they would like to invite the high official to be the guest speaker at their graduation ceremonies.

'You're late, Bandong,' the superintendent answered. 'Five other towns have already invited me. But we can still take a raincheck, okay?'

The rich couple kept on looking around since the governor had not yet arrived.

'I didn't see him yesterday,' Don Severo said. 'His secretary is here, though.'

'Well, the guests might get hungry if we keep on waiting for him.'

'Then we should start eating. We've got a lot of food.'

'Very well then.'

After a signal from Donya Leona, the guests began the feast. Everyone grabbed a plate and cutlery and served their food, except the two head tables, where the guests were served. They also had their own bottle of whiskey and the servants at their beck and call. They did not need to stand up because the food was being brought to them.

'There's nothing like this in the provincial capital,' said the treasurer.

'This isn't a village feast but the feast of a first-class city,' the judge decided.

But in spite of their praises, Donya Leona noticed someone's absence.

'It's too bad that the governor wasn't able to make it,' she told the mayor and the judge.

At these two tables, talk was rife about politics, business and the last price of unhusked rice.

'Donya Leona once again hit the big jackpot,' said the treasurer. 'There's no more unhusked rice in the capital.'

'Don't worry,' Don Severo told the treasurer, since the old man didn't get his point. 'There's a lot in our warehouses, if ever you need rice.'

'Oh no, Don Severo,' answered the treasurer. 'What I meant was that you won big with the pricing.'

'Just enough to spend on another feast,' said Donya Leona, effectively cutting off the discussion on the price of unhusked rice.

On another table, Jun, Ninet and their friends Marybee, Bining, Pil and Dan were finalizing their plans for the following days. They would all go up to the mountain city of Baguio.

'Let's get our own cottage,' Jun suggested. 'It will be more enjoyable than staying at a hotel.'

'Okay,' Pil said and then winked at Jun.

'Amen,' added Dan.

The three women just looked at each other; they neither approved nor disapproved.

The teachers, along with Bandong, Pina and Mang Pablo, ate their food at a separate table. They were talking about the end of the classes, and what the teachers would do on their vacations.

Dislaw had visited their table several times, offering his service to Mang Pablo and the teachers.

'You should have the roasted pig,' he said, 'or the stuffed fish, or the salad. What else do you want, Pina? How about you, Mang Pablo?'

'Thank you, Dislaw. We cannot even finish the food on our table anymore,' the teachers said.

'We can't find fault with the service of Mang Dislaw,' a female teacher slowly said to a male teacher beside her.

'Dislaw is excellent at his speciality—serving others,' said the male teacher.

'Would he be able to win over the principal?' said another teacher in a loud voice, as if wanting Pina to hear it.

'Far from it,' said another teacher in a teasing tone.

Pina's cheeks turned red, but Bandong just ignored the banter.

After two hours, after the sound of the spoons and forks had subsided and the noise from the drunken guests had abated, Mayor Bartolo stood up and didn't want to miss the chance to give a speech. He had already sought permission from Don Severo to do so.

On behalf of the owners of the house, the mayor thanked the guests and mentioned the names of the high officials sitting at the head tables. He repeated the occasion for the feast, which had already been mentioned in the invitation. Then, he introduced the new doctor and pharmacist.

'It's a great honour for the town of Sampilong,' said the mayor, 'that the two children of its wealthiest family have returned here from Manila, bearing with them the fruits of their academic learning. Jun is now a medical doctor, while Ninet is a pharmacist. Let us congratulate them on their shining achievements.'

Loud applause greeted the siblings as they stood up to receive the warm wishes. They both went to Donya Leona and kissed the cheeks of their happy mother. The guests shook hands with them.

'Now, we can start dancing,' the mayor announced. 'Those who want to dance can start moving inside the house.'

Some of the guests left their tables and proceeded to the first floor of the big house. The others stayed in the yard.

Father Pascual and the judge had their arms draped around each other's shoulders as they walked.

'You should dance, our gentleman judge,' suggested the priest.

The judge looked at the minister of the church and then said, 'Sometimes, the priest and the judge are the same. You can't do openly what the others do, even if you also want to do them.'

'They've already judged you even if you're not yet doing anything,' the judge weighed in.

A stir was created by the arrival of Cookie, the enchanting singer of the orchestra. Donya Leona had thought it was because the governor had arrived, since the young guests flocked around the new arrival, but it turned out to be the nightclub singer.

'We like her better than the governor,' said one teenager upon meeting Cookie.

Cookie sang several songs in English and Tagalog.

The followers of Terpsichore found their partners. Those who danced were delighted with the hammock-like mellowness of the songs; those who just watched, felt likewise. But the onlookers' attention was riveted by three sets of dancers: Marybee and Jun, Ninet and Dan, and Bining and Pil. The people liked their suave moves on the dance floor.

Suddenly, when the next song came on, Jun went over to Cookie and started dancing with her in the middle of the salon. Their steps and movements matched, along with their gyrations. The dance floor slowly cleared, until only the two of them were left on the hallway, performing their own show.

'We seem to be watching a show at the Clover Theatre,' said one guest who had turned into a fan of the performers.

Don Severo didn't know whether to feel happy or sad, because based on what he was seeing, he couldn't decide where his son's talents lay: in being a doctor or a dancer.

Marybee had different thoughts, but what she could not say, eventually came from Donya Leona's lips.

'Jun even beat his own father,' she said in a voice heard by only those around her. 'Where else would he learn those gyrations except at a nightclub? This must be his partner there.'

'Don't act as if you were born yesterday,' said Mayor Bartolo. 'In these times, even priests have a good time in nightclubs. Did you know—'

But the mayor stopped short when he noticed that right behind him was Father Pascual, who could hear everything he was saying.

10

More than 300 guests enjoyed the hospitality and entertainment that were offered at the big yard of the Grande mansion that night. Delightful conversations, stories, jokes, repartees and contests were held on various topics. Various kinds of drinks flowed freely, nobody stopped drinking from the bar, which seemed bottomless. The orchestra also played incessantly without any breaks, and those so inclined never stopped dancing the night away.

The front yard was filled with people, as well as the terrace, the first and second floors of the house, the dining room—why, even the bedrooms and changing rooms.

A platoon of servants and house helpers rushed around to and fro, serving with meekness. Many of them came from the barrio and had gone there not to partake of the festivities but to serve. Some of them carried trays of dishes, others bore bottles of drinks and empty plates. They were seen walking fast or even running. All of them looked like puppets moving to the machinations of a puppeteer.

All of the festivities were held in the big yard surrounded by thick cemented walls. Outside, nothing could be seen except the heavy bar that bolted the door, and the gleam of light from the lanterns. The sound of the orchestra also cascaded outside the stone house.

Under the shadows of the walls were the big cars of the guests, except for a few whose sparse plate numbers indicated that they belonged to the top politicians and were therefore parked in the garage of the house owners. Food was brought to the drivers, but some of them freely entered through the gate and joined the guests in eating.

Amongst those who were not lucky to get an invitation were Andres and his wife Sedes. In truth, the Grande family did not know them, or if they did, they were not the kind of people they would treat with kindness. They were mere squatters. They lived in a rundown part of the town on the other side of the road, around three-fourths of a mile from the front yard where the major festivities were being held. In that humble home lived Andres, Sedes and their three children.

They lived along with other families of similar ill-fortune, in shacks built close to each other on land they didn't own. Andres' shack was made of galvanized iron roof with irregular cuts, plywood and castaway wood. On top of the grassy hill lived fifty families in shacks notable for their sheer look of poverty, similar to pigeonholes, where only the poorest of the poor would live. They all got wet when it rained, the water pouring through the holes in their roofs, and at night, only the light guttering from a half-coconut filled with oil, or a desolate gas lamp, served to illuminate their shacks.

They were not native to the place and had only moved there during the Second World War. They resembled small stones flung from a forest and landed there, where they built shacks and tried hard to sink roots and grow moss on borrowed land. They were all squatters, huddled beside each other on the land where they had all sought refuge from poverty and from the war.

Many of the men had no livelihood, not because they were lazy, but because there were more jobless men than available jobs. The women washed clothes, foraged for firewood, or worked as household helpers for the few foreigners in the town. Several times, Sedes had tried to look for work at the big stone house, even meeting Iska several times, but she had been unlucky. Back then, Iska was not yet close to her family.

Their family sometimes missed lunch or dinner. How could you feed a family three times a day when there was no rice harvested from the field, or wages from the factory? They wanted to work on the land, even if they were not used to it, but there was simply no space for them. They planted vegetables in their backyards, but these were not enough for their daily needs. Where would they get the rice? Where would they buy the other ingredients for their dishes? How would they fulfil even the most basic needs?

They tried everything they could to earn a living. They carried goods in the public market, dug up the earth and poured it into canals for three days or five days, but this would be followed by days of no work. That was their situation. The lives of the wretched of the earth. But in spite of such poverty, they had large families, the children growing like grass. And with every child added to the brood, the cycle of hunger and poverty continued, and they would just repeat the doomed and desperate lives led by their parents.

Just like Andres and Sedes, who found themselves raising three children in the squalor of the slums. Andres once thought that when the Lord told Adam and Eve to go forth and multiply, it was a curse for poor people like him. On the other hand, Andres was puzzled why the poor had many children while the wealthy only had a few. Was this also a destiny wrought by heaven, or caused by men?

Both of them used to work and tried to save as much as they could. Andres worked as a foreman in a construction company, while Sedes made umbrellas in a factory.

'I hope life would be kind as this till we have children,' Sedes would pray upon reaching their house every afternoon. After fixing dinner, they would eat together and rest.

'How many children do you want?' asked Andres.

'It depends on you,' Sedes answered sweetly.

And in the happiness of their lives together, they wanted to build a family and realize all their dreams. Both of them strove to have a child who would be the fruit of their dreams. After a few months, Sedes felt the pulse of life quickening in her womb.

After that, their desire to have their own plot of land became more intense, land on which they could build their own house. It's different when you have your own house, they told each other. Whether you eat or not, nobody will know; nobody will know if you've fought with each other either.

They worked even harder to earn more. They also scrimped on their needs, so they could increase their savings.

But their resources became scarce when Sedes became ill because of her pregnancy. Not only was she unable to work, they also had to spend money on her medication. When she recovered, she returned to work, only to fall ill again.

When the Second World War broke out, Sedes lost her child. This brought on a new round of expenses and extreme disappointment. All of their savings were whittled down, and the promise Sedes had made to Andres that all his seeds would be harvested came to naught. The Japanese Imperial Forces invaded the cities and the construction company where Andres worked was shut down. They looked like leaves that had fallen and been scattered by the wind.

What were they to do? Where would they go? What would happen to them? In the midst of a raging war, where violence reigned and cruelty prevailed, the ordinary people had no ability to answer the questions that faced the couple, as well as millions of other poor families.

Andres and Sedes were carried away by the rampaging currents that also bore away the rest of the people. They fled the city and went to the province. Andres remembered that when his mother was still alive, she told stories of having relatives in a province in Central Luzon, where her ancestors used to own vast tracts of land, but the lands had been lost and they had become poor for yet unknown reasons. And then, his mother's ancestor had died in uncertain circumstances.

Andres tried to recall the name of the town that was often on his mother's lips. Sam-pilo? Sampilok? Sampal—Sampilong? Oh, yes indeed, it was Sampilong. Right. Sampilong. What a strange name— like the sound of the Japanese soldiers slapping the people.

So when life became unbearable in Manila, one day Andres told Sedes, 'Let's go to Sampilong.' Before that, the man had already told his wife about his late mother's stories.

They didn't have a lot of things to take with them and soon, they set off for the province. They were able to squeeze themselves into a truck, but it didn't take them even halfway to their destination. The Japanese soldiers commandeered the truck and forced everyone to disembark. So, they proceeded to walk, then took a horse-drawn rig. The next day, they walked again, took a small boat, rode in a cart drawn by a water buffalo, and again walked many miles. After five days and nights, they finally reached Sampilong. After the days of liberation, when the Americans had left, travelling became more comfortable. A new bus could cover the distance between Manila and Sampilong in three hours.

Andres looked for his mother's relatives, but he didn't find anyone. Nobody seemed to remember his mother. She had still been a young child when she had left Sampilong, and the people's memories of her must have blurred. If only he could remember the name of his ancestor; but had no clue about that at all.

They found squatters when they reached the knoll overgrown with cogon grasses, who asked Andres to stay there if they had no other place to go. The area was big; only the cogon grasses needed to be cut and cleared. They could get water from a clear stream nearby. It was easy to forage for firewood and to build a house.

Sedes teased him after they had chosen the plot of land filled with cogon grasses. 'Here you have land, but no relatives.'

But pretty soon, the other squatters became almost like family. They got to know each other easily. Marcos was the first to welcome him. He was married to Intang, who had a brother named Kanor. Kiko lived in the shack over there, and he was married to Magda.

Marcos, Kanor and Kiko helped Andres build his own small shack.

'Are there no Japanese soldiers here?' Andres asked Marcos after a few days.

'There's a company of soldiers in town, housed at the school.'

They lived in a place shielded by several old trees. They could barely be noticed, if one were to look down from the first road downhill. They left the tall cogon grasses intact in that area, to shield them from the enemy. From where they lived, they could see the trucks of the Japanese soldiers coming and going, but they couldn't be seen by them from below.

When Andres had lived there for two weeks, two armed men came at dusk. They asked Andres where the couple had come from, why they had fled there, and what they thought of the war. They talked to all the men who lived in the squatters' area.

'Are you pro-Japanese or pro-American?' they asked.

'We are Filipinos,' Marcos said.

The men seemed to like the answer.

'If that is so, then we're united by the same cause,' they said and then firmly shook the hands of the men who lived in the squatters' area. 'Our oath is to not help the enemy.'

Since then, Andres and the other men on the grassy knoll became secret guerrillas in Sampilong.

During the war, there was hardly any soul in the big stone house hemmed in by high walls. The Grande family had relocated temporarily to Quezon City. However, on the rare occasions that they went home, they would throw a feast for the Japanese captain and his soldiers, offering them gifts afterwards. On the other hand, the guerrillas also did not harm their properties, because many of them were from the village, while the others farmed the lands owned by Donya Leona.

The only prize that Andres and Marcos got for being guerrillas was the satisfaction of having helped drive away the enemy. Aside from that, they didn't get any recognition, or accepted backpay, or any remuneration at all. They also realized that the nationalist villagers also got nothing for their sacrifices.

Andres went to the city when things had begun to settle down there, in Manila. He saw the ruins, and also the different squatters inhabiting what remained of the buildings, schools and stations. He learnt that many companies weren't yet ready to resume their operations. Nobody knew when they would reopen for business. Amongst them was his construction company. He wasn't even able to meet some representative who could apprise him of the situation. On the other hand, he realized that the city had become too crowded for many things—there was a lack of jobs, lack of places to live in, soaring prices of everything, and a throng of people walking around aimlessly.

Andres' hope of returning to Manila with Sedes and his family was doused with cold water. That was why he came back to Sampilong before he ran out of cash.

'My journey was a sad one,' he told Sedes upon arriving home, tired and hungry.

'If that is so—'

'Let's stay here for a while,' Andres said, while gently caressing the hand of his wife.

They looked at their three children asleep on an old mat on the floor. They realized they were not earning anything and the children were growing up and needed to be fed, clothed and educated.

'This wasn't our dream when we got married in Manila, right, Andres?' Sedes whispered in a low voice, as tears gleamed on her face.

'No, this wasn't it,' agreed Andres, 'but this is still love.' And he tightened his hold on the hand he was gently caressing.

11

Iska felt worse than someone scalded by boiling water when she learnt where Kosme had taken the basin filled with various kinds of food that the younger man had chosen from the long table. The head of the house helpers thought it would be to the important guests, but she learnt that Kosme didn't take the food there. Instead, the new Quixote had rushed to a small table that was separate from the rest, under the branches lit by several lanterns, where the new and proud Dulcinea sat.

Iska felt like she had been kicked in the chest. She went closer to check out the important guest who had been the recipient of Kosme's unusual service, and she realized who it was. None other than Dislaw's widowed sister, the flirtatious Cely.

The widow was well-groomed. She was wearing a dress sewn in the capital, and her well-done hair indicated that she had been to the beauty parlour. Iska realized that she had seen the newly opened beauty parlour in the centre of town and she had almost been inveigled to have her hair permed there. But she was disappointed to know how steep the price was for having one's hair done there. That was why she just heated some hairpins and used them to straighten her hair, since they curled from her forehead like the teeth of a wild pig.

Iska admitted to herself that Cely was still young, and more beautiful than her. The widow and Kosme were almost the same age. She was ten years older than the male servant. But for Iska, that wasn't important. What mattered was what this woman knew or what she could do as a woman, and consequently, what she, Iska herself, could offer to Kosme.

From her looks and behaviour, Iska knew that Cely couldn't even feed herself, and she was only good at giving temporary pleasure to men. In truth, her husband had died of a heart illness when they were but newly married. Their eldest child was still in the crib when the woman became pregnant again, and then the ill-starred brother-in-law of Dislaw passed away. When she became a widow, Dislaw took her in and she was put in charge of the household. However, she was often out of the house, as if an itch in her feet made her roam around constantly.

Iska had heard many things about Marcela, or Cely, her nickname. Rumours floated around that she had hardly finished her forty-day mourning ritual when she was already dating the chief of police, who was married and also had a regular mistress. This only stopped when the mayor talked to Hugo. Afterwards, the young widow was said to be seeing the three conductors of the bus that travelled to Sampilong from the capital. Talk reached Iska that Cely was courted—and even accepted the proposal—while travelling on the bus! From thereon, she would take the bus to the capital, and while she was there, the bus conductor would ask someone to cover for him while he went off for two hours with her, on their own journey in a motel room.

It was said that Dislaw had forbidden Cely from doing these crooked things. Aside from her being like a bus that one could take if needed and refuse if not needed, it appeared that the bus conductor was a passenger without a clear destination. In short, he was also a married man with children.

That was why the widow lay low for a while. But suddenly, she and Kosme became close. One day, Donya Leona ordered Kosme to fetch Dislaw from his house. But Dislaw wasn't here, and only Cely was present in the house. What happened to them must have been love at first sight. Kosme was invited upstairs and told to wait for her brother, who would be back soon.

When they talked to each other, Cely told him her life story, which she embroidered with additional bits and pieces. She was Dislaw's only sibling; God took her husband and left her with a child; she managed the household and cooked the food, did the laundry and cleaned the house; she would get bored at times and since she wasn't yet over the hill, she perhaps could still be mistaken for ...

Kosme wasn't a very sharp man, but he was also not dumb. From the words of the widow, he knew that she was opening a door.

He decided to butt in before she could finish, 'It's strange that I met you only now,' said Kosme as an opener. 'Perhaps you never left the house, nor even took a peek out of the window.'

He added to his preludes when he knew that the widow was thrilled, saying that only the blind or the dead would not feel attracted to her face and body.

In this way, the widow insinuated that even if she managed the household, she wasn't a lizard who only clung to the ceiling. Sometimes, she would rush to the town centre to buy ingredients for the dishes she would cook, or for other needs. She would even go to the provincial capital if what she needed could be found there.

Kosme wanted to know what he should call her because he didn't yet know her name at that point. She said that her name was Marcela, and Cely or Celing were her nicknames. She let Kosme choose what nickname he would use to call her. The man asked her the days when she would visit the town centre. Four days in a week, Cely said. Monday, Wednesday, Friday and Sunday. She also went to church on Sunday.

The man asked if she liked going to the movies. Cely said she liked watching movies, but she rarely did. She didn't like watching a movie in the town centre because the cinema hall was not air-conditioned and the seats were crawling with bugs. Meanwhile, it was difficult to go to the provincial capital and she didn't like watching a movie by herself.

'Then, I'll come with you to the movies,' Kosme offered. He finally got the wind in his sail and implied to her that he had his plans.

'Oh, I don't want to take up your time,' Cely feigned.

'You won't,' insisted Kosme, 'at least we can watch a movie. When are you free?' he suddenly asked, surprising the widow.

'Someone might get mad at you.'

Kosme made the sign of the cross over his heart and showed her his face, the one that he put on when Donya Leona came looking for the money missing from her bedroom. He said that he was single and Cely had nothing to worry about.

And that was the start of their close friendship. And the eggs hatched into chicks.

They met four days a week in the town centre, as if by happenstance, decided when they would meet again. They exchanged words and performed acts that only two people who were drunk on the wine of intimacy would do. They had gone to the capital several times to watch movies, and one day, they planned to go to Manila—they would eat, watch a movie and do other things.

All of these things had already reached the ears of Iska, but she just let the words enter her left ear and exit through her right. She also noticed that Kosme was often absent, even when the lady of the house had not asked him to run errands. But she thought that being young and lacking in experience, Kosme was easily swayed by something new, but that it would also pass.

But Iska's hopes were dashed. As the days passed, the widow became like a talisman sucking Kosme into her orbit. The head of the house helpers discovered that her relationship with the younger servant had turned to rust.

That was why she became deeply reflective. She quizzed herself until she discovered the beginning and the end of things. Cely was indeed the real widow, even as she was widowed by life. Cely was younger and fresher than her, and she looked like a thin fish losing its scales. Cely could still bear children, while she was infertile. Cely had no other master but herself, while she was tied to the cape of Donya Leona. And Kosme ... ah, usually a man has no sense of reason, governed as he is solely by his weakness, and his head can easily be trapped in a woman's snare.

There were times when Iska was pained by her loneliness. The moment she had finished her work in the big house—but was there ever a time when the work was done?—if she had survived another day of do-this and do-that from Donya Leona, and was by herself letting her tiredness subside in her room on top of the garage, Iska didn't only feel loneliness, but also pity for herself and her lot in life. She surmised that a poor woman in the village was luckier than her, like Beteng's wife or Tomas', because even though they were extremely poor and abject in life, someone loved them; they had husbands and children who shared their poverty with them, and gave them morsels of joy given away only by time.

Iska thought that someone like Sedes was indeed luckier than her. They were truly poor and lived in a shack with thin walls, in the midst

of similar shacks in the squatters' area, but they were a family of two
or three souls who survived and lived together under one roof, loving
each other, consoling each other, and happy even in the midst of such
dire poverty.

Iska and Sedes began to get to know each other deeply when they
met on the streets or at the town centre. More than once, the head of
the house helpers of the Grande family had confessed that she envied
Sedes because Andres was a good husband, as well as a loving and
caring father.

'I've no complaints about that,' Sedes would always reply. 'Whether
we share a meal or not, there's no other woman for Andres except me.'

Indeed, Iska and Sedes became good friends, such that when the
youngest child of Andres' had his confirmation in church, Iska was
chosen to be the godmother. At first, Andres didn't like it, but he
relented after Sedes insisted.

That was why from thereon, whenever Iska felt bad about Kosme
or Donya Leona, the moment she left the house of stone, her feet
brought her to the house in Tambakan, to visit her friend Sedes. There,
she would let unravel the tightness gripping her chest.

All of these reveries gathered together in the tired mind of Iska
when she saw, with her very own eyes, Kosme's betrayal. He actually
left what he was doing to take food to the widow. But still she restrained
herself, even if she felt that her breath was turning ragged. She didn't
confront Kosme, nor did she go anywhere near Cely, who was eating
the delicious food with much gusto.

Iska waited for the celebration to finish, the guests to leave, and
until they were already resting in each other's rooms atop the garage.
Then, she entered Kosme's room and unleashed her raw feelings.

'Oh, the widow had you all to herself, right?' she accused him. 'She
was the only one you served the whole night long.'

'She was a guest. Why won't I serve her?' Kosme defended himself.

'She was your guest!' Iska screamed. 'Why didn't you give her more
food to take home, aside from the grand spread that you had taken to
her? Why didn't you bring her home, then? And why didn't you sleep
over at her house? You should have done all that to complete your
betrayal.'

'Oh, there you go again,' Kosme said in a humble tone.

'Am I blind?' added the head of the house helpers. 'Okay, try me, but then don't repent in the end. I'm aware of the things that you do inside this house. I just keep covering for you; just go on. I brought you here. I can also ask you to leave.'

Iska must really feel bad, Kosme thought. He didn't have a lot of experience with jealous women, but the dried herring with thin scales wasn't joking, after all. Indeed, Iska had covered for him for the times he stole cash from Donya Leona; the times he wore the underclothes of Don Severo, and his other misdemeanours. If she couldn't contain her fury anymore, what would happen to him?

'You're very tired, that's why you've such a temper,' said Kosme as he caressed Iska's hand.

'Don't come near me,' she pretended to say in anger, but her annoyance was slowly subsiding.

She didn't complain anymore when Kosme took her to his bed and caressed her hair and her cheeks. In short, Iska was able to successfully blackmail the young servant.

She was indeed tired. She fell asleep quickly and wasn't able to return to her room again. The sun was already at its zenith when she woke up the next day. Kosme was still asleep beside her, snoring.

12

Sedes was a working wife and not merely a showpiece in the house. She helped Andres in running their lives. She was a kind mother to her children and her hands also did the laundry, patched their clothes and cooked their food. She also tried to work outside, if there was a chance for her to do so.

But there was no factory that produced umbrellas or cigars in Sampilong. There was no printing press, either, that would hire her to fold the sheets, or a bakery that would pay her to put biscuits in tinned cans.

There were only a few businesses owned by the Chinese, and very few houses that needed a laundrywoman, a cook, or a servant. Sedes tried to appeal to all of them for work, but she usually returned to their shack empty-handed, with a powder of dust on her feet. But she knew neither tiredness, nor lacked hope.

That was why during the morning when people were putting finishing touches to the work at the Grandes' house of stone, Sedes went there. She had been there once before, in the front yard, when she had heard that they needed someone to wash clothes. She had summoned courage in the face of the ferocious dogs. But Iska was the only person she was able to talk to. She had already known Iska and the latter wanted to help her, but they already had two laundrywomen. The one who had left earlier also returned after a few days.

'Maybe she could do something else?' Sedes asked. She could clean the yard, gather and crush the snails that clung to the walls, or flick away the earthworms and caterpillars on the plants and the petals of the flowers. Or maybe she could scrub the floor clean with half a coconut shell. But Iska confirmed that there was no available work for Sedes, for now. She said that sometimes, when someone was fired, or there was a celebration in the stone house and if the villagers didn't come to help, there would be an opportunity for her.

Because of this slim hope of finding work, Sedes returned to the house again. The ferocious dogs met her, but she wasn't afraid. Iska recognized her and drove the dogs away.

'How are you, Aling Iska?' she meekly asked. 'Is there work for me here?'

Iska shook her head. She gave Sedes advice.

'Don't come back here anymore, these dogs are ferocious. If there's a job, I'll call for you. You live at the Tambakan, right?'

Sedes' eyes darkened when she heard there was no work for her, but she didn't let it on.

'Thank you. Just look for Sedes, the wife of Andres,' she said, and then she took her leave.

Iska took pity on Sedes, whom she had then thought wasn't that poor. She had liked Sedes, and in the next few days, began to get to know her better.

When Sedes was leaving, she saw that indeed, there were already many house helpers. They could be found in the whole yard, around and inside the big house, in the garage, and in all the nooks and crannies of the vast house. The men and the women rushed around and worked without rest. Hiring her would be too much. She envied the people working there, for at least, they had some work to do.

'I'm sorry,' Iska said as Sedes walked away. The latter felt some sympathy from Iska.

Sedes surmised the grandness of the celebration from the work being done. She also heard Iska tell someone to ask what time the roasted pigs as well as the stuffed turkey would be delivered.

She applied for work not to get paid in cash—she only hoped to bring home some delicious food, even just a little. That way, her children could also have a taste of food like that. She recalled that ever since their children were born, they had never tasted roasted pig or honey-glazed ham, or stuffed chicken. When she had entered the yard of the house, she had thought this might be her chance.

Sedes walked quickly out of the gate. The same ferocious barking of the dogs that had met her earlier, rose in the air when she was leaving.

Andres left for the capital early that day. For one whole week thereafter, he left early for the capital and came home when night had fallen. For several days, he worked at the train station, or in the market. He received payment from the people he helped.

It was already dark when Andres left the capital to go home. Sedes quickly cooked the half kilo of rice that he had bought. That was going to be their dinner tonight, as well as breakfast tomorrow. The rice that Andres had got for helping in the fields was long gone.

'You didn't bring home any dish,' his wife noted.

'If I'd bought dried herring, then I'd still be out walking on the streets. I paid one peseta for my bus fare.'

Sedes went downstairs and picked some leaves from the yard.

'Our kids are sick and tired of boiled vegetables,' she said when she returned.

'Then, they won't have a problem,' said Andres, 'since they're not eating anything delicious.'

'I thought we'd eat something nice today,' Sedes said.

'Why?'

The woman narrated her visit to the stone house earlier that morning.

'Aling Iska wanted to help me, but she couldn't do anything,' she said.

'You don't get tired of doing this,' Andres said.

'Even Donya Leona's dogs are luckier,' Sedes said with a sigh.

'Luck doesn't only come from food,' Andres said, as if to himself.

'They invited a lot of people—all big shots,' the woman continued while turning down the flames in the clay stove. 'And there was a lot of food.'

'The lucky ones,' whispered Andres.

'While here we are, with our boiled leaves,' his wife said.

'I'm beginning to feel bad sometimes, Sedes,' the man said in a loud voice, his jaw set. 'Why is God doing this to us?'

'I just said those things, but I don't envy them for having them,' the woman said in a calm voice. 'I was just wondering why we seem to be unlucky.'

'Even though we have always worked hard,' Andres said with heat. 'Even though we haven't done anything wrong.' He continued, 'I don't want to blame God for what's happening to us. I know this is caused by people, by other people.' He said these words with much emphasis, through gritted teeth.

After a while, he calmed down and teased his sad wife.

'One day, we'll also eat roasted pig.'

Sedes' laughter was dry, but his joke had worked.

'Roasted pig?' she asked. 'What does roasted pig look like?'

And it was Andres' turn to laugh.

The rice was already boiling, so Sedes took some flaming firewood out of the clay stove.

'Just about anything will taste good on an empty stomach,' Andres said, as if to make up for what he had said about the roasted pig.

Then, he got the two tin pails near the clay stove. He had drawn water from a public faucet, a few houses away. The squatters used to draw water from the stream, but the stream wasn't always clean, and it dried up during the summer. The public faucet was the only benefit they had received from the municipal government since the American liberation, and it had been set up in time for the last elections. It was a big help to them, even if at times, the water came in trickles.

It took a long time for Andres to fill up the containers for their drinking water, as well as the big earthen vessels located beside their house. He took a bath under the faucet, and then rested upstairs for a while.

'The guests are now arriving,' he relayed the news to his wife. 'It looks like a procession of cars. The governor is also supposed to be coming.'

'If only we were invited,' Sedes teased. And she noticed that Andres was changing into new clothes. 'Are you invited?' she asked.

The man laughed.

'Where are you going? I'm about to serve dinner,' the woman said. 'The children are already asleep.'

'Kanor and company have invited me.'

'Where?'

'Just nearby. Wait for me, I'll be back soon.'

Andres went downstairs and upon turning onto the road, was met by Kanor and the other squatters.

13

A majority of the guests at the Grandes' big house had already finished their dinner. The dancing was at a frenzy on the first floor of the stone house.

Those who didn't want to dance gathered together in front of the buffet tables under the lanterns. Others walked with their arms draped around each other, taking a leisurely stroll around the yard.

Some teenagers could not be pried away from the open bar. They were loudly talking to each other, laughing in between bouts of drinking.

One drunken man who was slightly older than the rest of the crowd was happily recalling, 'I've failed the bar exams twice,' he said, waving his hand holding a glass of whiskey, 'because the examiners were very bright. But I challenged them that at this bar, they'll lose and later be found slumped under the table!' Then he drank the remaining whiskey and put his glass face down on the table. 'Bottoms up!' he said.

His company would later fill his glass with another round of whiskey.

Several servants came and went into the yard, bearing food for the drivers and the guards. Andres and his group saw several kibitzers who were able to enter the yard and help themselves to the food on the buffet table. From the open gate, they could see what was going on inside the yard and what was happening inside the house.

They only went there as curious observers, but the three squatters seemed to be seduced by the tables calling out to them—tables laden with food.

'Let's go inside,' Kanor urged them.

'No,' Andres said.

'Yes, let's have our fill,' said the third one.

'I don't want to do it,' Andres said, firmly.

'What will we lose?'

'And what will we get by just hanging out here?'

'And why will we just hang out here when the green light is on?'

When Andres still refused to budge, his two companions stood on both his sides and grabbed his arms, forcing him to go with them. So as not to attract undue attention, Andres just went along. The dogs were tied at the garage.

The guards were talking to the drivers who were eating inside the owners' cars. If anybody noticed them, they could be mistaken for farm tenants or servants.

Kanor and company directly went to the long table laden with the food from the fiesta. They grabbed one plate each and filled it up with the food. But Andres didn't follow them.

'Come on,' the two invited Andres, but he refused to budge. The two went on to eat.

Andres was salivating and his stomach was grumbling, but he restrained himself. He saw the excessive celebration and the delicious food. He remembered Sedes and their three children, who ate nothing else except the boiled leaves of sweet potatoes. He was almost tempted to do what he didn't want to do.

But he restrained himself. He couldn't eat all that grand food by himself. He wasn't even invited—the Grande family didn't even know him. Why had he even entered this yard in the first place?

As his reverie broke, Andres turned to walk away. His two companions were so busy eating, he wasn't even able to say goodbye. Kanor saw him and called out to him, but he didn't pay heed. He went out of the gate.

But he hadn't gone very far out when Kanor came. He was in a rush.

'Andres,' he called out.

He looked back and saw that the two men were carrying something. Kanor was carrying a head of roasted pig and a stuffed turkey in both hands. The other was carrying a bottle of Scotch whiskey and fried chicken. When they were near him, they said, 'Oh there, you can have

these,' and Kanor almost threw the head of the roasted pig at him.
He caught it so it would not fall on the ground.

Andres wanted to say something, to scold them, but the two
younger squatters had already run off. Without looking back, Andres
followed them.

Unfortunately, one of the guards saw them. He was alerted by
the sight of two unknown men carrying a head of roasted pig, stuffed
turkey, a bottle of Scotch whiskey and fried chicken. He suspected that
these men were neither tenants nor servants, so he had followed them.
He wanted to see where they would go and what would they do.

When the guard ascertained that they were not good guys, since
they seemed to be in a rush, he shouted at them.

'Hey, where are you taking that?'

When they heard the guard's voice, they thought that they
were being pursued. Kanor and his companion fled swiftly. Andres
followed suit.

The guard was met by a policeman, who asked what happened.

'Thieves!' said the guard. 'Thieves! Over there!' and he pointed at
Andres, who was running away swiftly.

The policeman blew on his whistle several times, but the group
didn't even look back once. The policeman pursued them, the guard at
his heels. His shrill whistle again rose in the air, but no one amongst the
absconding men dared to look back. The policeman got his revolver
out and fired two bullets in the air.

The drivers and those assembled on the yard heard the gunshots.
They were roused from the festivities and rushed outside. Several
drivers joined the pursuit, while the others honked their car horns.

But by that time, Kanor and company were gone. They had already
entered the tall cogon grasses. The policeman didn't even see them slide
swiftly in between the stalks of cogon. But those in hot pursuit saw that
one of the running men had turned and fled in the direction of the shacks
where the squatters lived. He had quickly entered one of the shacks. Even
in the darkness, it wasn't difficult to find where he was hiding.

The shacks only had faint lights. No human voices disturbed the
silence of the night there. Within a span of three minutes, the men

were sure into which shack the thief had fled. They neither called out nor issued a warning.

The policeman barged into the shack first, holding the gun in his right hand.

'Freeze!' he ordered in a loud voice.

The head of the roasted pig surprised him; it was resting on the table. The table was set in the middle of the small and narrow shack. The three young children had just awakened, and their eyes were widened. Their mother seemed to be preparing their dinner. On the table were several plates of rice and a bowl of boiled sweet potato leaves. The four looked obviously hungry, but they seemed to be waiting for somebody. Who else but the one being pursued by the policeman?

From what he saw, the policeman surmised what was in the mind of the man they were pursuing. In the beginning, he had thought that the thief had run away with money and jewellery, stolen from the guests and the owners of the big house.

He grabbed the head of the roasted pig. And when he saw Andres, his eyes widened and he spoke in a rough manner.

'So, this is it,' he said loudly. 'This is it.'

Andres faced the policeman.

'I'm arresting you in the name of the law,' the policeman said.

Andres didn't complain but calmly followed him.

'Where are your companions?' the policeman asked. But Andres didn't respond.

A throng of people were already gathered in front of the shack—neighbours who were roused by the commotion. Andres saw Marcos, but he didn't say anything.

Sedes was crying and wasn't even wiping away her tears. The three young children just watched everything unfolding before them, not understanding anything, until the youngest child started crying and tried to run after its father. Only the loud crying of the four could be heard when Andres finally left the shack.

The man caught by the policeman kept his cool. His steps were slow but firm. He didn't say a word to explain himself or weasel himself out of the situation.

'I've to arrest you,' the policeman said as they were walking. 'I'm just doing my job,' he said, as if to explain that it wasn't something he wished to do, but had to, in the name of duty.

From atop the walls of the grand house, they could already see the light coming from the hundreds of lanterns blooming in the big yard, along with the lighted bulbs hanging on an arch near the entrance to the house. The coloured lights spelt the word 'Welcome'.

As they neared the place, they could hear the sound of the orchestra playing, while in Andres' inner ear, he could still hear the cries of his three hungry children.

From their two steps of stairs, Sedes had stood looking at her husband whose hand was gripped by the policeman, until they finally vanished and melted into the shadows. Sedes remembered the joke that Andres had made in the early hours of that night, that they would eat roasted pig, and how they had laughed. But the roasted pig had now become the cause of the waterfall of tears, now cascading down her face.

14

Jun and Ninet, as well as their friends, were supposed to go up to the mountain city of Baguio, two days after the celebration at the big house. However, Donya Leona prepared a picnic for them by the fishponds. It would just be them, without any other guests.

A day before the picnic, Donya Leona had ordered Kosme to go to the fishpond and to relay to the overseer there that they were to arrive the next day. Kosme also took with him a list of things for the overseer to do and buy:

- Clean the two huts on both ends of the fishpond, the big one beside the dike and the small one near the last foothold.
- Fill the drums in the huts with clean water, along with the earthen jars for drinking water.
- Catch crabs and scoop shrimps.
- Harvest one dozen fat milkfish.
- Catch several river fish, including lady fish, moon fish, goby fish and mullet.
- Clean and put petrol in the motorized boat, and be present at the riverbank by 9 a.m. on the next day. Kosme will steer the boat which can accommodate twenty people.

As Kosme was about to leave, Iska hinted that maybe she should join the male servant and carry the things from the big house that would be needed for the picnic. But Donya Leona refused.

Iska thought it would be good for her and Kosme to arrive there a day earlier, so they could spend the night together. They had

had a good sleep there before, in the small hut at the edge of the footholds, which had felt like sleeping in a hammock swaying in the sea breeze.

Moreover, staying together in a peaceful place would somehow heal the wounds still festering inside Iska, from when she had caught Kosme serving Marcela. But Donya Leona forbade her to do so.

'Just stay here—you've a lot of errands to run here,' the old woman said.

Going to the fishponds on foot meant crossing the shallow part of the river near the bamboo groves, then going deeper into the river and finally climbing onto the first foothold. Then, they would have to walk for more or less an hour, until they reached the big hut near the dike. But if they took the boat from the riverbank, the entire trip would take only thirty minutes.

After Kosme had left, Donya Leona ordered Iska to prepare the things they had to take. She said they needed utensils and plates, as well as freshly picked papaya, desserts and powdered coffee.

'Put all of them in a carton box,' said the mistress of the house. 'Don't forget the sugar and milk as well.'

'They might not fit in one box.'

'Then use two boxes. We've many men who can carry them.'

After breakfast, the next day, the picnickers got ready. Dislaw drove the car with Don Severo and Father Pascual sitting in the back, while Cely sat in the front with her brother. Dan's friends were going to be riding with him. Iska and a younger girl were to take the jeep. The food and other provisions were also packed with them.

After arriving at the river bank, the cars were to be left in the rice warehouse owned by the Grande family on the outskirts of town. If one took the straight path, the warehouse was only five minutes away from the riverbank.

It was the first time Jun and Ninet's friends were passing by the town centre, leaving behind the village and the farmland, since they had arrived in Sampilong four days ago.

Sampilong didn't have much to offer to young people in search of something new and different to do. They only went there to join in the family celebration. On their trip from Manila, they also passed by many towns beside the national highway, and these towns were more developed than Sampilong.

But they didn't care for these things, for they were only concerned about making the trip and deriving whatever pleasure they could from it. Whenever and wherever the six of them were together, it was always an occasion for much cheer.

Sampilong had vast lands and vaster farmlands, but its town centre was narrow and small. It was surrounded by seemingly endless rice fields, like giant chessboards. The southwest part of the town had thick bamboo groves, cogon grasses and several tall hardwood trees. In the east, the river meandered, shaped like a snake, and the swamp was like a beast, filled with thick mangroves. Beyond these lay the fishponds, one of which belonged to the Grande family.

The first signs of the town centre could be seen in a few old buildings that the war had mercifully spared, as well as the new houses built in lieu of the ruined ones that had been cleared. The town centre looked like an island surrounded by rice fields, woodlands and the river. Except for how it looked, it resembled many other towns in the Philippines that had been sealed off from progress. That was why when the car first roared into the centre of town, Jun and company already knew how it looked in one sweep of their eyes.

There was the municipal hall, which was half the size of the Grandes' stone house. Inside this hall were the offices of the mayor, the vice mayor and the councillors; the police quarters, and a medical dispensary manned by a chronically ill doctor and a new nurse-clerk, his daughter. The hall also housed the office of the treasurer and two of his employees.

On the other side of the road slouched the ancient and mossy church that looked so different from the new convent, that it made her resemble a person in rags but wearing a shiny pair of black shoes. Farther down the road stood the old marketplace that should have been called a shed. The school house that was burnt down when the Japanese invaders used it as their headquarters, had been rebuilt after the war, but it still didn't have a library.

There were two stores selling a variety of items. These were owned by Chinese nationals who had married Filipino women who worked as sales clerks in the stores. There was another grocery store, also owned by a Chinese national. On the same side as the grocery store sat a strange establishment whose signage screamed two letter Ps. Under the P on the left, one could read the word Pharmacy and under the other P on the right was Parlour, for Funeral Parlour.

An old and cranky woman owned these two establishments. She didn't marry, owing perhaps to her sharp tongue. Her medicines were as expensive as her smile, and her coffins were as sad as her eyes. The signages were often the butt of jokes at Tinoy's barber shop. The scuttlebutt was that the real meaning of the first P was 'Please let this illness pass' while the second P stood for 'Parlour not for beauty, but for the dead'.

Meanwhile, a cinema hall stood near the bus station. It was built during the times of silent movies, and was open only three times a week. A group of noisy children were the only patrons of this cinema hall.

Between the church and the graveyard was the electric plant, which lighted up the town of Sampilong. There was also the cockpit, and a stone's throw away was the rice warehouse of the Grande family. The electric plant and cockpit were built using the capital of an association, whose primary investors were Don Severo, the mayor and the priest.

As Jun and his friends passed by the villages, they saw up in the front the houses of the well-to-do and the huts where the farmers lived. Those who owned their lands had well-kept houses, like Mang Pablo's family, Aling Oris and her nephew Bandong, as well as three or four other people who had rented their land and accumulated a little money. But the many others who had no land lived in abject poverty, which could be seen not only in their humble huts but also in the frail bodies of their children and the faces of the women, who looked older than their actual age.

In the village where Dan's car passed were the houses of Tasyo, Simon, Blas, Julian, Beteng and Tomas. All of them were neighbours, and they all worked as tenants in the rice fields of the Grande family. Mang Pablo and his family had a comfortable house with a yard tended by Pina's hands. They were located in the part of the village that was near the town centre.

Dinong was walking away from the inner street when he saw the two cars and a jeep whizzing past him. He recognized Dislaw as the one driving the first car.

'I saw them,' he later told his older sister.

'They're going to have a picnic at the fishpond.' Pina guessed.

'Why didn't Dislaw invite you?' he teased his sister.

'And who would have liked to join them anyway?' snapped Pina. 'I don't just agree to anyone who invites me,' and she put her two fingers together and placed them atop her nose.

Dan's car cruised past farmlands that lay fallow and paths that had got stonier as the summer was ending. Then, they reached the side of the river.

Jun boasted to his friends, 'All of that belongs to us.' And then his right hand swept across in the direction of the vast lands.

'Which of that is yours and which is Ninet's?' Dan quickly asked. Then he touched Ninet's arm with his forefinger. Before Jun could answer, Pil had already beaten him to the draw.

'What Dan wants to know is which of the lands would be his?' Pil's joke made the group burst into laughter.

The small motorboat was already waiting for them when they reached the river bank.

'They've been here for a while,' Kosme said, his right eye fixed on Iska while the left one glanced at Cely.

They quickly transferred their things to the small boat and asked the women to board first.

The jeep and cars were left in the care of the servant who wouldn't join the picnic, so they could be taken to the warehouse.

The group was delighted at how the small boat was like an arrow speeding down a straight path on the water, until they had reached a wider expanse of the river. They only slowed down to round a curve or avoid a clump of mangroves. In less than thirty minutes, they were already beside the dike of the fishpond.

After disembarking, Donya Leona talked to her brother, Father Pascual.

'I've my regrets now,' the woman said. 'I should have extended the footholds to cover five more hectares until they reached the swamps. We'd have incurred the same expense anyway.'

'You just let go of a big property,' the priest answered.

Earlier, Donya Leona had closed the footholds and claimed the river, creek and swamp that belonged to the government and used to be open to everyone for fishing. But she had set a parameter to her claims. She was also worried that the people who would lose their jobs would complain, and until now, her land claims were the subject of dispute.

Marybee turned on her battery-operated radio and held Jun's hand, inviting him onto the smooth, cemented floor of the dike.

'Can you teach me your dance moves with Cookie?' she asked in a pointed manner.

Jun just laughed and did as he was asked, but he ignored the barbed comment about the nightclub singer.

'Ahem, ahem!' Dan pretended to choke. Then, he and Ninet also proceeded to dance.

The three young women wore jeans and loose blouses, while the men wore shorts and T-shirts.

In one corner, Iska confronted Kosme.

'If that flirt does so much as come near me, somebody's going to drown today,' she warned.

While leaving the stone house earlier that day, Iska had noticed that Dislaw's widowed sister was also joining the trip. She felt as if her throat were filled with kernels of corn that were about to pop. She vented her fury at Kosme. The male servant felt as if he was standing between two foxes with pointed claws. When he was finally able to extricate himself from Iska's rage, he fled to the small hut at the edge of the footholds, alone.

The seafood laid out on the table was fresh and sweet, whichever way it was cooked. The picnickers feasted on the food and quelled their good appetites, except Cely, who felt she was burning under Iska's sharp glare.

'I'm eating more now, compared to the night of the celebration,' Donya Leona said happily.

'And why not?' agreed Don Severo. 'How could you eat when you were taking care of 300 guests?'

Afterwards, the women brought out the mahjongg tiles and set them on a table. The four women—Ninet, Marybee, Bining and Donya Leona—played. On the other side, Jun, Dan, Pil and Don Severo formed a quorum for poker.

'Oh, I've forgotten how to play this,' the old man said in a pretentious tone. 'Could you just play on my behalf, my brother-in-law?' he asked Father Pascual.

But Donya Leona swiftly punctured a hole in her husband's charade.

'Hey, if you learnt something at the university, it was how to play that devilish poker,' she said in a loud voice from where she sat.

The laughter that rose in the air after Donya Leona said those words had not yet faded when they were startled by Iska's scream from below.

'Crocodile! Crocodile!'

The three young women looked down and the three young men rushed downstairs. They found Cely thrashing about in the deep part of the river. They couldn't yet fathom what had happened because Kosme's lips were sealed. He recalled vividly Iska's threat about somebody drowning that day.

15

When Bandong arrived at the elementary school, Andres and Sedes were already there, along with their eldest son, Ato. They all went inside the office of the interim principal.

The school term was already over, but Bandong still went to work to solve what Mang Pablo had called as the school's problems. When Nana Oris noted Bandong never failed to go to school, her nephew said, 'It's better to work than to just play truant.'

Bandong already knew Andres. Even if the teacher was still young during the Japanese Occupation, he was already part of the resistance movement in Sampilong against the invaders. Andres was also in the movement, along with Tasyo, Simon and Blas.

Bandong had heard of what had happened to Andres during the night of the celebration in the yard of the big house. Andres was released after being held for a few hours at the police station, after eyewitnesses confirmed that he hadn't stolen the head of the roasted pig. Donya Leona didn't want him released because she and her husband didn't like the squatters, but Father Pascual had prevailed over them. The priest reasoned that the head of the roasted pig had been reclaimed, and Andres' wife always attended the Holy Mass every Sunday.

That morning, Andres and Sedes went to school to follow up on their request regarding their ten-year-old, who had not yet begun studying. The interim principal told them to visit him in school, so he could study the situation.

Bandong listed the name and age of Ato, along with his parents' names and where they lived.

'What do you call your place of residence?' asked the teacher.

'Gar—bage Dump,' Andres stuttered his answer.

The squatters explained that they were not the ones who had chosen that name for their residence, but those who lived in the town centre and the servants at the big house.

'They said we're like garbage that was dumped there,' Andres added.

'You should clean up your place then, and change its name,' Bandong advised. 'Even if people are poor, they shouldn't be seen as garbage.'

Then he turned to Ato.

'Do you want to go to school?' He looked at the boy who was wearing old but clean clothes, and no slippers.

'Yes, sir!' the boy swiftly answered.

'Very good,' Andres said, nodding. 'Time has passed, but you're not yet late. It's never too late for someone who wants to learn.'

'That's what we also thought,' agreed Sedes. 'It's painful for parents to not be able to send their kids to school.' She stopped because she seemed like she was about to cry. 'But the expenses, sir ... Why would I be shy to admit that even for our food expenses—'

The principal cut short what Ato's mother was going to say, and reassured her that they had nothing to worry about.

'Ato will start in Grade One, and the expenses are very minimal.' Bandong promised to take care of these expenses.

Two teardrops finally fell from Sedes' eyes, but what she heard lit up her face.

'We'll owe a debt of gratitude to you for the rest of our lives,' she said.

'Please ask us to do anything for you, and we'll repay your kindness,' Andres said.

'It's the government's obligation to educate all children,' Bandong answered. 'But the government will fail if the leaders and teachers like me don't do our share of the work.'

He told the husband and wife that they should come back and bring Ato when classes open, and that he would find space for him. He gave the child a small primer for Grade One, a pencil and paper pad.

'You may practise reading and writing,' he said. 'Please teach him.'

With excitement, Ato received the things given by the teacher, as if they were toys or food that he had wanted for a long time. He opened the first page of the primer and read aloud.

'Boy, gel, dog—'

'Oh, he already knows how to read!' Bandong said with admiration.

'He really likes to read,' the mother said with pride. 'He learnt it from his friends in the neighbourhood.'

From his closet, Bandong took out a bag made of abaca fibres and a basket made of rattan. He showed it to the husband and wife.

'The students here made these,' he said proudly. 'You can also make something like this,' he said, as if making them an offer.

'I know how to make umbrellas,' Sedes answered. 'If only we have materials—'

'That's what I meant,' Bandong clarified. 'We can make and finish these things. We shouldn't waste our time.' Then he turned to Andres and asked, 'Why aren't you earning a living now? What used to be your work?'

The squatter recalled his job before the Second World War, and why he rarely had work after the American Liberation.

'Our company completely closed,' he said. 'I used to be a foreman in a construction company. But now, I'm not picky, I can do any work. I can work as a carpenter, baggage carrier, anything just to earn money.'

Bandong praised Andres' humility. However, he reminded him that it wasn't correct to just wait for good luck and have no sense of direction.

'Look,' he said, and then he seemed like a professor guiding his students in an economics class. 'The government can't afford to give jobs to everyone. The politicians can make their promises, but you know where those promises lead.'

'That's why the people don't believe them anymore,' Andres said. But Bandong didn't make a comment and just pressed on.

'The industries also can't hire all workers and give them employment. There are so many extra workers here in Luzon, but people don't want to live in places where the land lies fallow. For example, Mindanao, Palawan, or Mindoro.'

When the teacher stopped talking, Andres took the chance to give his own opinion on the matter.

'Many people have gone there, but they've also returned,' the squatter said. 'Because the forests in Mindanao and elsewhere can't be cleared by just using one's hands. Equipment is needed, and they also need to eat before harvest can come—'

'That's true,' agreed Bandong. 'I'm not suggesting that people like you should go there. People are free to go where they want to go. But those who want to stay here should find ways and means to make a living.'

The teacher held the basket and bag up again and told them he showed them to tell the couple they need not go to Mindanao to find a livelihood.

'You can make these even inside your huts,' he said. 'Or you can make hats like these, traditional woven bags, mats, broomsticks, fans—'

'Where will we get the raw materials?' the couple asked.

'We can source them. There are offices in Manila that can provide them, and they'll even pay you when you finish the products. Or we can make it here, at our place. We can set up a cooperative whose members can give small contributions.'

'Your suggestions are good. I'll tell the people about this.'

'Please meet them as a group and discuss my proposals thoroughly with them.'

'We'll do that.'

Bandong stopped, stood up and went to a shelf. He returned with a book. He sat down, opening the book and turning its pages. The husband and wife just looked at him. Meanwhile, Ato had separated himself from the group, put the pad paper atop a desk, and started drawing with his pencil.

'Nobody should go hungry in this country,' Bandong read aloud when he finally found what he was looking for. 'Nobody should pick up garbage from the streets just to be able to live.' He stopped and scanned several paragraphs, then looked again at the couple. 'Do you know that the Philippines is bigger than all the New England states, which include the state of New York? Do you also know that if they combine Belgium, Denmark, the Netherlands, Portugal and Switzerland, they would still come out smaller than the Philippines?' He showed the couple a map of Europe and pointed out the five countries that he had mentioned. 'However, these countries are wealthy and their people live in comfort, especially the Swiss, Belgians and Danes.'

'And the Japanese,' Bandong snapped. 'We've more natural resources and industrial raw materials than Japan. But where is Japan now, and where is the Philippines?'

The couple was enchanted by what they had heard and were rendered speechless by the facts delivered by the teacher.

'Why are Filipinos poor?' he asked them, as if he were asking a group of students in class.

'Because here, the foreigners are king,' Andres swiftly answered.

'And who's at fault for that?' Bandong countered. He said that they shouldn't discuss the issue now but instead focus on the home industries that would help improve the lot of the squatters.

They all agreed that Andres and Sedes would start the initiative by thoroughly cleaning their area.

'You turned that place into a slum area,' the teacher accused them. 'It should be a habitable place for people, and you'll also be able to live in better conditions.'

Bandong reminded them that the land was owned by the local government and there was no sign that it would use the plot for any purpose anytime soon. But the plot couldn't be given away to the squatters, because the government didn't give away free plots to the public.

'You can rent it or buy it on installments,' he said. 'But first, you must clean up the place. Don't turn it into a mountain of garbage. Spruce up your homes and turn the place into a real village. When that happens, no one here will resent your presence. Instead, they'll treat you well, because you'd have proven yourselves worthy of such treatment.'

Andres voiced his fear that whatever the squatters did to improve the place, the Grande family would not change their intention to drive them away from the spot that used to be filled with cogon grasses and thorny weeds. Someone had suggested to the mayor and the chief of police that the remaining cogon grasses could easily be razed by fire, which would also burn down the squatters' huts.

Don Severo had allegedly said, 'They better leave, or else the flames will swallow them up!'

Bandong calmed their fears and told them to relay to the squatters to not be afraid either.

'You should all help yourselves and live in an honourable manner. Don't be afraid,' the teacher advised them. 'In due time, God will prove His presence to everyone.'

A funeral wake was being held in a poor hut in the village. It was the house of Julian, the farmer, and his wife Sepa had just died. Julian worked as a tenant on the farm of the Grande family.

The doctor wasn't wrong in his diagnosis that the woman had a lung condition and wouldn't live much longer. Sepa was the reason why Julian had gone to Donya Leona after the rice harvest. He had almost cried as he begged the woman not to get her share of the harvest first, because he needed to buy medicines for his ailing wife and pay the doctor's fees as well. But the woman had harshly told him that if Sepa's case was already terminal, then the doctor wouldn't be needed anymore, and the medicines would just be useless.

Julian had been so angry at the woman's coarse behaviour. If a water buffalo is ill, it's treated until it gets well. What about his wife, then, who was also the mother of his children? But the owner of the harvest had a heart of stone.

Sepa had fallen ill from the heavy work she used to do on the farms of Donya Leona. When they transferred the rice saplings from the seedbed to the paddies, her feet remained deep in the mud, whether rain or shine. She already had high fever when she went home one afternoon, and was restless.

Julian immediately attended to his wife. He got a face towel, dipped it in warm water laced with vinegar, and gave her a sponge bath. Then, he got another face towel dipped in the same mixture, and placed it on her burning forehead. He also made ginger tea and asked her to drink it. He also tried to make her take rice broth that night, but the ill woman's stomach couldn't take it.

Sepa's fever subsided a bit, but by dawn, she was wracked with cough—cough so persistent and so strong that tears fell from her eyes and snot was discharged from her nose. She complained of pain in her chest and when she finally expelled what was knotted in her chest, they found it was a lump of blood.

Mercifully, Sepa was able to sleep before morning came and when she awakened, she asked for food. But over the next few days, as the afternoon light began to die out and when the morning came, her fever returned and the coughs also returned with a vengeance. Julian repeated his home remedies several times, but they could no longer ease her pain or improve her condition. Then, he also tried herbal medicine, to no avail.

His wife continued to weaken as the days passed. He could no longer work in the fields. He didn't even have the time to do the housework. He was constantly bombarded with things to do, so much so that he had to ask his eldest daughter to quit her studies for a while to help out with the household chores.

Sepa drank the herbal concoctions and allowed the old man to put leaves on her skin, but they were all to no avail. That was why Julian was forced to fetch a real doctor who lived in the town. He quickly bought the medicines that he asked to give to Sepa. But her condition continued to deteriorate, and the expenses mounted.

At one point, Julian began to doubt the efficacy of medicines. That was why he and his children always knelt and prayed fervently before they went to sleep, and attended the Holy Mass every Sunday. They asked for God's mercy for their beloved Sepa. But she didn't improve and her body showed the ill effects of her illness.

What Julian feared, finally happened. One morning, he woke his four children up and calmly told them that their mother had passed away. The eldest one broke into sobs, followed by the younger siblings. And then they all rushed to where their mother lay. They all embraced her, kissed her, ran their fingers through her hair and touched her hand.

'Mother! Mother!' they all sobbed, like little birds lost in the night.

Goosebumps rose on Julian's skin, but he restrained himself. He felt as if a part of his body was gone. In front of him lay his other, now-missing self. Julian just cried in silence.

'Sepa, my wife,' he whispered. 'You'll be alive forever in our memories.'

Sepa lived a very brief life; she was all of thirty-four, but her love was great and her patience was long. She was the angel of this house in which they raised two young Julians and two young Sepas.

Like all ordinary women married to farmers, she carried on her frail shoulders the burdens of housework, as well as work at the farm. In spite of their poverty, she lived a happy life with Julian. Even though she was too weak, she would still try to do some housework, because she felt delighted if she could help out in the house.

Indeed, Sepa had died at thirty-four, but she looked much older than her husband's forty-three years, if you saw her sunken cheeks and her veiny hands. When she got married, Sepa stopped entertaining thoughts of trying to look younger than the man she had vowed to follow and to love.

The neighbours were roused by the crying of the children, and they immediately knew what had happened. A day earlier, the doctor from the capital had visited Julian's shack, and the neighbours had seen him leave with a glum face. That was why they immediately sprang into action.

Three women who were also married to farmers cleaned Sepa's body. She was first laid on a bamboo bed inside her hut. Then, the women looked for black clothes that the four orphans could wear. The four children just sat like stones in front of their dead mother, hardly moving at all.

The other farmers who were friends of Julian's also attended to the other needs. Tasyo, Simon, Blas, Beteng and Tomas, each went his own way to find ways and means to hold a decent wake. Even Ba Inte came early and gave Julian advice on what to do.

Then they all found wood for the coffin. They cut, planed, fitted, nailed and varnished it.

They put in front of the house a shed made of fresh coconut leaves and cut banana trunks. Wooden benches were then arranged in a circle, and a rectangular table was set at the end. This area was for those who would attend the funeral wake, since not all of them could be accommodated inside the shack.

They also borrowed two Coleman lamps and bought one dozen candles.

On the other hand, two pails of water were poured in a vat set on four rocks in the backyard, to boil water for the ginger tea. This tea was made using crushed slices of ginger and sweetened with a piece of brown sugar or molasses.

Before lunchtime came, the people who wanted to offer their condolences to Julian began to arrive. Almost all of them came bearing something to offer to him. Some of them brought traditional bags full of rice, while others came with fruits and tubers. Yet others came with trays of eggs and dried fish. Two men came loaded with firewood tied by strings, while one or two offered native white hens.

Beteng and Tomas came back carrying a fat pig. Julian also had a pig, but the people told him not to slaughter him, since it was a custom in the village for friends and neighbours to provide for the needs of a funeral wake, everything all the way up to the burial expenses.

'Where did you get that?' Julian asked the two men carrying the fat pig.

'Just around the corner,' said Beteng.

'It's easy to ask for donations for the dead,' said Tomas.

Before the sun had set, the coffin was already finished, its top and sides smoothened and varnished. They put a clean, white cloth inside as a lining. After dressing up Sepa's body in her wedding dress, they moved her from the bamboo bed to the improvised coffin. The women powdered her sunken cheeks and put some colour onto them. Then, they put a thin layer of lipstick on her lips. These were things that Sepa didn't do even when she was still alive.

'She looks prettier now,' one of the women admired the makeup they had put on Sepa.

'It seems she's just asleep,' said another woman.

The eldest daughter added an old crucifix that their mother always touched. It was placed in between the crossed arms of the dead. On top of the coffin, the orphans placed a bouquet of wild and beautiful flowers that they had gathered from outside.

The coffin was then placed on top of a table in the middle of the narrow shack. Julian was carrying his youngest daughter and just stood in front of the coffin. From where the grieving widower stood, he thought that Sepa no longer looked gaunt and suffering. There was almost no more trace of the cruel illness that had ravaged her body. In her face could no longer be seen the cloud of sadness that had darkened it, sadness not for herself but for her husband and four children.

Julian recalled that Sepa knew the wings of death were whirring close by. Whenever this happened, she would ask: 'What would happen to all of you when I'm gone?' Even until the end, she wasn't concerned about herself, but only about them.

The shroud of suffering had seemingly been lifted from Sepa now that she lay there quietly, in her wake. Her wedding dress still looked new, because it was worn only once, on that lucky day when she got married. Julian still seemed to hear his wife's vibrant voice, she who knew the privations of being a farmer's wife, but nevertheless promised to serve him and make him happy. But the lips that had spoken those vows and the fervent eyes that had promised to keep them were now closed and folded by peace. The body that had fulfilled those promises was now a cold corpse, while the life-giving soul had risen to go live in a place that no mere mortal's mind could reach.

On the other hand, Julian reflected that Sepa would no longer have to face the realities of the ugly world she had left behind. There seemed to be a slight smile on her closed lips; it felt strange to say but this pitiful wife and mother was comfortable lying in that state inside her poor coffin.

'God of all creation,' Julian began to pray, 'please accept the soul of my beloved Sepa.' And then the widower made the sign of the cross, before he finally turned away from the coffin.

He could see the strange ways of people when confronted with Sepa's death. When she was alive, she never experienced a single act of care, admiration and affection, but these were now being showered onto her, in death. Praises were heaped on her now that she lay in state.

'Sepa was very kind!'

'Sepa was very hardworking!'

'Sepa was a holy woman!'

'Sepa was the perfect neighbour!'

'Sepa was a role model wife!'

'She was a distinctive mother!'

They talked about her sweetness and her lack of hypocrisy when dealing with people in the village, and her kind courtesy while dealing with one and all.

That night, when people were already crowding the house and the benches in the yard were bursting at the seams, Dislaw arrived. He made sure everyone heard the sound of his jeep before he alighted from it.

He climbed up the stairs, went straight to Julian and said in a voice loud enough for everyone to hear, even the dead woman herself, 'We offer our condolences to you for your loss, Julian. Here is a contribution from Donya Leona, and here is mine.' He gave to Julian one bank note with the image of Dr Jose Rizal, the national hero, and another bank note with the image of Apolinario Mabini, the Brains of the Philippine Revolution against Spain.

'Thank you, Mr Dislaw,' Julian acknowledged, but it couldn't be known whether his eyes shone with hatred or with tears. He immediately recalled the time he had almost knelt in front of Donya Leona after the harvest, asking her if he could keep his complete share of the harvest to buy medicines for Sepa, but the rich landowner had stoutly refused.

As if in response to Julian's thoughts, an eyewitness saw the contribution of Donya Leona and said, 'Two pesos only for the wife of her tenant? Someone is really tone deaf.'

17

As the night darkened, the energy of the people at Sepa's funeral wake ironically kept increasing.

Before Dislaw arrived, Teacher Bandong, the father and daughter Mang Pablo and Pina, and Ba Inte were already there. Ba Inte had arrived early in the morning, left, and then came back again. After having dinner, Pina and the other single women of the village went to the wake. Bandong brought along Nana Oris. All of them made their donations, but only Julian knew how much. They weren't like Dislaw, who had proudly brandished before everyone the Rizal and Mabini bank notes donated by Donya Leona and himself. Aside from Pina and Nana Oris, many other women were also busy helping around.

'I'm thinking of the children whom Aling Sepa has left behind,' said Pina to Nana Oris.

'They'll survive,' answered the old woman. 'Wasn't Bandong that age when he became a complete orphan?' and she indicated with her hands how small her nephew had been then. 'I was able to bring him up by myself.'

'But you're well-off,' said Pina.

'It all depends on how you steer your life.'

Nana Oris intentionally mentioned the name of Bandong, and it made the young woman's heart jump. Nana Oris had liked Pina ever since she was a child. On the other hand, Pina had had yet another chance to weigh the qualities of both her suitors, Bandong and Dislaw, on this occasion.

Most of the women were upstairs, while the men were clustered in one part of the yard. Upstairs, the conversation revolved around life in the village, at how swiftly the rice grains had vanished, the spiralling prices of goods, especially of viands and clothes. On the other hand, the men downstairs were exchanging views on what was happening in the town centre, municipal and provincial politics, the difficulty in finding a source of living, before returning to the topic of how swiftly the rice grains had vanished, along with the spiralling prices of goods.

Meanwhile under the makeshift shed, the young men and women didn't concern themselves with the grave topics being discussed by their elders. They seemed to live in a different world focused only on the present moment, with neither a past nor a future. Their benches were close to each other and everyone was telling stories, cracking jokes or teasing one another. In their merriment, they seemed to have forgotten there was a funeral wake going on.

Someone suggested that the young people should play *juego de prenda*, the game of fines, played during funeral wakes.

'Yes, why not play juego de prenda?' many people said in unison.

'Oh no, I'm not good at singing,' said one young woman.

'Then you can serve your fine by dancing,' advised the person sitting beside her.

'I also don't know how to dance.'

'Then you can do a striptease,' said a young man beside her.

'You're shameless!' she said, then hit the young man with her fan made from woven anahaw leaves.

All of them decided who would serve as the king, and decided on a man who looked like a large bat hanging from the trellis of bottle gourd.

'What an ugly king,' observed another young woman.

'How else should a king be, if not scary?' snapped someone near her.

The designated king sat behind a rectangular table at the back, and began.

'Everyone should keep quiet so we can hear each other,' he requested. 'Are you ready now?'

'We've been ready for a while.'

'The king's butterfly escaped and landed on a jasmine flower,' the king said.

'Da butterply his not in da plower,' said a young woman. People near her restrained their laughter, for by her accent, the speaker obviously came from another province.

'So where is it?' asked the king.

'Da butterply his with da king.'

The king pounded the table with his fist and said that nobody should counter the king.

'That's the rule,' he said.

But the jasmine flower did not relent, and continued countering.

'So wat is dat, only the king rules?' she asked. 'In our town of Hapalit, heveryone rules, not just da king. Hay don't want to dyoin hany more!' She said, stood up, and then stomped her feet.

'All of us should follow the rules and decisions of the king. The king is the king. Be prepared and we'll start again.' Then he continued, 'The butterfly flew again and landed on the white *sampaguita* flower.'

'That flower isn't here.'

'Where did it go?'

'In the cashew tree.'

No one answered.

'Cashew tree?' the king called.

'The *cahews* tree isn't here,' said the young man who was called.

'What *cahews*? Cashew,' corrected the king.

'Cashew,' the teenager repeated.

'Where did it go then?'

'It landed on the butterfly pea flower.'

Someone laughed at the mention of the flower shaped like a woman's genitals. And why on earth did this flower's name belong to an ugly woman? She was confused and stopped cold in her tracks, and couldn't answer anymore.

After six people had failed to answer, the king ruled, 'Let's stop and pay our fines.'

'The butterfly pea flower will sing,' commanded the king.

'May I just drink a cup of ginger tea?' requested the butterfly pea flower.

'It should be boiling hot,' the king said, and everyone tittered.

The other fines given included playing the guitar, reciting a memorized poem, and a woman was even asked to kiss the hand of everyone who joined the game, in a gesture of respect usually reserved for elders.

Dislaw was watching from the back, and when it was her turn to kiss his hand, he suddenly put it in front of her face without waiting for her.

'Oh my,' the woman said. 'And I don't even know the last thing touched your hand.'

And there was laughter loud enough to wake even the dead.

Meanwhile, Ba Inte and Mang Pablo were joined by those younger than them but definitely older than those who joined the game of fines. Tasyo and the other farmers were in this group. It was a tradition at such gatherings to seek wisdom from those with more life experience, so naturally, everyone turned to Ba Inte.

'Pablo, were you already born when the river here was still wide and deep?' Ba Inte asked Pina's father.

'I just heard about it, Ba Inte, but I never really saw it,' said Mang Pablo.

'Yes, you're much younger,' the old man reflected. 'You're as old as Severo and Leona.'

Ba Inte then lighted the end of his cheap cigar, sucked deeply, and the smoke floated out of his nostrils before he spoke again.

'I'll tell you about the crocodiles in this town,' he started, which made the group excited. 'I was already alive at that time. We used to take a bath in the river,' he said while pointing to the area where the old river used to snake. 'By then, it had turned into a narrow and rather shallow stream. But when one day, a crocodile attacked a young boy; the river seemed to have been cursed.'

'Did the crocodile eat the boy?' asked one of the listeners, his voice fraught with fear.

'Yes,' confirmed Ba Inte. 'We didn't believe it was possible until the day it happened.' He looked afar. 'The river was connected to a wide swamp,' the old man continued. 'The mangroves and cork trees grew in such luxuriance that the swamp looked like a forest. There used to be a lot of fishermen then. Some people gathered river snails for food, while the others picked fallen mangrove branches for firewood. Nobody used to own that area before.'

'What happened to the crocodile?'

'Without any warning, the crocodile left the swamp and went ashore,' he continued his narration. 'It lay down in the mud, covering its body and only showing its head. Its eyes were closed and its mouth was wide open. The animals suddenly began to vanish. The moment they went to the swamp to look for food, they themselves became food for the greedy crocodile.'

'Did the crocodile prefer to eat people?' asked a curious observer.

'It preferred to eat dogs and pigs, but if they weren't available, then people would do,' said Ba Inte. 'But there are also people who drink the blood of other people.'

'Those are leeches,' said one voice.

The rest kept quiet to allow the old man of the village to continue with his story.

'I already mentioned one child who was attacked by the crocodile. Soon after, another boy was attacked; this time, a boy who was just foraging for firewood. The boy screamed in pain. His companions saw everything. They ran back to the village. The older men rushed back with spears and machetes. They searched the swamps and the nearby river. The others took the boat and thoroughly searched the waters. They caught two crocodiles, small ones, but not the one that had attacked the children.'

'So, the child wasn't saved?'

'No,' Ba Inte shook his head. 'After a few days, the people in the village burnt the weedy areas and woodlands. The place was ablaze for a while, as if there was a big fire going. A wall of bamboos was built on one side of the river, so that the crocodiles could no longer enter the area near the village. The river slowly became narrower and shallower.'

'Is it true that a crocodile sheds tears when it's about to eat a person?' asked a young man.

'That's what they say,' answered Ba Inte. 'It seems it sheds tears before it kills. It raises its tail and creates a noise, and it appears to be weeping. But that's just a ruse so that someone would come near it. And pity the one who comes near.'

'From then on, has the crocodile vanished from this place, Ba Inte?'

'Some of them have vanished, but some remain. Some crocodiles even left the swamp and went upland—'

'Huh?'

'Don't be surprised,' the old man said firmly. 'They went upland to live in the big stone house.'

Ba Inte's last words were met with loud laughter by those who understood the reference.

'Oh, this Ba Inte,' said Mang Pablo with a smile, breaking his silence.

'And from then on,' said Tasyo, continuing the tale of Ba Inte, 'only the tail of the crocodile moves.'

It was Ba Inte's turn to be surprised, that was why Tasyo stared at the old man.

'Here comes the tail, it's coming here!' and Tasyo signalled with his lips whom he was alluding to.

Dislaw arrived while the group was still laughing.

'Why are you happy when someone is dead?' noted the caretaker of the Grande family.

'We're the opposite of the crocodile,' answered Simon. 'The crocodile cries when it's about to eat someone. We do the opposite and follow the saying that one should have a happy face on a sad day.'

'Phew!' Dislaw said with a hint of insult, as he sat on a bench offered to him by a farmer.

18

Someone at the back asked Ba Inte to finish his story.

'It's finished,' the old man said. 'The river became narrow and shallow. Almost all the crocodiles have vanished.'

'And thereafter, everyone in Sampilong lived happy and peaceful lives,' added Dislaw.

'No,' said Ba Inte. 'Because when the crocodiles vanished, the farmers' bond of unity also vanished.'

Dislaw butted in, 'Perhaps, they all went to a place where there were no more dangers.'

Ba Inte shook his head and said, 'No, the lack of unity is a weakness, and weakness is a dangerous thing.'

'Don't you like the unity shown here as everyone consoles Julian?' asked Dislaw.

'They're consoling him because someone has died,' the old man said as a rebuke. 'A person dies only once, but he lives for a long time.' He fixed his stare at Dislaw and said with bitterness, 'It's been said that unity is only seen when someone dies. Take, for instance, Sepa—can she still appreciate this show of unity?'

'But the soul of a person doesn't die,' protested Dislaw.

'The living needs to stay united.'

'When there's an enemy, yes. Like during the Second World War.'

'But there's always a struggle to unite for,' said Ba Inte. 'People don't run out of enemies. Sometimes it's nature; oftentimes, it's his fellowmen. People weren't united even during the war. Even in this small town, there were people who supported the Japanese.' Ba Inte stopped, trying to figure out the effect of his words on Dislaw when he said there were people who supported the Japanese, and then continued, 'Some people took advantage and even became rich. They only helped themselves, right? What I mean is, back then, our enemies were the Japanese. Today, our enemies are the wrong practices, the burden of poverty, envy … Ah, sometimes, peace feels heavy on one's shoulders because your oppressor is one of your fellowmen—someone whom you put in power …'

Ba Inte let out a deep sigh as he uttered the last words.

'Then we should keep the farmers' unity alive,' Simon suggested firmly.

'Unity?' Dislaw snapped and expressed his fears. 'You'll just put another burden on yourselves. What happened to the previous association? You chose leaders who weren't from here. You paid in terms of both money and harvest. They taught you violence, to go against the law. What happened to many of those people?'

When no one answered, Dislaw deepened his thrust against the union.

'Your harvests vanished because of your unity. Some got caught with firearms. Others went to jail. Some were killed, and a few killed people themselves as they followed the wrong ideals of bad leaders. Is this good? Now you want to form another group. For what? Who will you fight against? My friends, they who sow the wind will reap a storm.'

Bandong heard the commotion downstairs, so he left his delightful conversation with Pina midway. He arrived just as Dislaw issued his threat and Tasyo answered sharply.

'It's hard for you to know our needs,' said the farmer. 'We're just tenants on the land; you're the overseer of the landlord—'

'What's the difference?' Dislaw said, without letting the farmer finish what he was saying. 'Don't the landlords trust you as well? And as for me, I'm just the landlord's employee.'

'Heaven and earth,' Tasyo answered. 'We serve, while you represent those whom we serve. Although the bounty comes from the same land, yet we're different. We work tirelessly using our water buffaloes. But we're more tired than the beasts, because they're there only to help us.'

Tasyo looked around and noticed that everyone was listening to him with rapt attention.

'The heat of the sun burns our faces,' Tasyo added, 'the harsh rain dulls our bodies. We skip our meals. We fall ill. Often, there's no doctor and no medicine. We die young. Like Sepa.'

His hand touched his face, as if to touch a passing shadow. Then Tasyo continued.

'On the other hand, the landowner lives a comfortable life. He doesn't sweat. His children have things in excess. Only a blind person can't see the big difference.' He took a deep breath and said, 'You're against our unity because you're different from us.'

Tasyo then saw Bandong coming.

'Here's Teacher Bandong,' he said, causing the people to look back at the young teacher, who just stood at the back of the group. 'He's not a farmer, nor does he lease his family's land. He's a teacher. Yet, he knows what's right, and is a friend to all. Let's ask him if a unified organization of farmers is right or wrong. Could you please explain to us, Teacher Bandong?'

All eyes were then fixed on the young teacher.

With a smile, Bandong raised both his arms and begged their indulgence to not be included in their discussions. But some onlookers who were watching the card games came nearer to him and when he looked up toward the house, there were several women, including Pina, looking at him. Mang Pablo, who was downstairs, was also watching the proceedings intently.

'We just want to know your honest opinion, whether you agree or disagree with us,' Tasyo implored. 'Mang Dislaw thinks the union is excessive. He pointed to the bad things it had brought before. But I think it's time to form a new union. We just need clarity from you, Teacher Bandong.'

Dislaw was about to speak before the teacher could start, but the others asked Dislaw to stay, saying the discussion would be no good without him there.

'The Constitution of the republic is clear on the matter,' Bandong began, 'of which group of people can form an organization. It's a right given to everyone, and it can't be refused. We also have freedom of expression and of free assembly, to meet and seek redressal for our grievances.'

'But what if the organization's aims are against the law?' Dislaw snapped.

'The government has the power to intervene and suppress,' said Bandong. 'It has police powers. I'm talking about your rights, since the question is whether they've the right or not to form a union. More than myself, I think you can answer this question better, based on your experience.'

'We're aware of that,' said Tasyo, 'but we want to know your opinion on the matter. You're different from Mang Dislaw. We know that on this matter, you will not just side with one of us.'

'That's true,' Bandong said. 'I'm a teacher but I don't only teach; I also try to learn endlessly. Based on my readings and observation, it's but natural for people to form a group, to bond together as one. That's the truth.'

Nobody opposed what he said, so Bandong continued.

'Whether to build something or to destroy it, people work together. The country has one government that belongs to us all, even if we follow different religions, or belong to different parties. The businessmen, sugar planters, coconut growers and rice farmers could form their own organizations. There are professional groups, as well as student and veteran groups. Even women have their own clubs and organizations now. Here in our small town, we have different groups: the Caballeros of Colon for men, the Hijas de Marias for women, the Parents' and Teachers' Association, even the landowners have ...'

Simon took advantage of the chance to talk when Bandong took a break to breathe before speaking again.

'But there's no organization for farmers,' he said.

But Dislaw didn't want to be beaten to the draw, so he added, 'Maybe because it's not necessary.'

'There were organizations in the past,' Ba Inte reminded them.

'They were all affiliated to a national organization,' added Blas. 'But they were crushed by those in power. The cowards fled and some also betrayed the group.'

'Like a form of suicide,' Dislaw said in a loud voice, to lord it over the rest of the group whose voices were now raised, arguing their points. 'They followed the promptings of those who wanted to sow disunity, they used violence, and then they lost their minds.'

'The sins of the few aren't the sins of all,' Simon defended his point.

'A drop of acid in a glass of water,' Dislaw said in derision. 'Form a new union and it will happen again,' he warned.

'Experience is a good teacher,' said Tasyo. 'We know what to learn from the past. We know the changing colours of the chameleon and the sly traps of the crocodile.'

'It's up to you if you want to continue,' said Dislaw with emphasis, 'You've been burnt before, and now you want to play with fire again.'

And then the Grande family's overseer turned his back on them and left, without even saying goodbye to Ba Inte or to Mang Pablo, the father of the woman he was courting. He was visibly angry because he had seen that the farmers now had the gall to argue and stand firm in their beliefs. Simon, Tasyo and Blas didn't argue with him in the same manner that they just had. And if ever they did talk back, it was in a meek and humble fashion. But now, they appeared rock-solid in their arguments with him. They even asked Bandong for advice, and he had the gall to pretend he was fair and square about it all, when everyone knew his ancestors had also farmed the land. Who else would this pretentious teacher of schoolchildren side with, except peasant folk like himself?

Dislaw left in a huff, and like before, he left with the roar of his jeepney ringing in the ears of those he had left behind.

19

Pina and the other women went downstairs and offered ginger tea, rice cakes wrapped in banana leaves and steamed rice cakes to the people attending the funeral wake. That was why the conversation, the music and other forms of whiling away the hours stopped, and everyone proceeded to eat or drink.

'Where's Mang Dislaw?' asked Julian, who was behind the women offering the food.

'He left without permission,' Simon said. 'He was annoyed with the discussion and since he couldn't win it, he simply left in a huff,' he said in a sharp voice.

Many of them disapproved of Dislaw's behaviour, but they were already used to his boorishness.

'Such a short temper,' said Blas.

'It's more appropriate to say he's like a fly that has learned to sit on top of the water buffalo,' said Ba Inte. Then, he looked at Mang Pablo and made a snide remark, 'And he's even courting that beautiful woman.' He then pointed his lips towards Pina, who was distributing the snacks.

Mang Pablo just scratched his head.

'He'll surely make a report to Donya Leona,' Beteng made a guess.

'And what will he report to her?' asked Simon.

'That the farmers are planning to organize into a union, and from the looks of it, the rich woman, the mayor and the chief of police will think we intend to mount a revolution,' Beteng said.

Laughter erupted at what Beteng said.

'So, you'll revive your union?' asked Bandong.

'The farmers' organization should neither turn cold nor simply die,' Tasyo said firmly. 'If it's dead, then it should be revived; if sleeping, it should be awakened. I repeat that it will be our fault if we aren't united.'

Ba Inte joined the conversation again and he said, 'I told you the story of the crocodile, because this is what I wanted to hear from you. If the people in the village weren't united, the crocodiles would still be rampant today.'

'Social justice has long been on everyone's lips, but what kind of animal is this?' asked Tasyo. 'We cannot tell. What is the difference between it and the chameleon or the crocodile? When election comes, they say they want to bring the government closer to the people. But we don't really know what that means. In our experience, when the leaders come to the people, either the latter's money is lost, or they get hurt.'

'Indeed, that is what happens,' agreed Blas.

'There are laws on wages and the division of the farmers' harvest,' continued Tasyo, 'but these are merely laws written on water. Whatever the landlord likes, becomes the law. They are in cahoots with the agents of the government, since they can easily be placed in the pockets of the rich so they'll keep quiet.'

'When there's silver, there's liquor,' added Blas.

'It's just too bad that Dislaw is no longer here, because I want to hear his thoughts on these matters,' Tasyo said with added vigour. 'Let me repeat: only the blind, or those pretending to be blind, can fail to see the big gap between the farmers and the landlord. One is neck-deep in debt, while the other is rolling in wealth. The farmer lives in the hut, while the landlord lives in the mansion. Look at this village,' he said, indicating the place with a sweep of his hand, 'whose huts have faucets and toilets, electricity and gas stoves; a radio, piano and refrigerator? All of that, and more, can be found in the Grandes' house that's made of brick and stone.'

Everyone remained silent, and since no one spoke after Blas and Simon, Tasyo continued.

'How many times did the doctor visit the now-dead Sepa?' he asked, prompting Julian to stand up and leave, even if the query was neither directed at him nor required an answer from him. 'How many times did she get medicine from the pharmacy in the capital? Why didn't she get to stay in the hospital for even a day? What will happen to the children of Ka Julian, what will be their future, as well as those of our children? Why can't they go to school, and if ever they finish their elementary school in the village, why can't they study further afterwards? Has anyone in the village taken up programmes of study at university like Jun and Ninet? Has anyone in this village ever owned a car, had money in the bank, lived a life of abundance just sleeping well and waking up to another day of comfort? Has anyone of you ever gone on vacation anywhere, or have even gone to Manila just to watch a film at the cinema?'

'Everything that Tasyo is saying is correct,' Ba Inte said slowly to Mang Pablo, 'but according to Captain Melchor, one's destiny is already fixed from birth. Allegedly, one can't undo what the heavens have decided for them.'

'Only they can change their destinies,' said Mang Pablo.

Everyone's attention returned to Tasyo, as he piped up again.

'But the farmers work heedlessly,' he said. 'We are penniless from birth, like our parents, and like the children who'll follow us.' He stopped when he saw Ba Inte whispering something to Mang Pablo. 'When did you stop working in the fields, Ba Inte?'

'I wouldn't have stopped were it not for this devil of an arthritis,' said the old man. 'The farmer only stops working once he's dead.'

'And Ba Inte isn't a tenant farmer like us,' Tasyo clarified, and then added, 'But he isn't a crocodile.'

'There's clear injustice in the way the farms are run,' said Simon.

'Isn't it clear, Mang Bandong?' Tasyo repeated and looked at the teacher who had just been quiet since Dislaw left.

'Indeed, there's a lopsided arrangement for sharing the fruits of the earth,' answered the teacher.

'See?' Tasyo said. 'Lopsided. Someone has a feast, while the other endures famine. The one who sweats on the land ends up poor and hungry. What then should we do?'

Tasyo answered his own question without waiting for anyone to do so.

'The problem should be solved,' he said. 'But the landlord won't make the effort to look for the solution, nor would the agents of government. We should do it, we who are oppressed. We can change things through our union; by being united.'

'Let's set it up as soon as possible,' Blas suggested.

'After the funeral,' added Simon.

'We can meet here again,' answered Blas.

'Please tell Mang Julian,' Simon suggested. 'Tasyo, you can be the president.'

'Not me. You may elect someone else,' Tasyo demurred.

'Is there anyone better than you?' Simon asked.

'Indeed, there's no one,' Blas concurred.

'The strength of the union lies not in its president or leader, but in all of its members. The members shape the leader and the things that the group can accomplish,' said Tasyo.

'The members should be guided and the leader should shape the organization's initiatives,' added Simon.

'Give emphasis to the ideals of the union—of unity, of the group's mission and its vision,' added Blas.

'I'm for Ka Tasyo.' Simon repeated his earlier call.

'Me, too,' added Blas.

'Teacher Bandong, please serve as our adviser,' Simon suggested.

'It's against my work as a teacher,' said Bandong.

'But you're with us, aren't you?' asked Simon.

'Tasyo earlier said that I don't side with anyone,' Bandong said and then he closed one eye.

'Those are just words,' Tasyo corrected himself, 'but you really belong with us.'

'Ba Inte will be the adviser,' said Beteng.

'Please don't disturb me in my retirement,' the old man said. 'Choose someone without arthritis and someone who can still run.'

'And Pina will be the treasurer,' Beteng said again, and said loudly the name of the woman who was carrying a tray of steamed rice cakes and rice cakes wrapped in banana leaves right then.

'I think I heard my name,' said the woman while looking at Bandong.

'They want you to be the treasurer,' he said.

'That can't be. I'm not even a member.'

'As long as one lives in the village, he or she is a member.'

'And why do you need a treasurer when you don't even have any funds?' she teased them.

The men laughed and she laughed with them.

'That's why we want you to be the treasurer,' said Tasyo with a smile. 'So even if the union doesn't have money, at least you've money.'

And the woman joined them again in their laughter.

By then the night had darkened further, but the milky light of the moon shone. The hot weather was cooled down by the wind that made the leaves on the trees flutter. The game of fines had stopped, and the young men and women were clustered together in conversation. The guitar played in a desultory manner, and the player never finished playing a song whole. A few chickens crowed, and the tail of a water buffalo flicked away the mosquitoes biting at its flanks.

The sun had risen, shining on those who had stayed for the funeral wake. But sleep never seemed to overcome them. Only Ba Inte took his leave early, along with Mang Pablo and Pina. Bandong dropped them home.

Julian took the chance to sleep for a while in a corner of their house. On his arms and thighs rested the heads of his sleeping children.

'It's hard to lose one's mother,' a woman observed.

The preparations for Sepa's burial were also made by the same group of neighbours and friends who had attended the funeral wake without sleeping a wink. The men alternated shouldering her coffin on the way to the cemetery. Julian followed them, holding on to his young children. Everyone walked in the intense heat of the sun in the first hours of noon.

Before Sepa's coffin was lowered into the ground, an old woman from the farms uttered the prayers for the dead. Tasyo spoke briefly and said that they weren't just burying a sweet wife and devoted mother, but also a martyr to the cause of farming.

'May the earth fall on her lightly.'

20

Mang Pablo and Teacher Bandong waited for more than an hour for the members of the PTA, but only a few came and they never reached a quorum. Even Dislaw, who served as the treasurer, didn't show up.

'I'd informed everyone about the meeting,' said Mang Pablo in an annoyed tone.

'I know why many people couldn't make it to the meeting,' said Bandong, as if remembering something. 'Our meeting was held at the same time as a cockfight and an event at the church.'

'Oh, no wonder then,' said Mang Pablo. 'How can they turn their attention to us when there's a call from God from one end and a pull from the devil from the other?' he added in a teasing manner.

'Better to have our meeting on a day with no other event clashing with it,' suggested Bandong. 'On a Friday night, for example.'

'I think that's what we need.'

More people attended the next meeting, and the discussion was energetic. Forty people had arrived in the hallway of the school before Mang Pablo began the meeting. Dislaw was there, as well as a few farmers, Andres and several other squatters. It was a Friday night.

Mang Pablo said that he deemed it necessary to hold a meeting even if the school term was already finished because of a few important matters that needed deciding. He added that it was a better time to meet now, rather than when the classes were already about to start. He also informed the body that Mang Putin was ill and needed to rest, and that Bandong would serve as his temporary replacement.

The presiding officer asked the secretary to read out the agenda of the meeting. The first item was where to spend the 1,000 pesos that the group had collected.

'There are two suggestions or proposals on the table,' explained Mang Pablo. 'First, to build a wall around the land occupied by the school, and second, to buy books for the school library. Both are good suggestions, but we don't have money for both the proposals. That's why we've to choose which project to do first.'

Dislaw immediately stood up without even asking permission from the presiding officer. He said in a loud voice that the wall should be built first.

'We need a wall at times like these, he said. 'Earlier, we used to build walls so that foraging animals won't enter our property. Now, we need a wall to keep out people with bad intentions.'

He stressed on 'bad intentions' while looking at the group of squatters.

Dislaw reminded them that many, if not all, schools in the province and the capital are surrounded by walls.

'Not just schools,' he added. 'You may go to Manila, Quezon City, or any other important city. All the big houses are surrounded by walls, steel matting, or even barbed wires. Times are dangerous and a wall is an effective deterrent against crime. In truth, you can even check out the churches—they are now all surrounded by walls.'

It seemed that Dislaw was able to persuade everyone to side with him, but they quickly changed their minds when Bandong spoke.

The principal spoke in a calm and gentle manner.

'I can't question the good intentions of the people who built walls around their properties, And I don't oppose the building of a wall around our school, either. But this afternoon, we're deciding between a wall and a library. The wall will keep out those with bad intentions; and it will be decorative as well. On the other hand, the library will enrich the minds of those who want to drink of its rich spring. Our town is quiet and there are no wandering animals. I also don't know about the people of ill will whom Dislaw is talking about—'

Dislaw suddenly stood up and confronted Bandong.

'No people of ill will?' he said in a loud voice, and then started openly insulting the teacher, 'Haven't you heard of incidents happening outside the school that involve young pupils? Aren't you aware of the thievery in the yard of the Grande family on the night of the celebration? Since the squatters started living here—'

'Gentleman!' said a loud voice from behind the gathering. A man had stood up and was asking to be heard. Dislaw looked at him and he recognized Andres.

'What do you want?' Dislaw said without the honorific reserved for older people. His eyes were blazing.

'Dear Presiding Officer,' Andres turned to Mang Pablo, 'permission to speak, please.'

'But I still have the floor,' snapped Dislaw and then he queried, 'Before I continue defending my proposal, what right has this man, who has disturbed me, to attend this gathering?'

Mang Pablo explained that Andres and his group had been invited to attend the meeting. He added that they had been living in Sampilong for many years after the Second World War ended. In fact, they also served as guerrillas against the Japanese—an honour that other people couldn't claim.

'Many of us know them,' Mang Pablo said to end his defence of Andres.

'If anyone can just enter a gathering like this, then we don't really need a wall for this school,' Dislaw shouted and then he walked out.

Andres also left his spot and was about to follow Dislaw out, but Tasyo quickly put his arm around him and stopped him. Andres was mollified.

Mang Pablo restored order to the meeting and proceeded. Some people left the gathering, perhaps worried about any trouble that might come if they stayed there, even if Dislaw had already walked out. But the majority remained.

Andres asked to be allowed to speak. Briefly, he explained how they came to Sampilong, how they helped the people fight against the Japanese, how they strove to live with dignity in the middle of their hardship, and how strong their desire was to join and help the majority in developing the town.

With humility, Andres also narrated what happened when the policeman caught him with a head of roasted pig in his hut. His story about the roasted pig was met with loud laughter.

'I saw the excessive luxury, the extra food that wasn't yet touched and would surely just go to waste, but I didn't dare steal it,' said Andres. 'When I was already out of the front yard and going home, someone gave me a head of roasted pig. And suddenly, the word "thief" rose in the air, followed by gunfire. We've been living in this town for many years, and not even once could you have accused me of doing something that would stain my reputation.'

Andres had his head bowed low when he finally sat down. Two farmers went to him and patted him on his shoulders.

After a while, the presiding officer piped in again.

'What our friend Andres did,' said Mang Pablo, 'was just to follow the law of life. The real sin against God and fellowmen is to steal food that the poor are about to put into their mouths.'

Tasyo propped up Mang Pablo and added that an empty stomach is more dangerous than dynamite.

'What is the worth of a head of roasted pig?' he asked, and then also answered, 'There was a time when herds of water buffaloes vanished, granaries of rice were emptied and their owners couldn't be traced anymore. They say it's better for the water buffaloes and the rice to vanish, rather than have the heads of those who make us suffer.'

Tasyo also gave his opinion about the wall.

'Those who build walls are those who have something to fear. We in the village don't even build fences, nor do we lock our doors at night. Perhaps because we have nothing to lose.' Tasyo waited until the volley of laughter had subsided. 'While in Manila,' he continued, 'the houses are hemmed in by walls, the doors are locked and the windows barred, but still thefts happen night and day.'

When at last the votes were cast, the proposal to buy books for the school library won.

After a while, Tinoy, the barber, stood up and said that if everything in the agenda had been covered, then he proposed that the new principal be allowed to speak.

'Before we part ways, we want to hear the programmes planned by Teacher Bandong for his administration,' said Tinoy. 'New king, new ways of being. I'm not saying he'll completely change the way Teacher Putin ran the school, but we hope he can bring some changes to improve the school.'

Everyone listened in rapt attention as the new principal spoke.

'As all of you know,' Bandong began, 'my appointment is temporary. But because I have been entrusted with this position, even if only for the time being, I won't fail to serve you in small ways.'

Bandong looked into the eyes of the people in the audience before he continued.

'I want to implement three plans as soon as possible. Their success depends on the help of everyone and of the leaders of Sampilong. It's just too bad that our mayor isn't here today.'

'First, I want to have seats for all the children who want to go to school. If the parents can't pay for their education, then the government must provide for them. They shouldn't be charged matriculation fees and should be given free books.'

'Second, I plan to open a night school for the older people who want to learn reading and writing. They should learn to do so, and we should help them. It's hard to be poor, but to be poor and ignorant is to remain shackled to the depths of poverty. Once the older village folk have learnt how to read and write, their eyes will be opened, and they will no longer be fooled and oppressed. Then, they'll also become aware of their obligations. Does anybody here disapprove of these suggestions?' asked the principal.

'Dislaw is no longer here,' answered Tasyo, which drew laughter from everyone. 'Dislaw always opposed everyone else's suggestions.'

'I move for the approval of these suggestions,' said Tinoy, the barber. 'Please pound the mallet now, Mang Pablo.'

'My third proposal,' continued Bandong, 'needs the support of everyone, especially those who live comfortable lives in this town. I propose that we start what we call "home industries". Do you know what that means? Traditional bags, baskets, brooms made from coconut midribs, hats, and other products. There are many amongst us who are willing to work, both men and women. If we could only raise capital, just a small capital at first—for example a few hundred pesos—it will be a big help for our villagers who aren't earning anything at the moment.'

Several hands were raised, indicating they approved of the proposal.

'Thank you and it seems there is fertile soil for this seed,' Bandong happily said in acknowledgement of the support. 'Through your concern, as well as your hard work and talents, who knows, maybe one day, Sampilong will be able to make money from these home industries, much more than it could ever make from its farms. The villagers will benefit from this, especially those without income, like some of the families in the area where our friend, Andres, lives.'

After Bandong had spoken, Andres stood up to confirm what the young principal had just said.

'I've already met with my neighbours and they've assigned me to speak on their behalf. We support this proposal. We're ready to start, even tomorrow, if needed. We want to work and earn money. Whether you like it or not, many of us were also born in this village, therefore, we are also natives of this place, like all of you. Our children will grow up, study and live here. That's why you have to help us find a livelihood. The proposal put forward by Teacher Bandong is a challenge as well as a source of hope. You already saw how we helped all of you during the Second World War in our fight against the Japanese conquerors. We won't abandon you, whether in good times or bad.'

Right there and then, the PTA raised several hundred pesos. They all agreed to form a cooperative and gave Bandong the right to continue with the process.

For the first time, the group was able to propose plans not related to the usual topic of entertainment. And according to Tasyo, it was because Dislaw had left before the meeting was finished.

21

The cool weather and the picturesque view in the mountain city of Baguio were not enough to calm the restless bodies and bored minds of the young people like Jun and his friends. After a few weeks, they decided to leave behind the chill of the mountains.

'Baguio is small and there's nowhere to go but go around,' groaned Jun when he was seized by boredom.

However, during the first two weeks, the city of pines had brought them extraordinary pleasure and joy.

The festivities at Mansion House, the famous tourist spots and sights, and the people they met were delightful in the early days. But for the siblings, Jun and Ninet, who weren't strangers to Baguio—like most wealthy families—and visited the place often, the beauty of the aforementioned city was almost commonplace.

A number of times, they had already climbed the steepest ridge of the zigzag at an altitude of 5,000 feet. It was a lovely and cool place perfumed by pine trees. From there, they went to the hills and caves, and breathed in the cold wind which felt as if it were coming from a refrigerator in the dark depths of the caves. They drove—and sometimes walked—around the famous Burnham Park, where they enjoyed strolling before the sun set at dusk, and danced in its elegant auditorium in the evening.

They raced up Mount Mirador and counted each of its 225 steps. They stopped, knelt and prayed at the oft-visited Lourdes grotto. They visited the observatory of the Jesuit priests at the top of the grotto. They also visited the monastery at Dominican Hill and caught up with the kind Dominican priests.

They bathed and swam in the swimming pool of the Asian Hot Springs. Later, they watched the gold mines under the Mines View Park, one of the richest in the world, and marvelled at the miracle of nature and the industry of man. They went on a motorbike ride to the magnificent rice terraces of Banaue, which resembled a very long staircase going up the rainbow, green during the rainy season, and golden before harvest time in summer.

They visited the Philippine Military Academy at Camp Allen, but didn't stay long and quickly turned the car around, back to the city. The reason was the swift approach of some handsome cadets whose sheep's eyes looked like they were about to fall off, while staring at the three young women on board.

'Officers and gentlemen, really,' Jun, who was driving, sneered and sped up the car.

The six friends lived in their own cottage with various amenities for vacationers.

Sometimes they were all there day and night, drinking and dancing to radio tunes. Sometimes they played mahjongg and beat each other.

There were days when they couldn't be found together at the cottage or anywhere else. They would separate without letting each other know where they were going. They would return to the cottage at midnight or dawn, and would often not see each other even at the breakfast table.

In short, they drained the contents of the cup to the last drop. Thus, the six of them became even closer, and the love that was nurtured in the hearts of the lovers grew even more intimate. They all but indulged in a honeymoon, although they didn't try the dress rehearsal irresponsibly, since for the very modern youth that was just part of their calisthenics.

Ninet lost her coyness around Dan. She no longer hesitated sending off or greeting the young lawyer-to-be with a kiss. 'Darling' and 'honey' were now their pet names for each other.

Pil and Bining became more confident of their plan to be together forever, once Pil became a doctor and the young woman a teacher.

Both of them were extremely excited to make their dreams in life come true, like fruits beginning to ripen.

Meanwhile, Marybee was persuading Jun to tie the knot before the young man headed to the United States after passing the medical examination. Marybee could stay in the Philippines until she finished her studies in banking, or she could go with Jun and continue her studies overseas. Marybee had indicated that she hoped that if she gave birth to their baby, it would be in the United States.

'My son will be an American citizen even though he would be Pinoy,' Marybee said, her eyes twinkling at the prospect of the extraordinary fate of her firstborn.

'He's going to be like the "United Nations",' Bining teased.

The breeze in Baguio was always humid, but it seemed to fuel the fire in their hearts even more. And they wouldn't have gotten bored, except for when the summer heat in Manila and other plains became maddening, and many more guests flocked to the city in the mountains. One morning, they could not enter the church because the worshippers were crowded all the way outside the door. One morning, Dan turned on the shower in the bathroom and no water came out.

'Our vacation here is over,' Jun informed his companions. And everyone seemed to agree.

Back then, government, business and society were already in Baguio. Of course, vices and exploitation were also present.

'Baguio is small,' Jun repeated, 'and now it's hot as well.' What he wanted to say by hot as well was that it was getting too crowded because of the sheer number of tourists from the lowland provinces and the cities.

If it were up to Marybee, the daughter of a rich Chinese family—even though she had no idea how her father had made his fortune or how he had entered the Philippines—everyone vacationing in Baguio during the summer months—March, April and May—should first ask permission from the authorities concerned. They should also make sure they had enough money and were good people.

It was really annoying for Marybee to sit in the chairs of Burnham Park beside students in cheap sweaters smoking non-imported cigarettes, or women who worked in the cigarette factories in Pasay or San Francisco del Monte, sorting through watermelon seeds.

'Did you see that bus of excursionists, singing that tawdry song, "Kaka O Kaka", over and over? When the bus stopped in the park, they came down, laid their wrapped food on the grass and started devouring it.'

Marybee followed up her story with squeezing her pointed nose with two fingers, and then laughing, her narrow eyes disappearing.

'Ah, the one Dan and I saw at the Pines Hotel was even better,' Ninet reported. 'We were having breakfast there one morning.' She turned to her boyfriend and said, 'Do you remember, darling? He was said to be worth a million dollars, because he cracked the "big deal" in Tokyo. The way he carried himself—in his ring finger was a solitaire diamond, twinkling like Bining's eyes. He was dressed in a tweed suit, but he looked like a Pinoy who came from Hawaii.' Ninet stopped laughing for a while. 'He also had breakfast. Would you believe that he jabbed the round bread with a fork, and it rolled like a golf ball and the waiter had to chase after it? Hahaha!'

'Nouveaux riches!' puffed Dan, and waved his hand as if shooing away a fly.

Bining, who wasn't very talkative like Ninet and Marybee, also had a funny story which had happened recently in Baguio.

'I witnessed this dance at the Mansion House,' she said. 'The wife of a politician from the Ilocos region dressed like an Ifugao (a member of the indigenous peoples who lived in the mountains). A friend saw her and asked why she was dressed like that. "Someone wore Chinese clothes who looked Chinese, another who dressed like a geisha and looked Japanese," explained the politician's wife. "I'll try to look like an Igorot." "Well, lady," replied the friend, "if that's all you want, you don't have to wear that costume." The politician's wife turned away with a frown.'

'Hahaha! I laughed too,' Pil said, and they all giggled not at Bining's story but at Pil's mimicry.

When their companions were about to leave Baguio, Pil and Bining planned to go directly to Manila, but were persuaded by Jun and Ninet

to drop by Sampilong again, because the siblings were also going to go
to Manila before June.

'What else are we going to do in Sampilong?' Pil asked.

'Eat and sleep,' replied Ninet.

It was Pil's turn to drive the car and he didn't speed much. Besides,
they had to make a stop at the capital of the provinces as they passed.

'The Philippines isn't just Manila and Baguio,' Pil said, as if he was
a tourist guide, whenever they stopped their car. 'Like Jun,' he said.
'He will travel to America, and maybe to Europe. If you ask him about
the Philippines, besides Manila and Baguio, what will he say?'

'And Pasay City,' Dan added.

'Where the nightclubs and cocktail lounges are,' Marybee added
with a scrunched-up nose.

Jun kissed his girlfriend in return for her jibe.

It was already dusk when the dusty car was greeted by the barking
of dogs in the yard of the large house. Their arrival was unexpected,
so Donya Leona greeted them with surprise, 'I thought you'd never
come home.'

Ninet kissed her mother and said, 'Oh Mother, Sampilong is better
than Baguio these days!'

'Told you so,' said Donya. 'There's your dad insisting that we go
up there. I said, If you're just going there to gamble—just gamble in
the provincial capital.'

22

Before breakfast on Sunday, Donya Leona woke up the three young women who were still sound asleep, and told them to get up and get dressed.

'We will all go to church,' the lady announced. 'Father Pascual has requested our presence.'

The guests already knew that the parish priest of Sampilong was Donya Leona's elder brother.

She also had Jun and his two friends woken up.

'I don't mind being criticized for other things, just not being told I'm a bad Christian.' The madam would often repeat such things to herself, as if being a good Christian completely erased her other flaws or defects, or that going to church once a week was a true measure of being a good Christian.

When they were dressed and some of them were having coffee in the dining room, she casually questioned Ninet.

'Did you go to church in Baguio, my child?'

Ninet boasted that they never missed church on Sunday morning. She didn't add that amongst the royals of the city in the mountains, going to church was not only a religious duty of the faithful Catholic, but also involved showing off social status. There, one usually flaunted new outfits, expensive clothes not worn in Manila, and fancy cars, which would be parked around the church.

'Too bad I couldn't go to confession,' Marybee said as they left.

'Me, too,' Ninet replied.

Bining held back agreeing with her two girlfriends; she could only look at Pil. She was perhaps thinking that Marybee and Ninet couldn't possibly be planning to confess to their worldly ways in Baguio.

Donya Leona was wearing a skirt and blouse, looking as if she were attending a party. This was her ritual whenever she attended Mass. The three young women were dressed elegantly and according to the latest fashion. They wore different colours, though appropriate for the occasion. One of the practices that the modern girl couldn't forget was proper dressing and grooming. Don Severo was in a formal native wear while the three young men wore long-sleeved shirts and ties, resembling Jaycee members.

The church was already crowded when they arrived, but a space was reserved for them in the front. The Grande couple had donated six benches and pews, at Father Pascual's request, but with the agreement that one of them would be placed in front and reserved for their family, even if they were not attending Mass. So Donya Leona wasn't worried that they would have to stand in the aisle, even if the church was full of people, because there were sure to be seats for them that others could not use.

When the Grandes and their guests arrived, almost all of the glances followed them, and suppressed whispers filled the air. The first topic of discussion was who amongst the three young women was the most beautiful, and the second was who amongst the two—the one who looked like a sweet orange and the one who looked like a nearly ripe mango—was Jun's girlfriend, and third, which of the two bachelors was going to be Ninet's husband.

The mother and daughter, Sabel and Pina, had been kneeling for a while on one of the benches in the middle, so a lot of people couldn't avoid making a comparison between the village belle and the three city girls. Not a few thought that Bandong could be compared to any of the three young men who owned the hearts and affections of the three young ladies who accompanied them.

'Pina is mine,' said a farmer.

'No matter which one of those four, it's like you've won a sweepstakes prize,' said another.

'If the snake is lucky, even luckier is the—'

'Hey, shut your mouth and remember we're in the house of God.'

'Amen.'

And the chatter of the talkative ones stopped.

Father Pascual began the Mass with the help of two young sacristans. He wore a white linen cassock topped with a white chasuble. A cross hung on top of the chasuble.

The priest entered the sanctuary, made the sign of the cross, and ascended the altar. He kissed the white marble in the middle of the altar a few times. Then, he went to the right side of the altar and read the Introit. He then moved back to the center and recited the *Kyrie eleison* and *Christe eleison*, 'Lord, have mercy on us; Jesus Christ, have mercy on us.'

It could be noticed that amongst the companions, Donya Leona was the only one earnestly praying and following the ceremony. She opened and folded her missal, flipping to the next page by turning it with an unusual rosary blessed in Rome, a gift from her sibling priest. Sometimes she would count the beads of the rosary while reciting her prayers.

In one corner, it seemed Don Severo was getting impatient and feeling hot, fanning himself incessantly with a palm leaf fan. Perhaps, he would have been less bored if it wasn't rude for him to light a cigar. He would wonder at the connection between the good priests, sacred ceremonies and the extraordinary poker skills of his brother-in-law when he wasn't wearing a robe.

Meanwhile, sitting next to each other, Jun and Marybee continued to talk, as did Ninet and Dan, only stopping when they knelt. They hardly followed what Father Pascual was doing, as he read the *Epistolary* and a part of the *Gospel*. They seemed surprised when the old priest faced the crowd and in a sonorous voice, began delivering his sermon.

Father Pascual took his subject from the book of Matthew in the *New Testament*, which tells of a rich man who left his country and entrusted his wealth to three servants. He gave the first servant five talents, the second two talents, and the third only one talent. The first invested and doubled his five talents; the second invested and increased his assets as well. But the third was foolish and buried his only talent in the ground.

When the rich master returned from the journey, Father Pascual repeated Saint Matthew's account of how the master discovered what had happened. He praised the two servants and rewarded them, while chiding and ridiculing the third servant. The priest read aloud the four verses of the twenty-fifth chapter of Matthew, which went:

'You wicked and lazy servant, you know that I reap where I did not sow, and gather where I did not scatter;

'If so, you should have invested my money with the bankers, and when I came home, I would have received what was mine with interest.

'Take the talent from him and give it to the one who has ten talents.

'For to everyone who has, more will be given, and he will have an abundance; but from the one who does not have, even what he has will be taken away.'

Later, Father Pascual compared this parable to what was happening to the tenants in the field who, even though they had a small plot of land, were reluctant to work and unwilling to work hard and strive for more so that could reap an abundant harvest. He advised them not to be envious of the landowners, whose five talents had become ten, because they were wise enough to increase their wealth.

'The third servant had no one to blame but himself since he was lazy and foolish. So, what the Lord had given him, he took it back and entrusted it to someone who knew how to take care of it.' Father Pascual emphasized the lesson of this subject and in the end, he instructed, 'Nourish what little you have been given, let it flourish and multiply. Because it would be more painful if, due to your neglect, the owner who entrusted you with one talent, takes it back. May it be so.'

Donya Leona's face looked happy as she listened and tried to understand her brother's sermon. She turned a few times to where the tenants and squatters were. She seemed to be telling them, 'You've heard the command of the Lord directly from the mouth of his representative.'

The farmers remained quiet and their faces didn't even turn sour from what they had heard. However, some were troubled about the possibility of Donya Leona having suggested the sermon to Father Pascual. Until then, they hadn't tried to fathom the secret of the siblings, a tiny spark in the deep mystery of faith. Nevertheless, the priest had enough wisdom and kindness to sense which topic was the right one to discuss in front of the parishioners from the countryside.

The passing around of alms' bags followed. The two sacristans went down together and each one went down either side of the long hall. They held a bamboo stick with a big open bag made of cotton, at one end, and as they walked down the aisle, they thrust the bag in front of those who wanted to give donations. So they looked like two fishermen who were catching bream and shrimp in the cloudy waters of a lake.

After the consecration and the blessing of the chalice with the holy wine and the paten filled with the holy host, those who had gone to confession the previous day or in the early hours of that morning raced to kneel at the foot of the altar to receive communion. Donya Leona knelt with her knees together and shoe heels aligned, her eyes closed and mouth open, looking like a true matron genuinely doing penance. The rich woman's sincerity in communicating with God at that precious moment couldn't be underestimated, because she believed that it was extremely necessary to wash away the sins of the past week in order to have the right to commit new ones in the coming week.

A farmer watching Donya Leona as she prepared to receive communion thought to himself, 'Perhaps, that's what the crocodile Ba Inte was talking about looks like.'

23

Bandong had to leave for Manila, along with Pina and her teenage brother, Dinong, as did the couple Andres and Sedes. Their purpose had to do with the home industries cooperative.

In order to save time, they took a horse-drawn cart to the capital and when they got there, transferred to a bus going to Manila. The bus would only pass through Sampilong four times a day, and sometimes not at all.

It had been some time since the last detailed events in the town. The cooperative had been established and had raised part of the necessary capital. Teacher Bandong had been elected the president of the organization and Pina, its treasurer. Dislaw bought a share not because he believed in the goals of the cooperative, or agreed with them, but because he couldn't refuse the young woman's offer, aside from wanting to be a member and having the right to fight against the movement, as well as Bandong and the squatters. Thus, he threatened to play the role of a traitor.

On the one hand, the squatters were ready to shoulder the promotion of the home industry, which was going to be funded and managed by the cooperative. They had cleaned up their entire area, laid a canal that drained the water so that it didn't get muddy, dug a garbage pit, and in the distance, also made a toilet like the one used in Antipolo and other places, fenced with ashes constantly being poured into it to avoid bad odour.

In the middle of the crowd of shanties, they built a beautiful hut like a bower made of bamboo and dry cogon grass, with a roof and open wall frames. The hut wasn't expensive, as the materials used had just been taken from an area in Sampilong. That became the gathering place for the neighbours in the afternoon and evening, when they had no more work for the day, and if they had any problems they wanted to discuss and resolve.

'This is our "centre",' Andres had said to Marcos, Kiko, Kanor and other helpers when the hut was finished and in use.

Teacher Bandong praised them when he first saw the positive developments in the squatters' area. He greeted Andres and the tenants.

'Who would still call this a dump?' he said. 'This is now a new village.'

Since then, the old dump was baptized as the New Village.

Bandong's purpose in going to the capital city was to make enquiries and evaluations related to the cooperative's proposals. He consulted the shareholders and they agreed that it was necessary, and the only reason many didn't join in the trip to the city was to save expenses.

'Be careful and come home early,' Aling Sabel strictly instructed the siblings when Bandong came to fetch them. Pina wasn't new to Manila, as she had stayed there for a long time when she was studying dressmaking and other household skills.

It was only seven in the morning and the sun's rays had not yet erased the chill of the dew on the grassy plains, so the journey was comfortable and interesting.

The group was first going to visit the revived Social Welfare Administration (SWA) to find out what kind of help and support it could give to their cooperative. They wanted to borrow the services of a home-industry employee.

They would then go to the Bureau of Commerce to find out the corresponding steps for registering and operating their cooperative, as well as for purchasing materials at a fair price and selling their products at a profit. They would also get a list of where they could deposit their products in bulk.

Afterwards, they would visit some markets to see what goods were in excess and in short supply in the home industries, which products sold fast and slow, as well as the prevailing prices of those goods.

'We'll conduct a census directly,' said Bandong to his delegation when they got off the bus at the parking lot in Manila. 'We'll panic if we only rely on the official census,' he added.

'The price the newspaper says is different from the price you find in the market,' Andres pointed out.

'Prices are unstable when production is weak,' explained Bandong. 'What I mean is, if there isn't enough supply to meet the demand. There are many buyers, but there are few goods. Moreover, there's the greed of the profiteers.'

'In my opinion, what's happening is not just a result of poor production but of wrong production,' said Andres, who Bandong felt, even before, was ahead of his fellow squatters because of his keen observation and intelligent judgment.

'Wrong production?' repeated the teacher. 'What do you mean?'

Apparently, Andres was ready with an answer.

'When we get off the bus,' he said, 'what do we see on Folgueras Road, on Azcarraga Street, all over Tabora and Ilaya, but stores on all sides selling clothes, fabric, cotton and all kinds of dresses? That's only in Tondo, and even more so in Binondo, Santa Cruz, Quiapo, Sampaloc and Paco. People need clothes, indeed, but don't they also have the same need for food? Children don't have milk, mothers don't have meat, and there's not enough rice, even in our own Sampilong, where rice is the main product. That's what I call wrong production.'

Bandong patted Andres on the arm and said with a smile, 'We have "free enterprise" my friend. Everyone is free to do what he wants, as long as he doesn't violate the law. He's free to invest his money, free to make a profit and lose money. If he wants to make and sell shoes, then that's up to him. If he wants to make and sell bread, that's also up to him.'

'He's free even if he causes harm to many?' Andres asked.

'There are laws that establish what freedom entails,' said Bandong, 'but it has become the government's policy to relax industries and businesses, because they should be patronized for the good of the people.'

'It seems that such regulation should be changed, and the government should set limits to what and how much an industry can produce,' suggested Andres. 'Thus, waste can be avoided, and it will be possible to fund first what is really needed.'

Bandong shook his head, but smiled as he answered the squatter's leader.

'In order to do that, the system or structure of government must first be changed. Instead of democracy, a dictatorship should be implemented.' He laughed as he directed a question towards Andres, 'Do you want a dictatorship?'

'We've a lot of investment in democracy,' Andres quickly retorted. 'Let's admit that democracy has its flaws and defects, including what I referred to as wrong production, but that proves its inclination towards the greater good.'

'You're right, my friend,' Bandong agreed. 'We've the same belief in that regard. And,' he added gently, but without doubt, 'the Filipinos will suffer even more under other systems.'

While the two men were talking, Pina and Sedes were busy watching the goods on the sidewalks, most of which were made in other countries, as well as the usual dolls and children's toys.

They decided to go first to the office of the SWA. In an effort to appeal to the many people who were unemployed, the SWA had opened a workshop dedicated to home industries. The trainees were working when the manager brought them there. Pina and Sedes saw that most of the makers of baskets, hats, artificial flowers, abaca slippers, and other daily items were women. Bandong asked for a report on how many products each worker made in a day and how much they earned in a week.

'It depends on their job,' said the manager. 'They can earn a lot if they produce many items and do it well.'

Sedes and the others bought some products to use as samples at the cooperative centre in the New Village. Bandong, on the other hand, reached an agreement regarding the deputation of one Social Welfare Administration personnel there, who would initially act as a guide for setting up the home industry in Sampilong.

From there, they went to other places they needed to visit. While walking through some of the main streets, the group noticed that Manila was very different from the last time they had been there. There were almost no traces of the destruction and ruins of the last war. Proudly standing were lofty buildings once brought down by the bombs and cannons of the two contending powers. On the other side of the Pasig River, they saw the post office building and the city hall standing again. New and innovative bazaars, shops, restaurants and cinemas had cropped up once more.

And the vehicles, all kinds of vehicles, were like a swarm of ants that had been disturbed and running close to each other, meeting each other, going this way and that with no idea where to hide. There were no gaps in the procession of trucks, buses, bulldozers, wagons, cars, jeeps, tricycles, and carts. It was clear that the motor vehicles were kings of the roads, because they barely gave any time to the people crossing, with their horns blaring and the speed of their acceleration.

Pina thought, as they stood for a long while at the corner of two roads, that Manila must have the most motorized cars in the whole world. When he mentioned this to Bandong, the teacher exclaimed, 'And imagine we don't have a single car bolt factory!'

Pina and Sedes talked about the danger of the city streets, especially for children going to and from school.

'My daughter, I lived here in Manila for a long time,' said Sedes. 'But now, I prefer Sampilong. There, you can walk with your eyes closed without fear of dying prematurely under the wheel of a motor vehicle.'

Pina saw a man crossing, holding a white cane, who didn't seem concerned about the vehicles. 'The blind can also walk here,' she said to Sedes and pointed to the man. 'He's blind, but safe. The truth is that the blind are indeed more careful than the sighted, that's why you don't hear about accidents where the blind are run over by cars.'

'Blind or sighted, I don't trust those Lucifers,' said Sedes. It was unclear if she meant to imply the drivers were Lucifers. She continued, 'I'll only cross if the traffic policeman is watching me.'

'Why will the traffic policeman look at you?' said Andres, teasing his wife. 'He only watches white legs and the passengers of a low-numbered car.'

24

It was already noon when Bandong and company were done with their many errands, so they decided to eat at a restaurant.

'I'd like to go to a Filipino food stall,' suggested Pina and looked around the area where they stood. She couldn't see the food stall she was looking for.

'We will starve if we keep looking for a food stall in this place,' warned Bandong. 'It's all restaurants, noodle shops, refreshments and kitchenettes.'

'We're either Americanized or Sinicized,' Andres said.

'Manila, the capital city of the Philippines, is owned by foreigners,' Bandong quipped.

He told them to look around in all directions and observe the hotels, restaurants, jewellery stores, clothing stores, grocery stores, and various other businesses and places of interest, and all of them were in foreign hands.

'There is no Filipino,' he added, except at the small barber shops, newspaper and magazine stalls on the corner, some funeral homes and some cinema houses that didn't screen Tagalog movies.

They entered a typical restaurant and once they were seated, they were approached by a waitress, who seemed to be from the southern Philippines, going by her accent. They were presented with a menu. The teacher handed it to the young lady and said, 'Please order now, Pina.' Pina looked at the menu and returned it to Bandong.

'You do it,' she said. 'There's no stew.'

'This is what is called *macao* cooking,' explained Bandong. 'Cooked food is just mixed and sauteed again.'

Bandong offered the couple Andres and Sedes the menu to choose what they like, but they insisted that the teacher take care of it.

In the end, it was Bandong who ordered all the food. While waiting, they continued to talk.

'Now, our fellow citizens are slaves of the Chinese,' said Andres when the server turned her back on them. 'In the past, the Chinese were scrap merchants. Now, they're the masters of many Filipinos. The Filipinos are now the ones carrying around baskets and buying old shoes, bottles and newspapers.'

'Never mind a server like her,' Bandong said, 'she really has nothing and wants to earn a living somehow. But there are powerful Filipinos, who even have government positions, and yet are Chinese dummies. So, I ask: who's to blame for what is happening? Is it the Chinese or us, too? Those people came here with only a shirt and a pair of trousers.'

Andres was about to answer, but just then, the waitress placed the tray of food on their table. At the same time, the flies swarmed.

'I thought Manila was the cleanest place in this part of the world,' said Pina while shooing away some flies that landed on the plate of noodles. 'There are no such flies in Sampilong.'

'It's clean because of propaganda,' replied Andres.

Suddenly, they were interrupted by someone asking for alms. It was a middle-aged woman, bodily healthy, carrying a baby who was mere skin and bones. Pina handed her a twenty-centavo coin.

'If that woman was working and had left the child at home,' said Sedes, 'they wouldn't be wandering around.'

'How do you know if the child is her offspring?' Andres was suspicious. 'Maybe she just borrowed it from someone for begging.'

'Even that is possible?!' Pina was amazed.

'Here in Manila, all rackets are possible,' testified Bandong as if he was a Manila native. 'By the time we go home, we'd have met about twenty beggars, men and women. I'll bet none of them are blind or lame. Better yet, they would have clear eyesight and strong knees.'

'So why do they ask for alms?' Pina asked. 'Do they want to be beggars?'

'Because begging pays well,' explained Bandong. 'Who said there were three kinds of jobs? First, there's real work, second is stealing, and third is begging. Of those three, begging is the easiest.'

'But it's shameful,' insisted Pina.

'If that's what you think, then know that in the vocabulary of many, there's no such word as shame,' said the young teacher. 'That's why not a few grew up, got rich and famous—that is, succeeded—and their only investment was shamelessness.'

Bandong was speaking loudly, so Pina spoke softly to remind him, 'Please don't shout, Teacher Bandong.'

The one who was reminded then smiled and lowered his voice before he spoke again.

'Your reminder is always like cold water on a kindling straw,' he said to the young woman, whom he adored.

Suddenly, a sweepstakes ticket vendor approached them.

'Mister, get an underdog ticket,' said the vendor who was dressed like a girl, but didn't look like one at all. When Bandong didn't respond, the ticket vendor repeated, 'This is your lucky day, Mister. The draw is on Sunday.'

Then she turned to Pina.

'What about you, Miss? This might be your lucky day ... Choose a ticket.' And uttered in succession, 'Manueluy-Mantaring-Millar (Money-Fate-Success).'

After the persistent seller left, there came another one, and pulled at the sleeve of Bandong's shirt. Later came another beggar, and before they could start on the second dish, another child craned its neck towards the table and demanded that they give him what they were eating. He had a bag full of money.

Then a cigarette seller came.

'Do you have a Filipino?' Andres asked.

'What Filipino, sir?'

'The one made here, our cigarette.'

'No, sir. I don't sell that.'

'Why not?'

'They don't sell, sir.'

After eating and when Bandong was paying the server, he noticed that the amount charged on the receipt was more than what was printed on the menu.

'Why is this?' asked the teacher.

'Prices have been raised for a week now,' said the waitress in her Visayan accent. 'Everything is expensive now,' she added.

Bandong paid nevertheless, for fear of wasting time arguing about the anomalous amount for what they ate. It could even be said that provincial people like them didn't know how to eat at a Manila restaurant …

'All goods are expensive now,' Sedes complained, 'but many aren't earning at all.'

'Those who earn do not get a wage increase, despite the high cost of living,' Andres added.

'It isn't surprising that products from other countries are expensive,' said Bandong, 'but local products are also very expensive.' He mentioned fish, vegetables, bananas and others.

When they left the restaurant, Dinong, Pina's teenage brother, finally spoke. He asked his sister if they could watch a movie.

'No sir,' the young woman declined. 'We'll get home late.'

'But I only came along to watch a movie,' Dinong sulked.

'You were allowed to come along to accompany me,' Pina said, correcting him.

'To keep an eye on you,' Bandong whispered to the young woman and she smiled.

Bandong declared that, although he was old-fashioned, he believed that the tradition of a chaperone accompanying a young woman when she went out was outdated. Pinang said, on the other hand, that it was an old custom that never got old, especially in a time of extreme audacity, when the line between old age and youth, women and men, seemed to have disappeared.

It was as if Pina had alluded to a vision, because when they were walking through the crowd on Avenida Rizal with both Sedes and her in the front, followed by Bandong and Andres and Dinong behind them, a teenager dove like a spear and snatched the bag hanging on Pina's right arm. The young woman screamed, but the bag was gone. However, Bandong and Andres quickly caught the crook, cornering him when he turned into an alley.

The teenager pleaded and cried, saying he had been forced to do it because his mother was sick. Andres was almost moved and remembered when he was chased and caught because of a roasted pig's head. He was about to intervene when the policeman Dinong had called arrived. They were followed by Pina and Sedes.

When the policeman saw the young thief, he recognized him and slapped him on the head and yelled at him.

'You never learn, you animal!'

He then turned to Bandong and Andres, and told them that the shameless teenager had a long criminal record. He asked if Pina was the owner of the handbag, handed it to the young woman, and asked her to see if anything was missing. Pina checked her bag, took out and counted two hundred-peso bills and a few trinkets. She was sure that nothing had been taken.

The teenager swallowed and the policeman turned pale when they saw the bank notes inside the handbag. The law enforcer recorded the reports he needed, the name of the person robbed, the names of the witnesses, and their addresses. He informed them that they would probably receive a court summons to try 'this animal'.

Pina declared that she did not intend to prosecute since nothing was taken from her, and she might not be able to go to the city on the day of the trial because she was from the province.

'Fine, I'll take care of this,' said the policeman and waved at a passing cab. The young woman insisted that he accept a five-peso bill for the cab.

Before the cab got to the police station, the law enforcer and the teenager got off in an isolated area.

'Stupid,' shouted the policeman when they were alone, 'don't let them catch you again.'

'Okay, boss,' promised the young culprit.

The policeman took out a pack of Chester cigarettes and they lit one each before going on their separate ways.

It was already nighttime when the five travellers returned to Sampilong. They were tired from going around the whole day and their common experiences, but they were happy. Their happiness stemmed from the reality that they lived in a small but quiet town, and not in Manila—the vastness and progress of which were full of hardships and troubles.

25

Sepa had been buried for several weeks when another gathering was held in front of Julian's house. It seemed the attendees were the same ones who went to the wake and the funeral. But this gathering had a different purpose. They accepted the invitation to a farmers' meeting.

Tasyo, Simon and Blas arrived together. Tomas and Beteng followed. Then the women came. Before the conversation started, Ba Inte arrived, carrying a cane made of Chinese bamboo. Some leaseholders who were allies of the tenants also attended.

'Let's start the meeting, Tasyo,' Julian urged when the gathering was already dense.

'Why not you?' Tasyo replied to the host.

'It's your turn, Tasyo,' said Simon.

Thus, without delay, Tasyo sat down in front of a small table, which was also used by the king in the game of fines on the night of the wake for Julian's late wife.

Some benches were easily filled by the women attendees, so the men remained standing or patiently crouched down. Others placed a mat on the ground and sat on it.

'Comrades, we have called you to this meeting,' the one presiding over the meeting began, 'to revive the unity of the farmers here in Sampilong.'

'Will Teacher Bandong not be attending?' an attendee asked.

'Teacher Bandong is an ally,' Tasyo replied, 'but he's the head of the public school, so it's not appropriate—'

'And what about Dislaw?' asked the questioner.

'Comrade, this is a meeting of farmers; we don't need the child of the landlord here'.

This was met with loud laughter, and the men giggled even more when Tasyo couldn't tell what the meaning of the said words were, and asked.

The table continued to present the objectives of the meeting.

'You must remember that I mentioned at the funeral of Comrade Sepa that she was a martyr of labour. The farmers have many martyrs amongst us, and they didn't die of illness. Their lives were taken by the bullet, by the knife, by the prison. They were victims of extreme cruelty. Look at their names on the crosses in the cemetery. Many have no signs. Even though they most certainly died, there remained no traces of how or when. We all know for sure that they suffered for the cause of the farmers' desire to live like human beings and not like water buffaloes.'

Tasyo stopped when a jeep with three policemen on board sped past outside.

'Few of you will recall that we used to have unity here among the farmers, as part of the general society,' continued Tasyo. 'You must also know how this unity was destroyed by the enemies of the working class. We have been calm, patient and indifferent for a long time.'

'We've displayed the patience of the water buffalo,' Blas tried to interject, but Tasyo didn't pay attention to him.

'But now, comrades, our actions will answer a challenge. Eye to eye or heart to heart. Dislaw has reported to his master, Donya Leona, that we will organize into a union. You were witness to what happened here on the night of the wake. Dislaw angrily fled the polite meeting. When the Donya learned of our plan, she sent word and threatened that if anyone working on her land joins the union, they'd better pack up and find a new place to live in.'

The simultaneous murmurs of the attendees prevailed, and many indicated that they couldn't be intimidated or denied their right.

'Let her just try,' one shouted hotly.

Tasyo continued, 'It's our right and freedom to organize. You heard Teacher Bandong mention the Constitution's provisions regarding this matter. Now we must decide. Do you want us to continue to be poor, serving masters? Or should we be free farmers, who are treated as human beings and respected by the landlord? Shall we build a union or not?'

Everyone's cry resounded resembling a powerful decree, 'We will build!'

'All those in favour of building a farmers' union in Sampilong, please raise your right hand,' the president called out.

The unconditional cry from earlier was confirmed in passionate unity—all right hands reached for the sky as if taking a holy oath.

'Everyone agrees,' Tasyo said, and the applause was almost deafening.

Unity was established and they elected at once the leaders who would steer the future course of the union. Tasyo was elected president without opposition; Simon and Blas were made vice presidents; Julian, the secretary; Pina, the treasurer, and Ba Inte, the counsellor. Pina wasn't there, and after all, she wasn't a farmer, but they nevertheless agreed that the kind young lady would not refuse the work. The fact that Pina had the same position in the new cooperative was not a hindrance.

'Now that we already have a union and you've elected me as your president, even though I shouldn't have been,' Tasyo said, 'the first thing we'll do when we get home later is to pack up and find a new place to live in.'

A few happy laughs were heard at the joke made by the elected president of the farmers.

'Is that really what we should do, Ba Inte?' Blas asked the elderly counsellor, and everyone's attention shifted to him. Ba Inte didn't participate in the discussion, and was reluctant to take on the responsibility entrusted to him.

'It's your turn to talk, Ba Inte,' reminded the table.

Ba Inte left his corner and sat next to Tasyo. He pinched his lit cheap cigar with two fingers before speaking.

'My answer to question of Blas,' he said, 'is a story. And this is the life of Kabesang Tales, from the novel *El Filibusterismo* by the late national hero, Dr Jose Rizal.' The old man stopped, then he looked up as if he was recollecting what he was going to say, then continued his slow speech. 'Kabesang Tales, who was just Tales then, chose a part of the forest outside the town. Nobody owned the forest.'

'He cleared and cleaned his land. While working, his wife and eldest child were struck with illness, which eventually led to their deaths. When the land was planted and the crops were ready to be harvested, the field that was once a forest was claimed by the friars' corporation. They claimed it was within their property boundary. However, Kabesang Tales was allowed to harvest on the condition that every year, he would give a small donation—only a small one, about twenty to thirty pesos.'

The old man took a puff of his cigar first. He noticed that the audience was eager to listen.

'A kind person avoids trouble, and because he didn't know Spanish, Kabesang Tales agreed to the condition. Besides, he realized that it was hard to hit a pan with a clay pot. Kabesang Tales father, Tandang Selo, who was still alive at that time, reminded him, "Just think about those thirty pesos falling into the water and being eaten by a crocodile."'

'So crocodiles eat money?' a woman attendee wondered aloud.

'Animals, humans, money—they all go into the crocodile's mouth,' Ba Inte replied.

Some of the men giggled, because they remembered Ba Inte's story about the crocodiles that went up the land of Sampilong and never returned to the river.

'Please continue with the story of Kabesang Tales,' Tasyo urged him on.

The old man took another puff, but the cigar was no longer burning. Tasyo lit a match and brought the flame close to the cigar Ba Inte was smoking. Ba Inte blew smoke and continued.

'Another year passed and the harvest was once again bountiful. The friars increased the donation and made it fifty pesos. Hmmm! Poor Kabesang Tales paid again, perhaps hoping that he wouldn't lose more money. Tandang Selo advised, "Just imagine that the crocodile has grown."

'But when the fee was raised to 200 pesos, which was a true tax and not a donation, Tales refused to pay. He no longer listened to his father's advice, which was, "The crocodiles' relatives have also arrived". Instead, when the friar took over the land, Tales stood watch around the field with his gun. He carefully said, "I'm ignorant and weak. But I cleared these fields; my wife and child died helping me. That's why I won't give it to anyone, nor allow it to be taken from me, without him first doing what I did. If anyone tries to take this land, he must first spill blood on it and bury the corpses of his wife and child here.'

And then Tales would aim his gun at whatever he thought was the figure or shadow of the friar.

26

It was as if the male and female farmers were hypnotized listening to the courage that was displayed by an initially oppressed Filipino—Kabesang Tales—against the friars' greed. They admired his bravery in defending his cause.

The brave image of their ancestors seemed to rise in the pupil of their eye, reprimanding them for their cowardly surrender of their great heritage.

'This land used to be a forest cleared by our parents,' Ba Inte mused after a long pause. 'They tilled and enriched it. While those who emerged as the owners when the land was already productive, from the friars to the Grandes, were the ones who enjoyed it greatly. The only thing we inherited was servitude. And if we try to escape such oppression, all we incur is our land being taken away from us and we being driven away from it. I don't know how much longer the poor can endure this.'

Those who were close together talked and exchanged opinions amongst themselves, but Tasyo pounded on the table, since the meeting wasn't over yet.

He said emphatically, 'What we want is justice, nothing but that. But for a farmer, justice is intertwined with the land. For him, the welfare of the land is the fulfilment of what is called social justice.'

Julian stood up and presented an idea, 'I remember the initial campaign was to buy farmlands under dispute. Isn't it time to revive that?'

'Buy, but how?' a female member asked.

'The government will buy it and then divide it amongst the farmers,' explained Julian. 'On installments, at the purchase price. The farmers' bond is their harvest.'

'As far as we are concerned, that's what we really want,' said a leaseholder. 'A leasehold tenant paying a fixed amount to the owner of the land so that the tenant would take care of the farming, all the work and the expenses, while the landlord would get all the produce.'

One who had a wavering belief in such a programme spoke out.

'That would be great if it happened, but maybe man will reach the moon first.'

'If the government has the desire to do it, it can easily be accomplished,' insisted Julian.

'Where is the government going to get the money to buy such vast lands? Your government might lose the desire just dealing with the Grandes' land.'

Tasyo caught onto the last question and assisted his secretary in explaining properly.

'Look, fellow tenants,' said Tasyo. 'The government doesn't need to buy all of the farms. First, the landowners have different characters and systems. In short, they're not all like Donya Leona and her husband.' His addition of the husband to Donya Leona's name as if the former was tied by the shoelace to the latter caused some laughter.

'So, what should be bought first are the farms that have conflict—'

'Is there any land without conflict?' a farmer interrupted.

'Hold on,' Tasyo stopped him and repeated what he said, 'The farms that are under dispute should be bought first. Now, the buyer does not need to pay in full. Set the accurate value of the land first, and that will be the basis for calculating the average annual yield or income. That's easy to do, since reports do not lie.'

'And the witnesses are alive—the tenants themselves, of each farm,' Julian added.

'So, it's clear,' Tasyo stressed. 'This is what the government must pay the landowner first, every year, until it's fully paid.'

'That would be good if the landowner would agree to such a condition,' an attendee expressed his doubts.

'If he doesn't agree, he will be hurt further,' Tasyo retorted. 'What will he earn while an altercation is going on? As the saying goes, it's better to have a fish in the basket, than that which still needs to be caught.'

It seemed that the one who asked the question wasn't satisfied, and in his desire to squeeze all the juice out of the topic being discussed, he argued again.

'Another thing is that the government is different from the leaders,' he pointed out. 'What I mean is that the landlord's side will be given more weight in the leaders' decision-making. The truth is that not a few leaders are friends and relatives of the landlords, aside from being landlords themselves.'

Tasyo recognized the bitter truth expressed by the farmer comrade in his argument.

'What our brother mentioned cannot be simply shrugged off,' he said. 'It's true that the leaders are the government. But it's also true that if they want to stay in the government, they should listen to the people, especially those who live by working on the land. They can't deny that in a democracy, the influence of a few mighty ones can't prevail at all times. All exploitation comes to an end.'

'In theory ... ,' said a sneering voice from the back.

Tasyo got annoyed, so he pointed his finger at the one who was mocking him and sternly said, 'Remember, when the lowly ones truly unite and learn to use their strength, the landlords and leaders will be forced to act sensibly.' Tasyo took a long breath without anyone contradicting him, then asserted, 'Now, let's resolve our stand. Do you agree with us reviving the initial campaign of land purchase as mentioned by brother Julian?'

Ba Inte preempted the others from answering the table's question.

'Good, good,' said the old counsellor of the farmers. 'But let's slow down. Let's not try to cross the bridge until we get there. What I mean is let's prioritize what needs to be prioritized first. Why did we revive the union? So that we can come together, unite and become strong. Let's assess ourselves first. Are we bound together after electing leaders? Are we united? Are we strong? Those are questions that we cannot answer right now, but with time, with experience ...'

They immediately saw the wisdom in Ba Inte's advice, but the old farmer added to his speech.

'So, before we surge like a blaze of cogon grass, let's look back at the past and carefully examine the future.' He raised his Chinese bamboo cane and pointed it toward the distant woods beyond the fields. 'I didn't tell you what happened to Kabesang Tales—later, he was forced to go to the mountains and join the bandits.'

A few long 'ooohs' and 'aaahs' escaped the women's lips, but Simon wasn't amongst those who were scared.

A bitter smile appeared on Ba Inte's dry lips.

'That's also how the landlords, friars and government saw it,' he explained. 'Disobeying the law, even an unfair law, is called banditry. And often, when the oppressed choose to follow a law imposed by the rulers and the rich, they call it rebellion.'

'So sometimes, the only choice an honourable citizen can make is to go to the mountains—or go to jail,' said Blas.

'That's what the late Dr Rizal learnt when he first returned to the Philippines from Europe,' testified Ba Inte, who could easily recall what he had seen, heard and read. 'In order for a Filipino to be honourable at that time, he had to be imprisoned. Because at that time, the truth was forbidden and reason was persecuted.'

'In every era, wickedness reigns; that's how it is,' Tasyo also chimed in. 'Many of us witnessed it under the Japanese. Although the truth is that evil didn't end with the defeat of Japan and after the war—'

'History repeats itself, but nothing much changes,' said Blas.

'As long as the crocodiles don't disappear, the danger won't go away,' said Simon.

'But when will the crocodiles disappear?' Ba Inte asked. 'When the stork has turned black and the crow has turned white.' The old man choked, laughing softly at his metaphor and ended, 'But there's no doubt the worms will eat me first ...' And lit his cigar stub again.

As the day cooled down, the conversation, the plans, the aspirations and the threats became more heated. Tasyo reminded them that it was getting dark, and that Julian might have to prepare dinner for them instead of a light snack.

'We should celebrate, comrades,' the president concluded. 'We have made great strides in this first meeting. We've formed the union and discussed its important goals. Next time, we can outline our petitions from the landlords, as well as the government. But I agree with Ba Inte's advice. Let's not surge like blazing cogon grass, and first of all, let's assess ourselves. That's the key to all success.'

The women helped in serving the rice cakes and ginger tea, the only meagre fare that Julian could provide. The members of the new association enjoyed their meal together.

While they were eating, the jeep of the three policemen sped past again, heading back to town. The farmers weren't worried because each one of them believed that he was with everyone, and everyone was by his side.

27

A big bamboo arch festooned with fresh leaves and strips of coloured paper was hung above the street, indicating that something was afoot in the place where the squatters lived. The words 'New Village' were spelt on the front of the arch.

The new centre of the home industries was going to be inaugurated. Father Pascual was invited to bless it, while Mayor Bartolo was requested to address the crowd on the said occasion. Everyone waited for their arrival with excitement. But when the appointed hour came, the two guests didn't show up.

At the last minute, the priest sent word that he was ill and needed bedrest, while the mayor said that he had suddenly been summoned to the capital for an important meeting and would return home to Sampilong very late.

However, the programme of ceremonies could no longer be cancelled or postponed. They went ahead even without the blessings of the priest, and Teacher Bandong was asked instead to address the crowd. The representative from the Department of Social Welfare also came. The beautiful Pina cut the ceremonial ribbon.

The new thatched hut built in the middle of the new village served as the exhibit area for the products made by the people living in the humble shacks. As planned, they had now finished the baskets, bags, anahaw fans and woven hats, slippers made from abaca fibres, as well as hats made from the native buri plant—all of which were made by hand. Moreover, Andres said they would also be making flowers made from small shells, assorted bags and other items, as soon as they got the raw materials for the new array of products.

They also showed the fruits and vegetables newly harvested from the plots of land tended by the people, planted in their gardens or in trellises set up in their backyards. Several pigs and chickens that they fattened were also proudly displayed to the delight of the crowd, because two hens seemed to be having a competition on the number of eggs they could lay on the spot.

Everyone who attended admired the fruits of the organization's efforts. There was Mang Pablo, as well as the leaders of the new farmers' organization, and a big delegation from the village. Amongst the guests were the few well-off people living in the town centre, who had gladly contributed to the seed fund that had gone into creating the home industries' products. They all saw the happy results of a good vision that was implemented by everyone involved, with care.

'These products are similar to the ones now being sold in Manila,' said one enthusiastic observer at the scene.

'And these are even cheaper and more durable,' added a second observer.

Dislaw was also there, and he was the one who had brought the messages from both the priest and the town mayor. He was hovering near Pina, very much like a pesky fly who had smelt something sweet. He had another reason for coming—and it wasn't to join in the celebration that day, but to spy on it for Don Severo and Donya Leona.

'Check on the exhibition of the squatters and make a report to me,' the rich woman had said as Dislaw was leaving. This remark meant that she was the one who had prevented Father Pascual and Mayor Bartolo from attending the inauguration of the centre.

'Giving attention to trash like them means giving them the importance they don't deserve,' the haughty woman had said in an annoyed tone.

The Grandes had long resented the presence of the squatters. Their revulsion deepened when they heard that the people had cleaned up their area, built a centre to showcase the products of their home industries, and made further moves to ensure their permanent presence on the land.

'These people are shameless and beginning to treat us as if we were driftwood,' Don Severo also said in a brash manner. 'Better leave this place than allow them to do as they please.'

But it seemed that the squatters in Sampilong were beginning to prevail, propped up by people everywhere.

For the first time, the dirty place on the hill overgrown with cogon grasses was filled with joy. Indeed, there were no musical bands, no fireworks, no grand spread served in every house, the way it was done at the usual fiestas and festivities. But pure and unalloyed laughter rose amongst the people, and gladness gleamed in their eyes.

The place seemed to have changed overnight from what it used to be only a few months ago. The humble huts now looked like houses, even if their poverty still showed. Gone were the potholes on the roads that were filled with water and mud; the clotheslines and basins of clothes in front of the huts; the clumps of riff-raff and trash.

Today, the people wore clean and newly washed clothes, even the children. And on everyone's faces shone the happy rays of hope. Like an ugly blindfold, fear, defeat and despair had been taken away from their eyes. Irrefutable was the miracle that had dawned upon their lives, situation and identities. Now, they were recognized as people with a sense of purpose, who could build things and give shape to their dreams, through their own talents and hard work.

In his opening remarks at the inauguration, Andres said that everyone was seeing the beginning of a new day, a metamorphosis in their lives. They had changed from living amidst a heap of rubbish to a new and vibrant village. He briefly sketched the history of the place, how those who were turned away to be homeless and hopeless, had found a place to live in; the sufferings wrought over the years; the horrible conquest of the Japanese during the Second World War; the hurtful snobbishness of the rich in the town; and the farm workers' happy alliance for their cause of change.

'But our consciousness was changed,' Andres said in a voice filled with pride. 'For we're not vagabonds just thrown into a place heaped with rubbish. We are people who have moved here, driven by the winds of change and prepared to start a new life.' The leader of the squatters thanked Teacher Bandong for sowing the seeds of trust in the humanity of the seemingly hopeless people driven there by fate.

Andres also admitted that their situation in the new village wasn't yet tenable, since they were living on land that they didn't own, and that was why they were pinning their hopes on the sense of social justice and charitable hearts of the leaders of the town, in a way.

'We're squatters, yes,' he declared, 'but we don't deign to possess the land that doesn't belong to us. When we arrived, this place was a forest that nobody tended to and cleaned up. We cut the wayward shrubs and tangled vines. We set up our humble huts, began planting our small gardens and started our new lives. Many of our children were born here. Now, we're hoping for renewed understanding from you, our friends, as well as care from the government.'

Andres stopped speaking for a while and repeated his last sentence. Then, he looked with affection at the eyes of the people around him and ended, 'And if the words of the Holy Book will be followed—that the gifts of the Lord belong to everyone—then this place should be a legacy we can pass on to our children.'

For his part, Teacher Bandong also spoke briefly and praised the people of the new village. He said that the inhabitants weren't the only ones who should rejoice, but also the town's authorities for their important contribution to the progress of Sampilong.

'May our good start be the beginning of healthy and prosperous home industries for our village,' he began. 'These industries will serve as the keys to our development. Like an ordinary plant, we sowed the seed, planted the sapling and took care of it until it sprouted leaves, flowered and bore fruits. In fact, we're now starting our new lives, like fruits beginning to form.'

The last words of Teacher Bandong seemed like an answer to Andres' clarion call.

'Have faith that your dreams will come true as soon as possible. What you built and worked hard for, will be yours forever.'

The representative from the Social Welfare Department also spoke and said they would gladly support the products that came from the hardworking men and women of New Village.

'There's a big market for the products of the home industries,' he reassured them.

The inauguration was thus concluded, but the showcase wasn't only for one day. For the whole week after, people from the other villages visited New Village to look at the products and buy whatever they fancied.

Ever since the raw materials had arrived and been distributed to the members of the cooperative, Andres no longer had to go to the capital every day to scrounge around for work at the bus station and the marketplace. He now served as the inspector of the cooperative, while Marcos worked as the foreman. He accepted the delivery of the raw materials and apportioned them to the members of the cooperative, which served as the new spring for their livelihoods. And as the clear signs of growth showed, the old dumping ground not only became a new village that was on its way to progress, it also became a model for other villages to follow.

After the inauguration, Dislaw insisted on taking Mang Pablo and Pina home in his jeep, after which he went to the big stone house to make his report. The Grande family felt as if a thorn had slashed their throats when they heard Dislaw's report. Dislaw even exaggerated the role played by Bandong in organizing the squatters, as well as the farmers.

'That man is dangerous,' Don Severo said.

For Donya Leona, things were no longer trivial. The farmers had organized their union despite her threats, and she saw it as an obstacle to her plans. These were the two weapons that people who disliked her could use against her.

The tenant farmers used to just bow their heads when the Grande family ordered them to do something. Even if they complained and came one by one, still, the orders of the Grande family were followed. Earlier, everything that was needed in the village was sourced through Donya Leona and paid for in installments. In this way, she was able to charge them whopping interest rates. The rich woman was worried that she could no longer continue her business because of the union and the cooperative.

That was why she listened intently to the report delivered by Dislaw, starting from the meeting held in the house of Julian, up to the inauguration of New Village. Even if only the tenant farmers had met at Julian's house, Dislaw still knew what the agreements were, because he had planted spies in the organization. Even in a flock of sheep, there would be some animal donning a different fur.

The names that Dislaw mentioned were no longer new to Don Severo and Donya Leona, but now there were inscribed in black and bitter letters: Bandong, Tasyo, Andres, Pablo, and all the rest of them.

'They want war,' Don Severo shouted, 'then they should prepare for one. Who are they scaring?'

'Someone is pushing those fools to do these things,' said Donya Leona. 'It's really easy to lure the blind into a place filled with red ants.'

28

After Dislaw left, the Grande husband and wife talked seriously. They just kept on whispering to each other, as if the mystery of what they were talking about should not be heard by the servant bringing food to them.

'I'll talk to my brother, the priest, and you talk to Bartolo, the mayor,' Donya Leona said with finality.

Only they knew what they later told the two powerful men in town. But one could surmise it involved the squatters, whom they hated, and the farmers, who were now turning stubborn.

After a few days, there were guests for lunch in the big stone house. The Grande husband and wife invited Mayor Bartolo, Father Pascual, and the judge in the capital. They consulted the judge on matters of the law, even though they also had their own lawyer.

Jun and Ninet were already back in Manila by then, to prepare for their examinations. The two siblings didn't know a lot about the transactions and operations of their parents. All they knew was that their family had vast lands, lots of money, and they could easily get whatever they asked of their parents. They were raised to be picky and uppity. Jun and Ninet didn't have a relationship with their tenants on the farms, that was why it could be said that they lived in a world of their own. For the siblings, they had a mother who was an angel and a father who was a saint.

Before lunch started, the priest and the judge seemed to be having a contest on drinking and eating as much of the finger food as they could. In truth, both of them could drink vast amounts of alcohol and never got drunk easily.

'Don't ever think, dear judge,' said Father Pascual, 'that my drinking at Mass made me a seasoned drinker. I was already the champion drinker at the seminary, even before we celebrated the first Mass, which we sang.'

The priest of Sampilong recalled that priesthood wasn't his original vocation of choice when he was still a young man, but he could not say no to the wishes of his parents.

'I can't remember now who between my parents was more adamant that I become a priest,' said Father Pascual, 'but before you could bend them to your will, they had already bent you to theirs.'

Donya Leona nodded at the description offered by her brother, but she didn't speak a word. She knew her brother's recollection was correct, because even she herself didn't like Severo at first. But then, Captain Melchor told her that she should prepare for her wedding, because her father had already arranged a match for her.

On the other hand, the judge said that he wasn't originally a hard drinker, and had even tried to stop drinking, especially in the last few years. He had problems, including high blood pressure and irregular heartbeat.

'I drink because of my need to,' he said, 'and many judges are forced to be friends with alcohol. Because for most of us, our worst enemy is our conscience. We judge a case, but our conscience judges us in turn. If you become used to drinking, you begin to forget; even your conscience becomes dulled.' And the judge was the first to laugh aloud at what he had just said.

Father Pascual and Mayor Bartolo were also compelled to laugh.

According to the mayor, drinking was part of his work as a politician, who had to drink and pay for other people's drinks.

'Especially paying for other people's drinks,' he said, 'here in our town, they look down on a politician who doesn't get along well with other people. You should be game and have the qualities of a man on the streets. It's all right if they call you ignorant, greedy or immoral. All of that could be forgotten if you know how to dance to the song; in other words, if you know how to win the game of fooling other people. And the first lesson in fooling people is to ply them with free drinks.'

'It's hard to be a politician,' mused the judge.

'But that would change if the people's eyes are opened, if a new generation—' said Father Pascual.

'Maybe when a tortoise begins to fly, perhaps that would happen,' Bartolo interrupted with a sigh. 'But the thing with politics is that it's like gambling or taking opium—the deeper you are into the habit, the more you want to extricate yourself.'

'It becomes a vice,' said the judge.

'Or an illness,' added the priest.

After lunch, they began smoking expensive cigars in the hallway on the first floor of the big house. When the rich man and woman were seated in front of the guests, Don Severo revealed the real reason for their invitation.

'We want to consult you on an important matter,' he began.

Everyone listened with rapt attention, but nobody spoke; they waited for the rich man to continue.

'The other day,' he continued, 'while we were looking at some papers, we were surprised to see an old document.' Don Severo stopped and watched the interest generated by his revelation amongst his guests. 'The old people left so many documents, land transactions, pawned items, loans that had not yet been paid, things we no longer pay attention to. But this document is different; it completely caught us by surprise.'

'What document?' asked the judge.

'A document that states that the Spanish ancestors of Captain Melchor, *es desir*, that is to say, the grandfather of my wife and of Father Pascual, received a big plot of land from the King of Spain. The vast land is located in Sampilong. From the description and size of the land, it includes even the hilly terrain covered with cogon grasses.'

'This hilly terrain is now occupied by the squatters,' explained Mayor Bartolo. He stopped for a while before he continued, 'But all along, I thought it belonged to the municipal government.'

'That's what we all thought,' said Don Severo. 'In truth, we just ignored that land before, because it was rocky and overgrown with tall grasses. But now, it's different—'

'It's now clean and orderly,' the mayor confirmed. 'It has been planted with different crops and is now called the New Village.'

'I was even asked to give my blessing to whatever it is,' said Father Pascual who spoke up only then. It was noticeable that the siblings, Father Pascual and Donya Leona, who would most benefit from the document being discussed, just listened and didn't join the discussion.

'Please wait for a while,' said Don Severo as he went to the library. He came out with a big folder.

'This is the document,' he said. He took out from the folder a thick piece of paper that looked like parchment, on which something was written in Spanish, more or less, describing the matter that Don Severo had discussed earlier with his guests. At first glance, the paper looked dated and the letters written in an old script. He gave the document to the judge.

'What's the problem?' he asked after a cursory study of the document.

'There's no problem except to certify and declare who the real owners of the land are,' answered Don Severo. 'It's clear that its only and real heirs are my wife, Severa, and my brother-in-law, Father Pascual.'

A long silence fell upon the group until the judge offered an opinion.

'If nobody else claims the land, then there's no problem transferring it to the real heirs. You should prepare a petition.' Then he looked at Mayor Bartolo. 'What do you think, Mayor?'

'My point is we have to respect and follow the law,' said the prime administrator of the municipality. 'When earlier we thought that the land belonged to the municipality and no one was interested in it, what more now?'

Father Pascual just behaved as if he didn't care about the topic at hand, even though the Grande husband and wife had first shown the document to him. They had also asked for his approval on what they intended to do.

'But what about the squatters?' the mayor asked suddenly.

'The squatters have no right,' the judge said. 'They can only stay there at the mercy of the landowner. They can be driven away if the landowner wishes to do so.'

'That's what I want to happen,' Donya Leona said, finally uttering what was on her mind.

Before leaving, the men drank one more glass of liquor, as if they were toasting to a celebration or victory. They were all clear on the next steps that would be taken.

Dislaw was the first to float the news that the land where New Village was located—as well as the land further beyond—belonged to the siblings Donya Leona and Father Pascual. They had inherited the said land from their Spanish ancestor, who was the father of Captain Melchor, according to an old document. Dislaw broke the news to some teachers, as well as at the barber shop owned by Tinoy, and to whoever was willing to spend time listening to his tale.

After a few days, the news also spread that the squatters living in New Village would be asked to leave. The hilly terrain that used to be covered with tall cogon grasses, clumps of shrubs and trees and a tangle of vines was now clean, and it would be rented out to a rich Chinese in the capital. It was rumoured that he would use the land for some kind of business.

The sudden and fearsome news reached Andres and Bandong. It also reached the ears of the people in the cooperative, as well as the farmers.

Andres and Marcos swiftly went to the principal, along with Tasyo and other comrades.

'We think someone is behind this,' Andres said. His eyes had turned red.

'Perhaps, but we should wait to see what they do.'

'There are still vast lands in this town that don't belong to the Grande family,' Tasyo said in consolation.

'But we worked hard to turn the New Village into something else,' Andres said with despair. 'If anything happens ...'

29

Like the whiplash of summer lightning came the summons of the judge in the Court of First Instance in the name of Andres and the other squatters. They were being called to face an investigation, because the owners of the so-called New Village wanted to know who gave permission to Andres and company to build their huts, plant their gardens, cut trees, build a canal and do other things to improve the place. The new owners had already filed a civil case so that the squatters would leave the place, and the reason for the investigation was to give them a chance to explain why they should also not face criminal charges.

Andres and the other squatters did not think that the news that Dislaw was going around spreading would be so quickly followed by a case filed by the Grande family. That was why they were so unprepared.

The group formed by Andres rushed to the office of the mayor for guidance, but the mayor said his hands were tied and that he could not possibly interfere in a case proceeding. If the land belonged to the government, as they all thought it was, then he said he would allow the squatters to remain there, as long as the land wasn't being used for a commercial or public purpose. He added that was what happened before, with the hilly terrain remaining overfilled with cogon grasses, until the squatters came and settled there after the Second World War.

'You better face the new owners and settle the dispute with them,' advised Mayor Bartolo.

'But you'll no longer fight for the right of the municipality?' Andres asked.

'What right?' and the mayor raised an eyebrow. 'Naturally, the owner has the original right in land disputes.'

Andres reminded the mayor that when they decided to settle in the hilly terrain, the mayor gave them permission and even encouraged them to do so. 'That's good, so you can clean up the place where the snakes live,' the mayor had said then. He just reminded the new settlers not to make trouble, avoid littering, and never do anything that would violate the laws laid down by the conquering Japanese military forces. A squadron of Japanese forces were staying at the public elementary school at the time.

The mayor gave them the same encouragement when Andres and the settlers decided to improve the place. They set up a public faucet, and later on, the squatters were persuaded to clean up the whole dirty place, set up their home industries and a centre as well. In truth, Mayor Bartolo had even praised them when they invited him to attend the inauguration of the centre and make a speech. He even said he would attend the event, but he never showed up.

'You suddenly abandoned us, Mayor,' Andres said in a hurt voice.

Why was he now sitting there, his arms akimbo, looking like he didn't care about his constituency? Didn't he, as the mayor, promise them—when they happily told him about the New Village and the home industries—that he would work for the land to be parcelled out and given to them by the government, to be paid for in monthly installments?

Mayor Bartolo was unhappy with the words spoken by Andres and Marcos, but he pointed out, counting the events with his fingers, the new conditions under which they were now operating. The new owners had come, and wanted the land to be returned to them.

'I want to help you but that would be impossible,' said the mayor. 'The government can't buy the land because it doesn't have the funds to do so. And if there were funds, the money would certainly go to more worthwhile projects.'

Up to this point, and to the other issues that Andres and company had presented, the chief executive of Sampilong had only this to say, 'I'm sorry, I'm sorry, but I can't do anything. It's not in my hands ...'

Several times, Andres and his group met with Teacher Bandong, Mang Pablo and Tasyo. They asked questions and sought advice.

Their tempers flared and then they subsided. Someone suggested that force might now be an option, but more people said that cooler heads should prevail.

They also met several times amongst themselves, the leaders first with each other, and then later, with their respective families. They discussed the matter thoroughly. They studied properly the steps they could take. They thought of seeking an audience with the provincial governor and meet with a high government official in Manila. And if they failed, if they could no longer be controlled and if they never tasted what they called social justice—Andres and Marcos, Kiko and Kanor and a few others, discussed in secret what they would do—then so be it.

Ba Inte shook his head when he heard about the dire straits the squatters were in.

'This is just a repetition of what the Spanish friars did to Kabesang Tales in the novel by Dr Jose Rizal,' he said. 'When the land was just a forest, nobody owned it. When it was cleared and planted and the rice was ready for harvest, suddenly an old document showed up. The crocodile has finally bared its fangs.'

The so-be-it of the fuming squatters meant different things.

'That's why the ant is easily crushed,' Marcos said, metaphorically.

In truth, the squatters weren't alone in their struggle. The principal of the elementary school, the president of the PTA, the union leader of the farmers, all of them said they would support the fight against the bodyguard of lies and unreason.

'Count me in,' Bandong told Andres concisely, even if ill feelings against the situation still knotted in his chest.

Mang Pablo also said he would help in whatever way he could.

'I don't have any respect for anyone whose only god is money,' said Pina's father.

'Don't say that,' argued Aling Sabel when she heard what her husband said. 'Donya Leona is one of the biggest donors to the Catholic Church.'

'She thinks she can save her soul by donating a pittance out of the vast amounts that she has stolen from the poor? Moreover, she does it because of her elder brother, Father Pascual.'

Tasyo was rather rash. He saw that the Grandes only had ill feelings for the farmers and squatters, whom they treated shabbily. He suggested that the farmers and squatters work together to defend themselves against oppression.

When the court hearing began at the provincial capital, you couldn't drop a needle amidst the crowd that thronged the hallway of the Court of First Instance. Only a few people were left behind at New Village, like the elderly who would have mobility difficulties, as well as the children whose parents had decided to leave them behind. Tasyo also remained at New Village, along with other inhabitants. The Grande husband and wife didn't face the squatters, but their two lawyers were present, as well as Dislaw.

As soon as the judge opened the trial, the two lawyers presented the old document that proved the ownership of the land as belonging to the ancestors of the siblings Donya Leona and Father Pascual. He read in Spanish the royal grant of the land given by the King of Spain, as well as the translation into Tagalog requested by the judge so that the farmers could understand what it contained.

The lawyers sketched the history of the land, how it was given to the father of Captain Melchor for his sterling services rendered to the King of Spain. They also lamented that the squatters had used the land for their own benefit without seeking permission from its real and legal owners.

'Now, the owners want to use their own property,' the lawyer said, 'and it's illegal for the squatters to stop this.'

Andres and company had no lawyer; he had only himself and Marcos to serve as their spokesmen. They knew that they would be muted if they wanted to appeal to the judge using the diktats of the law, so they chose to appeal to the jury's conscience and good heart, to humanistic ideas and spiritual notions.

'Perhaps we can't find justice through laws,' said Marcos whose eyes were already gleaming with tears, 'but is there no pity in the hearts of people, and is the love of fellowmen simply a humble flower on one's tongue?'

He told the court that they had developed the land and the said village over the course of many years, watered the land with their own sweat and tears, their bodies wounded by thorns and the sharp leaves of cogon grasses, bitten by snakes, which had even led to the death of some of them, afflicted with fevers again and again, and always hounded by poverty—and this was before they could begin planting in the soil and eking out some small livelihood, deep in debt despite their ceaseless labours. On the other hand, the new owners just came out of nowhere, had not a care in the world, didn't even take a peek at the land they were now claiming as their own; their feet not stained with the mud, nor their hands with blood from cuts. The owner who laid claim over the land was wealthy, comfortable and already in possession of vast tracts of land in Sampilong, while they, the squatters, had nothing except this small plot of land on which they had pinned their hopes to have a roof over their head and the means to build a somewhat decent life.

'Where's the justice in this?' Andres asked with firmness in his voice. 'Where's equality?'

The judge restrained Andres and sharply reminded him that they were not having a meeting in the town square.

'The owner of the land is charging you in court, bearing with them proof that they own the land,' said the judge. 'Before I start the trial, I'll give you time to prove that they're wrong and you're right. That's the only thing I want to clarify. But I won't allow you to defend yourselves as if you're making a speech similar to the harangues made by politicians in public.'

Andres made an apology to the court and said he didn't intend to be disrespectful toward the honourable judge and the Court of First Instance. But he said he was carried away by the tide of his emotions from the oppression of the poor by the rich.

'If we can't say in court everything we want to say, including our deepest wishes,' Andres said and his voice rose a pitch higher again, 'then where under the vast heavens could the plight of the poor be heard?'

The judge pounded the mallet on his table and he pointed toward the seat where Andres was asked to return.

30

The buzz rose amongst the groups of squatters that the judge had not looked fairly and squarely at the two opposing sides in the case. He had accepted everything that the two lawyers of the Grande family had presented, but had chided Andres and Marcos for narrating their sorry plight before the court.

During the recess of the hearing, the judge called Andres to his room. The leader of New Village saw that the two lawyers of the Grande family were already there.

'I want to give you all the opportunity,' the judge said. 'You should get a lawyer to defend you in court.'

Andres said that they wanted to do that, but they didn't have the funds. They also heard the lawyers were expensive for civil cases. The faces of the two lawyers representing Donya Leona and Father Pascual turned red.

'Even for civil cases, there will be lawyers who will work for free,' said the judge. 'There are many good people in this profession.'

At the end, Andres said they would try to find a lawyer, but he let fly the snide remark, 'But we're not sure we can get lawyers as brilliant as the ones hired by the Grandes.'

That afternoon, the group of squatters promptly met with Teacher Bandong and told the principal about what had happened during the court hearing at the capital. Andres said that they would need a lawyer when the trial properly started.

'If not, I'll be perpetually told to return to my seat,' he said with a smile.

Teacher Bandong furrowed his forehead to think. He riffled in his mind through the names of lawyers they could approach. None in Sampilong. In the capital, there would be two or three lawyers, but they were of middling talents. They were also under the thumb of the judge, and the Grande lawyers could easily put them in their pockets. Suddenly, Bandong remembered someone. A lawyer friend with whom he had stayed at the dormitory in Manila, when they were both studying. They had since met several times and even exchanged letters after their graduation.

Bandong hit his right fist on his left palm and happily said, 'Yes, we'll have a lawyer.'

He got his memorandum and looked for the lawyer's name and address.

'A. Reyes, with an office in Escolta, Manila,' Bandong read and underlined the telephone number.

'Here's your lawyer,' he told one of his guests.

'How much—' Andres began to speak.

'I'll pay for it', said Bandong. 'If the lawyer and I are still friends, he'll be on our side.'

They agreed to leave for Manila in the morning.

Bandong, together with Andres, set out for Manila and they told Marcos and the rest of the squatters not to tell anyone about the purpose of their visit to the capital. First of all, Bandong didn't want it be known that he was supporting the cause of the farmers since he was working as the interim principal of the elementary school. Second, it would not be good if the Grandes came to know of the steps being taken by the people of New Village. But Dislaw still found out about their departure, for he saw them enter the bus bound for Manila. It seemed that the Grandes' overseer had been spying on Andres, watching his every move, as well as that of the principal.

However, Attorney Reyes was not in his office when Bandong and Andres arrived. According to his assistant, they could meet the lawyer if they returned to the office at two o'clock in the afternoon.

The two took the occasion to go to the Register of Deeds to check if the area where New Village sat was listed in the name of an owner. They were hardly attended to by the clerk, who kept asking who they were and what the purpose of their query was. Then, he said that all the records had been deposited in the warehouse and it would take more than a week to retrieve them. He told them to return after a week and then turned his back, as if the two were borrowing money like beggars.

'That's the way government employees treat people,' Andres said in a hurt voice. 'They act like lords and not servants of the people.'

Bandong recalled the irregularities in the Register of Deeds that had led to troubles and controversies, especially those in Mindanao in southern Philippines and in other places, where people opened tracts of land under the homestead system. After years of hard work and sacrifice, the people found out that the forest they had cleared and planted with crops belonged to someone else, many of whom were high government officials, who didn't even spend money or sweat to develop the land.

Bandong and Andres also went to several markets to ascertain the prices of the products that they were making in their home industries, and which they had recently presented at their showcase at the centre. They were happy to know that the products were popular and their pricing was competitive. Andres thought that if Donya Leona wasn't the epitome of greed, then the squatters would surely have a better future.

'If not for that witch, our future would be as smooth as the sky,' he said.

Bandong said that whatever the outcome of the trial, the squatters should still continue what they had already started.

'For sure,' said the principal, 'people bear in their hands their own future. The rays of the sun reach all places.'

They had lunch later, and Bandong noticed that the prices of food had risen again. After a while, they walked around Avenida Rizal and then returned to the lawyer's office in Escolta.

The principal recalled to Andres what he had said when they had come to Manila earlier, that the most prominent city of the country was owned by foreigners.

'Let's look all around us, at the visible evidence,' then he looked to his left, and then to his right.

All the stores had foreign names and sold branded foreign goods. They were also owned by foreigners.

'The only Filipinos are the salespeople—and the customers,' he said. 'We're being fried in our own lard,' Andres said.

They then returned to a discussion about the many problems regarding economic production, the Filipinos' lassitude, as well as the hardworking and cunning foreigners.

'The foreigners do well in business and they succeed fast,' said Bandong, 'because they're hardworking, persistent and patient. Look at the Chinese and their variety stores. You could buy anything in the past. A little fish sauce, a little vinegar, a smidgen of salt, a head of garlic, soy sauce, pepper, even small nails for your wooden clogs. They sold everything, even in small amounts, and their profits kept on multiplying. You cursed them, and they returned your curse with a smile. You hit them on the back of the head, they never hit you back. They just toiled hard, plowed their money to buy more items in their stores, then saved the rest of their money. And then, their small stores became grocery stores; the noodle shop became a hotel; the corner stall selling textiles became a departmental store.'

Bandong compared these traits of behaviour to the snobbish Filipinos, who had no patience and couldn't care less, and were driven by the overweening desire to make a lot of money from small capital—and in the shortest time possible.

Andres agreed with these things and added that the Filipinos, instead of making their own products and selling them far and wide, were just content with engaging in the small trade of buying and selling finished products.

'They would buy land not to farm it or build on it, but to resell it at a higher profit; they would then buy a house and lot, only to resell it for a higher profit,' Andres said.

It was almost two o'clock in the afternoon and Bandong saw that even though they had walked slowly, they were almost in front of the lawyer's office. They entered and met Attorney Reyes, who still remembered his roommate who had stayed in the same dormitory as him.

'We haven't seen each other in a hundred years,' said Attorney Reyes in a happy tone. The principal introduced Andres, and the three of them sat down in the office.

Bandong said that he was still teaching, although he had recently been promoted as interim principal of the elementary school, and was still single because no one wanted to be with him, at which they all laughed.

Attorney Reyes was married and had three children, and a queue of clients always formed outside his office. In truth, while he was talking to Bandong and Andres, three other clients were already waiting outside.

'If trial cases before a judge were an industry,' said Attorney Reyes in a joking manner, 'then we could be considered a top industrial country.'

Bandong then went on to business and told his friend the reason for their visit. The lawyer checked his schedule and saw that he was free on the day of the hearing of the squatters, so he agreed to defend them.

'I'll be there,' he promised.

Then he asked Andres about the relevant details of the case that he should know about. He asked how many years Andres and his group had lived in what they now called New Village, the condition of the place when they had first arrived, and the improvement they had made. Then, he asked Bandong for details about the Grande family.

He also discussed the so-called old document that was the basis for the Grande siblings' claim to the land.

'Have you seen the document?' he asked Andres.

'The judge showed it to me,' Andres answered and recalled how it looked. 'It was on thick paper and it looked old; the Spanish words were written in deep black ink, and it had a stamp as well as a seal.'

'I want to examine this document,' said Attorney Reyes. 'There are many fake documents like that. But some shrewd people use them and even judges are fooled. Let's see.'

Bandong and Andres looked at each other, but the words on the tips of their tongues were the same: 'We think so, too.'

'They should have incontrovertible proof that the document is genuine,' Reyes continued. 'We'll then try to prove that it's fake. We'll get the facts from the Embassy of Spain here in the Philippines. If they don't have the facts here, then we'll get them from Madrid itself. They've a complete record there of all the lands given by the King of Spain to their subjects in the former colony.' He stopped for a while, and then added, 'I just wanted to give you an idea of the fight we'll mount against them.'

Andres and Bandong were filled with gladness by the time they left the office of Attorney Reyes. They could foresee a miracle in the offing in the oncoming clash between the clay pot and the wok. The two felt as if the bus they had boarded to bring them back to Sampilong had wings.

31

Donya Leona felt like a powder keg that had suddenly been lit when she read the demands of the farmers who were members of the union. They had presented the list to her and she couldn't stop cackling like a hen at the cursed names of Tasyo and the others. Even the names of Teacher Bandong, Mang Pablo and Ba Inte were included in her volley of angry words.

Dislaw had brought the farmers' list of demands to the rich woman. After reading it, she threw it in the direction of Don Severo.

'I can't believe the demands of these shameless people,' she said in an angry voice. 'Read it, Severo.'

And even if Donya Leona had already gone through it, Don Severo still read it aloud with emphasis. But there was an evident tremor in his voice.

'With respect, the union of farmers ask the following of Don Severo Grande and Donya Leona Grande. First, the landowner should pay for the cost of the seeds, since the seeds are part of capital;

'Second, after every harvest, the landowner will give enough fertilizers for the farmers to use in the next planting season;

'Third, lend money to the tenant farmers during the planting season until two weeks before harvest, in the amount whose total cannot exceed half of the farmer's share of the harvest, and the interest for which should follow that laid down by law;

'Fourth—'

Don Severo didn't continue reading the rest of the demands, for he had already crumpled the paper and thrown it on the ground in front of Dislaw. For his part, Dislaw decided to stand between the rich man and his wife.

'Why did you even accept it and bring it here?' he demanded from the overseer.

'They forced it into my hands earlier, when I was leaving the farm,' explained Dislaw. 'I accepted it so that you could hear about it immediately.'

'If they had brought this list here, they would have seen what they really needed to see!' threatened Don Severo.

'That's not just a challenge but an outright rebellion against us,' Donya Leona said of the demands. 'I told them that I'd take them off the farms the moment they set up a union. What did they do? They set up a union, and now they've even filed a petition. Clearly, they want to see how far we'd go!'

'They're hard-headed now and strong-willed,' the rich man said. 'They're not afraid to go hungry.'

'Because someone is pushing them,' snapped Donya Leona. 'I'm sure that Bandong is behind this, as well as Pablo and that old man Inte. Right, Dislaw?'

'You're right, ma'am,' swiftly answered the overseer. The colour returned to his cheeks, which had become ashen earlier. 'Haven't I told you that Bandong is the adviser of the union? And during the funeral wake, they all ganged up on me.'

'Bandong shouldn't involve himself in the farmers' affairs,' said Don Severo. 'He's the principal of the elementary school. And why does Pablo always take the side opposite to ours? He is also a landowner. Inte should just shut up, since the earthworms will soon eat him up. And Tasyo, Julian, Simon, Blas—all of them grew horns while working on our lands and now, they want to gore us!'

'Let's not allow them to work on our farms. That's it!' decided Donya Leona.

Dislaw was quiet, and then he said, 'If you won't allow them to work on your farms, then no one else will work on your farms.'

'Oh, really?' snapped the rich woman, her eyes flashing with extreme hatred. 'Would the farms die if they don't work on it? I hope lightning strikes them.'

'Shameless people!' said Don Severo, and then he pounded his fist on the table. 'They're challenging me? They will reap what they sow!'

Both the husband and wife kept quiet for a long time, as if weighing in their minds the gravity of the situation. Then, Dislaw coughed and said, 'If I may, I'm going to take my leave.'

'Watch them closely, the tenants on the farms and the squatters on our land—'

'I'll do that,' he said and he was about to leave, but then he bowed down and picked up the piece of paper containing the farmers' wishes. 'What do I do with this?'

'Throw it away,' ordered Don Severo, but when the overseer was about to leave, he said, 'Just leave it here.'

Dislaw put the paper on the table and covered it with an ashtray so the wind would not blow it away.

'Drop by the town hall and tell the chief of police I want to talk to him,' said Donya Leona.

'I'll go there now,' Dislaw said and then he finally left.

That night, the barking of the dogs announced the arrival of a guest in front of the big stone house. Kosme met the guest, Chief Hugo, and brought him in front of the hallway.

Hugo was a corpulent man whose head looked bigger because of his long hair, and his two arms looked like paddles. He looked more like a goon than an agent of the law. He was just a sergeant in the police office, but when he chose Donya Leona to be the godmother at his wedding, he was immediately made the chief of police upon the resignation of his predecessor. He rarely spoke; he used his fists instead of words.

He respectfully kissed the hand of his godmother and godfather.

'Dislaw told me that you were asking for me,' he said as soon as he had sat down.

Donya Leona made him read the list of wishes given by the tenants in the farm.

'This is too much,' said Hugo.

'These people want to exchange places with us,' Donya Leona began. 'They want to give the orders and us to follow them.'

'It's bad for the farmers to acquire a little learning,' said Don Severo in a snide manner. 'During earlier times, when their parents didn't know how to read and write, my parents didn't have any trouble, neither did your father and mother. Am I right, Leona?'

'Well,' the rich woman began in a boastful manner, 'if my parents were still here, they would have been lashed all over with a stingray's tail. And my parents won't stop until they would be crawling and asking for forgiveness. I saw them do that once.'

'The times don't bode well,' agreed the chief of police.

'The world turned upside down during the Second World War and during the arrival of the Americans to liberate us,' Donya Leona said with disappointment at a vanished past. 'The penniless stole and they suddenly had money. The tenants stole the harvest and wanted an equal share of the harvest. The landowners were scared. The farmers bore firearms and used them without heed. The squatters began to occupy private property and never wanted to leave after the war. Have you heard, Hugo, about the case we have filed against the squatters in the hilly terrain?'

'Yes,' said the chief of police. 'It's the topic of everyone's conversation nowadays.'

'What are they saying?'

'That the squatters got a lawyer to defend their case.'

'What will they get even if they have ten lawyers? Reason is on our side.'

'What I heard is that they won't leave, whatever happens.'

'That's the way snakes think,' said Don Severo in a loud voice. 'But can they do that? What will you do, Hugo, as the chief of police, if the judge orders the squatters to leave the place?'

'I will follow the order of the court.'

'Exactly. But what if they fight back?'

Hugo smiled and showed off his two big arms shaped like paddles.

'Then they'll get hurt,' he said firmly. 'Woe to those who would go against the law and fight the police.'

'It has already happened in Manila,' Donya Leona reminded Hugo. 'The squatters couldn't do anything. The police just demolished their huts and that was the end of everything.'

'That's what we'll do in the squatters' area when the order of the judge comes,' said Hugo. 'Operation Demolition.'

'Well done!' Donya Leona said in a happy tone.

Then, she called for Kosme and asked Hugo, 'Have you already eaten your dinner, my godson?'

'Yes, my godmother. I've had dinner by the grace of God.'

'Then, you now have time to drink.' She turned to Kosme and said, 'Bring us a bottle of whiskey and ice from the fridge.'

Kosme returned with the order of the rich woman and gently put the things down for the chief of police. Then another order was issued to him.

'Also take out one sealed bottle of whiskey. I will give it as a gift to my godson.'

'Oh, my godmother, that's too much—' Hugo pretended to say while taking a swig of whiskey from his glass.

'We've a lot of whiskey. And all imported. If you need a bottle, just send word to us.'

'Thank you, my godmother.' And Hugo continued to drink.

The rich husband and wife then narrated to the chief of police their plans for the squatters in the hilly terrain.

'At first, they look like two separate issues,' Don Severo said in a calm tone. 'But in truth, they're just one. Both of them are linked to the issue of land. The farmers want to get the rice harvest; the squatters want to grab the land. What sort of businessman would agree to these conditions, and which government would allow it?'

Hugo would sometimes look up from his copious drinking, to pretend that he was listening intently to his godfather. He would nod and then drink again.

'That's why we have laws, judges and police forces,' continued Don Severo. 'If not, what then would reign over this country?'

Hugo's eyes widened when he saw the vein pulsing under the ears of the rich man.

'What will reign?!' Don Severo repeated.

'Anarchism!' snapped Donya Leona.

'Yes. Troubles, communism, banditry,' added the rich man.

Hugo stood up, as if startled by the series of -isms fired into the air. He swiftly swallowed the whiskey in his mouth, and it was clear that the spirits of anarchism and communism weren't lording over his mind, but the stronger spirit of the whiskey. But he tried to make it appear as if his mind was still clear and his knees not buckling.

'These troubles won't reach us here in Sampilong,' he shouted. 'We won't allow troubles here. It's either them or me. But my dear godfather, my dear godmother,' and then he bowed slightly and showed them his revolver, touching it, 'I'm a sharpshooter.'

Don Severo also stood up and managed to get Hugo to sit down again. He tried to get the empty glass from the chief of police, but his hand was tightly gripping it, and instead, the guest grabbed the whiskey again and poured it into his glass. And then, he took another swig without pausing to breathe.

32

The hours were moving swiftly, but Chief Hugo did not seem to notice it, while the Grande husband and wife kept on looking at each other, as if to say it was time to end the meeting with the chief of police. Donya Leona didn't think it seemly to continue conversing with a drunken man, especially the chief of the police forces.

Nevertheless, Don Severo emphasized to the chief of police the real feelings of his family regarding the matters at hand. 'We'll drive the squatters away,' he said.

'Do you ... want it done ... now, my godfather?' the chief asked, seemingly ready to launch into action.

'When the order from the judge has been handed down,' Don Severo clarified.

'Indeed,' the rich woman said. 'I won't allow the tenants to work again on the farms,' she added.

'I ... am ... here to help ... you, my dear ... godmother,' said Hugo.

'Don't abandon us, my godson,' Donya Leona said.

The chief of police quickly stood up, but almost fell over when he tried to snap his shoes together into place, and then raised his glass as if to make a toast to the couple. Then he put the glass on the table, got the revolver from its holster, making the couple take a step backward, took out the magazine of six bullets, and then put them on his palm as he began counting.

'One, two, three, four,' he counted and while he did so, he pointed at the gun with his forefinger. 'Six bullets, my dear godfather and godmother,' he said, and then he returned the bullets inside the magazine and returned the revolver to its holster. Only then did Don

Severo and Donya Leona breathe a sigh of relief, for they had frozen with fear while watching the actions of the drunken man.

'Six ... only six bullets in this re ... volver. There are other rounds of bullets ... in my ... belt,' he said in a boastful tone. 'Count how many ... heads of the squatters and troublesome farmers ... will ex ... plode.'

The couple allowed the man's drunkenness to dissipate a bit before they said that the meeting was finally over.

'Therefore,' Don Severo said while Hugo leaned on the back of the chair and put his paddle-like right arm on his forehead, 'we've already made ourselves very clear on the matter.'

The chief of police immediately opened his eyes upon hearing the words of the rich man. It seemed that light had finally won over the darkness in his mind, and he said with clarity, 'It's very ... clear, my godfather. You may now sleep without being disturbed, my godmother. Whoever amongst them causes trouble will get it from me.' Then, he put his right arm in front of his neck and made a slashing motion.

He tried to walk as if measuring his sense of balance, until he finally exited through the door. But before he could go downstairs, he turned around and bowed low at the waist.

'Good night,' he said in farewell.

'Accompany him downstairs,' Donya Leona told Kosme, who was then entering the room, 'And he left his bottle of whiskey,' she added, pointing at the bottle for the servant to carry to the chief of police.

Don Severo was laughing at his wife when the chief of police finally wended his way out of the front yard, followed by the loud barking of the dogs. 'If they're unlucky, they'll meet Hugo in this state of mind,' he said, referring to the troublesome farmers and squatters. 'Those who cross paths with a drunken man are dead meat,' he added.

'The dead should be buried,' said Donya Leona while humming a tune as she went to the kitchen.

Hugo was able to return to the police headquarters without any mishap. He asked for a cup to hot water, which he drank, and later washed his face with some warm water. Then, he took a nap for thirty minutes and when he woke up, he was already feeling better.

That night, he ordered two policemen to guard the big stone house. He told them to scrutinize every guest and make sure they weren't carrying guns.

In the meantime, a silence floated in the air, similar to the moments before a strong tempest arrives.

The New Village was peaceful the morning after and the sun blazed over it. But the people were agitated to see Dislaw later at noon, with Kosme and a young man inside a jeep.

The jeep stopped as Tasyo and Simon were passing by. The eyes of the three inside the jeep met those of the two who were walking. Tasyo spoke up first and asked about the list of requests that they had sent over to the Grande family through Dislaw.

'What did your master say?' asked Tasyo, laying emphasis on the word 'master', which annoyed the caretaker.

'I don't know if they've an answer or not,' Dislaw answered with a smirk.

'Because we won't work unless there's an answer.'

'I also don't know if they still want you to work the farms or not.'

'Is that so?'

'Yes.'

'They're really tough, huh?'

'They own the land.'

'If not for us, snakes will roam on their land.'

'Even if snakes roam there, they won't die of hunger.'

'Perhaps, because they became rich feeding off the blood of the poor.'

'The Grandes were already rich from the beginning.'

'There's no such thing as inborn wealth—everyone was born naked.'

'They didn't steal anything.'

'No?'

'No.'

'That's what you say.'

Tasyo laughed loudly and was followed by Simon. Dislaw was so annoyed, his temper flared up. He jumped out of the jeep and confronted the two.

'What are you laughing about?'

'Why do you look as if you're the butt of the joke?' he said to the caretaker, whom he used to talk to with deference.

'You're too much,' said Dislaw.

'You're the one who's too much, and thus should be put to order.'

'What do you mean?'

'Only lightning doesn't take revenge.'

'You'll just get in trouble.'

Both of them would have lunged at each other if Simon had not prevented them from doing so. Kosme also got down from the jeep to prevent the fight. Tasyo knew that his arms were strong and he could easily trash Dislaw like a sack of rice. But Dislaw knew that his revolver was fully loaded and just one bullet would stop the rashness of this foolish farmer. It was good that cooler heads intervened.

Dislaw climbed back into his jeep while Tasyo continued walking. But when the jeep was beside Tasyo, the caretaker let fly another threat.

'One day, you'll get your due desserts,' he said, and then he swiftly drove off in the jeep.

From thereon, things became more tense. Dislaw rarely ventured into the farms and even if he did, he came in the company of two or three people. He also kept a gun handy inside the jeep, aside from his own revolver.

The humidity of the air was palpable in both the old barrio and the New Village. But the heat didn't come from the sun that was quickly setting, but from the intensity of the feelings welling up within the people.

The villagers temporarily stopped their former habits of talking freely and openly to their neighbours. These days, the voice of the village crier who announced the latest news and happenings had gone missing. The boisterous crowds that used to gather in the barber shop and in front of the variety store had disappeared. People still talked, of course, but only amongst themselves and with much care. At times, they communicated only through signs.

'Please don't spread the word,' was the usual request made to those who had just been given the latest news.

'Go only when the sun has set,' was the usual advice given to someone with whom one had set a meeting.

The villagers had taken away the calm veneer and now went about their business carrying a sharp machete. It seemed as if when a man set out for the day, he didn't expect to meet a friend, but rather an enemy, who might challenge his masculinity.

It was already time to plow the fields and prepare the seedbeds to plant the grains of rice, but the water buffalo just kept on gaining weight grazing in the pastures, and the plow that was hanging in the open space under the huts began to rust. It seemed that people were trying to postpone their work or were determined not to work at all, anymore.

Meanwhile, in the New Village, the other people continued working in the home industries, but they no longer worked in the centre during the afternoons and evenings. Even the children couldn't be seen roaming the hot and dusty streets. Only Andres and Marcos bustled about, bringing raw materials and collecting finished products. And then afterwards, they would meet with Bandong.

On the other hand, the big gate in the front yard of the Grandes' stone house remained closed, and there was no hour when the ferocious dogs weren't let loose to guard the empty spaces. The two policemen whom Chief Hugo had assigned were always there, every day, aside from the security guards whom Dislaw had hired from the provincial capital.

One of the police jeeps kept paroling every day, as if it was on surveillance and tracking down an assassin, and its three or four occupants always carried rifles that were to be used at the first opportunity.

'It seemed we're back in the time of war,' said Blas at night in the secret place where they met.

'It seems like we're under the rule of the Japanese military forces again,' answered Simon.

'We're like guerrillas again,' said Tasyo.

Suddenly, a long whistle tore through the silence of the night. The light in the hut died and one by one, the farmers walked away in silence from their secret meeting place as the thick curtain of darkness fell.

33

One morning, Mayor Bartolo was seen rushing to the big stone house. Even though he hadn't set an appointment, the Grande husband and wife were eager to meet with the mayor of Sampilong.

When they were face to face, Mayor Bartolo said he was worried about what was happening. 'Fragile peace hung at the end of a thread,' he said. He was the chief executive; he was supposed to keep the peace and order in the town. But this issue lay not in his hands but in the hands of the Grande husband and wife. It also lay in the hands of the farmers and the squatters.

Could there be no peaceful resolution to these troubles? Could the two opposing forces not find a middle ground?

'There are many nights when I can't sleep,' said the mayor, 'and white hair had begun to grow on my head.' He blamed this on the deep troubles caused by the issue on the farm and of land ownership.

Mayor Bartolo was Don Severo's cousin and Donya Leona was his cousin-in-law. He reminded them that, for obvious reasons, he would side with them. He knew—and had evidence to prove it—about the acts of the chief of police. But if things came to a head, who would lose more? May God not let it happen, but if the troubles continued to fester in the town, the terribly poor farmers and the homeless squatters wouldn't suffer more. These people were only looking for someone who could help them. But the Grande family would be at the losing end, because they were a big and prominent family and people in the whole town looked up to them.

That was why if Don Severo and Donya Leona would agree, he would like to talk to the farmers led by Tasyo. He would say that the Grande family was willing to meet with the farmers' representative or with Tasyo himself, to study their list of requests. Moreover, he would meet with Andres and the squatters and tell them that the Grande family wasn't closing its doors on the discussion over the land in New Village.

'Believe me when I say that a good discussion will lead to good results,' said the mayor, who was filled with fervent hopes for a peaceful resolution of the issues.

The Grande husband and wife listened intently to the suggestions of the mayor and when he was finished, Don Severo asked, 'Do you already know the demands of the farmers?'

'Hugo has told me about it.'

'First, we can't recognize their union,' the landlord said firmly. 'It will just cause further troubles.'

'We've already had a bad experience with that in the past,' added Donya Leona.

The mayor lit a cigarette, took a drag and then released a wreath of smoke, before speaking. 'I've a different opinion,' he said. 'If I've land, I will allow people to form a union.'

'Huh?' the Grande husband and wife almost spoke at the same time and they scrutinized whether the mayor was pulling their legs or not.

'You can say that because you don't have a farmland,' said Don Severo.

'Believe it or not,' the mayor insisted. 'Look. If there's a union, then I won't have difficulty dealing with different kinds of people, because one policy would bind them all. Second, I'll know what they feel, because it would be brought to my attention. It's similar to the petition that they had sent to you. I'm not saying I would give them everything they want, no dice. They'll have to go through the eye of a needle. Third, I'll use the union as an instrument for good fellowship, and this will lead to a higher yield in the harvest, better care for my farm, et cetera.'

'Our experiences have been the opposite of what you just said,' said Donya Leona.

'Do you know the reason?' asked the mayor and he answered his own question. 'Because you're at odds with the union. You fight with them and don't want to recognize them. That's what you're doing even now.'

'Therefore—'

'You've to deal with them.'

'Put them on the same pedestal as us? Treat them like business associates, is that what you mean?' The vein began to throb beneath the left ear of Don Severo.

'You deal with them and they'll be like meek sheep. That never fails, my cousin.'

The Grande husband and wife reflected on the suggestions of the mayor, all of which were against their beliefs. For a long time, they had ignored the farmers' pleas, since listening to them would diminish their stature and giving in to them would be treated as an act of surrender. It would make them look bad and, therefore, they weren't keen on doing it.

But on the other hand, they also thought about the delicate situation that hinged on peace and order, and how they would be on the losing end if things went haywire. What greater tragedies could befall those who've nothing to eat? And weren't these people their tenants and their servants? People who would immediately follow their orders and keep quiet when scolded. Why were they afraid to talk to their tenant farmers? Would they lose in a rational discussion? Would they be at the losing end in a battle of wits?

That was why Don Severo's tone of voice softened when he spoke again to the mayor.

'Very well then, since you insist—'

'For the good of everyone,' said Mayor Bartolo.

'You may bring Tasyo here,' Don Severo decided.

'But only Tasyo,' said the rich woman.

'The others might join him, like Simon and Julian.'

'Very well then. Three people.'

'How about the squatters?' the mayor asked.

'We'll deal with them at another time.'

'You may talk to them at another time, but I might tell them that you'd like to meet with them, too. We can set the date later.'

'If that is what's good in this situation.'

The lines that had furrowed the forehead of Mayor Bartolo vanished when he left the front yard of the Grande family after their two-hour meeting. He believed that in that brief time, he had lessened the tension in the town because he had persuaded the landowners to meet with the farmers and the squatters regarding their issues. He was hoping that by meeting with each other, both parties would arrive at a consensus that would be amenable to everyone.

Mayor Bartolo was telling the truth when he said that he was indeed partial toward the Grandes. Not only because they were his relatives, but also because of matters involving his livelihood and politics. The honour and dignity of his office was at stake and his name hung in the balance, because if trouble erupted and blood flowed, he would be held responsible by the powers-that-be and everything would fall on his head as the town's chief executive.

Therefore, he was keen that the two parties meet on common ground. And it seemed that he wouldn't fail. That was why he was smiling widely and silently giving himself a pat on his shoulder for a job well done, as he returned to the municipal hall in the centre of the town.

That very same afternoon, Mayor Bartolo called for Tasyo and his group, as well as Andres and his associates. He told them that the Grande husband and wife had agreed to meet with them. The mayor reminded them that he wouldn't allow the town to descend into chaos and the government would maintain peace and order, no matter who got hurt in the process of doing so. He said that in his opinion, a civilized discourse was better than hurling warnings and threats as if the opposing forces were roosters girding for battle in the cockpit.

'Isn't honey sweeter than vinegar?' the mayor asked the squatters and farmers, in a rhetorical manner.

'You should tell them that, Mayor,' Tasyo said. 'All of us here are now lying prostrate and all we want is to stand up.'

Mayor Bartolo used a different tactic to persuade the poor people of his town to mend fences with the Grande family.

'The Grande family is rich,' he began. 'They won't go hungry if nobody works on their farms. They've other sources of income and various businesses in this province, as well as in Manila. But you've nothing else to lean on, except this farm. You'll lose your livelihood and your families will suffer.'

'Indeed, we already lack so many things,' answered the leader of the farmers, 'and we're even deep in debt. We're just seeking redressal because our families are suffering.'

The mayor advised the farmers' group to present their requests to the Grande husband and wife during the meeting, aside from those already listed in their petition, but that they should do so with restraint.

That was the same advice he gave to Andres—that when their turn came, they should strive to arrive at a consensus with the Grande family.

'We're naturally patient and restrained,' Andres said, 'but we can't let it pass when our very beings are insulted.'

They all met under a trellis of the fragrant milegwas flowers with smooth and wide leaves, in the front yard of the Grandes' big house— the landlords and the farmers' representatives. Mayor Bartolo came with Tasyo, Simon, Julian and Blas. Dislaw met them at the gate and brought them to the location of the meeting. Then, he fetched the Grande husband and wife, who were waiting on the first floor of their big house.

The mayor was glad at the beginning of the meeting, for Don Severo and Donya Leona warmly greeted the farmers and even enquired after their families. Even Dislaw and Tasyo shook hands, as if they had not had an altercation recently.

'My wife and I decided to meet you here,' began Don Severo, 'because it's cool and windy here. The fresh air might be able to help us, right, Mayor?'

Those in front of him agreed and gave him a smile.

Don Severo said they had read the list of requests but before he could respond to them, he would like to mention some things. He narrated the story of their working together in the farms since the time of their parents to themselves to their children and future grandchildren; the way they treated each other not as strangers but as familiars; the sincerity and trust they have afforded each other.

Then, he talked about the obligations of the landlord, the taxes imposed by the government, the expenses of the operation of the farms, the charitable contributions and donations given to tenant farmers for all their needs, including the loans that were given and would never be completely paid off.

'Now that the taxes have risen and the yield of the farms is low, you want to add to our burdens?' he said in an accusing tone. 'Have you forgotten the ways of our old relationship?'

The members of the union were stunned by the direction being taken by Don Severo. Tasyo recalled that in the analysis done by the farmers' leaders and the early organizations of farmers' groups, the issue of paternalism by the landlord often showed up. The idea that the relationship between the landlord and his tenants was like that between a parent and a child, handing down old clothes, a few doses of medicine, donations for the dead, a little charitable deed on this or that occasion. But over and beyond everything, the landlord refused to give social justice to the farmers, as well as the right to think freely for themselves and act accordingly.

This was uppermost in Tasyo's mind when he answered Don Severo.

'I won't deny everything that you've said,' Tasyo began. 'But we aren't asking for pity, nor charity. We are asking for justice. The pity and charity are good deeds that come from you. On the other hand, our cause is social justice, and it's a right that we're seeking.'

Don Severo's face turned red at what he heard, so he quickly shot back.

'In the farms, you don't own anything except your sweat. Everything else belongs to us, and don't speak to me about undeniable rights.'

Don Severo swiftly stood up, as if he was already ending the discussion. Tasyo and his group also stood up. The mayor tried to intervene, but his attempt was unsuccessful, for it was like trying to mix water and oil. The meeting quickly ended like a rice seed swallowed up by a worm.

34

Bandong felt a mixture of deep sadness and secret delight upon hearing the news that Teacher Putin had died at a hospital in Manila. He was saddened by the passing of a bright teacher and an honourable leader. Almost single-handedly, Teacher Putin had improved the elementary school in Sampilong after the Japanese Imperial Forces had left during the Second World War. On the other hand, Bandong also felt restrained delight, because now he could be appointed as the principal of the school, and not just in a temporary capacity. It had not yet been six months since Pina had made a promise to him, a promise that was occasioned by the grave illness of the principal.

Nana Oris uttered 'Jesus Mary Joseph!' upon hearing that Teacher Putin had died, and then said a short prayer for the dead.

'Poor Teacher Putin,' she said. 'When will he be buried?'

'His remains will be brought here,' Bandong said. 'His widow will decide on his burial date.' The family of Teacher Putin had a house in the centre of town.

The old woman looked at her nephew and said something filled with hope.

'So you will now be the permanent principal, right, Bandong?'

'If God wills it, auntie.'

That night, the young man visited the house of the woman he loved. The recently departed principal was a friend of Pina's father's and they helped each other at the PTA.

'We'll honour him during the funeral,' Mang Pablo suggested.

'Indeed, we should,' agreed Bandong.

Afterward, the old man expressed the hope that Bandong would be appointed as the permanent principal of the elementary school, so that he could also broach the subject of his suggestions to improve the school. Bandong said that the first thing he wanted to do was to give space to the young children of appropriate age, who would be enrolled at the elementary school.

'The children become more numerous and the school becomes smaller.'

Mang Pablo believed that this issue should also be attended to by the leaders of Sampilong.

'The government shirks its responsibility as long as there are unschooled children roaming the streets,' Bandong said, and the head of the PTA agreed with him.

When Pina left her room and entered the living quarters, her father stood up to leave and give privacy to his daughter and their guest. Bandong thought that the young woman seemed more beautiful than before.

After the warm greetings, the young principal said in a sombre tone, 'Teacher Putin has returned, but inside a coffin.'

'A good teacher has died,' Pina said sadly, and then she added, 'He didn't even make it through six months, right?'

In their minds, they recalled what they had earlier discussed about this issue, in relation to Bandong's proposal to Pina.

'I told you that six months would be a long time,' Bandong said with a hint of accusation.

'I hoped he would recover and regain good health within six months,' the young woman said in a half-whisper.

'I asked you then, what if Teacher Putin didn't recover and you said your answer would not be affected by how long or short the next six months might run.'

'That's true.'

'It's the sixth month now, Pina.'

'It's not yet enough ...' the young woman said, while thinking, 'And why are you in a hurry? Teacher Putin still has to be buried, you'll be appointed as the permanent principal and classes will start soon. You'll be facing a mountain of challenges.'

'You're the first of my priorities.'

'You must do first things first.'

'But Pina, you're—'

'Later,' she said, with what seemed like finality.

'You always make me suffer and offer me no sympathy,' Bandong complained.

Pina gave him a little smile that lifted the corners of her mouth and she said, 'But I thought I was helping you.'

'In what way?'

'By giving you time.'

'Or wasting time ... letting the days slip by just like that ... every time we postpone what should be decided on now ...' the young man said with feeling.

Pina didn't respond.

'I need your love,' the young man said. 'I can't walk in the dark when I'm not strong, my faith falters.'

'I might become a burden on you,' she said to divert the conversation. 'What I mean is, by giving you time, you can focus on your obligations at the elementary school, since you're currently completely free and unhindered by—'

'Why, don't you agree with the things that I'm doing?' Bandong butted in.

'I agree and I want you to succeed.'

'Then why do you leave me high and dry?'

'Do you want the prize to come ahead of the victory?' Pina gave him a meaningful smile.

'I understand you,' and he let out a deep sigh, 'but you can't take it away from me if I'm filled with anxiety.'

'You've nothing to worry about,' the young woman said, and then she gazed at him.

'My rival is strong and powerful.'

'Who?' Pina pretended she didn't know.

'Who else?

'I can't be taken by force.'

'I thought so, too.'

'Then, what are you worried about?'

'You don't need to ask,' Bandong said. 'You're aware that I have loved you ever since ... That you're very important to me. Why won't

I be afraid when you still don't belong to me? Ah, Pina, I'm always worried about what my rivals would do—they who've more to offer than me. I also envy the wind that plays with your hair, the sunlight that kisses your cheeks, the garland of flowers hanging around your neck, and all the other things touched by your hands.'

Pina laughed a little and said, 'Are you reciting a poem for me, Bandong?'

'Yes, Pina,' the young man admitted, 'because what you're hearing is the throbbing of my heart, the prayer of my soul.'

'Until when will this last, I wonder?'

'Until the end of time.'

'If so ...' Pina restrained herself from saying what she had wanted to say, and just looked out of the window.

'If so?' Bandong enclosed Pina's right hand within his hand. But Pina pulled her hand away and stood apart from him, although she had left a small, white and fragrant handkerchief in his hand. Pina rushed back to her room.

Just then, Aling Sabel came out from the kitchen, bringing with her some snacks for the guest.

'You're all alone here,' the old woman said. 'Where's Pina?'

'She's doing something inside,' Bandong answered.

The young woman went out of her room again after Bandong had taken a drink. Her smile wasn't generous and tears seemed to have coursed down her cheeks. She had put a fresh layer of powder on her face.

The two didn't speak, but their hearts did all the talking for them. Later on, the young man asked permission to leave. When he reached out for Pina's right hand, he said in a gentle tone, 'I'll now carry your handkerchief around with me.'

'If that's what you want,' she said, the words barely audible from her lips.

'I'll take care of it, as if it were pawned to me,' said the young man.

But Pina's lips remained sealed and the only answer she gave to him was a meaningful look.

Bandong went downstairs but felt as if he was floating above the ground. The moonlight shone like silk. And the light coming from the two stars looking out of the window, that the young man saw when he looked back, was enough to guide him as he walked home. It was a gift from her, which the darkness could never snatch.

Bandong saw Mang Pablo taking in the air in front of their house and he bade the old man goodbye.

'I heard that the discussion about the farm didn't turn out well,' said the old man as Bandong was turning to leave.

'That's what I also heard.'

'How about the issue in the New Village?' the old man asked.

'That's also unclear,' the young teacher answered.

Mang Pablo was shaking his head when Bandong finally left. By then, the moon had hidden beneath the clouds and the cold northern wind had begun to blow.

'This isn't good, this isn't good at all,' Mang Pablo said in despair, and he wasn't just talking about the weather but also about the threat of a tempest on the farms and in the New Village.

The old man turned and swiftly ascended the wooden stairs.

35

Several days had passed but Mayor Bartolo didn't follow up on matters with Andres regarding what they had agreed on earlier. The squatters also waited for their turn, but later, they were told that the meeting with the Grande family may no longer come through.

And that was, indeed, the decision of Don Severo and Donya Leona in the face of the sad result of their meeting with the farmers' leaders. They assigned Dislaw to inform the mayor about their decision.

'It's hard to deal with fools,' said Don Severo to his wife.

'We wouldn't even bother talking to them if Bartolo wasn't so insistent,' the rich woman said, as if blaming the mayor for what had happened. 'If they can't follow our conditions, then they should leave. Could they take the farm when they finally leave?'

'That's why I also do not want to meet with the squatters anymore,' added the rich man.

'What for? It will just be a waste of time.'

'Because their situations are different,' clarified Don Severo. 'The farmers have filed a petition against us, while we're the ones who have charged the squatters in court.'

'But you said they're the same: both issues have to do with land. Why do we have to include the squatters? We've known these tenant farmers since childhood and now they're goring us with their horns. What more can be expected of these squatters? They seemed to have come from hell itself. They'll have to deal with the judge.'

The husband and wife decided that it would indeed be wise to let the judge take care of the matter. Don Severo blithely dismissed Dislaw's report that the squatters had hired the services of a lawyer, and it was the meddlesome Bandong who had found the lawyer for them.

'They'll lose even the shirts on their backs,' was Don Severo's reaction, and then he laughed.

'But they barely have clothes on their backs, so what shirts can they still lose?' snapped Donya Leona.

'What I mean is that they'll grovel all the more. Have you seen a rich man lose against the poor in court? The rich can end up poor after the case is finished, but how can the poor win a case when they don't even have money to hire a good lawyer? Impossible!'

'Then why did the judge allow the case to proceed?'

'I don't know what show he's putting on,' Don Severo said and then he frowned. 'Maybe he wants to meet with me again?'

'You already met here in the house and even went out together one night. What else does he need?'

'That is okay. Didn't we go to Manila together, the other night? Myself, along with the judge and Attorney Amargoso?'

'I remember that you didn't return the change for the 500 pesos I gave you that night.'

'Change?' and his eyes widened. 'Oh, 500 pesos isn't enough. Will the car move if there is not enough petrol?'

***

The remains of the deceased principal were brought to Sampilong, and were transferred to the elementary school from his house, for the honours. Tinoy and his friends met at the barber shop on their way to the funeral wake that night.

Tasyo, Julian, Simon and Blas came from the barrio, while Andres, Marcos and Kiko came from the squatters' area. They were going to attend the programme that the PTA had organized for Teacher Putin.

The two groups greeted each other and gave updates in a spirit of camaraderie and joy.

'The mayor didn't meet with us again,' Andres told the farmers. 'He just relayed to us the message that we should just settle everything in court, with the judge.'

'That's better,' said Tasyo. 'It's just a waste of time to deal with people with crooked ways of thought. He called for us and, according to the mayor, he wanted to discuss our petition, but he just gave us a sermon filled with insults and blame.'

'Isn't it enough that both our groups met with the mayor at the town hall? In short, nothing came of the mayor's plan.'

'What will we do now?'

'The red flag is up.'

'Should we continue the fight?'

'Yes and may the stronger party win.'

Later, Tasyo repeated his suggestion for the farmers and the squatters to join forces so that they could fight together, since they both dealt with the same issue of land.

'We're together in the fight against the Japanese during the Second World War,' the farmers' leader recalled. 'The war has ended, but the oppression and injustice continue.' Tasyo stopped for a while when Tinoy pointed towards Dislaw, who was driving past in a jeep then, going around the town square.

'Bad deeds are bad deeds,' he continued, 'whether done by the Japanese, the Americans, or our fellow Filipinos. Evil isn't measured by the slant of the eyes or the bow shape of one's legs. It should be stopped dead in its tracks. That's why it's time for us to join forces.'

They immediately accepted Tasyo's suggestion after Andres had told them how the squatters felt about the whole situation.

'We're amenable to joining your group, not because your situation is much better than ours,' Andres said. 'But because we believe in the unity of the oppressed, and for us in the labouring class, it would be sheer madness not to help each other. We're called squatters, trash people, snakes roaming a land that isn't ours. But my dear friends, we're also Christians and we're afraid of the wrath of God. But who are the ones destroying the Seventh Commandment of the Lord, which is "Thou shall not steal"?'

Andres' eyes roved around the people gathered during the meeting, and when no one piped up, he mentioned the real thieves.

'Not Tinoy, the barber, who expends sweat for every grain of rice he eats. Not you, Tasyo, or anyone else amongst the four of you, for even if the harvest is bountiful, your families still suffer from the pangs of hunger. Not us, the squatters, who built our huts on three hands' spans of land just to be able to live. They're the puppets who stole lands that are so vast a crow cannot fly over them; such is their greed. Who stole the lands? Is it the person who stole a can of rice grains, or the one who stored corn and rice in his granary, and would only sell them once the prices were sky-high?'

The words rushed out of Andres lips swiftly, like water flowing from an open faucet. But they served like sharp knives wounding the feelings of those listening to him. That was why he became fervent in his wish.

Just then, a group of people who were going to the funeral wake of Teacher Putin passed by, and Tinoy reminded everyone that it might be time for them to leave.

'I'm not driving you away,' the barber said.

However, Andres didn't stop until he had put an exclamation point at the end of his speech.

'We agree,' he said. 'My two associates, Marcos and Kiko, and myself represent the New Village.'

'Now, it's a done deal,' answered Blas. 'The three people present here represent the farmers. I just pinch-hit when someone is absent for meetings.'

'Me, too!' said a laughing Tinoy to Blas.

All of them wended their way to the public elementary school, but they continued talking while walking.

'At first, we should have a group that will form the framework of our organization,' said Tasyo. 'For example, a group of seven people. Three from your group, Andres, and three from ours. The seventh one should be the presiding officer and for this position, we can ask—' then he stopped for a while, dredging his mind for a name. 'Ah, yes, perhaps we can request Teacher Bandong to join us?'

'Teacher Bandong would be perfect,' said Andres swiftly. 'But he might not agree. He already leads a cooperative and now, he is going to be the permanent principal.'

'We can still try to convince him. He is our only friend who has the ability to preside over us, and he is someone we can all trust.'

'We don't have any doubts about that. He's the enemy of injustice and a friend of the oppressed. But I was just wondering if we should get him involved ...'

'Let's leave it up to him.'

The programme started as they reached the school and all the seats had already been taken. A platform had been placed in the front part of the hallway, and the coffin was set there. Around the coffin were wreaths of flowers from several organizations, as well as from the leaders and friends of the departed. The memories of the family in the shape of a cross of fresh flowers was placed on top of the grey coffin.

The widow sat in the front row, between Mayor Bartolo and Mang Pablo, who led the group that would honour the deceased principal. Pina, on the hand, sat between Bandong and Dislaw. At the end of the first row sat a teacher who served as the adviser of the committee that was to honour the deceased.

As happened in similar situations, all the good and noble qualities of the deceased principal were extolled by those who spoke beside his coffin.

'If Teacher Putin were a politician,' Tasyo whispered to Andres, 'the speakers giving eulogies would be forced to tell lies.'

'And what do you think of the mayor's speech?'

'Was he talking about the good qualities of Teacher Putin, or was he talking about himself?' asked Tasyo.

After the programme, Dislaw offered to drop Pina and Mang Pablo home, but Pina thanked him and said that she would stay for a while. She said she would go home with the other people in the barrio. Dislaw threw a dagger look at Bandong and in the flash of his eyes, you could almost see the words 'a mere barrio'.

In a private conversation after most of the people had already left, Tasyo told Bandong about the meeting between the farmers and the squatters. Bandong praised the initiative, but demurred when told he would be the perfect person to lead the Committee of Seven.

'You know I really want to help all of you,' the teacher said, 'but it might be wrong for me to lead the group. Please think about it carefully.'

Then, the teacher gave suggestions on the important steps to be taken by the united group. He said, 'It would be good to fight against the excesses of the landlord, aside from helping each other lead better and more comfortable lives.'

'The women in the barrio can also make money from the home industries,' added Bandong. 'One problem in the farm is lack of income. One suggestion would be to exchange the rice of the farmers for the products made by the squatters in a barter system of trade.'

Tasyo and Andres agreed that it was a good suggestion that would help both groups of people.

At the end, Bandong told the groups that if they wanted to sustain their united organization, they should promise to avoid the path of violence and should always be measured and peaceful in their dealings.

'I was also a guerrilla fighter during the Second World War,' he reminded everyone. 'During wartime, the sword and fire ruled, and force was met with force. But in times of peace, we should use reason as a weapon and the law as the means to obtain our ends.'

Tasyo and Andres said almost in unison that the poor people would always follow the law, but since the laws are crafted by the rich, oftentimes, they go against the laws of nature and of God.

'But what if the laws made by people trample on the laws of God?' asked Andres.

'Then, we should give to God what belongs to God, and unto Caesar what belongs to Caesar,' advised Bandong.

36

An unexpected thing happened at the burial of Teacher Putin. Andres met Ba Inte—or rather, the more proper way to put it would be that Ba Inte found Andres. We could surmise that this might be just an ordinary happening, if it didn't lead to something of a miracle.

'So, you're Andres,' Ba Inte said while looking intently with his still-clear eyes at the face and form of the person who led the New Village. They had already seen each other on several occasions before, but they hadn't had the opportunity to sit down and have a real discussion.

'Yes sir, this is Andres,' the leader Tasyo said with respect, after the oldest farmer had scrutinized him. Bandong had earlier introduced him to Ba Inte.

'I often hear your name during meetings.'

'Likewise, Ba Inte. I also hear yours. Everybody knows you in this town.'

'Because I'm already ancient,' and Ba Inte laughed softly. 'I'm the Methusalem of Sampilong.'

'But you still seem strong, Ba Inte.'

'I'm now like dried-up earth. I'm already over the hill, young man. If you only saw me in the prime of my life.' The old man looked far, as if tracking times past. 'In this town, I was the only one who was not oppressed by Captain Melchor, the fierce father of Donya Leona.'

Ba Inte still had a full head of hair and it had turned silver. His skin was bronzed and on his forehead and cheeks, you could see the lines wrought by the years. But he still stood straight and only leaned forward a little because he was carrying a cane. The arthritis had sapped a lot of his inherent strength.

Andres recalled his mother and his ancestors. His mother was born in Sampilong and his ancestors used to own land there. Ba Inte might still remember them. His mother was named Martha, but he didn't know the name of his ancestors. His mother also mentioned his ancestors' name to him, something attached to the appellation of 'Kabesa', but Andres' memories had been erased by the passage of the years.

He resumed his conversation with Ba Inte.

'Ba Inte,' Andres said and his left arm supported the old man, who had begun to walk. Ba Inte was holding a cane made from Chinese bamboo. 'I'm the son of someone who's also from Sampilong.'

'Huh?' the old man was surprised. 'I had thought you only came here during the Second World War.'

'Indeed, and we came here because my mother was born here.'

'Who's your mother?'

'Her name is Martha.'

The old man stopped for a while and thought. From amidst his treasure trove of memories, he tried to recall the name that Andres had mentioned.

'Martha ... Martha ...' But it seemed like a telephone cord without a connection. Ba Inte shook his head.

'I can't recall anyone named Martha,' he said.

Andres then repeated the story of his mother. That she was a young child when she left for Manila. She was an orphan and her ancestor had taken care of her. This ancestor had vast tracts of land in Sampilong and was indeed a rich man. But he became poor and Martha didn't know what had happened. And then he died, with the reason for the loss of the lands still unclear to everyone. When the ancestor died, Martha was brought to Manila—this Martha who then became Andres' mother. She grew up in the city and got married there.

'Is your mother still alive?' asked Ba Inte.

'She's been dead for a long time.'

'What's the name of your ancestor?'

'She mentioned it to me, but I've forgotten it.' Andres' palms touched his face, trying to dredge a name from his memories. 'Oh, yes. All I know is that the word Kabesa is attached to his name.'

It was Ba Inte's turn to reflect. He mentioned some names.

'Kabesang Juan, Kabesang Pemyo, Kabesang Tunying, Kabesang Resong—'

Suddenly, he lifted his cane and when he put it down, it was pointing at a small mound of earth on the road. He looked at Andres' face intently.

'Wait a minute, it might be Kabesang Resong, ah.'

Andres just kept silent.

'Didn't your mother say Resong—Kabesang Resong?'

The leader of the squatters tried to recall the name, when suddenly, Ba Inte made a clucking sound with his tongue. He released his hand from Andres' grip and tapped him on the shoulder, saying, 'You're right!' and to prove that he was on the right track, he added, 'Your name is Andres. And Resong is a nickname for Andres. Didn't your mother tell you why you were named Andres?'

Andres' heart throbbed in his chest, but he could only answer, 'I don't know' as to whether or not his mother had told him or not why he was given that name. Ba Inte looked at Andres' face again, this time more intently, gazing deeply at it, without batting an eyelash. Then, the old man put his hand on the shoulder of the younger one.

'There's a facial similarity,' Ba Inte concluded. 'Your eyes, your mouth.' And then he finally rendered his judgment, 'You're indeed the grandson of Kabesang Resong.'

'How about my mother, do you still remember her?' Andres asked.

The old man quickly answered, without any shred of doubt.

'Oh, yes, the young girl whom Kabesang Resong was always carrying in his arms.'

Before they separated after the burial, Ba Inte told Andres to see him at the first opportunity.

'I'll be there,' Andres promised.

***

Ba Inte always woke up early. But he still didn't have time to go down and take a walk to soak in the sunshine by the time Andres was already arriving with his wife Sedes.

'Have you had breakfast?' asked the old man of his two guests.

'Yes, we're already done, sir, thank you.'

Andres introduced his wife Sedes to Ba Inte. She had also wanted to personally meet him whose name had been on the lips of all the farmers and squatters. She was excited to hear from the old farmer himself the extent of the truth of what Andres had told her about his mother.

They sat down inside the house. Ba Inte's house was old like himself and it was made of different materials. The posts looked ancient and hewed from hardwood that had grown in the forest; the roof was made of thatch; the walls and floor from wide plywood the colour of chestnuts. His house stood near the old river. Ba Inte owned his farm, which he had inherited from his father, and which his father had inherited from his ancestors, but now they didn't have any heirs. Ba Inte never got married.

Indeed, the house was already old, but like Ba Inte, it was still solid and strong, despite the whiplashes of time.

The grey-haired farmer stood up and from his wide window, then he pointed his farm to Andres and Sedes.

'Since my arthritis started, I haven't been able to attend to my farm,' he said.

From the window, one could also see a vast expanse of land made of different plots that had dried and cracked. The remaining stalks from the previous harvest still stood on the farm, but their colour had begun to resemble the brown earth. Small shrubs had overrun parts of the farm. It could be noticed that since the last rice was harvested, no hand had plowed the land and prepared it for planting.

'That vast land until the wide parts beyond—all of them belong to the Grande family in this town,' said Ba Inte.

'A crow can't even fly over the vast lands,' Andres said to himself in admiration, and then wondered, 'But why do they still want to grab from us the hilly terrain formerly overgrown with cogon grasses?'

They returned to their seats. Ba Inte expressed delight at the couple's visit, because they could then discuss a very serious matter.

'I've no more doubts in my mind,' Ba Inte continued, 'that indeed, Martha was the name of Kabesang Resong's granddaughter.'

He showed Andres a thick book of lists that contained names, dates, numbers and other details of various people.

'I retrieved this from my old wooden trunk,' said Ba Inte.

Andres looked at the item that Ba Inte had pointed out, and later asked Sedes to read it as well, 'Food prepared for the feast of Kabesang Resong's granddaughter (Martha). 26 October.'

'That's my own handwriting,' said the old man.

After Andres had looked at the list and returned it to him, Ba Inte said, 'Thank God that the grandson of Kabesang Resong is alive. That's easy to prove, and we'll do it.'

Ba Inte dipped into his memories. Then, he narrated the things that he remembered about Kabesang Resong, his kind treatment of the farmers, the townspeople's love for him, and his relationship with Captain Melchor's father. Andres and Sedes listened with rapt attention and didn't interfere with flow of the old man's memories.

'But it's wrong to say that Kabesang Resong became poor and died because of unexplained circumstances,' Ba Inte said firmly. 'He was rich until the very end, but he suddenly died and left no last will and testament. Because your mother was a minor and she lived far away, the Spanish father of Captain Melchor contrived a document to show that Kabesang Resong's land had been pawned to the Spanish family. That was easy to do during those times.'

'So, my mother's story is true?' asked Andres, his eyes filled with wonder.

'More or less.'

'See, Sedes?' he said, turning to his wife who had always doubted the veracity of his stories.

'I'd thought that this story was already a closed book,' said Ba Inte. 'But now you're here, Andres—seemingly like Kabesang Resong in new form. Thus, the book will be opened again.'

'You mean to tell me that I can reclaim those lands?' Andres said with extreme excitement.

'What reclamation?' Ba Inte answered. 'You won't only get back the lands, you'll also get back the profits from the collective harvest and the interest that has accrued over the years. You're the real heir of those lands.'

'Oh, my God!' exclaimed Andres and embraced his wife. Both of them were gripped with a feeling they couldn't place, whether deep joy or confusion. They were both on the brink of tears.

'You're rich, Andres—Don Andres!' said Ba Inte and he pressed the hand of the squatter.

37

'You're rich, Andres. Rich, rich, rich!'

The words of Ba Inte tolled like bells in the mind of Andres, almost making him deaf, telling the squatter that, he was, indeed, an heir to vast lands. He wasn't startled by the prospects of unknown wealth, but with the sudden change that felt like a miracle, similar to the change in Aladdin's life. It was very much like a dream—difficult to understand and stunning.

Andres looked again at the tracks of land that, according to Ba Inte, were owned by the Grande family, and asked, 'Which of those lands used to belong to my ancestor?'

Ba Inte spread his right hand, seemingly to encompass the land: 'Half of that. And your ancestor owned land in other parts of the town as well. Perhaps, he even owned the hilly terrain that used to be overgrown with cogon grasses, where you now live.'

After that, all of them lapsed into silence. For a few minutes, the old farmer and his guests reflected within themselves about the possible consequences of what they had just discovered.

Ba Inte looked back and dipped again into the well of his memories, when he was still very young and Captain Melchor and Kabesang Resong were already advanced in years. He was witness to the opposite character traits of the two old men. The first acted like a king, ruling over his kingdom with a severe hand. Meanwhile, the second understood the plight of his tenant farmers, who planted the rice and nurtured it to fruition, as well as the plight of his sharecroppers, who helped in the harvest and only asked to be paid in sacks of rice. While he was still young, he was deciding which footsteps to follow in running his family's own land. He decided to follow the ones charted by Kabesang Resong, whose dealings with the farmers and exemplar in life he had kept to since then.

'There was a big age gap between Kabesang Resong and I, but he had always been kind to me,' recalled Ba Inte.

On the one hand, Andres was ruminating on the big and startling changes that would happen in their life, as well as in those of the squatters in the New Village and the farmers in the barrio, if ever they seized back the lands that belonged to his ancestor. But before jumping into a future that wasn't yet sure, Andres first thought of the initial, practical steps that needed to be taken. This, that, those—his mind always worked like this.

On the other hand, Sedes' mind wasn't as complicated, since she only thought about the wishes and feelings which were natural to a woman and a wife like her. She wanted a wide yard with flowering plants, an elegant and comfortable house, the luxuries of life she had seen in the house of the Grande family, a good education for her three children, and the other windfall that, she hoped, would happen as soon as possible.

When Ba Inte spoke again, he said that Andres would have to tread a difficult path, if he intended to start the process of reclaiming the land owned by Kabesang Resong. Similar thoughts flitted in the minds of the husband and wife, roosting there like birds.

'It's not as easy as cutting down stalks of cogon grass,' Ba Inte reminded them. 'It won't be a mere adventure; it will be a real struggle. The Grande family will do everything in their might they won't have to return even a hand's span of land—'

'I can almost see it,' Andres agreed. 'They're even grabbing the small plot of land we do have, what more of the vast lands that they've already stolen?'

That was why Ba Inte and Andres agreed not to make public the fact that the grandson of Kabesang Resong was alive and would reclaim the land grabbed from his ancestor. Andres decided to first initiate the legal processes to settle the issue. He needed to gather all the documents and reports, as well as interview all the witnesses, hire a lawyer, secure themselves and set aside money for the expenses, amongst others. They should surprise the enemy. They needed to do all of these things *and* file a case in court, without anyone spying on them and finding out.

Andres thought not only about his own security but also that of Ba Inte, who would serve as the primary witness in the case. He thought of talking to Kanor to help the old man at all times. If the news spread early and reached the ears of the Grande husband and wife, even Father Pascual or Saint Teofilo himself, of the Catholic Church, wouldn't able to stop the Grandes from resorting to violence. That was the usual route they followed.

'A very sensitive situation,' repeated Ba Inte without fear.

'I'll turn night into day just to secure all of us,' Andres said. He reminded Sedes not to tell anyone in the New Village of the revelation that had come from Ba Inte.

'Whatever happens, this revelation is like a gift from God,' the old farmer happily said.

'I'm lucky that you're still alive, Ba Inte,' Andres said. 'If not, this land-grabbing would've been buried under the earth, and the injustice would just continue on.'

Andres told Ba Inte as they were about to leave, that they would go directly to Teacher Bandong. They sought the permission of the old farmer to inform the young teacher about their recent discovery. Andres felt that Teacher Bandong would help boost their case, aside from the fact that he could be trusted.

'You're right,' agreed Ba Inte. 'Bandong is an honourable person.'

While walking, Andres and Sedes felt as if their lips had been sealed. They walked swiftly, but swifter still were the thoughts running in their heads. Their hearts boomed and they glanced at each other and smiled while their feet half-walked, half-ran on the dusty streets that seemed to grow longer as they traversed them.

'Dear God,' Andres whispered to himself, 'am I just dreaming, or have I finally lost all my senses?' He pinched one of his arms and his fingernail almost broke his skin. But he was awake, and he was sane.

'Oh, holy God filled with grace,' Sedes prayed. 'Please help us and make sure that everything we heard from Ba Inte is true.' She also prayed to the Blessed Virgin Mary in the provincial capital as well as

Jesus of Nazarene in the Quiapo Church and the Our Lady of Peace and Good Voyage at the Antipolo Church.

The couple felt as if they had won the first prize in a lottery, like one who already knows the winning numbers and holds the ticket in their pocket, yet doubts everything until they've received the prize money.

Teacher Bandong was surprised to see them almost out of breath, the words flying from their lips like wild birds. The teacher thought that Andres had come to seek advice about the situation in the New Village, but then Andres said there was another reason for their visit.

Bandong was all alone in the house at the time because Nana Oris had gone to the market to buy food.

At first, Andres was still hesitant to tell Bandong about the real reason for his visit, for it seemed similar to the fantastic metrical stories of faraway kingdoms in ancient times that didn't have a place in the modern world. Bandong might just think that he had lost his wits because they were being driven out of the New Village.

Nevertheless, he gained courage from the sheer concentration with which Bandong listened to him, the young teacher prodding him on to continue when he faltered. At last, Andres was able to relate the full story to Bandong, from the time he met Ba Inte to the old man's memories of Andres' late mother, the sudden death of his ancestor Kabesang Resong, and the 'disappearance' of the vast tracts of land that he owned, whose ownership had since been transferred to Captain Melchor. He also narrated the account of the documents and signs that Ba Inte had shown to him when they had visited the old farmer that morning. There seemed to be no doubt that Martha, his mother, was the grandchild of Kabesang Resong, who had left for Manila after her ancestor died and had not inherited a single square metre of the vast lands.

Andres said that when his mother was still alive, she repeated to him stories of his rich ancestor who owned lands in Sampilong, which was why when they fled the city during the Second World War, it was to Sampilong that he and Sedes came, and the first thing he did was to look for his mother's relatives. But he didn't find anyone.

Later on, Andres told Teacher Bandong of his plans, as advised by Ba Inte. He asked him for help. Bandong assured him of his support.

'This is a matter of justice,' said Bandong, 'and events have now brought us to face the strong enemy of justice in this land.' He was referring to the Grande husband and wife.

Bandong was happy that his high estimation of Andres in the beginning had been confirmed, in spite of the abject poverty he lived in. This recent development merely shored up his confidence in Andres.

'I often think,' said the teacher, 'that you, Andres, are not an ordinary person, and I wasn't fooled by the poverty that enveloped you.'

'The blessings of good fortune, if it comes to pass, won't change my beliefs,' confirmed Andres.

'I believe in that, and I know you'll never alter your beliefs.'

Gladness rose in the face of Andres when he spoke again. 'That's good, since we can both work together and help the people thereafter. Please trust that I will help you in your plans for the school and for the town.'

'Thank you, Andres. May you win in both of your cases.'

'You're part of our issues, and you'll also be part of our victories.'

Just then, Nana Oris arrived with the ingredients she had bought from the market for lunch. When the couple was about to go downstairs, the old woman said, 'Why will you leave now when it will just take a few minutes for me to cook?'

'We can have lunch some other time, auntie,' said Sedes, using the formal title for an older woman. The couple could no longer be stopped from going home.

The sun was already at its zenith, its rays touching the window-sill of the humble house. Earlier, Andres had looked at the ball of sunlight when they were walking through the front yard of Bandong's house. He quietly told himself that whatever golden blessings come to him, he would use not just for himself but—more importantly—for the happiness of those around him.

Bandong and Andres clasped each other's hands tightly.

'I'll be more energetic in working on our common projects,' said Andres.

'May you and your wife be blessed, as well as your whole clan,' replied Bandong, and he walked with them out of his front yard until all of them had reached the street glittering with sunlight.

38

Classes would start at the elementary school, the next day. As was his usual habit even if it was still vacation, Bandong was already at the school before eight o'clock in the morning. But the hardworking interim principal wasn't alone. He was meeting his fellow teachers about the forthcoming schoolyear and the problems of the school, the students and the teachers.

'Our first problem is a recurring one,' said Bandong. 'I'm referring to the many new pupils who are enrolling in our school. We need at least five new classrooms and seven new teachers.'

He showed them the long list of new students who would start studying that schoolyear, and the names of those on the waiting list, who could not be accommodated in the previous year. Most of them belonged to the age range between eight to ten years old.

According to him, there was a revolving door between the superintendent and the mayor. If he was talking to the first, he would be advised to seek help from the local chief executive. And the latter would always reply that the job of the national government shouldn't be shouldered by the local government unit.

'I'm like a basketball being thrown from one person to the other,' Bandong complained to the teachers. 'But I thought that we could resolve this at our level if there's no other way.'

He stopped for a while and waited for any suggestions from the group, and when none came, he offered his own.

'We can hold classes even under the shade of trees,' Bandong told the surprised group. 'That's for the kids who are already old enough. As for the teaching staff, I'll also teach and the others can work overtime, taking two more classes. We need to make some sacrifices, fellow teachers.'

No one ran counter to the suggestions of Bandong to avert the crisis of the elementary school of Sampilong, even if the solutions he offered were only temporary. The teachers agreed to sacrifice more for the sake of the children. Almost all of the teachers were natives of the barrio, and they knew most of the kids' parents—both those who were already enrolled and those just coming in.

In the midst of their discussion, who would suddenly appear but a man wearing a white, long-sleeved shirt and a black tie, thin of body and pale of lips, resembling a frail dragonfly. His pair of thick-lensed glasses hung over his flat nose.

'Gud-morning,' the man greeted everyone in English when he arrived in the room where the meeting was being held. 'Mister Bandong Cruz?' he asked while looking at Bandong, who was sitting at the head of the main table.

Some of the female teachers wanted to laugh, but they just controlled themselves.

Bandong stood up and ushered in the guest. His height of five feet and eight inches almost overshadowed like a big tree the guest, who was five feet and two inches.

'I'm Bandong Cruz,' he said in the Tagalog language. 'How can I help you, sir?'

'Ay am Mister Henry Danyo,' said the guest in English. He gave a letter to Bandong. 'Leter prom di superintendent,' he added.

Bandong offered him a seat at the head of the table, before he opened the letter. He read the typewritten letter in English.

Bandong's face became serious and his brow furrowed.

The superintendent's letter introduced Mister Henry Danyo to Bandong. Mister Danyo was to serve as the new principal of the elementary school in Sampilong, to take over the position of late Putin Reyes. The letter ordered Bandong to turn over to Mister Danyo all the properties and papers of the school that had been entrusted to him.

The letter also asked Bandong to go to the office of the superintendent in the provincial capital to clear up some things.

Bandong almost lost consciousness after reading the letter. He felt as if the blow of a hammer had thundered over his ear. His eyes were clouded over by a grove of fireflies and his knees turned to water.

Nevertheless, he steeled himself. He didn't want Mister Danyo to notice the ill effects of the letter on him. The other teachers were waiting in excitement to know the letter's contents, but he didn't tell them about it. But the other teachers could feel that the letter in Bandong's hands contained a piece of bad news, although they could never have known the reversal of fortunes that it contained.

'Very well, then,' Bandong told the guest and then later said to everyone, 'Dear ladies and gentlemen, I introduce to you Mister Danyo—Henry Danyo—who will be the new principal of this school. The superintendent has appointed him as the principal to take over the job of the late Teacher Putin.'

Mister Danyo stood up with his chin raised in the air and bowed his neck stiffly before the crowd, before he sat down again.

This announcement was followed by long 'ooohs' and 'aaahs' from the women, the words seeming to slip out of their throats. Some of them turned pale, while the others reddened. There were those who frowned, others who shook their heads, while some put their palms on their foreheads. No one amongst them looked happy about the announcement and no one thought of standing up to greet Mister Henry Danyo.

Bandong told everyone that the meeting was over. He reminded everyone that classes would start tomorrow, and wished everyone good luck.

When Mister Danyo was left alone, he walked back and forth in the office, looked at the photographs on the wall, then went to the toilet and closed it from the inside.

Bandong then went directly to the provincial capital. He went to the superintendent and told him he had received the letter.

'There are complaints against you,' the superintendent told Bandong.

'Complaints?' asked the teacher in amazement. His hunch was proving to be correct.

'Serious allegations,' said the superintendent.

'From whom?'

'A big shot in Sampilong.'

'Ah.'

The superintendent retrieved a memorandum made up of two pages and gave it to Bandong.

'Here.'

The young teacher took it, went to a corner of the office and sat down to read it. He first looked at the name of 'the big shot from Sampilong' who had signed the letter, then proceeded to read the following accusations against him:

'That, while an interim principal of the elementary school in Sampilong, he meddled with the farmers' organization; that, he pushed them to write a series of disturbances against the landlords;

'That, he also connived with the squatters and pushed them to illegally use, stay and even claim ownership of the land owned by the landlords;

'That, as interim principal, he refused the building of a wall around the elementary school to protect it from stray animals as well as people with beastly behaviour;

'That, he provided capital and that he leads a business—the cooperative of home industries—which is against his work ethics as a principal of the elementary school;

'That, he is sowing radical ideas in the minds of the teachers and students, ideas that go against the grain of accepted norms and principles in society, that is why he should not be entrusted with work as an interim principal, because he poses a danger to public peace and order.'

Bandong's smile had soured by the time he reached the end of the list of grievances against him. The letter was signed by Hugo, Dislaw and a lieutenant. The young teacher already knew who was behind the accusations against him. It was like a nail whose slim body is embedded in wood, but the head could be seen by everyone. Who was Hugo, the chief of police? A godson by marriage to the Grande husband and wife. Who was Dislaw? The overseer of the Grandes' properties. Who is the lieutenant? Another minion of the Grande family.

Dislaw had two reasons for accusing Bandong. The first was for the sake of his master, while the second was a personal reason, since he was also courting Pina.

Bandong didn't stand up from his chair while he was reflecting on the situation. His aims were honourable and his conscience was clear, he told himself. But there were still people who got mad at him. But this didn't surprise him. In the battle between good and evil, one could not just join one side without being the object of an opponent's attack, and it would be worse just to sit in the middle, because then one would risk being squeezed between the two opposing forces.

Nevertheless, he wasn't afraid. On the one hand, he was even grateful, for now his real enemies had revealed themselves.

He went back to the superintendent and returned the memorandum.

'See? These are serious accusations, right?' asked the superintendent, raising his face from the papers he was reading on his table.

'Sir, it depends on the colour of the lenses one is using,' said Bandong with respect.

'Very well then, please answer this letter within seventy-two hours,' ordered the primary head of teaching in the province.

'You'll get my answer, sir.'

The superintendent leaned on the back of his swivel chair and looked at the beleaguered teacher.

'I won't stop you from working,' he decided. 'You can continue teaching while the investigation is still ongoing. That's my consideration for you.'

But Bandong objected.

'Sir, I'd like to ask for a vacation of two weeks,' he said. 'It would be hard for me to teach while this issue remains unresolved.'

'If that's what you want, then that's fine with me,' the superintendent relented.

Bandong bade his farewell and said he would return after three days to submit his defence. He was given a typed copy of the accusations levelled against him.

The superintendent also felt bad about what happened, because he was aware of Bandong's stellar record and knew the young teacher had a very bright future. But he was being accused and the ones doing so were powerful.

About his being a principal, the superintendent thought that Bandong would no longer accept the post even if he was found not guilty and it was then offered to him. A powerful person had lobbied with the provincial governor for Henry Danyo to be assigned to the post. The governor himself had talked to the superintendent about it, and asked that it be done as a personal favour to the governor.

'My friend, I've already promised this appointment to someone,' the governor had whispered to him. 'You may ask a favour of me next time.'

'Sure,' he swiftly answered. 'Can I say no to my boss?'

At the time, the superintendent was thinking of the additional teachers' positions that he had requested to be funded. That was why he couldn't shy away from this situation, very much like Eve being tempted by the serpent.

39

Bandong walked around the park in the provincial capital to let the intense heat inside him subside. He felt like some kind of fever was welling up inside him. His eyes and breath seemed to be filled with fire, and melted steel seemed to be coursing through his veins. He wanted to lunge at people whom he had met on the street, and beat them up. His hands were itchy. He wanted to kick his feet and bury his teeth into someone's flesh. Perhaps, that was how running amok felt.

But the dark clouds in his mind quicky vanished upon the appearance of light. The storm inside him subsided like water in a crystal glass, and he was able to smile at the two children who were like a dog and a cat at the end of the road, alternately munching at a stalk of sugar cane.

He remembered Pina, Nana Oris, his friends in the barrio and New Village. He was hungry, so he went into a small canteen and had his lunch.

Upon reaching Sampilong in the first hours of the afternoon, he decided to drop by the elementary school before going home. Mister Danyo was still there. Bandong greeted the new principal, fixed the papers on his desk, putting some inside a big envelope and crumpling the others and throwing them into the waste basket. He covered some books and put them on top of the envelope.

'Mister Danyo,' he told the thin dragonfly, 'these table and chair are my personal properties, but you may use them if you like.' He said that he would be on vacation for several days.

'Olrayt,' said Mister Danyo and looked at Bandong through his eyeglasses that were as thick as goggles.

He turned over the properties of the school, like the list of teachers and students, several books and keys, to the principal. And then he left quietly.

Nana Oris didn't notice anything new with him when he reached home. She was surprised when he told her that he had just come from the provincial capital and was already done with lunch. He didn't tell his troubles to his surrogate mother. Without a doubt, she would feel very bad about the fact that he hadn't been chosen as the new principal, and was even being asked to answer to a slew of charges against him. If someone would tell Nana Oris that Bandong was short of a role model in any situation, she wouldn't believe them and would just say that the person was angry at her nephew.

That was why Bandong thought that it would be better not to inform her of the matter right now, to save her from the despair. He just told her that he had asked for a vacation for two weeks to give him time to prepare a comprehensive report. He said that he didn't do this report earlier, since he was only asked to do it recently, for which he had been summoned by the superintendent and had to go to the provincial capital.

'You're taking a vacation just when classes have started,' noted Nana Oris. 'Maybe that's why some teachers were looking for you earlier. But they didn't tell me the reason.'

But from Mang Pablo and family, Bandong didn't keep the sad events a secret. In truth, the people living in that house already had inkling of what had happened, although they weren't yet clear on the specifics. When the teachers who had gone to Bandong's house passed by, Mang Pablo caught wind of the news.

The leader of the PTA realized that the teachers were surprised and saddened by the king-like order of the superintendent. However, they couldn't display their misgivings openly. For them, Bandong was the only proper replacement for Teacher Putin. Although they didn't know the real abilities of Mister Danyo, they thought of him as a dragonfly who had been carried there by some ill wind, and therefore, couldn't bring any good tidings.

After they had arrived at the elementary school that morning, the teachers had indeed gone to visit Bandong at his house. But he wasn't there and Nana Oris didn't know that her nephew had gone to the provincial capital. That was when the teachers met Mang Pablo and told him about their bad feelings.

Until then, they didn't know that there was a slew of complaints against Teacher Bandong, which was why a replacement for him had been sent to Sampilong. The teachers suspected that politics was the root cause of the abominable events.

'What's more important than seniority and efficiency?' asked a male teacher with anger in his voice. 'If they didn't like Bandong, I'm next in the hierarchy, why didn't they assign me? Suffer, poor soul, because you don't have a strong patron.'

'Just look at that Henry Danyong,' said a spinster, poking fun at the new principal's name. 'How can we find motivation to work with him?'

Mang Pablo was the first to tell Pina that the new teacher had been sent by the superintendent in the provincial capital. The woman felt as if a knife had been struck in her heart. A well of emotions filled her, born out of pity for Bandong and ill will towards someone else. She just went to her room, closed the door behind her, and wept. Aling Sabel was surprised and thought that something was gravely wrong; when she heard the reason for her daughter's tears, she proceeded to calm her down.

'Oh, I thought that something serious had happened to you,' the mother said. 'You've been mewling and mewling as if you've lost a kitten.'

Aling Sabel had known that Pina favoured Bandong over Dislaw, whom she liked for her daughter. The reason might be obvious: Pina had known Bandong since he was a child, but she had only met Dislaw recently.

Pina felt embarrassed when her mother noted her behaviour, so she quickly wiped her tears and calmed herself. When she left her room, the traces of grief were gone from her face, except for a slight swelling of her eyes that made them look even more attractive. She had regained her composure.

When Bandong called out his greetings that night, all of them knew that half of his news would be about the new principal. But they weren't aware that the other half was more disturbing. Bandong was being asked to answer to a slew of serious accusations hurled against him, and was now under investigation.

Pina almost burst into tears again. She was smiling at her suitor, but he felt that despite her lips parted like a rose and the thin film of powder on her face, she felt melancholy because of what happened to him.

'Your eyes are swelling,' Bandong noted, when only Pina and he were together.

Pina admitted that she had wept when she heard the bad news earlier, that the position held by Bandong had been assigned to someone else. Pina's revelations went right through Bandong's heart.

'If there's any good thing that this situation has brought to me, it's the realization that you also have feelings for me,' he said with gladness. 'But please, don't cry. This is just a trial for all of us. I've nothing to fear because my conscience is clear. The only thing I want to know is if your feelings for me will dampen because of what happened.'

'You just became a bigger person, in my view.'

'Thank you, Pina. Your trust will be my strong and enduring shield.'

'Now that they're accusing you,' the woman said, now shorn of her demureness, 'now, I cannot deny to myself or to you how I feel. Please remember that I'm always ready to—'

'Oh, Pina! I'm the luckiest of them all,' the young man said, as he almost gripped her hand in his. But instead, he quickly fished for the small white handkerchief that Pina had recently given to him and used it to wipe her away her tears. 'Now, I'm ready to fight, and to win.'

'You're not alone, Bandong,' Pina said with clarity, and she made him happy with a moist look in her eyes that was filled with so much love, the way Magdalene looked at Jesus when she washed His feet with perfume and dried them with her long hair.

Their sweet words stopped when Tasyo and the other farmers arrived, looking for Bandong. They wanted to hear from Bandong directly what they had found out.

Pina left the men to discuss things by themselves. Aside from Bandong and Tasyo, the other men included Mang Pablo, Julian, Simon, Blas and Aling Sabel's brother, who was also a farmer.

Bandong confirmed to his friends that what they had heard was, unfortunately, true; that he was under investigation for some grave accusations and he told them one by one what these accusations were and who had accused him; that he was no longer the interim principal of the school; that he had asked for a leave of seventy-two hours to prepare his answers to the accusations hurled against him, as well as prepare for the other things that needed to be done.

'My vacation isn't a vacation,' he said. 'How can one who's in a fight have a vacation?'

'It's easy to find the fire by its smoke,' Mang Pablo said in a metaphorical manner, referring to the plot against Bandong. 'We can easily see the dark hand of the Grande in this.'

'The claws of the crocodile,' said Simon.

'What they're doing to you is like hitting a water buffalo, while we are being whipped,' Tasyo said in a meaningful manner. 'This attempt against you is like a sword raised against the farmers as well.'

'They're more afraid of you,' said Julian.

'Or I'm more hated,' Bandong added.

Blas had wanted to apologize for Bandong being implicated in their problems because they had asked the teacher to serve as their adviser in the organization. But Bandong quickly disabused the notion.

'You and I have nothing to repent for,' he said with firmness of conviction. 'Your union, our cooperative, the struggle of the squatters to improve their lot in life—all of these things were impelled by one reason: to live a more comfortable life and be given justice in this land. As Mang Pablo had said once, this land isn't owned by a handful of landlords, or a slew of foreigners; this land is ours, we are the true children of this land—we who plowed her and made her spring riches for us all. If that's bad, if that's a sin, indeed, then I'm ready to take full responsibility, and to suffer.'

The people around Bandong confirmed to him that his struggle was the struggle of everyone else as well, because their one, common enemy had now been revealed.

'Rapacity and greed without end,' Tasyo said.

'By the crocodiles,' added Simon.

In the end, Bandong outlined the steps he would take to answer their accusations. That it was not true he was meddling in the farmers' organization, because these people had their own inherent intelligence, bravery and sense of honour, and they knew that setting up a union didn't mean stirring disturbance, but rather, just tapping into the rights of those engaged in labour. That the local chief executive of Sampilong had encouraged the squatters to pursue their desire to improve their lives and therefore, the squatters should be applauded for this since they turned their once-hilly terrain into a model for other villages to follow. That the honourable people of Sampilong had not organized home industries to earn private profit only for themselves, for they were neither businessmen, nor usurers. Rather, they set them up as a source of livelihood for those who are jobless, and for his work with the cooperative and the home industries, Bandong didn't draw any salary at all. That he was asking those who had conspired against him to point out the dangerous ideas and illegal acts that they claim disturbed the public peace and order.

Bandong wasn't yet finished with his defence when those around him absolved him of any guilt.

'Not guilty!' said Tasyo, as if he were a judge.

'If only you were the investigator and the judge,' said Bandong.

'I absolve you not because I am siding with you, but because you're not guilty,' repeated the president of the farmers' organization.

Just then, Aling Sabel and Pina entered the room, bearing refreshments and snacks for everyone.

Pina went to Bandong and gave him a teaspoon and small plate, followed by sweet words that nobody else heard. 'If I were the judge, you would stay behind bars forever.'

'Forever in the arms of your love,' the words slowly left Bandong's lips.

40

It seemed that the new principal and Dislaw had already known each other for a long time. This was uppermost in the minds of many when classes started the next day. Mister Danyo was busy that day; teachers and parents and children were waiting outside the principal's office. But when Dislaw arrived, he just went directly into the office of the principal.

'Congratulations, Henry,' the caretaker said and gripped the hand of Mister Danyo as the latter stood up to shake Dislaw's hand. 'I just dropped by to see if I could help you with anything.'

The principal pointed his two fingers at his head, then squinted his eyes and looked at Dislaw through thick eyeglasses.

'Dats rayt,' Henry answered. 'Kent yu loket e gud pleys ay ken bord en lads? Its difikult to meyk ey long trip ebery day.' Mister Danyo and his family lived in another town in the province.

'Are you looking for a place to rent all by yourself?' asked Dislaw.

'Alon, yes. Payb deys ey wik. Ay plan to go hom on Praydi afternun en bi bak Mondi moning.'

'You don't want to stay in my house?'

'Big trobol to yu, Dislaw.'

'No trobol at ol,' Dislaw was forced to speak in English as well, then reverted to Tagalog because he was not fluent in English. 'Don't worry about it. My house is big. I only live with my sister, who is a widow and his only son. Marcela cooks very well.'

'Rili, ay don't want to boder yu, poks,' but since Dislaw was insistent, Mister Danyo had no choice but to give in.

'Olrayt, ip yu insist en ip der's no beter pleys.'

Before lunchtime came, Dislaw fetched the principal and brought him to his house. Cely cooked a wonderful meal. And after lunch, Mister Danyo was shown to the room that had been prepared for him.

They did not discuss how much the board and lodging would cost. Indeed, Cely cooked well, but she also directed her moist gaze at the principal.

In truth, the Grande overseer and the new principal had just met recently. They had met twice at the provincial capital. The first was when Don Severo had asked Dislaw to visit the provincial governor, and the second was at the office of the provincial superintendent, when he lodged his complaint against Bandong. During their first meeting, the governor introduced him to the principal, and during the second meeting, the two had a long conversation.

'Henry, you should meet Dislaw,' said the provincial governor, 'since you're moving to Sampilong.'

When the new principal and Dislaw met in the office of the superintendent, the latter told Dislaw, 'Dislaw, have you already met Mister Danyo?'

The two happily shook each other's hands and the principal said that he was a friend of Dislaw's.

'Perhaps, you don't know it yet, Dislaw. But Henry will be the new principal in your town's elementary school.'

The caretaker pretended he did not know anything about it, and showed gladness upon hearing the news.

'I had thought of that,' Dislaw answered, 'and now it has been confirmed.

'It's still off-the-record, and you're the first one to hear about it.'

'Mister Danyo will find Sampilong waiting for him,' preened Dislaw. 'These documents are proof that they were not happy about the temporary appointee at our school.'

Mister Danyo's eyes bulged behind his goggle-thick lenses upon hearing Dislaw's words against Bandong.

'I hope all of you will help Henry,' pleaded the superintendent.

Dislaw promised that they would give the new principal all the help that he needed, and even boasted that he had a high position in the PTA.

'If you will be the new principal, then I will be the new president of the PTA,' he said.

They did not part ways until it was lunchtime. While having lunch, Henry asked for information about the elementary school, the teachers, Bandong, the town's leaders and chief executive, and other important things that he needed to know. Dislaw obliged and told the new principal everything that mattered, and more. He made it appear that after the Grande family and the town mayor, he was the most important person in the whole town of Sampilong. If he had wanted to be the chief of police, he could have easily assumed the post, but why would he do that? He was the trusted overseer of the Grande family of their vast lands, he handled their court cases in the capital, he collected the money they lent to the farmers, he ordered everyone around. He was also the keeper of the Grande family's secrets, especially the secrets of Don Severo.

'Yu ar ten in wan,' said Henry, and thus, the two became even closer.

Dislaw then told Mister Danyo about the accusations he had heaped against Bandong when he visited the provincial superintendent. He called the interim principal a fake and boastful philosopher, and a dangerous radical who was in alliance with the farmers in the field and the squatters who lived outside the town centre.

'His time is up,' Dislaw said and followed up this statement with loud laughter.

That was why when Dislaw and Henry Danyo parted ways that afternoon from the restaurant where they had had lunch, they resembled the twin shells of a clam in their closeness. Dislaw was happy because now, Bandong could no longer walk in the town with his head held high. Henry was also happy, since he needed a powerful ally in the town of Sampilong, a place he had never known, and where he was a stranger to everyone.

Lately, Dislaw had been visiting the provincial capital more often. Once, he brought along the chief of police and the lieutenant as additional signatories to the affidavit of complaints that he had filed against Bandong. But sometimes, he would just go there alone and did not use the jeep. Instead, he took the bus.

One day, Bandong and Dislaw almost met each other at the office of the superintendent. The interim principal was entering the office as the overseer was about to leave, but the latter saw who was coming, backed out and fled. Bandong did not see him. Bandong's face was grim and he seemed to be looking for someone to punch. Even though Dislaw avoided Bandong, he told himself that he was not a coward, and why would he be afraid? He always carried a loaded gun with him. Nevertheless, the chief of police was not with him that day, neither was his assistant Kosme, and he thought it would be better to let Bandong be and release the anger clotted inside him. The day would come when they would have a duel.

While going back home to Sampilong as well, he made sure to avoid the young teacher who looked hot-headed that day on the brink of an explosion. Dislaw just strolled around the provincial capital looking for things to buy, and took the last bus bound for Sampilong in the late afternoon.

While inside the homebound bus, Dislaw could foresee the effects of his accusations against Bandong, especially on his relationship with Pina. Bandong's downfall would bring him luck.

'He'll stop pursuing her, if he has any sense of shame at all,' Dislaw thought to himself. 'And Pina, if she has any sense of propriety, will also close her doors to the stupid teacher.'

Dislaw decided that he would ramp up his offerings for Aling Sabel. Everybody in the family knew that the old woman liked him for her daughter, while Mang Pablo was neutral and Pina had not yet decided.

'In that family, only Aling Sabel has brains,' Dislaw mused. 'The old woman knows that if I marry Pina, their life would vastly improve.' Dislaw remembered the words that Donya Leona used to keep him under her heel: 'Do well, Dislaw, and when we close our eyes forever, you will be amply rewarded.'

Dislaw thought very highly of himself and thus was blind to how others perceived him. To the fact that Pina avoided him and liked Bandong. Many of the observers had placed their bets that in the Bandong–Dislaw tournament, the former would wave the victory flag, while the latter would be left to bite the dust. Dislaw was not aware of these bets. He had keen eyes, ears and nose when matters pertained to the Grande family, but a cataract covered his eyes, his ears were stoppered and his nose was stuffed when it came to his love for the most beautiful maiden in Sampilong.

Nevertheless, the rash Dislaw had an ace hidden up his sleeve. He had decided that if he could not win Pina through the usual ways of courtship, then he would force himself on her.

'If I can't get her through fair means,' he thought, 'then foul would be it—and they should not blame me for what I will do.'

There was a noisy gathering at Tinoy's barber shop when Dislaw passed by before dusk fell.

'Here comes Dislaw, rushing again,' said the barber to those around him.

'He's already late,' snapped another, without taking a look.

'Late or lost?' someone asked in a snide manner.

'Already late because Bandong has beaten him to Pina's door. You saw him pass by earlier,' and then the one who spoke laughed, 'and he has lost, because what he wants to grab already belongs to someone else.'

'As if you're a witness.'

'Teacher Bandong is already sitting in the nest.'

'Don't be so sure. A spoonful of rice that one is about to eat, can still fall.'

'How can it fall when it's already being chewed?'

'But Bandong is the one who got caught. Isn't he the one being investigated?'

'You're taking the talk into another direction. We're talking about Pina and not the position of the principal. When Bandong lost his position, Pina clung to him even tighter.'

'Or is it Pina's control over Bandong?'

The laughter was loud in those parts as Dislaw passed by. But he just continued walking and ignored the group, even though he had an inkling that they were talking about him. He knew that these poor souls envied him, so he never formed a bond with them.

Before going home, Dislaw went to the big stone house to make his report to the Grande husband and wife.

'Why wasn't Bandong suspended?' asked Don Severo.

'I don't know with the superintendent,' said the overseer. 'He said it's no longer needed. The only thing you wanted was for him to not be appointed as the principal.'

'That's all right,' agreed the rich man. 'There are several ways of skinning a chicken.'

'And how is the new principal?'

'He's doing well.'

'What does that mean?'

'He's part of our camp: he will do everything that we want him to do in the school.'

'Well done. If that's the case, then bring him here one of these days.'

41

Since Henry Danyo lived in Dislaw's house, the overseer of the Grande and the new principal of the elementary school met in mind and character, such that they resembled a pair of shoes. They had almost no differences in thought, in taste or in action. On the other hand, Cely continued to cook for them three times a day, five days a week, to the delight of Mister Danyo. However, the smile of the seductive widow and the moistness of her gaze directed at him began to dissipate as the days passed.

Cely had discovered early on that she was attracted to men who were of robust build and filled with energy. Those were the kinds of men that made her blood run. Aside from looking like a thin dragonfly, Mister Danyo was also as cold as the tail of a lizard that had been cut off from its body.

Nevertheless, Cely found she had less free time since she had to cook for them and clean the house. Earlier, Dislaw used to take his meals at the big house, while Cely and her son contented themselves with eating what was in the pantry. But now, she had to prepare good food all the time for Mister Danyo. Because of this, the only free day when Cely and Kosme could meet, was on a Saturday. Mister Danyo went home every Friday and returned on Monday morning to Sampilong.

When Kosme would visit her, Cely would answer him with snide remarks.

'You have Iska near you. And it's good if we don't see each other often ...'

'Why?' Kosme asked, thinking that the new principal must be having an affair with Cely.

'Because then we'll have greater appetites when we're together.'

'Have I ever given you the cold shoulder?' Kosme said in an accusing tone.

'No, that's why I won't exchange you even for a dozen Mister Danyos ...'

'Do I detect a threat there somewhere?'

'None. I'll show you everything on Saturday.'

That was why even if their rendezvous became less regular, their lovemaking was filled with moans and grunts whenever the two had a chance to tumble around in bed.

On the other hand, Dislaw had decided that he should now take advantage of Bandong's 'shame', as well as of the impending investigation of the accusations levelled against him. He was planning to force Pina into deciding.

One night, Dislaw took Henry with him when he visited Pina.

'I want you to look her over and see if, like a fighting hen, a spur can be attached to her so she can fight,' said Dislaw, when he invited the principal to come with him.

'Ay am an ekspert in looking tings ober, but not in attaching a spur,' answered Henry.

'I'll take care of attaching the spur, since I won't allow you to do that anyway,' Dislaw said in a teasing tone. He also added that Pina's father was the president of the PTA.

'Yu told me dat alredi, bat it's gud that I mit him.'

As usual, Dislaw took the jeep of the Grande family when he visited Pina.

Mang Pablo's family welcomed them with graciousness and treated them with hospitality. Upon hearing the roar of the jeep, Aling Sabel immediately went down the stairs to welcome the two guests. Dislaw gave a souvenir to the old woman, which he had bought when he had visited the provincial capital.

In truth, Mang Pablo and Pina were excited to meet the new principal who had been assigned to the elementary school of their town. Mang Pablo because of his position in the PTA, and Pina because she wanted to see what were this person's advantages over Bandong and if he had something that the younger man did not have. She only had the highest admiration for Bandong's stellar qualities.

Pina still treated Dislaw with civility, even when she began to hate him upon learning that he had levelled the accusations against Bandong. The maiden from the barrio could not be faulted with displaying bad manners towards her guest, even if she felt revulsion for him.

After the initial greetings, Aling Sabel left them. Mang Pablo and Mister Danyo talked in one corner of the house, while Dislaw and Pina talked in the inner part. The head of the PTA and the new principal exchanged views on the problems of the elementary school. On the other hand, Dislaw asked Pina about his proposal. Even now she called him 'Mister Dislaw', which he resented.

'I'm already tired of waiting, Pina,' complained Dislaw. 'Till when ...'

But Pina didn't answer him, as if she did not hear anything. That was why he repeated his entreaties.

'I hope you'll give me an answer soon, Pina.'

'I've already told you, sir, to turn your attention to someone else, but you are stubborn,' the woman calmly said.

'But your heart is harder.'

'It's your fault.'

'Why? I'm the one who has suffered and waited for so long. Why are you doing this to me? Don't you trust me?'

'That's not the point, sir.'

'Or is there a luckier one . . ?' The words from Dislaw's dry lips were obviously stained with jealousy.

Pina just kept quiet and rearranged the flowers in the vase in front of her.

'Just level with me, Pina,' Dislaw pleaded. 'Do you already have someone else?'

For the first time, the woman raised her face and gazed into the eyes of her male visitor.

'What do you think?' she asked, in answer to his question.

'I'm not a prophet,' Dislaw said in a hard tone, afraid that their conversation would end on a sour note.

'That's why I said—'

'But what did you say?'

'That you should turn your attention to someone else—'

'That won't happen.'

'I'm sorry, Mister Dislaw.'

'What are you sorry for, that you're leaving me with hurt feelings, with defeat?'

'I can't do anything.'

'Don't turn me down because I'm not used to losing.'

'What do you want me to do, then?'

'Choose me, or nobody else.'

'Excuse me?'

The wind coming from the farm was cold, but Dislaw was sweating. He took out his handkerchief and wiped his face.

On the other hand, Mang Pablo and Mister Danyo were having an animated conversation. The new principal could speak the native language of Tagalog fluently and he spoke it now, otherwise he would have had difficulty conversing with Mang Pablo in English. But now they understood each other perfectly, even if they sometimes had different opinions on an issue, unlike Pina and Dislaw, who crossed swords even if both of them spoke firmly and honestly.

'That's too bad!' Dislaw said with disappointment, and then he bit his lower lip.

Pina was looking outside the window, into the distance.

'Just remember—' Dislaw said, and it seemed as if a thorn had slashed his throat.

'What is it, sir?'

'If you don't become mine, I won't allow you to belong to anyone else ...'

'Mister Dislaw!' Pina was about to stand up, but the blazing eyes of the man stopped her cold in her tracks.

'Remember that!' and the two words rolled and stopped abruptly, like the two front wheels of the jeep. Dislaw raised his polo shirt to reveal his revolver, which caught the sharp eyes of Pina.

'I don't accept defeat,' the man added and touched his revolver.

Pina's eyes turned red, as if tears were about to flow from them. Her forehead was furrowed, like slivers of the moon that had turned pale on the horizon. Then she stood up and left.

'Pina!' said Dislaw.

Later, Aling Sabel went inside the main room of the house, carrying some barrio food for the new principal. Pina also entered and helped her mother offer the snacks to the two guests. She never went back to sit in front of Dislaw again, and the man also joined the conversation going on between Mang Pablo and Henry.

After eating, Mister Danyo looked at his watch and said, 'May God, itl olredi leyt,' he told Dislaw. 'Let's nat trobol dem tu mats, besayd ay wud bi ap irli tomoro.'

'Let's go, then,' Dislaw stood up. He went to Aling Sabel and bade her farewell.

'Please visit us again,' Mang Pablo said. When the guests were gone, Pina rushed back to her room.

The moon had completely vanished from the sky, but the night sky was lit by the stars. The wind came in waves and the crickets answered each other's chirping in the night. The fireflies were like lanterns, flitting here and there, lighting up the trees as if for Christmas.

'Dislaw, yur laki,' said Henry when the jeep had started to move. And he added that if he were still single, then Dislaw would have a competitor.

'Pina is beri priti,' concluded Mister Danyo.

'Beri priti,' Dislaw said to himself.

'Yu ar saying sumthing?' Henry asked.

In answer, Dislaw just stepped on the accelerator and the jeep flew.

42

In a small and forgotten town like Sampilong, a local chief executive was like a goldfish swimming in a crystal bowl. Especially so if people did not expect him to land that seat and the one people had expected, did not win in the elections. This was what happened to Mister Danyo, the newly appointed principal.

His personality became the focus of everyone's attention; many found faults with him and only a few praised him. The look and form that only a mother could love, the manner of walking as if there was a bulging kneecap lodged in his wide-opened armpits, his speaking in pidgin English even if talking to someone not conversant in the foreign language, and the thick eyeglasses that sat on his flat nose, were the butt of jokes for those who disliked him.

Even though they did not read his curriculum vitae and neither did Dislaw talk about it, the people who were questioning his appointment found out soon enough. He graduated with a degree in Education from a university in Manila that belonged among the so-called 'diploma mills'. He had taught for many years as a regular teacher in his hometown, far from the provincial capital. He was nearly thirty-five years old, married and had several children. His redeeming quality was that his brother was a businessman, who was a strong leader and a friend of the governor.

'You better be influential with the governor,' was the phrase on the lips of the members of the PTA.

'Now, what really matters is your pull with those in power,' snapped another one. 'It doesn't matter what you know, but who you know.'

'I'd much rather prefer Bandong to be the principal.'

'Likewise.'

'But even though you want it, you're not influential with the governor,' teased another.

'Well, we may not be influential, but we're voters,' countered the one who was pro-Bandong.

'But the elections are still far away.'

'Excuse me. In politics, every day is a campaign day. You can count the ways of politician which don't smack of campaigning.'

This was why, on the first day of the school opening, you could say that Henry Danyo was the most popular person in Sampilong. Popular not because people favoured him, but because he was the subject of many snide remarks.

Whenever a group of people gathered together inside the barber shop or in front of the variety store, in the town centre or the barrio, the conversation was either happy or sad, whenever Mister Danyo was the topic.

'Teacher Ebeng said that Danyo is strict,' Tinoy, the barber, said with a smile. 'It seems that Danyo doesn't know how to laugh.'

'The one who doesn't know how to laugh is a dog,' observed another one whose hair was already till his ears, yet he was still refusing to get a haircut.

'Well, dogs smile when they wag their tails,' said another who seemed to be engaged in the trade of black magic.

'Why don't you show it?' asked the barber.

'What do you think I am, an animal?'

Laughter erupted from the crowd and the conversation meandered everywhere, only to return to its original topic. They seemed to be going around in circles, and this was how they happily passed the time, seemingly without any sorrow and not minding the many disappointments in their lives. People called life in the barrio a mixture of the good and the bad: good, because the people could seemingly forget their poverty, even if this lead them to accept their poor condition; to indifference and lack of ambition.

But even the teachers who had worked with Bandong and seen his efficiency, and the parents who knew more than the rest of the crowd, were unhappy with the way the principal ran the school.

Many new students were not allowed to enroll and the new principal did not seem to care about this. Ato was one of those who had been refused admission, the son of Andres and Sedes, whom Bandong had promised to accept.

'Wat kan ay du?' Mister Danyo defended himself against those who had complained. 'Dis hayer problem is nasyonal, en nat ey mir local wan. Wi nid more titsers, mor klases, ay admit: bat olso, we nid moni en mor moni. If the government say no moni, en its tru, siyal wi dig it awt ob awir on paket? I am sori. Wi ar titsers, edyukeytors, but not martirs.'

With this speech, Mister Danyo let the curtain fall on the hopes of the poor students who would be forced to roam the streets because the government had shirked its responsibility to educate them. He also dismissed Bandong's suggestion to resolve the issue of the lack of classrooms. He suggested that if there were no classrooms, then classes could be conducted under the shade of the trees. The elementary school was filled with trees that gave generous shade to all. Different teachers could alternate teaching these classes, since there was also a lack of teachers in Sampilong.

'Isi tu sey, but hard tu du,' said Mister Danyo, with his lower lip jutting out. 'Impraktikal. Di superinten den wud redyek di plan. Don't insist on di imposibol. Kresi aydiya, dat wan.'

On the other hand, Teacher Bandong had already prepared his answers to the allegations hurled against him. He took his written answer to the superintendent. The latter scanned Bandong's reply, all of three pages, until he reached the last part signed by Bandong.

'Okay,' the superintendent said, putting the letter in a box on his table. He included it in the file that contained the allegations that had come from the chief of police of Sampilong, Dislaw and the lieutenant.

He looked at Bandong and then asked, 'Do you want to go back to teaching now?'

Bandong explained that the vacation leave that he had asked for had not yet finished.

'I can go back to teaching later, sir,' Bandong said in a respectful tone. 'I'll inform you as soon as my leave is up.'

'It's up to you.'

The superintendent was an old leader with a kind soul and a sense of justice. He harboured no ill will against Bandong, and in truth, he even secretly admired Bandong's stellar qualities. Even though he had not yet read the latter's written response to the allegations, he had already studied the allegations and ascertained that they were rather weak. He also deduced the real motivations of the people who had hurled the allegations against the young teacher.

'It's all there, between the lines,' he had thought to himself.

When he assigned Bandong to become the interim principal to replace the ailing Teacher Putin, he had wanted the young teacher to get the plum position in a matter of time. The deceased teacher Putin, his fellow teachers and the members of the PTA had high respect for Bandong, as head of the school and a model citizen. Mayor Bartolo also had a high regard for Bandong.

However, the power-play of politics took over, whose tentacles never failed to grip everyone and squeeze them dry. The elected high officials acted like kings and queens in the chess game of politics.

The superintendent recalled that he had started as a regular teacher, become a principal, been promoted to supervisor and now was the provincial educational leader. He was a career man in the real world of education. He was the first amongst his peers. But in the chessboard of politics, he was only a pawn, or a horse—a rather ordinary being. He was not attached to any politician, and sometimes helped in the coming and going, the push-and-pull movements, of the queen and other powerful players.

'Career man?' said the superintendent, and a bitter smile dawned on his lips at the term he had used to call himself. He remembered that the career men here blindly followed the dictates of those in power, so that they could keep their jobs and continue with their chosen careers. Once he stopped agreeing to what they wanted, he might find that his appointment papers were not even enough to buy a ticket to see racehorses.

In short, the present superintendent was a gentleman with a conscience. He had no doubt that reason was on the side of Bandong, but since he was a career man who had a family to feed and still had many years left before he could retire with a pension, what else could he do? Go with the flow, be like the bamboo bending with the wind, so he could secure his position and shield his office from other political acts.

'You can also ask me for a favour.' He still remembered the words of the provincial governor, a bitter pill that he had to swallow. *Give way and you will also receive something in return.*

Feed them one of your pawns if you want to continue playing the board game. What could he ask of the governor? More funds for his department, new positions for teachers and staff, confirmation for the positions that he had approved, new schoolhouses in the far-flung areas, school and office supplies, amongst many other necessities. And who did not want to become a 'partner' to their boss?

He only snapped out of his reverie when Bandong spoke again. The young teacher was bidding him farewell.

'Don't worry. I will fast-track the process,' was all he could say.

'Thank you, sir.'

The pawn had left, leaving the knight alone. He again looked at the chessboard of politics and discerned how far or how close he was from the seat of power now.

43

The people walking on the street where the elementary school was located, all paused and stared at the mountain of sand and the piles of rocks in front of the lot. A group of students was chasing each other around the rocks, as if in a race to see who could climb and slide down fastest.

That morning, two dozen sacks of cement and piles of lime had been delivered.

The people tried to discern what the construction materials were for. Perhaps, some people thought, more classrooms would be built to accommodate the overflow of students who wanted to enroll in the elementary school. Others thought that a wing of the school would be built, to house the library.

When noontime came, five people began to work. They separated the sand, thrust spades into it to loosen the clods, added lime, mixed cement, poured water and then mixed everything thoroughly. Then they set up iron pillars on both sides of the lot and strung a piece of string as a guide. Then, they began putting the rocks and hollow blocks in front.

Mister Danyo went out of his office, his hand draped around the shoulder of Dislaw. They talked to the workers and Dislaw gestured with his hands, while the principal just kept on nodding.

Finally, those who were passing by knew what was going to be built.

'A wall,' one of them said.

'Oh yes, they'll build a wall around the elementary school,' confirmed the other person.

Later on, a member of the PTA and a teacher who had seen the construction, went to Bandong's house and told him about it. The member of the association said he had presented a proposal during the last meeting and everyone had agreed that they would not build a wall.

'Are you sure about this?' Bandong repeated his question.

'I just came from there,' said the member. 'Five men are now working on it and Mister Danyo and Dislaw the Eagle are also there.'

Bandong quickly changed his clothes and rushed to Mang Pablo's house. The president of the PTA was both surprised and annoyed.

'They should have told me,' he said.

'I'm sure Dislaw is behind this,' Bandong answered.

'But they might use the school funds for this.'

'I've confirmed this several times—the school doesn't have funds,' said Bandong, who knew what he was talking about.

'Let's see,' said Mang Pablo, and then he went to his room to change into formal clothes.

Bandong saw that Pina came from the kitchen and went to her room, a sheet of cotton with printed flowers wound around her body. She obviously had just taken a bath. Her hair was loose till her shoulders, and the shape of her body could be seen within the wet cotton sheet. She was too shy to go to the receiving area and instead proceeded to her room. Bandong compared that sudden sight to that of a kid who had seen almost-ripe mangoes dangling from the branches of a tree so close to him.

The three then went on their way to the school: Bandong, Mang Pablo and the member of the PTA. They already saw the evidence of what was happening, even if they were still far away. Mister Danyo and Dislaw were there, surveying the scene as if they owned everything within their sight.

'Good morning, Mister Danyo,' those who had arrived greeted the new principal.

The principal turned, squinted through his thick eyeglasses, and drily said, 'Gud moning.'

They ignored Dislaw, who likewise ignored them, his hand planted on his hip. His polo shirt was tucked in, exposing to everyone the revolver on his hip.

'Mister Danyo, we came here because of the wall,' Mang Pablo began.

'Wat abawt?' asked the principal.

'We just want to know who will pay for that wall.'

Mister Danyo looked at Dislaw, as if seeking the answer from him.

'The Parents' and Teachers' Association, Mang Pablo,' Dislaw snapped from the swamp of his silence.

'Parents' and Teachers'—our group?'

Dislaw nodded and turned his face sharply away from Bandong.

'And who decided on this?'

'That's what the majority wanted,' Dislaw said rashly.

'What? Weren't you also there at the meeting?'

'I left.'

'Because they didn't want to follow your suggestion.'

'Because many of those who came to the meeting were not members, the squatters who are the enemies of the law. The—'

'That's not true!' cut in Bandong, who had decided to join in the discussion.

'Are you calling me a liar?' Dislaw asked.

'Yes.'

'What?'

'The association had voted on a proposal, and it wasn't the wall!'

'How many of you voted for it?'

'The people in the meeting.'

'A meeting without a quorum.'

'Don't be so rash, Dislaw,' Bandong said and stepped forward towards him.

Mang Pablo quickly grabbed Bandong's arm and the old man spoke again. Behind them was the member who had told them about what was happening in the school.

'Therefore, the association's money was used to pay for these materials?'

'The money that belongs to those who want the wall,' Dislaw snapped.

Mang Pablo's annoyance was like a piece of rubber that had hardened and turned into iron inside his chest. He was stunned by what was happening and the insolence of the Grandes' overseer, who had just come from his house the previous night and was courting his only daughter. On the other hand, Dislaw intended to show his real crass self because Pina had turned down his suit, and now that Bandong— his rival—had his arm draped around the shoulder of the old man.

'Don't continue with this,' Mang Pablo told the principal, who for so long had been looking like a matchstick in between the opposing forces.

Mister Danyo again looked at Dislaw for an answer, but instead, Dislaw turned to the workers and spoke.

'Hurry up with your work,' he ordered as his defiant answer to Mang Pablo.

'We'll approach the courts,' warned the president of the PTA.

'We're prepared to face you in any court!' shouted Dislaw, who had seemingly lost all semblance of good manners.

Mang Pablo was filled with anger and did everything to control himself from slapping Dislaw, while the anger inside Bandong was welling up like soldering iron being heated by burning charcoal. The member who had reported the matter stood ready to calm down everyone, but he knew which side he would be on if a melee erupted.

The voices of those debating had reached fever-pitch, such that some teachers went out of the veranda of the elementary school to check out the source of the noise. One or two passersby stopped, but then continued on walking.

'This doesn't look good,' surmised one of them and then rushed to the town centre, in the direction of the police station.

Some cooler heads tried to calm down the opposing parties, telling them to resolve the issue in a peaceful manner, or appeal to the higher authorities in the provincial capital, or to the judge.

'They can go where they want to go,' Dislaw sneered as Mang Pablo and Bandong turned to leave, as a concession to those who had tried to calm down everyone.

Upon hearing this, Bandong turned.

'I want to talk to you, one on one,' he said to Dislaw, who looked at the teacher as if he were a fly he could easily crush.

'Anytime, just choose the place,' the Grandes' overseer said firmly.

'Prepare yourself for our next encounter.'

'We can meet easily. This town is too small for the both of us.' Dislaw snapped and then added, 'But—'

'But what?'

'You've to finish with the investigation against you.'

'You're the one I want to finish off,' and Bandong raised his arm.

Dislaw grabbed his revolver but Bandong beat him to it and twisted his arm.

A loud shout stunned them all.

'Stop!'

Chief Hugo jumped off his jeep. He had been fetched by the passerby who was agitated at the argument he had seen and reported it to the police to prevent any untoward incident from happening.

The chief of police asked what the matter was and then he told everyone to go their separate ways. Mister Danyo put his arm around the shoulders of Dislaw and then brought him back to the elementary school.

Mang Pablo and Bandong also started to go home, along with one or two companions.

The five workers just stared at the chief of police, as if asking him what they should do. But the chief of police ignored them and returned to this jeep, without conveying what needed to be done.

Bandong and Mang Pablo separated in front of Tinoy's barber shop. Mang Pablo went home alone.

It was already high noon and the heat of the sun was made more intense by the humid air. While walking, Mang Pablo felt that the blob of rubber that had turned into iron inside his chest, was growing sharp points that lacerated his heart. He was having difficulty breathing.

Before the old man could climb the stairs of his house, he had to sit down. He gripped his chest and called out in a ragged voice, 'Sabel—Pina—please help me!'

44

Mang Pablo's jaws were already hard and his pulse almost gone when Pina and Aling Sabel found him sprawled on top of their wooden stairs. His hands fell to his sides, seemingly boneless and his tongue seemed to have retreated and he could not speak.

The two women brought him into the house with the help of Dinong, who had come from the neighbour's house. Then, they made him lie on his bed, with his head propped up on three pillows. Aling Sabel took off his formal clothes that were already soaked with sweat. Pina got a glass of water and tried to make her father take a sip. When she failed, she just touched her fingertips on the water and wet her father's dry lips with it. Then, she placed a wet face towel on his heart.

They all decided that Mang Pablo was in a grave state. They told Dinong to rush to the municipal hall to fetch the old doctor.

Aling Sabel was in deep shock, since it was the first time she had seen her husband in such a condition. Mang Pablo often boasted about his good health and claimed that illnesses avoided him. That was why in front of her husband, who was still breathing but already unconscious, she began to cry. Pina also began shedding tears.

The ferocity of the attack had somewhat subsided by the time the doctor fetched by Dinong arrived. He checked the sick man, before giving him an injection. His prognosis was that Mang Pablo was in a serious condition—he had a heart problem. To receive the needed medicines and care, he had to go to the hospital in the provincial capital, the doctor said. If it would not be too expensive for them, it would be better to take him to a good hospital in Manila.

'We should take care that he doesn't have another heart attack,' said the old doctor, while writing the prescription. 'It's bad for him to get angry, get tired, or surprised. He needs to be calm.'

After the doctor left, the family discussed the best course of action, given the medical emergency and their financial condition. They decided to take Mang Pablo to the hospital in the provincial capital. The expenses did not matter, as long as he could get the best medical care.

They still didn't know what had happened to Mang Pablo, just before his heart attack. He felt well that morning and was in good spirits until he left the house with Bandong. Even when he was coming home, he had not complained of any malady, since Bandong had taken good care of him.

Aling Sabel's brother borrowed a jeep and after lunch, they all proceeded to the provincial capital. Aling Sabel and Pina sat on either side of the ailing Mang Pablo.

Many guests came to the house of the family that night to know the latest medical situation of Mang Pablo. The siblings Pina and Dinong were left alone in the house because Aling Sabel had stayed in the hospital to take care of her sick husband.

Tasyo narrated what had happened earlier that morning, which had led to the sudden illness of Mang Pablo. Tasyo was not in the lot earlier that morning, but this was what he had heard from people who had witnessed the quarrel in front of the school. Only then did Pina realize that her father and Bandong had almost come to blows with Dislaw.

'Dislaw's tail is becoming longer,' Tasyo warned and in his mind, thinking back to all the abuses of the Grandes' overseer, like what had happened during Sepa's wake, the meeting of the PTA, the accusations hurled against Bandong, and the building of the wall around the school, which was Dislaw's suggestion, using the money of the association and going against the majority's wishes.

'And his schemes against the farmers and squatters don't seem to be those of a human being,' said one guest.

'In this life, only lightning won't seek revenge,' Tasyo said firmly.

Suddenly, Bandong and Andres came to console the family of Mang Pablo and wish him a speedy recovery. The guests asked Bandong what really happened regarding the wall being built around the elementary school. Bandong narrated that he and Mang Pablo had gone there to ask who ordered the building of the wall and who would pay for the expenses, because they knew that the association had arrived at a consensus to build a library instead. An angry altercation then ensued, with Dislaw treating Mang Pablo with boorishness and even threatening Bandong by pulling out his gun. Chief Hugo had then appeared, blown his whistle and asked them to go their separate ways.

According to Bandong, he had no inclination that Mang Pablo was already feeling unwell while they were going home, otherwise he would have accompanied the old man on his way home.

***

It was already ten o'clock on the next morning. Pina was alone in the house, working on her sewing machine. Dinong had just left the house to go to the provincial capital. He took a change of clothes for Aling Sabel and several things needed by his ailing father. If the old woman wanted to come home, Dinong would take over and watch over his sick father in her stead. He and Pina had agreed that she would visit later in the afternoon, since she still had to finish sewing a dress that a customer had asked her to make.

Her uncle had gone on ahead to his farm to work and her auntie had stayed in the store. Pina bought some things she needed from her aunt's store. Her uncle helped her father on the farm, and they lived on another street, near their house.

The day was humid and even if the sun was already at its zenith, dark clouds had quickly gathered on the horizon.

Pina was concentrating fully on what she was doing to such an extent that she did not hear a vehicle stopping in front of their house. The visitor was already on the landing of their stairs when she noticed him. She was surprised to see Dislaw. He did not call out his greetings but instead came directly into the house. Pina swiftly stood up and did not know what to do. She was all alone in the house and it was the first time that someone had entered their house when she was alone. She could not decide whether to ask Dislaw to sit down, or to leave.

But the man did not wait. He just sat down and leaned against the back of a chair.

'I came here because I want to—' began Dislaw.

'I'm all alone, Mister Dislaw,' Pina said.

Gladness spread on his face upon hearing she was all alone.

'If possible, can you visit at another time—'

'That's good, so we can have a serious talk,' snapped Dislaw, ignoring Pina's plea. 'I only want to talk to you,' he added.

'But Mister Dislaw . . .' the woman said.

'I've heard that Mang Pablo is ill. I commiserate with you.'

'He's in the hospital, sir,' Pina said, but she did not let on that she knew the reason for her father's heart attack.

'I'll visit him later,' Dislaw said.

The insolent soul wanted it to appear as if he did not have anything to do with Mang Pablo's illness. In truth, he had already heard what happened to the old man, as well as his being taken to the provincial hospital for medical treatment, Aling Sabel's not coming home on the previous night, and earlier, he had seen Dinong take the bus bound for the capital. He had hoped that Pina would be all alone in the house and that was why he had come, and he was correct.

Pina just stood behind her sewing machine and never took her eyes off Dislaw. But her heart boomed in her chest and the guest might have seen the quiver in her hands. So he would not notice it, Pina gripped the back of the chair on which she sat to do her sewing.

'Sit down here so we can talk,' Dislaw said after a few moments of silence.

'We can talk another time,' Pina insisted. 'Please leave me alone.'

'I won't pass up this chance,' Dislaw decided. 'I won't leave until we have come to an agreement—now!' The man's voice was hard.

'Please leave, Mister Dislaw.'

'Answer my question.'

'Please leave. Have mercy on me.'

'Have mercy on me as well. I won't leave—'

'What do you want?' Pina asked, her voice almost drowning in her throat.

The barrio girl was brave, since she had grown up in the remote parts of Sampilong where people have wills of steel born and are bred by circumstance. But a different situation now faced her. She was a single woman and she was all alone; her suitor was now in front of her, one she had turned down, and appeared unwilling to accept defeat or refusal, and would likely not respect her situation, since he was now shorn of a gentleman's manners. Pina groped for her pair of scissors sitting on top of the sewing machine.

One step, two and three, and the man's blazing eyes locked onto the pair of scissors. When the man was near, Pina took a step back and gripped the pair of scissors tighter. They looked like two fighting roosters girding themselves for a standoff, preparing to slash each other with their steel spurs.

'Is there any other lucky guy?' Dislaw asked, seemingly chewing his words and turning to her with his eyes filled with fire.

'You should leave now! Leave me alone!' the woman pleaded.

'No!' And like a big fox, Dislaw suddenly leapt on Pina and grabbed her hand which was holding the pair of scissors. 'Tell me it's Bandong!' Dislaw said in anger.

Pina freed her hand from his grip, and the pair of scissors fell to the floor. As Dislaw was about to pick it up, the woman fled, ran to her room and tried to shut the door. But she could not shut it, so she just propped it closed with her body.

Dislaw pushed the door once, twice . . .

'Open it,' he ordered.

'I'll scream if you don't leave,' came a threat from inside the room.

Dislaw took a step back and with all his might, pushed the door open with his right shoulder, which made Pina fall and almost land on the bed.

Pina grabbed something on top of her dresser and threw it at Dislaw. He went nearer and embraced her, then put the palm of his hand on her mouth. The woman fought back, clawing at him and kicking. But the man was strong. She could not scream because his left hand was on her mouth. Her lips seemed to have been sealed shut by a pair of pliers.

Meanwhile, the man's right hand gripped the woman's body tight and struggled to pin her down on the bed. Dislaw straddled her. He was like a python that wanted to squeeze her, destroy her. She felt that the man was not filled with lust anymore, but with revenge, or a combination of the two. She was sure it was no longer love. A man in love would never do such a thing. Dislaw's behaviour was like that of someone who had lost his mind.

Pina's tears began to fall, but she felt that blood was spilling from of her eyes and flaming oil was flowing from her lips.

She was breathing hard and felt as if her chest would explode. She felt suddenly weak, and almost could not move.

'Oh my God! Please save me!' she screamed in silence, for no words came from her lips. Her mouth seemed lifeless now that Dislaw's hand had covered it.

By then, the darkness had overcome the light, and suddenly the rain poured down in torrents. But neither Dislaw, nor Pina noticed the change in weather. The place and time seemed to have been erased for both of them.

Pina closed her eyes and her arms fell to her sides. It seemed that her heart would stop beating. She wanted to die.

When Dislaw noticed that the woman he was raping was no longer fighting back nor protesting, he took away his hand from her mouth and kissed her lips. Then his cruel hand went to her breasts. He ripped her dress and wanted to expose her body. In a moment, the woman's enticing body was exposed, in spite of her weak condition.

As if coming out of a deep nightmare, Pina turned, used her arms, feet and teeth. Filled with hatred, fear, shame and grit to protect her honour, she shut her eyes and pushed the man on top of her with all her might, and was able to free herself from his grip.

'Viper!' she snapped.

45

Bandong was left behind by the bus bound for the provincial capital and it would be two more hours before the next bus would leave. He wanted to visit Mang Pablo in the hospital.

Bandong looked at his watch and saw that it was already almost ten o'clock in the morning. He thought that since he still had a lot of time, it would be better to visit Pina for a while, in case she had some message for her father. He did not ask when the young woman would visit her ailing father, and he better ask her now to see if she could join him in the visit, or he would just wait for her arrival later in the hospital. Bandong was not aware that Dinong was one of the passengers on the bus that had recently departed.

The young teacher had gone down to his house early that day, and he had paid a visit to the New Village. He thought that everyone was still asleep in Pina's house when he passed by. The window in front was closed, unlike before when it used to be open early in the morning, and he saw as he passed it by, her smiling face already radiant in the open window.

Bandong talked to Andres and Marcos about the issue in the New Village that was now the subject of litigation in the court. Attorney Reyes attended the hearing recently, but he did not have the notes and evidence he could use to favour the squatters, to rebut the claim that the old document produced by the Grandes was fake. The offices he had consulted had not yet answered Attorney Reyes, which was why they could not present anything in court. The judge reminded them that the court would only accept evidence—not opinions and hearsay. Apparently, the judge had already met again in private with Don Severo.

On the other hand, Bandong learnt that Andres had already collected the necessary information about his late mother and Kabesang

Resong, his ancestor. Andres had also reposed his trust in Attorney Reyes regarding his case; his attempt to reclaim his ancestor's land that had been grabbed by the Grande husband and wife.

Bandong was delighted to know that the people in the New Village had not lost their hopes. They were even invigorated by the recent events and invested more energy into making products for their home industries. They had all agreed that this livelihood did not have to depend on where one lived, but on the hard work of those who made the products.

'We might lose our land,' said Marcos, 'but we won't let go of this livelihood.'

From the New Village, Bandong then proceeded on his way to the provincial capital, but he missed his bus. The bus between Sampilong and the capital only travelled four times a day. Bandong stopped briefly at Tinoy's barber shop to chat. Tinoy then reported that he had earlier seen Dislaw's jeep going in the direction of the barrio.

'That man is a traitor,' added the barber. 'Be careful, Teacher Bandong, because he always carries his gun.' Tinoy was keenly aware of what had happened at the elementary school and of the altercation between the two men.

Bandong just shrugged his shoulders at the reminder given by the barber. He then proceeded towards Pina's house. He noticed that the light of the sun had been darkened by the thick clouds beginning to spread across the sky. *It might rain*, he thought. And so he walked faster.

On the way, he met two carts that had come from the farm, bearing hay and cut pieces of wood. The occupants of the two carts were seemingly engaged in a race, perhaps to avoid the rain. Even from afar, the young man had already seen the jeep parked in front of Pina's house—Bandong recognized the jeep.

'It's Dislaw,' he whispered to himself, and then was worried why the boastful overseer was there at that time. 'We'll meet again,' he said, as if he would face him in a game that he would surely win. But then, he reminded himself that such an encounter should not happen in the house of his beloved, so decided against making the encounter that morning. He shook his head.

Like voices recorded in a cassette tape, he still remembered his exchange of words with Dislaw. 'Prepare yourself for our next encounter,' he had challenged Dislaw, to which the latter had answered, 'We'll easily meet, since this town is too small for the both of us.' And now, after a mere twenty-four hours, they were fated to meet again. But this time, in Pina's house, with his beloved as a witness. *No*, Bandong reflected.

But then, he seemed to be impelled by some hidden force—he half-walked, half-ran towards his destination. Dislaw was not inside the parked jeep. The window was open, but there was neither the radiant smile nor lovely face to be found there.

Bandong called out his greetings in front of the open window once; no one answered. He repeated his call, this time in a louder voice. No one answered again. But this house had never been bereft of occupants. The jeep was there. The window was open. *Where is Dislaw? Where is Dinong?* And like an answer to his volley of questions, the heavy rain fell.

Bandong climbed up the stairs. He looked inside the house. He noticed that the chair in front of the sewing machine had fallen. His gaze fell on the pair of scissors on the floor. And in his mind, he seemed to have heard Pina's plea. Quick as lightning, he turned to look at the woman's door. It was half-opened.

A thud surprised him. He leapt towards the room. And through the open door, he saw a scene that turned his blood into ice. Dislaw was straddling Pina and she was fighting back, but what could a chick do in the face of an eagle's cruelty? In that split second, Dislaw had wanted to fulfill his darkest wish.

Bandong's left hand grapped Dislaw's collar, turned the man around to face him, and with his fist, hit him on the lips. Dislaw could not ascertain whether he had been bludgeoned or struck by lightning. He fell on the floor and lost consciousness.

Bandong quickly raised Pina, checked her over and brought her out of the house. He got a glass of water and made her drink it. However, as the glass of water touched the lips of his beloved, a voice from behind surprised them.

'Don't move!'

Quicker than the falling rain, Bandong turned and threw the glass at Dislaw. The latter ducked and fired his gun. Pina screamed. But the bullet missed its mark and instead of hitting Bandong, it went through the wall.

Before Dislaw could fire again, Bandong had already grabbed the gun. They fought for its possession. A second gunshot erupted, went upward and through the roof. Then, Bandong gripped and turned Dislaw's left arm, causing the gun to fall. It fell with a thud on the floor, and Bandong kicked it away.

The rain continued to pour, drowning out the sound of the bullets and no one outside noticed the commotion in Pina's house.

Pina's strength had returned. She then stood up and went to one corner of the house. She seemed to be watching the fight between the two men, as if in a dream. She could not move away; neither could she come nearer.

The two men struggled and fell on the floor. Bandong was hitting Dislaw with his mighty fists, while the latter's feet kept on kicking in the air. He wanted his shoes to land on the sensitive parts of his opponent's body. Meanwhile, the lips of the traitorous overseer were bleeding and a cluster of dark berries seemed to have bloomed in his eyes. But still he fought, wanting to prove that he, Dislaw, never shied away from a fight.

Suddenly, with both his strong hands, Bandong was able to grip his opponent's neck. He closed his fists and tried to strangle Dislaw. It looked like the neck of a chicken being squeezed by a python. Dislaw's eyes began to bulge.

Pina was frightened at what she saw. It was the same fear that had gripped her earlier, when Dislaw was trying to rape her. Bandong might kill someone. Dislaw was already helpless. His body already lay flat on the floor and only his feet struggled, which was why he looked like a rat caught in a trap, with its tail being the only thing moving.

That was why Pina went to Bandong and with terror, she shook his shoulders.

'Bandong,' the woman called out, but he did not mind her, or he might not have heard her. It seemed that the young teacher had lost his mind, or his sense of restraint.

Pina was filled with terror. She knew that she could not stop Bandong from realizing his intent to kill Dislaw. She ran out of the house; she was confused. She would seek help outside.

The falling of the rain had already thinned by then. Pina did not know where to go. Thankfully, she was not far from her house when she saw her uncle, who was coming home from the farm.

'Uncle Ipe! Uncle Ipe!' she shouted.

She quickly told him what was happening. The farmer rushed and went up the steps of the house, two at a time. Pina followed suit and ran after him.

Pina's uncle had to use his unusual strength to pry loose the iron-like grip of Bandong around Dislaw's neck. Dislaw's face was already turning blue, his tongue was hanging out and it seemed like he was not breathing anymore. That was why the older man had to pry Bandong's hands from Dislaw's neck. The traitor's body shivered and then he stretched his body flat, like that of a dead person. They thought he had already died.

Bandong sat on a chair and placed his two hands on his face. Pina got a glass of water and let him drink from it. She also got a towel and wiped the sweat flowing from the face and neck of her boyfriend.

Meanwhile, Uncle Ipe applied what he had learnt to bring Dislaw back to consciousness. He massaged Dislaw's arms and body, the way it was done to the drowning, but he thought his efforts would come to nought. Suddenly, Dislaw moved his arms, and then he stopped cold again. He raised one of his feet, as if he wanted to rise, but then his foot fell again on the floor. Then one of his eyes opened, then both, but he quickly closed them, as if the light was blinding him. Then he inhaled air sharply and his chest heaved.

'He's alive!' Pina's uncle exclaimed.

Bandong raised his head and threw a sharp look at the figure lying prostrate on the floor. He wanted to stand up while staring at Dislaw, but Pina restrained him.

'Bandong,' said the woman, as she caressed the dishevelled hair of the man.

Bandong turned and his eyes met those of Pina's. In that one look, they exchanged the promise that sealed both their hearts and souls together. It seemed as if Bandong had whispered to Pina, 'My love' and the woman had responded with 'My life'. They could no longer control their feelings, so they embraced tightly, and Bandong kissed Pina's lips for the first time, a kiss that was seemingly endless.

46

Donya Leona's mouth fired like a machine gun when she learnt of what happened to Dislaw, whose lips had swollen like tomatoes and eyes had turned the colour of Java plums, the moment he got off the jeep he had parked in the Grandes' garage.

'It's better if you had just died,' the rich woman shouted, 'for the shame that you have brought upon us. Now, you'll be the butt of everyone's jokes.'

What had happened in Mang Pablo's house had spread like wildfire, and Kosme had promptly informed the Grande husband and wife about it, after hearing about it in the town centre. Cely had also heard about it because she was with Kosme at that time.

Dislaw had received first-aid at the town's dispensary and was interrogated at the police station. Before Dislaw could proceed to the Grandes' house to return their jeep, the rich couple had already been apprised of the situation.

'Now that we need him to help us in our cases and other things, this fool wants to swallow something else,' screeched Donya Leona.

'It's better if we send him to Manila,' said Don Severo. 'He can help Ninet there.'

'We need him here,' she countered her husband's suggestion. 'We need him to help us with our troubles at the farms, with the squatters, the errands to be done in the provincial capital. There are only the two of us here. Who else can we rely on? Kosme isn't like Dislaw.'

'Indeed,' agreed the rich man, 'but what did the beast do? Rape is not a light crime. And can you fix things with Pablo or Bandong? If you want him to go to Manila, then so be it. If not, I might be the one to kill him,' Don Severo decided in the end.

The husband and wife got mad not because their overseer had got into serious trouble, but instead because of the embarrassment he had caused them, which might even implicate the Grandes. Dislaw was not just anyone; his name had gained currency because he was the overseer of the prime family in the province.

If only he had succeeded in his attempt on Pina, or he had killed Bandong, or even just defeated him in their fight—then it would have been a different matter. He would emerge as the hero and not the heel, and people would admire him instead of laughing at him; fear him instead of heaping scorn upon him. The overseer of the Grande family had tried to rape a barrio girl and was beaten black and blue by a mere teacher—in the eyes of the Grande husband and wife, this was the height of shameful behaviour.

That was why when they came to face with Dislaw and saw evidence that confirmed Kosme's news, a dog freed from its tether in the backyard could not have eaten the words that Donya Leona flung at Dislaw. Dislaw was speechless; he looked worse than a kid who had been caught stealing.

Don Severo ordered Dislaw to leave for Manila the next morning and stay in Ninet's house. Ninet had already passed the board examinations for pharmacists and had just opened her own pharmacy in the city.

'Just stay there for a while and help out Ninet,' the rich man said. 'You can also heal your wounds there.'

Donya Leona had wanted her daughter to return to Sampilong and open a pharmacy in the town centre, but Ninet had refused.

'I'd rather not open a pharmacy here,' snapped Ninet. 'I don't want to compete with the pharmacy and funeral parlour owned by the sour spinster who already looks embalmed, even if she's still alive.'

'Well, you do have a point. We have to civilize your townmates first, Severo,' the rich woman had later assented.

That was why the person renting the first floor of their house in a famous district in the city was asked to leave, so that Ninet could open her pharmacy there. And that was where she lived and worked now.

On the other hand, Jun had passed the board examinations for medical doctors and had left for the United States. He would stay there for two years, and was supposed to specialize in the treatment of cancer patients. However, Jun had winked at Pil and Dan when he had said that he would 'specialize in the treatment of cancer patients'.

'I hope you don't come back with cancer yourself,' Pil teased him, since he knew Jun and his predilections very well indeed. The young Grande scion had barely passed his board examinations.

On the other hand, Marybee didn't want to leave Jun's side before he left for the United States, saying that she would follow her boyfriend there at the first opportunity to do so. But Jun had not even left Manila for a few months when Dan's telephone constantly rang—and who would be on the other end of the line, except Marybee? One night, they stayed in the club for a whole night, and one Sunday afternoon, they were all by themselves in a resort in the cool mountain city of Tagaytay. Marybee even introduced Dan to her father as a rich Chinese and the old man later told his family that they needed a lawyer more than a doctor.

All these things were not unknown to Ninet, but since she was a modern woman, she reasoned that losing Dan would never amount to a real loss, since there were ten others who could replace him. She would not want for suitable suitors. Ninet wrote to Jun about the open relationship between Dan and Marybee, and her doctor-brother just wrote back saying that in the American city where he lived and in the university where he studied, three women were in love with him and they 'liked Filipino men a lot over here'.

'And they're not just mestizas, but pure whites,' he told Ninet in his letter. He said that white women only began falling head over heels for Filipino men after the Second World War, because of Bataan and Corregidor, the places where the American and Filipino soldiers fought bravely but lost to the overpowering might of the Japanese Imperial Army. As for Dan, Jun just gave this advice to his sister: 'Forget the past as quickly as you can, for life is short'.

In this group of friends and classmates, only Pil and Bining did not veer away from their original directions in life. Pil became a full-pledged medical doctor while Bining became a teacher. They later got married and fulfilled the promises they had made. They moved to a far-flung town in the province in the south, where there was neither a hospital nor a good clinic. Pil started a medical dispensary there, while Bining taught at the school.

'We've got a good start,' Bining wrote in a letter to Ninet. 'We can help the ordinary people here, while we also help ourselves. Isn't this the real purpose of healing and teaching?'

The next day, following the orders of the Grande husband and wife, Dislaw went to the city to disappear for a while and let things settle down. He did not want the situation to worsen and he did not want to add more fuel to the fire that was blazing in Sampilong. He would help out at Ninet's pharmacy instead.

On the other hand, Aling Sabel's family was meeting to ascertain what they would do in the face of Dislaw's beastly attack. Mang Pablo was still in the hospital and they decided not to relay to him what had happened, to avoid his situation from worsening. He was already regaining his strength, recuperating in the hospital. Bandong was present during the family meetings but he kept silent, since he did not want to preempt their decision, and let the family decide on the matter. In his mind, he had reason to go after Dislaw for his attempt on Bandong's life, but the young teacher thought he now had the upper hand. In fact, he had a reason to be proud, for he had defeated Dislaw and would have met certain death if not for the timely arrival of Tata Ipe, who pried loose his fingers that were gripping the neck of the Grandes' overseer.

'I can forgive, but my anger will never subside,' Bandong told Pina.

He thought that Dislaw was the kind of person who would never change or repent as long as he lived in the big stone house. Bandong recalled the series of misfortunes that Dislaw had caused him: he was always stabbed in the back; Dislaw always fought with him through both words and deeds; Dislaw hurled unfounded accusations against him, and lastly, he tried to dishonour the woman he so loved. If he did not arrive in time and Dislaw's evil deed had been done, Pina would have been dishonoured and destroyed, and Bandong would walk the streets crowned with dried bamboo leaves on his head.

But if that came to pass, it would not have been Pina's fault, and any woman would try to shield herself from the force and violence of a man. It would not be a cause of shame because she would have fought bravely and well, but still, it was different if a woman was still clean and pure. Bandong reflected that if Dislaw had succeeded in raping her, she would just turn away and leave him and follow the myth of the woman of the barrio, who rose up from the mud where she had fallen. Bandong would not blame Pina if this came to pass, but he would surely go to Dislaw and slash his throat. Even ten lives of this beast would never be enough to compensate for the happiness with Pina that he could have lost.

Aling Sabel did not like the thought of taking the case to court because, according to her, nothing truly bad had happened to her daughter, and she was more afraid of the loose talk that a court case would generate. The other reason, of course, was that the old woman had favoured the well-connected Dislaw for her daughter.

'If he repented for what he has done and asks for sincere forgiveness, then that's it for me,' said Aling Sabel, and then she added, 'Let us leave the matter to your father.' Pina just relented.

In truth, Pina was torn between her hatred for Dislaw and her shame for Bandong. Now, there was no longer any doubt that she loved the young teacher, not just because she owed him a debt of gratitude, but due to the spring of feelings unleashed by the latest events. It would already be too much for Bandong to ask her again about her feelings for him. But she was embarrassed that he had seen the ugly drama in her bedroom. She was lying dishevelled in her bed, fighting with all her might against Dislaw's embrace and kisses. Dislaw, whom she never loved and whom she now hated, had been the first man to embrace her; the first to touch her fresh breasts; and the first to kiss her fragrant lips. The poison of his acts could be cleansed with soap and water, but could she erase them from her memories, and from the fact that Bandong had witnessed all of it?

Thankfully, Bandong did not share the anxiety and the dark worries of Pina, and repeatedly reassured her of his love. His admiration for Pina's purity and beauty deepened even further, according to Bandong, because she had shown that it was better to die than be dishonoured.

Mang Pablo's family and Bandong were not alone in their thoughts about the dire event that had recently happened. The farmers in the barrio and the squatters in the New Village were also with them, along with the teachers who were terribly annoyed with Mister Henry Danyo.

'Dislaw the Eagle should not even attempt to visit the barrio again,' warned Tasyo.

'He really assumed the role of an eagle and tried to snatch a young chicken,' Simon said with a laugh. 'But he almost lost his sharp beak and his big eyes, since he fought with a bigger bird of prey.'

'If he gets lost and finds his way to the Tambakan,' warned Marcos, 'because he called ours a land of trash, we will turn him into a piece of trash.'

47

Mang Pablo left the hospital after a few days. He wasn't fully well, but the doctor at the provincial hospital said he was out of danger. The health of Pina's father seemed to have improved, for he remained calm when apprised of the beastly act done by Dislaw to his daughter.

He listened intently to Pina's report, to that given by his brother-in-law Ipe, and the words of Bandong. The old farmer drank water several times during the course of the compiled narration, but he seemed no longer weighed down by the ailment that had struck him down earlier.

Pina said that even on the night that Dislaw had visited along with Mister Danyo, he had warned her that if he did not win the young woman's love, she would no longer be of use to others. Pina was inflamed and had hurriedly left Dislaw alone, but she had not reported the matter to her parents, because she had known the Grandes' overseer to be boastful. She also knew how to take care of herself.

But that morning when Dislaw climbed the stairs of the house while Pina was alone, the young woman felt her blood run cold when she saw that the beast had intended to make his threat come true, she told her father. But as Dislaw was attempting to rape her, she thought that to defend her honour, she would even kill him—even if there was the possibility of her getting killed. And when she was almost rendered unconscious in her self-defence, Bandong came and saved her.

Tata Ipe then narrated that he was going home as the rain had subsided, when he met Pina with her hair dishevelled, her clothes torn, and running barefoot. The words tumbled out of her mouth and as soon as the farmer pieced together what was happening, he rushed to the house of Mang Pablo and almost jumped up the stairs. He found Bandong choking Dislaw, whose face was already turning blue, tongue hanging and eyes turning white as oysters. Tata Ipe used his strength to pry Bandong's hands off Dislaw's neck, and when he finally separated him from Dislaw, it took a while for the beast to regain consciousness.

'I thought the shameless one had finally died,' said Tata Ipe. 'But it seems that bad weeds don't die easy.'

What was funny, added Mang Pablo's brother-in-law, was that the moment he regained consciousness, the first thing Dislaw asked for was his revolver. And when he was going downstairs, his eyes were sharp and jaw hard, as if he was not afraid to commit another beastly act. He did not speak to any of the people who had arrived at the scene; who had been summoned by Tata Ipe's wife when she got home after selling her wares in the marketplace, returning when the rain had subsided. Dislaw was already naturally ugly, but at that time, he looked more like he was wearing an uglier mask of himself.

'If I was bearing a child and took a strange fancy for his looks, I'd have ended up giving birth to a half-human, half-horse,' said Tata Ipe's wife.

But it seemed that repentance wasn't in Dislaw's nature. Before finally taking the first step down the ladder, he even threw a glance like the sharp point of a knife at Bandong, who was seated on a chair, and at Pina, who was standing behind her boyfriend, her right arm resting on his shoulder. Even if he did not say it, imprinted upon the whole of Dislaw's being were the words, 'One day, we'll have another duel'. Those left behind were stunned by such a wanton display of boastfulness.

Dislaw left with the policeman to whom Tata Ipe had turned over the revolver which he had picked up off the floor and secured. Some farmers who had heard of what had happened, followed Dislaw and the policeman as they wended their way out of the front yard.

On the other hand, Bandong reported that he had met with Chief Hugo and enquired about the steps the police would take against Dislaw. According to the chief, aside from the investigation launched against Dislaw, none of the other interested parties had shown up at the police station to make their report.

'If you or Pina have a complaint to make against him, then you should do so,' said the Chief of Police and then he added, 'It seems that nothing serious happened after all.'

Bandong did not mention anymore what Hugo had said about how if they had complaints, Pina would have to undergo a medico-legal examination with a doctor. The young teacher almost lost his cool at Hugo's words, especially when he recalled that the Chief of Police had hurled the slew of unfounded accusations against him along with Dislaw.

But Bandong wasn't aware that aside from the unwanted embrace and kisses that she had got from Dislaw, what had really gutted Pina was the tragedy that would have befallen Bandong if he had been able to kill Dislaw.

The chief also added that Dislaw had left Sampilong and he did not stop his departure, since there was neither charge nor a formal complaint made against him.

'It's easy to bring him back here if the judge issues a warrant,' said the Chief of Police.

After hearing Bandong's report and asking for advice from Aling Sabel and Pina, Mang Pablo thought that the issue would just bring bad tidings. Even if they filed a case in court, they could already see what the decision of the judge would be, biased as he was toward the Grande family.

'The Grandes hold the nose of the judge in the provincial capital,' he said, shaking his head. 'Let's bide our time, because there are many ways of getting justice.'

The afternoon after Mang Pablo was discharged from the hospital, his friends dropped by his house to wish him well. Ba Inte was there, as well as the other leaders of farmers' organization, some leaders of the PTA, along with Andres and Marcos from New Village.

Everyone laughed when Ba Inte said that he could not visit Mang Pablo because his arthritis did not allow him to walk.

'When the rainy season comes, my legs and thighs are like rice fields being raked by a thousand plows,' said the old man in jest. 'I was thinking that if ever I did visit Pablo, then I might also end up in the hospital.'

'If that happened, then I'd bring you along with me when I was discharged from the hospital,' said Pina's father. 'In the poor provincial hospital, you'll only get well if you're not destined for the graveyard, and you will certainly die if it's your time to go.'

'Oh, this man,' said Aling Sabel, 'if we didn't rush you to the provincial hospital, worms would have been feasting on your body by now.'

'Don't worry, Sabel,' said Ba Inte, 'bad weeds like us live for a long time.'

'But Dislaw, the falcon, he's the real bad weed,' snapped Simon.

'No, Dislaw isn't a bad weed,' Ba Inte corrected him, 'Dislaw is the kind of beast that crawls on the weeds.'

Everybody laughed at the fine banter by Ba Inte, who was known in the village for his sharp wit. When they were partaking of the snacks that Pina had prepared, Ba Inte waved at Pina and when she came closer, asked the young woman the whereabouts of Bandong.

'He was here, a while ago,' answered Pina, 'but he left for the capital because he was summoned by the superintendent. He even rented a jeep to make sure he could reach the capital faster. He said he will return as soon as possible.'

'Maybe it's because of the charges filed against him.'

'It seemed that way.'

'Those charges will all come to nothing,' said Ba Inte. 'Those are just his enemy's delaying tactics so he won't end up as the principal.'

'No one believes in the charges filed against him,' Pina said with sadness.

'Everyone knows that. But what I want to know, young lady, is when are we going to have a feast at the long table?'

Pina's cheeks turned crimson, but she dodged the question with a smile.

'Oh, Ba Inte. Who's been telling you about these things?'

'My eyes are still clear, and even if my arthritis is killing me, my senses are still sharp. I'm lucky I'm not a dimwit like Dislaw.'

Pina finally laughed and told the old man in a soft voice, 'Don't worry, Ba Inte. You'll be the first to know.'

The guests had not yet left when Bandong returned from the provincial capital.

'I've got good news,' he said, greeting everyone with a face wreathed in a smile. 'All the charges against me have been dropped!'

Everyone whooped with joy and congratulated him. They said that was the result that they expected as well.

'That's great news! I also expected that those charges would be dropped,' said Mang Pablo.

Bandong went closer to Pina and whispered, 'Aren't you happy?'

'Why do you need to ask?' his girlfriend said with a smile and repeated what she had earlier said, 'If it was up to me, you'd be imprisoned forever.'

Bandong gently took one of Pina's hands, indicating his approval.

The young teacher continued narrating the details of the good news to his friends. Along with the dropping of the charges, the superintendent had also asked Bandong to return to his work as an inspiring teacher and assistant principal of the elementary school.

'You'll either be the principal, or bust,' Tasyo snapped.

Bandong looked at Pina, and then spoke up. 'I've the same opinions as Tasyo. I might not even return to teaching anymore.'

Silence fell upon everyone and they noticed Pina nodding, as if to say that she would agree to whatever Bandong decided on. The young teacher continued speaking.

'I'll be a farmer again. The farm of Nana Oris now belongs to me and it needs to be plowed—'

'You can also work on my farm land,' offered Ba Inte.

No one in the gathering countered Bandong's plan.

'Once Bandong becomes a farmer, he will truly become our leader,' declared Tasyo.

'If I may speak, my friend Tasyo,' said Andres, who had been quiet all along and only spoke up now. 'You should remain the leader of the farmers' organization. Your leadership is excellent. As for Teacher Bandong, yes, we need him. The farmers, the squatters, the parents and the teachers, as well as the ordinary citizens of Sampilong—we all trust him and pin our hopes on him.' Andres stopped for a while and then he spoke, louder this time. 'We've got bigger plans for Teacher Bandong. We want him to be the mayor of our town. He should stand in the forthcoming elections!'

In unison, everyone in Mang Pablo's house agreed with Andres. They gathered around the young teacher and said with pure joy, 'Long live Mayor Bandong!'

48

The case in the provincial capital became the talk of the town, but now, more people attended the hearing of the case lodged against the squatters in New Village. In the face of the rising number of people who wanted to watch the proceedings, the judge had no choice but to bar more people from entering the courthouse. A staff member told them to just stay outside and listen, and not make any noise.

Unlike the first hearing which was only a preliminary investigation, the court hearing that day marked the start of the trial. Almost all of the squatters had left the village at the crack of dawn to go to the government building that housed the court. Some of them went merely to observe, while others went as if they would to attend a rally, or a picket that was part of a big labour strike.

This issue had been the topic of conversation in the New Village ever since the squatters' leader had received the summons from the court. Likewise, the farmers also talked about it often, especially once the squatters and the farmers had forged an alliance. The men went to attend the court hearing, taking their wives with them.

On the other hand, the Grande husband and wife did not show up, which was only to be expected, according to the huge crowd that had gathered outside the hall of the judge. What they noticed, though, was the palpable absence of Dislaw. In the earlier hearings, the boastful overseer had his arms draped around the shoulders of the two expensive lawyers hired by the Grande family. Father Pascual also came with them. Dislaw acted as if he was the head of the jury that was trying the case, which was why his absence was noticeable that day.

'How can he show up here when he's hiding? He's supposed to be in Manila,' said one farmer in response to the enquiry of someone who asked about Dislaw.

'I heard he is in the hospital because he was almost in his death throes when Bandong let him go,' said another squatter.

'He thought he won't get caught?' asked another man sitting at the back.

'That beast is lucky that Bandong didn't castrate him,' snapped one woman from the farm.

When the court clerk announced the start of the proceedings, the judge had just sat at his high table that was set on a wooden platform. The crowd was thick inside the hall and outside of it, and even the long passageway was filled with people. You could not even drop a needle amidst the throng of people.

The two opposing sides in the case sat in front of each other, on the left and right sides of the judge. On the right side sat the two lawyers of the Grande family, along with their witnesses, including a gentleman who was wearing a tie and who looked like a professor of Criminology at a university. Chief Hugo was also there, along with the treasurer of the province. The treasurer had nothing to do with the case, but he was a friend of the Grande family's and had come to watch the proceedings, perhaps to make a report about it later to the rich couple and curry a favour or two in return, later.

On the left side, Attorney Reyes sat between Andres and Bandong. They were in the same row of seats as Marcos and Tasyo, and in the back could be seen Sedes, Kiko and Marcos' wife, as well as Simon, Julian and Blas.

The clerk of the court read the charges of the Grande husband and wife and Father Pascual against the people, who had allegedly laid claim over the land they owned in what was now known as New Village. Attorney Reyes swiftly stood up, asked permission from the court to speak, and asked a question.

'Are the ones who have filed this charge also present here—the Grande husband and wife and Father Pascual?'

The side of the ones who had filed the case in court were surprised. The first lawyer said that the three people were not present, but they could be summoned to appear in court if needed.

'They're the ones who filed the case, therefore, they should be present here,' insisted Attorney Reyes.

'Don't meddle with the way we do things here,' said the other lawyer in an irritated tone.

'We need them here.'

'And why?'

'To serve as witnesses for their defence.'

'Witnesses? On your side?' asked the lawyer of the Grande husband and wife.

'If you'll permit, Honourable Judge,' said Attorney Reyes, addressing the judge. 'Please send a subpoena to the Grande husband and wife and to Father Pascual as well.'

The judge took down notes in his memorandum, but did not speak.

Then the lawyer of the accused presented their most important evidence, the old document that said that the King of Spain had given the land in question to the ancestors of the Grande family. By virtue of this document, the alleged owners of the land asked the squatters to vacate the land where they had built their shacks without permission.

The lawyer of the Grandes then painted a picture of who the squatters were.

'These are rash people who will go anywhere, stay there, and build their shacks on lots they do not own. They have no rights to these lands and they know it; they do not even seek permission before building their shacks on these lands. They did all of it in violation of the law, and while there, they did things that went against hygiene and health conditions, against morality and good behaviour, until the land that used to be clean was turned into slums filled with garbage, breeding illnesses, and a nest of disorder.'

Attorney Reyes again swiftly stood up and protested against the insults heaped by the opposing lawyer upon the people living in New Village. He asked that the words by of the opposing lawyer be struck from the records of the case. But the judge did not side with him.

'Let those words stay in the records,' said the judge.

The Grandes' lawyer continued with his tirades against the squatters.

'We don't know the origins of these people. They've no logical abilities and understand only the logic of violence.'

Attorney Reyes protested against this accusation, but the judge did not side with him again.

'They don't pay rent,' added the lawyer of the Grande family, 'they don't pay taxes, they don't contribute anything to the government, to the place where they have built their shacks—which they are now destroying. In truth, they have no source of livelihood and in this way, they are just a burden—a difficult and dangerous burden; a knife aimed at peace and public order of a country that is honourable and calm. They should not just be driven away, they should be imprisoned, so they can no longer pose danger to society, and can no longer infect other people with disease.'

Attorney Reyes again stood up and made a motion to have the insulting words struck down from the official records of the case, starting at the first words uttered by the opposing lawyer.

'We're here to present evidence and arrive at reason in these proceedings, not to insult other people,' he said, but his words again came to nought.

The lawyer of the Grande family then followed up with the presentation of their witness. They first introduced someone who looked like a professor, who was allegedly an expert on calligraphy and handwriting. He then made a presentation on the old document, saying that the paper was made of parchment; the ink that was used estimated the age of the document at more or less 100 years old, and then he certified that it was a true, genuine and complete document.

Another proof that he cited was the signature of the King of Spain in red ink, which the expert claimed could not be used by just anyone during those days because they were forbidden to do so. Only the kings and leaders of the state could use the red ink in their signatures. He added that the seal that was used by the king was also beyond reproach, then adding other details pertaining to science, and using Latin words to describe the chemistry, photography, microphotography, ultraviolet details, X-rays, and other arcane things dealing with the quality of the paper and the colour of the ink—details that only he understood.

The expert gave his testimony for more or less one hour, but Attorney Reyes only asked him two short and pointed questions, which caused laughter in the room.

First question: 'As an expert in the art of handwriting, are you also an expert in detecting which signatures are real or fake?'

The expert thought for a while, and then he said, 'Perhaps.'

Second question: 'How much were you paid to serve as an expert witness?'

Answer: 'That's a secret of my profession.'

Chief Hugo and the lieutenant also served as witnesses and gave testimony against the thievery and the illnesses rampant in New Village and places nearby, ever since the squatters had set up their shacks in the place. The two witnesses wanted to prove that the squatters were a group of people who did not follow the rules of hygiene and the laws of the government.

In their defence, the lawyer of the Grandes compared the situation of what happened during the Japanese regime to the so-called ways of democracy. He said that since the country was ruled by a government of laws, the laws should apply to everyone, without fear or favour, without being partial to anyone. Everyone was supposed to respect the laws and follow them.

'Is it right for the government to be soft on those who violate the laws?' asked the lawyer of the Grande family in a loud voice. 'Should we give way to those who do not respect the rights of others? Is it right that those who follow the government, pay their taxes, promote agriculture and business, be the ones to fall victim to the lazy, whose vices and sins should not be encouraged and rewarded?'

He called upon the court to side with propriety and honour those who owned the land in question. He cited the rules enshrined in the Constitution of the Republic that promoted the rights to property, and maintained that the Constitution should be upheld.

'Moreover, the old document that was signed by the King of Spain and is in the possession of the Grande family isn't just a piece of wet paper,' the lawyer said.

He even read the Bill of Rights, or the list or rights of every citizen, that said no one should be deprived of life, freedom and property, except through the operation of the law, and everyone has the right to equal protection under the law.

'Therefore, any property cannot be taken by someone else without appropriate payment given to the owner of the land,' he read aloud one provision in the Bill of Rights.

'Now, all of you can see,' the lawyer said, and then he looked around at the people in the court, at Attorney Reyes, at the group of squatters and ended his gaze at the judge, 'now you see that property is as important as life and freedom, according to our Constitution. Now, you also see that the government by itself cannot sieze someone else's property, even for public works, unless the landowner has been properly compensated. Why, then, would we allow the squatters to get, claim and use private land—a violation that even the government cannot commit?'

Whispers filled the place so that the judge had to pound his mallet on the table several times to silence the crowd.

'That's how much property is honoured and valued,' added the lawyer, 'because such property is the fruit of the hard work, talent, thriftiness, gallantry and other honourable virtues of those who own the land. This land did not come from bad deeds, not grabbed, not stolen from anyone.'

A buzz of noise erupted again amongst the people and the judge warned everyone that those who could not keep quiet, would be asked to leave the courtroom. He called the attention of the three guards to implement his order to maintain silence and order in the courtroom.

49

When order was restored in the courtroom, the lawyer of the Grandes launched a challenge about the matter at hand.

'We're choosing between two things,' he said. 'Between the owners of the land and the squatters. Between following the law and stepping on the law. Between what is right and what is wrong. Between justice and injustice. It's clear and unequivocal which between them we should choose. Is it going to be democracy or disorder?'

The lawyer fished a handkerchief out of his pocket and wiped the sweat from his face before delivering the last argument in his speech.

'Honourable Judge, for the sake of peace in the town and order in the government, because on this issue in the small town of Sampilong, depends the condition of the Republic, I hope you will give a lesson to all, whether they are big in stature or low; rich or poor; bright or dumb; and especially to those who lack the awareness that here reigns the rule of law and not of mere men. If this does not come to pass, it will adversely affect us all, Honourable Judge, because if reason loses in this battle, then disorder will rule along with anarchism, and even communism. That is why we should not give way to the enemies of democracy. The land should be returned to the Grande family, and may you serve unto the squatters the rule of law.'

Before the lawyer could sit down after his speech, Attorney Reyes quickly stood up. But the judge looked at his watch and reminded everyone that it was almost noon.

'We'll hold a recess and continue again at two o'clock,' he decided.

Most of the people left the court room immediately, their minds filled with their own opinions and hearts running riot with their feelings. They spoke with passion and argued with each other, and consequently, most of the things they heard ran counter to their beliefs. The small band of Grande followers were certain of their victory.

'You better prepare your things because you'll soon have to evacuate from the place,' Kosme made a snide remark within hearing range of the squatters, especially Kanor.

'You're a fool,' Kanor told Kosme, 'I might use an axe to split your face into two, later.'

'Oh, what a snobbish monkey we have here,' Kosme snapped and prepared for a fistfight.

Chief Hugo, who was behind them, intervened.

'If you're going to kill each other, do it in my territory,' he said, 'that way, I can easily bury the loser.'

The courthouse was filled to the rafters again that afternoon, when the hearing resumed. More people poured in, since they were hoping that Donya Leona would finally make her appearance. But neither she nor Don Severo showed up, and their lawyer later presented a medical certificate stating that the rich woman was ill and could not attend the hearing. She also sent a letter to the court, indicating that the best proof and witness is the presence of the old document.

The court accepted her letter, as well as her medical certificate.

The defence then presented their evidence and witnesses. One by one, they all sat as witnesses—Marcos, who first arrived at the hilly terrain to clear it; followed by Kiko and Andres, and finally, Teacher Bandong. Attorney Reyes had wanted Mayor Bartolo to appear, to show that the local executive had given permission for the squatters to settle in that place, but he also had an alibi for his non-appearance in the court.

'Now, we're getting the painful reward for everything we've done,' lamented Andres. 'We're being driven away and the roofs over our heads are being pried from us.'

Before he launched into a defence, Attrorney Reyes gave a history of the land, that it was given by nature to be a blessing for all and not to be owned only by a few people.

Attorney Reyes ended his tirade by reminding everyone that there are people who already have enough but still want more, and did not want to see other people living in even a semblance of comfort. They should read the biblical handwriting on the wall, because these words never failed.

'If you're not afraid of God and men,' the lawyer said with passion, 'then be afraid of history. History will not forgive you.'

The group of squatters could not help it. They burst into applause as Attorney Reyes took his seat back on the bench. The judge ended the hearing by saying that he would make his decision after both parties had submitted their memoranda.

The squatters and the farmers were filled with joy as they went home. They congratulated Attorney Reyes and Teacher Bandong.

The sun had already set when the people parted ways. Bandong and Andres took the last bus to Sampilong, while Attorney Reyes drove back to Manila.

50

The squatters of New Village felt worse than a gambler who had chosen a weak rooster in a cockfight. The judge gave credence to the authenticity and power of the old document, and since no other person was pursuing the ownership of the land, it was handed over to Donya Leona and Father Pascual.

Barely had the decision been made by the judge in the capital against Andres and his group, when the Grande husband and wife demanded for it to be implemented. They called for the chief of police of Sampilong.

'They still have an appeal,' said Hugo after Donya Leona had told him what she wanted to have happen. 'I'm not sure if we can drive them away now, but we can try.'

'The judgment of the court should be implemented until it's changed,' the rich woman gave her opinion.

'You and your policemen should go to the squatters' area,' ordered Don Severo. 'The use of force is part of reason,' and then he added, 'It's just too bad that Dislaw is not here. He could have helped you.'

'But your man can't even hit bull's eye,' the chief made a snide remark. 'He fired two shots that just went up in the air.'

Donya Leona called for Iska and ordered her to bring in a bottle of alcohol.

'Oh, I cannot take it, my dear godmother,' said Hugo. 'I don't drink when I'm at work. You know how it is, people might talk.'

'Very well then, just take the bottle with you,' and she ordered Iska to fetch a sealed bottle of Scotch whiskey.

That afternoon, Chief Hugo immediately went to New Village, along with six of his policemen. All of them were armed to the teeth.

Andres and his group were surprised, and the other squatters immediately formed a group. All of them went to the centre of the village.

'We are here to implement the judgment of the court,' the chief began, and showed Andres a copy of the judgment.

'But the case is still on appeal,' said Andres.

'I'm not concerned about your appeal,' snapped Hugo. 'Here is the judgment. You know how to read. Until it is changed, it has to be followed.'

'I need a firm and separate order for your act to proceed.'

'Are you wiser than the judge?'

'No, Chief, I just want to clarify the matter.'

'This is the right thing to do,' and he waved the piece of paper for everyone to see.

'But the case has no final judgment yet.'

'You're so repetitive,' said Hugo, who seemed like he was about to lose his patience. 'I'm giving you three days to dismantle your shacks. If not, I will order the police to do so.'

'You'll be in trouble, Chief.'

'Let us see.'

'Yes, let's see.'

One of the policemen then pushed Andres and demanded, 'Are you threatening us?'

Kanor and the other young squatters prepared themselves for a fight, but Hugo averted it by giving a warning to his men.

'Don't use violence immediately,' he said, then turned to Andres. 'You're really tough, huh? Who's your backer?'

Andres did not lower his voice and answered firmly.

'What are we fighting for?' he asked. 'We are poor, we are squatters, we are rubbish in the eyes of many people. We don't have money, no influence, no food. But we still believe that laws rule supreme in this country. And we should thank our stars that people like us still follow the rule of law.'

'Oh, the squatters claim they follow the law,' Hugo said in an insulting tone.

'Our only fault is that we're poor.'

'I don't want to argue with you,' snapped the chief of police. 'We'll come back in three days. Remember that. I do not want to see your rubbish when I come back here.'

Then the chief turned and left without farewell, along with his six policemen.

For a long time, those left in the centre of the New Village were quiet. Andres knew that the chief of police also knew it was wrong to order them to leave the place, and they couldn't be forced to leave without a court order. He knew that, but the chief of police came there not to follow the order of the court, but the caprice and whim of the Grande husband and wife, who had ordered him to threaten the people in the New Village, so that they would leave.

'My friends,' said Andres, addressing the people that had gathered around him, when Hugo and the policemen had left. 'The richest family in this town is at our throats. Because of that, we are now the enemies of the judge, the mayor and the chief of police. Our situation is difficult, but—'

'We're not enemies to ourselves,' said Marcos in a firm and clear voice.

'We're not alone,' added Andres. 'Bandong, Tasyo, and—'

'And reason is also with us,' said Kiko.

'And this!' Kanor said rashly, holding the sword in the scabbard hung around his waist.

Andres went to Kanor and put his arm on the young man's right shoulder. He reminded him that they should use reason first.

'That's only used when we no longer believe in the good and proper way to do things,' said the leader of New Village.

Things became worse when the supply of rice became scarce. This was felt even in Sampilong, which was a town whose primary product was rice. The last harvest was bountiful, but they could not understand why the supply of rice became as thin as water being filtered through a white cloth.

The forecast was that the situation would worsen in the coming months, since the farms had remained uncultivated. The request of the farmers was left dangling in the air by the unresponsive landowner, and after the failed talks, it seemed that an agreement would never be forthcoming at all.

Don Severo and Donya Leona hardened in their resolve that they would not go hungry even if their farms would turn into forests. Tasyo and the other farmers felt likewise; that they were used to being hungry, because whether they worked on the farms or not, they could not see any comfort under the unjust system of the farms.

'We want to turn our backs on the life of a slave,' said Tasyo to his associates. 'That's the issue.'

But in truth, there was enough supply of rice in Sampilong, but it was being hoarded. Most of the stocks were in the rice granary of the Grande family, while the Chinese merchants hoarded the rest. The Chinese could not buy more stocks of rice even if they wanted to, since they were being bothered by the police upon the orders of Chief Hugo, who served as the primary caretaker of his godfather and godmother, while Dislaw and Kosme did the actual buying of the rice.

It had been only a month since the rice was harvested and the respective shares of the harvest were given to the landlord and the farmers, but Tasyo and his associates were already saying that when the rains come, there would be no more rice in the fields. The price of a can of rice would surely shoot up to one peso since all the rice was stored in the granary of Donya Leona. When such a time came that the people had nothing to eat, that granary's doors would be pried open by the hordes of hungry people.

But the rain had not yet begun to fall in a steady fashion, and the hot breath of the sun could still be felt by everyone when complaints of hunger pangs began to be heard in the barrio.

'We're just eating congee,' said a husband and wife in the barrio to their neighbour.

'Well, at least you have congee to eat,' the neighbour answered in a sad voice.

One way the Grande husband and wife multiplied their profits was to buy all the rice when the price was still low, and this usually happened right after the harvest, and more so when the harvest was bountiful. The farmers sold all their rice in exchange for cash. That was when the Grande husband and wife would buy everything from the farmers. The price of the rice was often dictated by the seller and not the buyer. In this way, 1,000 sacks of rice could be easily be acquired and stockpiled in the granary of Donya Leona.

After a few months, when the supply of rice was low and the price was high, the Grande husband and wife would unload their rice in the market. The rice they bought at six pesos a sack could be easily sold for ten pesos a sack, or higher.

'This is an easy job,' boasted Donya Leona to Don Severo about her shrewd ways. 'It's really different when you have a mind for business.'

Don Severo was also happy, since he would have more money to spend on the cockfight in the capital.

In the meantime, the police were tightly guarding the barrio, because of the troubles in the farms and New Village, and because of the noise and complaints of the squatters. They were ready to act night and day, awaiting the orders of Chief Hugo.

But there were some things happening in Sampilong that the authorities could neither see or sniff. Or perhaps they were just callous or pretending to be blind.

They did not notice, or they completely ignored that when everyone had fallen asleep, a big truck would enter the rice granary of the Grande family, which stood between the church and the cemetery.

If one came closer, the figure of Kosme could be seen sitting beside the driver, while two other assistants from the stone house stood at the back of the empty truck as it entered the granary. After a few hours, the truck would leave the granary, but full. One could easily surmise that the sacks of rice stockpiled in the granary were being taken out in secret. Kosme and his group worked this way for several nights. After the truck had left the rice granary, it no longer stopped in front of the big house, but instead went directly to the provincial highway, in the direction of Manila, where Dislaw lived.

In turn, Dislaw would already be waiting for the loaded truck in Manila and would take it to the warehouse owned by Chinese traders.

He would be paid in cash right there and then, at a price that had been agreed upon by the Chinese and the Grande husband and wife.

After getting the bundles of cash, he would put it in a bag and tell himself, 'Loads of money.'

It was expected that he would turn over the money to Ninet, for her pharmacy business. Dislaw lived at the same address as her.

51

One day, Kosme went to the rice fields along with two of his assistants from the big stone house. They gathered the remaining hay on the fields that had been used to form mounds in the middle of the farms. They had brought a cart with them.

'What will you do with the hay?' asked one of the farmers.

'We need it.'

'You should leave some for us,' requested the farmer.

'Why?'

'We need it to feed the water buffaloes.'

'Then you should now eat your water buffaloes,' the servant of the Grandes said in a boastful tone. 'You're no longer working on the farms, why do you still need the water buffaloes? If you have no more food to eat, then you can have a feast eating those water buffaloes!'

'I will devour you first, you water buffalo!' said the angry farmer and was about to hit Kosme with the piece of wood in his hand. The two assistants Kosme had come with sprang to defend him, when the other farmers came and intervened, thus averting a fight.

'You'll get your justice desserts, one day,' Kosme warned the farmer, as he pushed the cart away.

'How brave the slave is,' said the farmer.

'And you? You hardly eat three square meals a day,' Kosme snapped. 'You devour the hay, you water buffalo.'

The two faced each other and were ready to resume their fight, but the others separated them. The three men working for the Grande family finally left, while the farmers walked back to their village. Kosme stored the hay in the rice granary located between the Catholic Church and the graveyard.

The sky was dark and the times were sad during the days that followed. The few people who had gone to the three stores owned by the Chinese went home early, as well as the few customers who visited the grocery store and the bakery, which were also owned by the Chinese. The pharmacy and funeral parlour owned by the stingy and termagant spinster whom Ninet had mocked, also closed its doors after the tolling of the bells of Angelus at six o' clock in the afternoon.

Even the policemen took rest after their dinner, since the nights were silent anyway and peace seemed to reign supreme everywhere.

Indeed, the whole of Sampilong was fast asleep. The shroud of darkness that had fallen on the rooftops, such that even the fireflies had got tired and sat resting on the smooth beds made of leaves. The thick silence was hardly broken by the shrill sound of the few crickets.

But in spite of this façade of peace and quiet, the little town of Sampilong was just like the other little towns in the whole archipelago, in the sense that not everyone followed the words of God and wished peace on their fellowmen. There were also dark schemes, petty jealousies, acts of oppression and utter lack of conscience.

It had been the habit of Father Pascual's assistant in the church to wake up at dawn while the priest and the whole town were still asleep. He always prepared the things needed in the convent and in the church early. As was his wont at dawn, he would open the small window of the convent before boiling water for coffee, to let the cool air in. He briefly glanced outside. What was it that he was seeing? The assistant was stunned. At first, he thought he had woken up late and it was already high noon. Everything was brilliant. He opened his eyes wider and focused his gaze on what he was seeing. It was not the sun, but fire. Fire, fire, fire! There was a big fire, and it was blazing to the very heavens.

The assistant made the sign of the cross, rushed to the priest's bedroom and knocked on the door several times. Father Pascual woke up.

'Father, fire, there's a fire!' shouted the assistant.

The priest swiftly bolted upright from his bed, and did not bother changing out of his pair of pyjamas into his house clothes. From the window of his room, he saw that a fire was indeed raging on, and it was quickly razing down a building.

'It must be outside the city centre,' surmised the priest.

He went outside his room. With his assistant, he stood looking at the angry tongues of flame and later said, 'It must be the electric plant, or the cockpit.'

He gazed at it again and then said, 'The rice granary—it seems like the rice granary!' he turned pale.

At that point, all they could see was a wall of flame blocking their view, and they could no longer espy which building or structure was burning. Father Pascual ordered his assistant to toll the church bells several times, to warn the still-sleeping residents about the big fire.

When everything had settled down and the day had advanced, it was clear that, indeed, the granary of the Grandes had burnt down to the ground. Nothing remained except embers and cinders. The whole building, as well as its contents of sacks of rice, had all been consumed by the fire. According to Donya Leona, the granary had contained 'thousands of sacks of milled rice and rice seeds, as well as assorted merchandise'.

Mayor Bartolo and Chief Hugo immediately sprang into action. They investigated the cause, but could not pinpoint the source of the fire. They sniffed around for evidence.

'There are signs that the fire was intentional,' said the mayor.

'That much can be seen in this dastardly act,' said the police chief.

When they talked to the Grande husband and wife, Donya Leona reiterated that the granary contained thousands of sacks of rice seeds and milled rice, aside from other important merchandise. Add to that the cost of the building, and the damage would reach one million pesos. However, everything was insured for only half a million pesos, and that is why she would lose a lot, Donya Leona claimed.

As for the perpetrators of the arson, the Grande husband and wife said they would not be surprised if their tenant farmers had been the ones to burn down the granary, since they had had an altercation with them a few days ago.

'Those people won't stop at anything,' Donya Leona said in an accusing tone.

Chef Hugo and the other policemen immediately went to the village.

Meanwhile, in a private conversation between the Grande husband and wife after the authorities had left, the rich woman boasted about what she had done.

'If something even did burn, it's only a few sacks of rice bran fit to be chicken feed,' she declared to her husband. 'Many Chinese businessmen got rich because of this scheme. Arson is their big business.'

This truth was known only to a few people; it was a secret sealed tightly in a box. While it might be true that some people knew that sacks of rice were secretly being ferried out of the rice granary, there were no witnesses and no one saw Kosme enter the rice granary two nights ago. Only Kosme's lover, Iska, knew everything. She had prepared the tin of petrol that Kosme had taken to the granary. She was even with Kosme until they reached the door of the granary. She never woke up and waited for him to return. And she was the one who met him when he returned to the big stone house at the crack of dawn, and the granary was already blazing.

We did not know if the chief of police had an inkling as to what had really happened. But his procedural steps indicated otherwise, for he immediately interrogated Tasyo and the farmers, especially the one who had had an argument with Kosme. They were all put behind bars in the municipal jail.

'You are angry with the Grande family,' Hugo accused Tasyo.

'If you will put the blame on those who don't like the Grandes,' answered the leader of the farmers, 'then you might as well accuse the whole town.'

'So, you are indeed admitting to it,' the chief snapped.

'I'm not admitting to anything and I didn't do anything,' Tasyo answered firmly. 'The farmer won't burn down the rice that's the fruit of his sweat and blood.'

'You said once in a gathering that you will target the Grandes' granary and that it will face the fury of those who are hungry, didn't you?'

'I didn't say that, but what the speaker meant was that he wanted to get hold of the contents of the granary; not burn it.'

'Therefore, you and the rest, all of you issued a threat.'

'Those who are hungry can perhaps say that,' snapped Tasyo at Hugo. 'They might snatch the sacks of rice, but to burn them? What sort of hungry person would burn food, and what sort of farmer who would destroy the fruits of his hardship? None of the arsonists were from the village.'

But Hugo just ignored the last words of Tasyo.

The police chief could not pry a confession from any of the farmers who had had an altercation with Kosme, either. On the other hand, the farmers implied that there was something suspicious about Kosme gathering the dried stalks of rice and hay, the day before.

'What would he do with the hay?' they asked. 'He didn't have a water buffalo to feed. In fact, they were the ones pulling their own cart. Couldn't he have used the hay as kindling?'

The word 'kindling' struck a chord inside Hugo, but he ignored it. He did not investigate Kosme, because he could not do so without the permission of his godfather and godmother. And how could he suspect and probe the servant of the one who lost property in the fire? Did the Grande family not lose one million pesos in the blaze, even if they could get half a million pesos back from insurance for the burnt rice and other merchandise?

Hugo detained Tasyo and the other farmers in the municipal jail, even though he did not have enough evidence to incriminate them. The chief of police warned that they would not be released until the real culprit had been caught by the net of the law.

He later when to his rich godparents to make a report on the results of his investigation.

'There is no shred of evidence against any of your tenant farmers,' he admitted to Don Severo and Donya Leona. 'I wanted to hit one of the farmers who had a disagreement with Kosme, if I could ...'

He added that the tenant farmers would not, however, be released from prison.

'They might accuse you of illegal detention,' Don Severo reminded him.

'That law is not followed in your town, my dear godfather,' said Hugo. 'When they can no longer endure the pain, these people will admit to the arson, even if they didn't do it.'

'Did you also throw the squatters into jail?' asked the rich man.

'Oh yes,' and Hugo suddenly stood up upon being reminded of what he had forgotten to do. 'Now, I will encounter those braggarts again.'

Hugo bade farewell to his godfather and godmother, then quickly returned to the town, along with six armed men. They rode a jeep that swiftly took them to New Village.

52

Kosme thought he was only dreaming. He could not believe what had happened had really happened. He had been asleep in his room when Iska had woken him up because Donya Leona had called for him.

He washed his face and changed into the clothes he had worn the previous day. Then he went to Donya Leona, who was waiting for him on the first floor of the big stone house. That was the first time Kosme had left his room since he had returned at dawn from the blazing granary.

Donya Leona was happy and was even humming a song. This only happened when her temper was not flared, which was a rare occurrence. She rarely smiled in front of her servants.

'Did you sleep well, Kosme?' she enquired in a gentle tone. Her servant nodded.

Iska was carrying a feather duster and she was dusting some of the décor in the house.

'Do you want to go to Manila?'

Kosme was surprised at the next question posed by the rich woman.

'What will I do in Manila?' he asked tentatively.

'Whatever you want to do—as if you were a tourist there. Do you want to go?'

'If that's what you want me to do, ma'am,' Kosme answered, although he was still confused.

'Very well then, you can leave after lunch.' She fished for something from the pocket of her dress. 'This is for your expenses.' She counted several bills for her servant. Iska looked at them from where she was working.

'That's 200 pesos,' added the rich woman.

'Is this all for me?!' asked Kosme in an unbelieving tone, and his body shivered as he accepted the money.

'Yes. You can buy whatever you want. You can buy new shoes and clothes. You can eat delicious food at the restaurants there. You can also watch a movie. Do whatever pleases you.'

Kosme almost kissed the rich woman's hands out of gratitude. When he returned to his room, he was still wondering if he was indeed awake, or was just dreaming. But the money was there, in his hands, and he counted it again. Almost 200 pesos, indeed. Five twenty peso bills, eight ten peso bills, and twenty ten-peso bills. This was already a treasure! In his whole life, this was the first time he had held such a big amount of money. And it all belonged to him, and he could buy whatever he wished with it.

Kosme only saw the goodness of the rich woman, but he did not foresee that what he had done at dawn would bring a million misgivings upon the Grande family. Kosme did not know anything about the mathematics of insurance, the link between wealth and fire, or the meaning of the secret deliveries of truckloads of rice in the dead of night.

Kosme had an inkling why Donya Leona had given him a reward, which was something he could thank her for by paying for a Mass in the church. He knew he had done a very good job, but he did not know what the Grande family intended to reap from what he had done.

On the other hand, Iska did not know if she should be happy with the windfall that had come into Kosme's life. She had heard the conversation between Donya Leona and her favourite male servant, seen the fat reward being handed over to him, and witnessed how he had counted it later. And since she was as shrewd as a monkey, she knew the real reason behind the reward.

When she returned to her room beside Kosme's, she waited for him to report to her about his grand handout. She was excited for Kosme to tell her personally about his reward, since that would've meant that she was indeed important to him. But Kosme kept silent, as if nothing had happened at all.

He did not even tell Iska that he was leaving for Manila. He did not invite her to join him, even if tokenistic. He did not ask her if she wanted him to buy something for her from the big city, or if she wanted a souvenir from his visit to Manila. And it would have been good enough even if Kosme had just told her that he was leaving for Manila, just so she knew. But Kosme left secretly, without bidding her goodbye, while she was still fast asleep. But he did not know that Iska was actually awake, and just lay there in his bed pretending to be asleep.

Finally, Iska realized that she had no reason to rejoice in the good fortune that had fallen into Kosme's lap. She was hurt to the bone.

'I've had no consolation at all from that beast,' the head of the house helpers sighed.

But the wound inside her seemed to have been singed with red pepper when she saw where Kosme was going before he left for Manila. He did not cross the road that went directly into the town centre. Instead, he turned right after leaving the big stone house, in the direction of where Dislaw lived. But Dislaw was not there, since he was also in Manila. Dislaw's nephew was not there either, since he was at school. The only one present there was the widow, Cely the bitch. It was obvious that Kosme had gone there to see her.

'Just wait and see!' Iska said in a rush of anger.

Iska was very much aware of the relationship between the two of them, and that was why she had almost drowned Cely during their fieldtrip to the fishpond. But she made herself believe that Kosme would choose her, and that she was the real lodestar in his life. Iska admitted that Cely was younger and prettier, but she could give Kosme many things that Cely could not. Moreover, Iska felt that the care and love she had shown to Kosme could overpower his desire for younger flesh.

Iska catered to Kosme's every whim. He did not really ask her for anything, but still, she provided him with different things to remind him of her: a new pair of slippers, polo shirts, undershirts and handkerchiefs. Sometimes, though, he would ask her for small amounts of money, which she would readily give. On the one hand, she did not ask for much, not even the real love that a man gave to his girlfriend. It was enough for her that she could be with him once or twice a week, cheer him up when he was lonely, or massage his back when he was tired.

But now, Iska felt a strange sensation filling up her being. She estimated that Kosme had been in Dislaw's house for more than thirty minutes. Thirty minutes spent with Cely. Many things could happen in half an hour; in fact, anything could happen in that span of time. Iska felt a tightening in her chest.

'The shameless ones are having their fill,' she said to herself with bitterness.

Later, Iska saw Kosme rushing to the road that led to the town centre. After five minutes, she saw the widow going in the same direction. Iska knew what was happening.

'And they're even going to Manila at the same time,' she said.

Iska felt worse than someone tied to a tree crawling with red ants. She often felt pangs of jealousy, but like a lit matchstick, they quickly vanished. But only now did she feel a jealousy like fire coursing through her veins, and she thought she would lose her mind. The naked truth about the man she had loved and taken care of was right there, before her very eyes. The two quislings were about to leave for Manila. There, they would spend the morning, afternoon and evening together. Iska did not know what to think anymore. She wanted to follow them. She wanted to grab a knife and slash the throats of Cely and Kosme, who in her eyes looked like dirty and despicable rats.

But the poor woman restrained herself. She reflected that what she wanted to do was bereft of reason, and people would just make fun of her. Who was she in Kosme's life? Who was Cely in Kosme's life? Nothing was clear, and nothing was certain.

'Calm down, Iska,' she could hear the voice of her conscience. 'Be patient, Iska. That seems to be your fate.'

Suddenly, she changed her clothes and told one of the servants that if Donya Leona was looking for her, they should tell the rich woman that she had just gone to the town centre to attend to something. But in truth, she did not know where she was going. She just walked to and fro.

When she finally managed to walk out of the stone house, she became frantic. She could no longer see the two of them. Then she crossed the road and went to New Village. She reached the exhibition centre, but there was nobody there. There were no workers happily weaving baskets and making bags, telling stories to each other while they worked. The whole place was dead silent.

She decided to go to the hut where Andres' family lived. She called out a greeting, but no one answered her. She turned and was about to leave when Sedes arrived, along with the wives of two other squatters.

'Hello, Iska,' Sedes greeted her. 'Where did you come from?'

Sedes invited Iska inside their hut, while the two other women went home.

But instead of Iska narrating her tale of woe to Sedes, it was Sedes who started relating her sad tale. Her eyes had turned red from crying and it was obvious something was weighing heavy on her mind.

'What happened?'

'Oh,' and Sedes began to cry. 'The police took Andres to the station.'

'But why?'

'He is being implicated for the burning down of the rice granary that belonged to the Grande family.'

'Do they have proof?'

'What proof? Andres was here all night long and never left the house. Our two kids had fever, that was why he was home.'

'Where is Andres now?'

'In the municipal jail. I just came from there. I took food for them. They have caught seven people—three squatters and four farmers.'

'Why were they implicated?'

'They said that the farmer and squatters were angry at the Grande family, but Iska, God knows that Andres is blameless.'

'I know that as well,' were the words that tumbled swiftly from Iska's lips.

Sedes was stunned. She grabbed one of Iska's arms and pressed for details.

'You know the truth? Why do you know it? Who burnt down the rice granary?'

Iska fell like a limp rag to the floor and decided it was now her chance to seek revenge on Kosme. As the Tagalog people would say, only lightning cannot exact vengeance. That was why when Sedes repeated her questions, Iska decided to spill the beans. She told her everything she knew. Sedes immediately stood up while still listening to Iska. When the latter finished, she invited her to come out.

'Where are we going?' Iska asked.

'To Teacher Bandong.'

'But I might get into trouble,' Iska voiced her fears.

'The blameless ones should not fear anything,' answered Sedes, and hope shone in her eyes, red with grief. Then she added: 'Those who burnt down the rice granary are the ones who should be afraid.'

When they arrived at Teacher Bandong's house, Iska repeated what she had told Sedes: the hauling of the rice granary's contents in the middle of the night and the journey to Manila, also in the dead of the night; Kosme's taking a can of petrol to the granary; the burning and the eventual return of Kosme to the big stone house when the granary was already ablaze. Iska also reported that Donya Leona gave Kosme 200 pesos before lunchtime, and Kosme's sudden departure for Manila along with Dislaw's widow sister.

'It's clear that they did it,' Bandong said as soon as Iska finished her report.

That night, Iska did not return to the big stone house. Bandong prevailed upon her to stay for dinner, and she slept in the same bed as Nana Oris.

The next day, when Sedes took food to Andres, she told her husband what Iska had revealed to her. Chief Hugo was surprised when he checked on the jail quarters and heard the group happily singing a song from the farm.

Early on the next day, Bandong and Iska left for Manila. They decided to meet with Attorney Reyes and a representative of a popular insurance company.

53

The events of the following days seemed to have wings. The native languor of life in Sampilong suddenly turned frenetic, and the former silence was broken by restless movement, protests, quarrels, court charges and accusations.

When Bandong returned from Manila, he brought Attorney Reyes back with him, and they shot two birds with one stone. Iska was left in the care of the security group that belonged to the insurance company. The moment they reached the capital, they quickly proceeded to follow the order of the court. Under the orders of the governor, the police did not touch any of the huts in New Village until after the court had handed its final verdict.

From the police quarters, they also secured the release of Andres, Tasyo and others, who had been kept behind bars without being charged in court. They had also been kept longer than the mandated twenty-four hours, after which a charge should have been filed against them in court. Because of this, Attorney Reyes was also able to file a case against Chief of Police Hugo and other policemen for illegal detention.

After Andres had been freed, the court proceedings against the Grande husband and wife continued, to reclaim the vast lands that belonged to Cabesang Resong, the ancestor of Andres' mother. It turned out that his land had been grabbed by Captain Melchor's Spanish father and its ownership was later transferred to Donya Leona. Aside from reclaiming the land, Andres also demanded 2 million pesos in damages, computed in accordance with the money accrued from the property since it was stolen by Captain Melchor's father, until the present day.

The news ripped through the town like a firecracker, and now suddenly, other witnesses besides Ba Inte appeared, who could testify as to what had really happened to the land. An old man who lived on the farm and two other women also came out and said they were willing to serve as witnesses. Several well-off members of the cooperative that had set up the home industries sent word to Andres that they were willing to collect money to pay for the court case.

Attorney Reyes confirmed his view that they had a big chance of winning in court, and when that would come to pass, almost nothing would be left to the Grande family. This had not yet happened, but joy already filled the hearts of the farmers and the squatters.

'Look at how a person's luck turns,' said Marcos during one gathering.

'It's not luck, but the revelation of the truth,' corrected Tasyo. 'The truth can't be buried forever.'

'That's why our bright future looms large now,' said Simon.

'Perhaps that's what Andres meant earlier, when he said they want Teacher Bandong to run for town mayor in the coming elections.'

'Now, Andres can buy the whole of New Village,' said Kiko.

'There's no doubt about that,' Blas told them his hunch. 'And I'm sure Andres won't be an abusive landlord.'

'We're not sure about that,' said someone in the group. 'Money changes people.'

'It all depends on one's upbringing,' Simon protested. 'Andres is a man of integrity.'

'Then he can be our new master,' continued the naysayer.

'There will be no more master in this town,' Simon said, 'because there will be no more slaves. We will help him as their equals.'

'How about the sharing of the harvest?'

'Sixty–forty.'

'No, seventy–thirty.'

'And the landlord will pay for the cost of the seeds.'

'And the fertilizer as well.'

'And there will be irrigation from now on.'

'That's for sure.'

'Then it will truly be like a cooperative from now on.'

'Indeed, a cooperative.'

'You should write all this down, Tasyo.'

Some people laughed, but Tasyo was serious when he spoke again.

'It would be too much to write these things down if the landowner is honourable,' he said. 'But it would seem as if it were all written on water like something to be forgotten, if the landowner turns out to be a crocodile.'

They heard someone clearing his throat, and then they saw grey smoke curling upwards from a cheap tobacco cigar. Then they noticed that Ba Inte was also there.

'The crocodile will finally leave this town,' said the old man. 'That beast only stays in a place where it can devour someone.'

And what Ba Inte said came to fruition. The people of Sampilong saw that the big truck that had carried sacks of rice to Manila for several nights, along with another big truck, were now being used to transfer the expensive furniture and other things that belonged to the Grande family. The two trucks were en route to the capitol city of Manila. The Grande husband and wife had finally decided to leave Sampilong.

Don Severo suffered serious bouts of insomnia and could not sleep well anymore. It seemed that he was finally being haunted by the shadows of his darkest deeds.

But that was not what they told their allies, like Mayor Bartolo and Chief of Police Hugo. They seemed unperturbed by the trouble on the farms, by their failure to drive away the squatters, by what happened to Dislaw and Iska, or by the noise created by the case that Andres had filed against them.

Don Severo said they were leaving because 'Ninet is alone in Manila'.

'Whether you like to admit it or not, we're no longer young and we need to rest now,' added Donya Leona. 'Bartolo can take care of the farms.'

However, the couple discovered that Manila could not serve as a hideout for them with their deficiencies, or as a soft hammock for those who wanted to escape from their inner torments. They could not go far, because their conscience was always with them; they could not escape the blame that came from their conscience.

To their utter dismay, the insomnia of Don Severo was not cured, and like the exponential interest of loan sharks, Donya Leona was felled by high blood pressure. When she began to recover, the woman could no longer speak. Her tongue was forever stilled and she could not walk, because half of her body had been paralyzed from the stroke. In short, the Grande husband and wife who had acted like the king and queen in character and been abusive, oppressive and uncaring towards other people, had now been reduced to an old man slowly withering because he could not sleep at all, and an old woman who was alive, but seemed already dead.

This fate had befallen Donya Leona because she had discovered two facts that went through her heart like a sharp knife: Kosme had been caught by the authorities in Manila, because Iska had reported him to the police; and Dislaw had fled with several hundreds of thousands of pesos that had come from the sacks of rice he had sold. It turned out that he had not remitted a single cent to Ninet.

To make matters worse, Kosme did not only admit to burning down the rice granary, but also that Don Severo and Donya Leona were the masterminds behind it. On the other hand, the police already knew where Dislaw was hiding, but according to their report, he had already spent a good part of the stolen amount on gambling and other vices.

As opposed to the torrent of ill luck that had fallen on the Grande husband and wife, fortune smiled upon the people of Sampilong.

Mayor Bartolo swiftly met with the members of the farmers' organization and agreed to their demands. That was why one afternoon, when the falling of the rain seemed endless, Tasyo and his group did not stop their work in the fields, following the water buffaloes as they plowed, and never seemed to tire as they turned the earth and prepared it for planting. Within the week, they began sowing the rice seeds and then firmed up the footholds of the rice paddies. Afterwards, they cleared the rows of stray weeds and deepened the canal so that the water could flow faster and irrigate the fields better.

'Even if we are late, the rice grains will still be robust,' Tasyo happily told his group.

Following his promise, Bandong tendered his resignation as a teacher and returned to the farm. He began plowing the field owned by Nana Oris. He also included the farm of Ba Inte in his care. Bandong did not stop working out even if he was not working on the farm, and that was why he did not find it hard to return to farm work even though he had been a teacher for several years.

One day, without warning, the superintendent of schools visited Bandong's house. He came directly from the provincial capital to personally meet with the young teacher. Bandong was just about to go to work on the farm, wearing a torn polo shirt, the hems of his old denims folded several times over, and wearing a simple hat made of woven buri leaves. He was surprised at the arrival of his unexpected guest.

When they were already seated inside the house, the superintendent brought out Bandong's letter of resignation.

'I personally came to visit you,' the superintendent said, 'to tell you I'm not accepting your resignation.' Then he returned the letter to Bandong.

The young man then explained that he had decided to focus on his work on their own farm, since no one else could work on it, except him. Bandong added that he had poured effort into becoming a good teacher, and he was happy to have been of help to the elementary school pupils in his town. But it seemed that what he had done, and what he was doing, was never enough. That was why he had incurred the wrath of his enemies and the educational heads had turned their backs on him.

'The land is the best friend a person can have,' Bandong said. 'You just sow a little and it returns thousand fold.'

'There are already many farmers in this town, Bandong,' the superintendent reminded him, 'but there are only a few good teachers. In the school, the students are like our plants. And they are the hope of this country.'

The superintendent plainly told Bandong that it was not true that they had abandoned him. In truth, all the accusations against him had been dropped.

'And I'm not asking you to return to your old job as a teacher, but as a principal,' added the educational leader. 'Henry Danyo can't get along with the people here. Even his fellow teachers don't like him, so he'll be transferred to another school.'

'So, it means—' Bandong looked directly at the superintendent.

'You will be the permanent principal.'

Bandong expressed his gratitude to him, but asked for two days before he could report for work. The two separated in jovial spirits.

That same day, Bandong met with his group, which included the members of the PTA as well as the leaders of the squatters and the farmers. They met inside his house.

He told the group about his dilemma, and sought their advice on the matter. Should he go back to teaching or should he continue farming? Ba Inte immediately gave his opinion.

'In the end, of course, it is Bandong who will decide on the matter,' he began. 'But I have a suggestion, which will link the two courses of action. My suggestion is that you accept the offer to work as a principal and serve for one year, and then resign the year after. Two years from now, there will be an election, and you should start campaigning as our candidate for town mayor.'

Ba Inte took a drag at his tobacco, smiled and then continued, 'I think this suggestion would please everyone, that on top of Bandong being a farmer and a principal, we also want him to serve as the town mayor of Sampilong.'

No one contradicted the proposal, and it seemed to have tied the group together as one. Tasyo and Andres, who had both suggested two different courses of action, shook hands.

'If that is what everyone wants, then I will do it,' said a delighted Bandong.

That night, Bandong and Nana Oris had an early dinner. Afterwards, they changed into their best clothes and went to Mang Pablo's house. Nana Oris carried a basket of fresh fruits along.

The family accepted them with delight. All of them sat around the long table in the house. Bandong told them about the visit of the superintendent and the consensus of the group on what he should do.

'Well done,' Mang Pablo said and made his apologies for not being able to attend the meeting held that afternoon. 'Your decision is right.'

Before everyone could speak again, Nana Oris took initiative.

'We are here to discuss an important matter,' she began, while looking down at the floor. Bandong stole a glance at Pina. 'If you will not embarrass me,' and then Nana Oris raised her eyes to look at Pina's parents, 'I would now like to be bold and ask for Pina's hand in marriage for my unmarried nephew.'

A long silence followed, with everyone seeming to scan the floor to look for the right words to say. Mang Pablo touched his lips, and looked at Aling Sabel and Pina repeatedly.

'It all depends on the children, Oris; their wishes will be followed.'

Bandong and Pina quickly looked at each other, and that look conveyed their eternal promise of a world filled with happiness and love.